D1461374

The Time Quantum

~ A NOVEL ~

DAVID STREETS

Fulton Books, Inc.
Meadville, PA

Published by Fulton Books 2021

ISBN 978-1-63860-504-1 (paperback)
ISBN 978-1-63985-769-2 (hardcover)
ISBN 978-1-63860-505-8 (digital)

Printed in the United States of America

CHAPTER 1

Joliet, Illinois
July 2018

Karen Butler was reported missing on the ninth of July. There was nothing sinister about it in the beginning. A friend from the university, Connie Cammaretta, had been calling her for two weeks with no response and finally contacted Joliet Police Department. A patrol car was dispatched to Karen Butler's apartment building on the southwest side of the city. It was a routine call.

The building manager, summoned from his air conditioner and his television set, snatched up the master key and followed the two officers out into the hot Midwest afternoon. By the time they had crossed two parking lots and climbed two flights of stairs, the men were perspiring. One of the officers knocked on the door of Karen's apartment. There was no answer. The manager unlocked the door and stepped aside to let the officers enter. The drapes were closed, and in the yellow half-light, the air felt oppressive and stale. The cops searched the four rooms, finding them all empty. The milk in the refrigerator was sour; the uppermost newspaper in the recycle pile was dated the third of June. They beckoned the manager inside.

"Do you know the girl who lives here?" one of the officers asked.

"No," the manager replied. "Well, I mean, I know what she looks like. She's blond these days, but she used to shave her head. Petite. Nice kid, as far as I can tell."

"Do you know if she has any friends in the building?"

"I wouldn't know. I only see her when she pays the rent. And she hasn't paid July's rent yet, by the way."

"Age? Any idea?"

He thought for a moment. "Maybe eighteen, nineteen."

The officer had already turned away. He surveyed the sparsely furnished living room, arms akimbo, sweat staining the armpits of his blue shirt. His partner held up one of several secondhand books that were lying on the coffee table and said, "Occult stuff." The first officer grunted. *Probably a druggie,* he thought. *Weed, maybe worse. A space cadet too. That's why the bedroom ceiling's painted black and hung with crocheted stars. Where would she keep the stuff? In a spice jar? A hollowed-out dictionary?*

"No," the manager said, intercepting his train of thought. "It's nothing like that. She's a normal kid. I'm sure of it. She's just a student on summer break. She's either moved in with her boyfriend or got a job out of town. Happens all the time around here. She'll be back in the fall."

Upon reflection, the officers seemed inclined to believe him. There was nothing more they could do in the apartment in any case, so they walked out, leaving the manager to lock up behind them. One of the officers knocked on an adjacent door and roused a fat man clutching a barbecue fork. "She's a nice girl," said the neighbor. "Never any noise, short blond hair, blue jeans. Gee, that's right, I haven't seen her for a while, now that you've mentioned it. No regular callers that I know of, no. Sorry, sir."

The officers returned to their squad car, turned the air-conditioning up high, and drove back to the station. They filed a report and handed it off to the watch detective. It took a follow-up call from Connie Cammaretta the next day to float the officers' report to the surface of Detective John Dietrichson's in-box.

"Ms. Cammaretta, yes," the detective said, fumbling through papers as he spoke. "You reported a missing person. A, er, Karen Butler?"

"She doesn't answer her phone. It's been two weeks now."

"Okay. Well, it says here that two of our officers went to her apartment yesterday. She wasn't there, and it looked like she hadn't been there for some time."

"Really?"

"Apparently. Can I ask, what is your relationship with Ms. Butler?"

"We both work at CIU, in the psych center. I'm a lab technician, and Karen's a student aide. We're good friends."

"And you last heard from her when?"

"I'm not sure. It must be at least a month ago. Our project's shut down for the summer."

"Who do you work for at the university?"

"Our boss's name is Harry Groh. And there's another scientist in the group called Frank Koslowski. We do experiments."

"What kind of experiments?"

"To do with sensory deprivation."

"What now?"

"Sensory deprivation. It's not easy to explain. Basically, the students float in a big tank of water and have strange visions, and we measure their brain waves."

"Right. And are there any other students involved in this project?"

"Only Karen at the moment. There used to be another kid called Dan Patzner, but he's no longer involved. Karen and Dan volunteered to be the experimental subjects. They earn some extra cash, you know?"

"Okay. Can you think of anyone who might know of Ms. Butler's whereabouts?"

"Not really. Well, her parents, I guess."

"Do you know how to contact them?"

"No."

"Well, thank you, Ms. Cammaretta, for your help. There's nothing more I can tell you at the moment. I'll look into it. I have your phone number. I'll let you know what we find."

"Thanks. It's strange that she would simply vanish like this without telling me."

The detective didn't get curious until after he had made a round of phone calls the following morning. The team leader, Harry Groh, had left for Europe on vacation right after the end of the spring semester. A headline flashed into Dietrichson's mind: "Disillusioned

5

Professor Elopes with Prize-Winning Student." It wouldn't be the first time. When Karen Butler's name was mentioned to Dan Patzner, the other student aide, he immediately became agitated. He said he wanted nothing to do with her anymore. He called her a witch. He said she had probably gone to the devil, in whose company she rightly belonged. "Virgin Sacrificed in Black Mass." Now that would be a first for Joliet. He pondered the significance of Patzner's remark and jotted down a note to visit him for further questioning.

Karen Butler's parents, when finally run to earth in Reinbeck, Iowa, reported that they, too, had become worried after failing to reach their daughter by phone. However, they could offer no explanation for her prolonged absence. They knew nothing about a boyfriend or an out-of-town job or any other reason for her to have left Joliet. Dietrichson's curiosity was aroused, but he was no closer to an answer.

He visited Karen's apartment in the afternoon. There were no clues to her disappearance—no diary, no calendar, and no revealing letters—not even an address book, just some unpaid bills from May and an invitation to a birthday party in June. He did, however, discover one rather puzzling thing: a guidebook to something called the Greenwich Observatory—Greenwich in England, he noted, not Connecticut. Across the top margin was scrawled an enigmatic message: "Beware! Beware! His flashing eyes, his floating hair." Did that mean Karen was in some kind of danger?

On a desk in the corner of the living room was a framed photograph of three people standing on the steps of a farmhouse: a pretty girl in her early teens with long blond hair flanked by a gaunt man and a thickset short woman. He stared into the face of the girl and whispered out loud, "Hello, Karen. And where might you be this fine afternoon?" Her playful smile seemed to say that it was up to him to find out where she was; she wasn't going to help. The stern features of her parents said that it was none of his damn business.

The coffee table in the middle of the room was strewn with poetry books—Byron, Coleridge, and Blake—and a collection of oddball works: Conan Doyle on fairies, a bruised copy of H. G. Wells's *First and Last Things*, a commentary on Nostradamus, and

Dunne's *An Experiment with Time.* Dietrichson snickered. *Yeah, Karen, wait till you have to earn a living.* He found the bed unmade, but there were no dirty dishes in the sink. When he had finished his search, he couldn't even decide if her disappearance had been planned.

Having some free time at the end of the day, he called the major airlines and the INS, inquiring after travelers to Europe by the name of Butler or Groh. This time, he struck gold. According to flight manifestos, Karen Butler, Harry Groh, and Frank Koslowski had left Chicago by American Airlines on the sixth of June for London's Heathrow Airport. *More than a month ago.* Coincidentally, the INS had just been notified by British immigration authorities that the three of them were no-shows on their scheduled return flight. Dietrichson was pleased with himself for finding a lead so quickly. He called Connie Cammaretta with the news.

"They're over there again?" Connie asked, sounding surprised.

"Do you know what they're doing?"

"They went over to England at the end of last year for some kind of new experiment. It was in early December, I think. Then again a few months ago, maybe April. But I didn't hear anything about a recent trip."

"What kind of an experiment?"

"I've no idea. They didn't tell me anything. You say they left the States at the beginning of June? Why hasn't anyone heard from them?"

"The British authorities want to know the answer to that question too."

"I wish I could be more helpful, sir. Jeez, that's weird."

"I'll keep on it."

Dietrichson called Central Illinois University. The director of the Illinois Center for Psychological Studies said he knew of no research trip to England. No foreign travel had been authorized for any of his staff in the past two months. All members of Harry Groh's research team were on leave for the summer. He regretted that he could be of no further assistance.

The mystery was getting international and intellectual, drawing it away from the realm of Dietrichson's experience. It was no surprise, therefore, when the Butler file began to sink back below the surface of the pile of burglary and traffic cases. It wasn't intentional on his part. He just gravitated toward familiar topics. A week passed, and he gave the case no more than a moment's thought. Then one day, the station chief called him into his office.

"John, were you assigned that case about the student who flew over to England?"

"You mean—let me think—Karen Butler?"

"Yeah, that's the one. Well, Chicago got a fax this morning from the American embassy in London and dropped it on us. Some PD over there says they've found the body of a US citizen." He put on his glasses and read from the fax sheet. "Deceased identified as Frank Koslowski of Plainfield, Illinois."

"I think that was the name of the third person. I can run and check the file."

"Remind me again what this business is all about."

"Well, apparently, this CIU student called Karen Butler flew to England in June with her boss, Harry Groh, and this other scientist by the name of Koslowski. The friend who notified us of Ms. Butler's disappearance thinks they might have been involved in some kind of science project—psychic stuff, I dunno—but the head of the center where they all work told me he didn't know anything about it."

"Well, the Brits have found the body of this Koslowski guy out in the sticks somewhere." He perused the fax sheet again. "Naked and hidden in some bushes by a church at a place called Hoyland. No idea where that is. Karen Butler is believed to have visited this church. They found her passport and some of her clothes in a cottage a mile away, near the coast. The cottage is owned by the uncle of some British professor who's also gone missing. No sign of the girl or her boss. No sign of anyone who knows what the fuck's going on."

"Isn't this FBI turf?"

"I haven't a clue, John, to be honest. I have enough trouble remembering how to deal with interstate flight." He paused and scratched his head. "I'll call External Relations and get us out of the loop. You just keep tabs on the missing Illinois residents. Check once in a while to see if any of them shows up at home."

"Got it."

*****

A week later, Detective Dietrichson was called upon to entertain Karen Butler's parents when they arrived from Iowa by Greyhound bus, looking about as lost and as country as two people possibly could. He drove them to Karen's apartment. He opened the curtains to let in some light. The mother choked back tears and began to clean out the refrigerator. Dietrichson told her to stop. The father was utterly bewildered. When questioned, he just stared at the floor as if ashamed not to know what had happened to his daughter. Dietrichson was sympathetic but could offer little consolation.

He drove them to see Connie Cammaretta, who told them what a terrific friend Karen was and cried along with them. Dietrichson mumbled that there was no reason to suspect foul play. Three despondent faces turned to him in unison. Karen's father said he couldn't afford to trace his daughter to England and wanted the detective to go in his place. Dietrichson said there was nothing he could do in that regard. He suggested they contact the FBI. The couple exchanged helpless glances, and he knew they never would. He said that he would let them know if there was any news. He drove them back to the bus terminal.

The case grew cold. He learned in due course that Frank Koslowski had indeed been killed. A verdict of murder by person or persons unknown was reached at the inquest in England, and Koslowski's body was flown home to the US for burial. Dietrichson checked periodically for the return of Karen Butler or Harry Groh, but without success. He presumed some international law enforcement agency was investigating the case—Interpol, whatever.

After a month, he took the manila folder with the red Butler stamp on the tab—thin and inconsequential as it was—and filed it under Inactive. Privately, he suspected that Karen and Harry were in love and hiding out somewhere. Maybe they killed Koslowski, maybe not. He was assigned to a double homicide in Peoria that occupied his attention for the remainder of the year. Of Karen Butler, nothing more was heard.

CHAPTER 2

Lincoln, England
1587

A funeral procession straggled down from the cathedral on the hill to the city below. At its head marched a pageboy carrying a banner of a golden sun surrounded by what appeared to be jeweled planets. Bringing up the rear was a pack of dogs, snapping at the heels of the mourners. A stray donkey accompanied them. The cortege seemed to have little sense of purpose or direction. It wandered from one side of the cobbled street to the other, dragged along as it was by a boy and driven forward by beasts. Mist enveloped the hilltop and obliterated the cathedral towers from view. As the party descended into the ragged metropolis, a thin rain began to fall. All in all, it was an inglorious end to a life.

The line of clergy, which surrounded the casket and seemed at times to be protecting it, was headed by William Wickham, Bishop of Lincoln, ecclesiastical overlord of the county and sometime confidant of Queen Elizabeth herself. Dean and canons and precentor and choristers shuffled along behind the bishop in hierarchical sequence. Damp but dignified, they held to the line. William Cecil, or Lord Burghley, being the highest-ranking noncleric, walked in the footsteps of the smallest choirboy. Behind him were the lesser nobility—Henry Clinton, Second Earl of Lincoln, and Sir Francis Willoughby among them—and their attendants. Such was the respect afforded Richard Crossly by the city of Lincoln as his black coffin nosed past the stables, alehouses, and crude shop fronts on his final visit to it this dreary September afternoon of a forgotten year in the late sixteenth century.

At the rear of the procession was a motley contingent, quite at odds with the rest of the party. Their robes were functional rather than ecclesiastical or ceremonial, their beards long and unkempt. Preeminent among them was the tall figure of John Dee, famed mathematician, occultist, and reputed necromancer. Clustered around him like moons circling a minor planet were Edward Kelley the astrologer, lately returned from Bohemia; the Polish alchemist Olbracht Laski; and lesser lights of the protoscience that was just then emerging from the Middle Ages.

That the deceased had felt a greater affinity for this irreligious band than for the guardians of the true faith was known to and resented by the vanguard, and only grudgingly had the sorcerers been permitted to walk in the cortege and then only at the rear. The nobility in the center of the line formed an uneasy buffer between the forces of Christianity and diabolism, the thorax of a long, disjointed insect creeping through the damp streets of the city.

Lord Burghley, who, as a young man, had accompanied Crossly on his fateful sortie against Hoyland Abbey fifty years before, was particularly resentful of the unbelievers. When one of them raised his walking stick to the dogs, he turned to scowl at him. Though now nearly seventy years of age, Lord Burghley was as prickly and unforgiving as he had been in engineering the execution of Mary, Queen of Scots, earlier that year. "They were the ones," he whispered to his son Thomas Cecil, nodding toward the back of the line. "They were at the root of it, Dee and Kelley. 'Twas some foreign magic they worked on him. If 'twere not for them, Crossly would be venerated today, not imprisoned in an inscrutable limbo along with the unbaptized."

"I know that many believe this, Father," Thomas replied, "but I am not fully persuaded."

The procession passed the wool market and was assailed by commotion from within. Local sheep farmers were haggling with cloth makers from Yorkshire in coarse northern dialects while the lilting tongue of Huguenot merchants floated in counterpoint. Deals were being struck; bargains sealed. At the sight of the cortege, the babble died down for a few moments then redoubled as soon as it had passed. The line of mourners straightened to avoid rainwater that was sweeping down the gutters on either side of the street. A flutter of wool danced across the coffin.

An old woman emerged from a doorway and paused to watch the cortege pass. Her eyes settled on the eyes of the only woman in the procession: Catherine Crossly, widow of the deceased. The onlooker was surprised. She expected to see signs of grief but saw only a world-weary, impassive face, the face of a woman who had shed her tears long ago and cared for life no more. The simple bonnet on Catherine Crossly's head served to channel the rain down over her ears, where it unraveled her hair and dripped onto her shoulders. The old woman reflected that the widow was not long for this world herself and emptied a pail of slops into the gutter.

Lord Burghley also gazed upon the widow but with more compassion. He had been a lifelong friend of the Crossly family and a solace to Catherine in her darkest hours. *She should let go,* he thought. *What Richard Crossly was once and what he later became is of no further consequence. Now is the time to let him go.* As he trudged through the rain, Burghley worried about her fate now that she was left alone with no children and no living relative whom anyone could call to mind. Tudor society could be cruel to a woman of advanced age with no male protector.

Two slovenly boys allied themselves with the procession, mimicking the upright bearing and solemn faces of the mourners. Lord Burghley dispatched an usher to teach them respect, but they kicked his shins and ran hallooing down the street. Lord Burghley grimaced at the unseemliness of it all.

At the southern gate to the old Roman town, by the Guildhall, the party halted in a stamping, steaming throng while horses were brought from a stable behind the Spread Eagle Inn. The bishop spoke some words over the casket, and the clergymen and choirboys began to retrace their steps up the hill to the cathedral.

"What is thy honest opinion of Crossly?" Bishop Wickham asked of the dean.

"I did not know the man," the dean replied. "I have heard what they say of him, but I did not know him."

"If, as some say, he bore the mark of Satan, then our ceremony today was blasphemous."

"The truth about him will never be known."

"Christian charity is the wisest course, and Burghley required it."

"Indeed." They nodded in unison as they walked away.

While the depleted party mounted their horses, the mourners from Lincoln bade farewell and dispersed to their homes. A carriage was furnished for Catherine to ride in, and Lord Burghley took his place beside her. Crossly's casket was strapped inside a makeshift hearse. When all was ready, Thomas Cecil swept pageboy and pennant up onto his saddle and led the riders out onto the heath in a whirl of mud and hooves and Godspeed from the dogs of the town.

The cathedral towers and the hills of the wold's edge faded quickly behind them as the party struck open country. Conversation lessened and then ceased entirely. For two hours, they rode across the barren, dyke-crossed fenland, eastward toward the sea. Slowly the rain eased, and the gloom of late afternoon stole upon them. At last, they came among the villages where Richard Crossly was well-known; and here, people were gathered in the streets with a purpose. Heads were lowered in respect as the hearse passed, and caps were tipped. Here, the talk was of Crossly himself, not his entourage, though the opinions expressed of him were curiously varied and led to more than one argument after the procession had passed.

"Aye, the Lord bless and keep 'im," an old woman remarked as the hearse moved through the market square of Hoyland village.

"The Lord won't be havin' nowt to do wi' 'im," replied a stout man with leather pads on his shoulders, who looked like he had carried more on his back than his brain could ever guess.

"That devil-maker Dee saw to it," chimed in his brother by his side. "Ironfist they called Crossly for a purpose. Ironfisted and stony-hearted he truly was."

"For shame," replied the woman, turning to them. "He was ever kindly to the church. He prayed in it each night to my certain knowledge and gave all the money he had to the restorin' of it."

"Prayed?" The man laughed. "Prayed? 'Tweren't no prayin' done to Abbot Gervase fifty years ago at the abbey, not by a long chalk. John's wife had an uncle who was there, eh, John?"

"Not no prayin', no. Her uncle was a pikeman in Burghley's troop. He stormed the abbey alongside o' Crossly. He said that when they finally dragged Crossly from out the fiery ruins, he was not the same man as the one that went in. Transformed beyond all belief, he said."

"'Twas the witchin', they all a-reckoned."

"And all those nights in the church thereafter? Sexton Palethorpe saw 'em with his own eyes—Crossly and them wizards a-dancin' with the devil. 'Tis true, right enough."

"Fifty years gone now," said the old woman. "Let 'im rest in peace."

At the gate to St. Neot's, the parish church of Hoyland, the stonemason quarreled with the sexton on the subject of the deceased's respectability and knocked him to the ground with a single blow, even as the cortege was awaiting word to enter the vestibule. Both men were aware of the time Richard Crossly had spent in the church during the latter part of his life, but the purpose of his visitations was in dispute. The stonemason maintained that Crossly was remorseful over his role in suppressing the monks of Hoyland Abbey. To earn salvation was the purpose. The sexton averred that the blackhearted Crossly who had torched the abbey on King Henry's orders was the same villain who had later cavorted in it with the sorcerers. To raise demons was the purpose.

They were in agreement, however—though both of them had been mere boys at the time—that a vast change had been wrought in the person of Richard Crossly at the time of the destruction of the abbey. Village lore was above dispute, and there was no denying that Crossly's later years were best characterized by reclusion. But when the discussion returned to saint or sinner, the stonemason felt the might of Christian right in his arm and knocked the sexton to the ground. "Speak no ill of the dead," he warned. "The man will lie in consecrated ground."

The sexton rubbed his chin and stared up at his antagonist. "If they must be a-buryin' 'im at all, then 'tis best they bury 'im face-down, the better to meet 'is maker."

Catherine Crossly turned her head to see the cause of the disturbance by the lych-gate. Then the curate brought word that preparations within were complete, and the pallbearers lifted the casket onto their shoulders and led the rest of the mourners into church. Thirty villagers rose from their seats, and the choirboys took up a dirge.

The interior of the church still bore signs of the days of suppression: beams blackened by smoke, cracked mortar high up on the walls, leaded windows unfinished, and pews not carved. *But the work is proceeding apace now,* Lord Burghley thought, supporting the arm of the widow as they walked. *Whatever wrong had been committed here, it had been wrought by the papists themselves. There had been no choice but purification of the avarice and debased ritual with a clear flame. Crossly was right then, and he was right thereafter. It was the common man who did not appreciate what King Henry had set out to do, and yet it was the common man who had the most to gain. The papists had sucked him of his wealth and chained him to a false ideology. Crossly was unblemished. If only Catherine could be consoled with these thoughts, perhaps she would find peace.* Lord Burghley sighed and helped Catherine Crossly to her seat.

The funeral service was long and tedious. Too many fine words were said about a man who was viewed circumspectly at best by the congregation. Either they already knew him worthy of the words and were embarrassed by them, or they guessed him unworthy and were annoyed. The clergyman administered the sacrament and said a final benediction over the casket. He snapped his prayer book shut. The pallbearers moved forward into the chancel, raised the casket aloft, and carried it over to the side of the altar, by the northeast wall of the church. In the wall was a niche carved centuries before. It was of good height and width but barely four feet deep. *Yet large enough for me to join thee anon,* Catherine reflected with a wry smile.

In front of the niche stood an elaborate stone sarcophagus waiting to receive the casket. As the pallbearers began the job of transferring the casket to the sarcophagus, Catherine Crossly and her friends turned away and left the church quickly as if the day had lasted too long and grown, even to them, distasteful. Outside, an autumn chill permeated their gowns and hastened their departure.

Edward Kelley trotted up to Catherine's side and spoke some private words of condolence. Then he asked, "Wilt thou stay on at Ketteringham Lodge, Lady Crossly? It is a capacious residence for a solitary widow."

"I will stay on," Catherine replied. "It hath served Richard and me well for fifty years, and it will see me out kindly. It was a gift from the king to Richard's father, after all, so I will not relinquish it lightly."

"Only, I have found that living alone in a great empty space irks me as I age."

"Do not fret over me please."

"May I escort you safely back to Ketteringham, my lady?"

"Lord Burghley will see to that, thank you, Edward. Get along with thee now and find conviviality with John Dee at the Red Lion. And treat Mr. Laski to some good English ale. Adieu, my friend."

Edward Kelley stopped, looking downcast, and let Catherine walk on. By the lych-gate, Catherine faltered. The stonemason started for her side but was blocked by those of higher birth. Nevertheless, he was close enough to see her regain her poise and to hear her cast these parting words to her husband and the fast-fading light: "Though I had but a moment to choose thee, I have no regrets. And though I now must live on without thee, I shall not weep. And though all else that I have known and loved was lost to me long ago, I will not be afraid. Only do I curse the deity who brought this cruel fate upon us both. Rest now, my love, until I may lie all-knowing beside thee."

CHAPTER 3

Hoyland Church
September 2017

Four hundred and thirty years after Richard Crossly's funeral and fifteen feet from the spot where his coffin had lain during the service, a young Englishwoman named Sarah Harcourt stood and admired a gleaming brass plaque set into the stone floor in front of her. She was captivated by its beauty. The design was exquisite. Each rivet on the knight's armor and each seam on the lady's dress—every curlicue and scallop on the border—was picked out in wonderful detail. Who could do such magnificent engraving these days?

When her eyes had had their fill of the fine workmanship, she stooped and placed two sticks of heelball and a roll of white paper on the floor beside the plaque. Then she reached into a canvas bag and pulled out tape, scissors, and a notebook and pencil, which she placed on the opposite side. Finally, she drew out a faded brown cushion and dropped it onto the flagstones at her heels. Satisfied with the symmetry, she sat down.

Brass rubbing was Sarah Harcourt's passion. She loved the idea of replicating a beautiful image simply through the pressure of a stick of wax. To transmute brass into paper, to change yellow into stark black and white, and to steal the soul of a knight and pin it on your living room wall—all these things were a delight to her. And there were memorial tablets in churches all over England just waiting for her steady touch.

Sarah took a deep breath and composed herself. She had learned that meticulous attention to detail produced the kind of clean, spare work that commanded a high price in the antique shops of

Bloomsbury, but it ran against her nature. In her daily life, she was impulsive to a fault. Those of her friends who had watched her hop nervously from one task to the next were convinced that neurosis had set in early. Sarah was tall and thinner than most people would think healthy. Her hair was auburn with ginger highlights. She had a certain kind of intrinsic beauty that was not enhanced by cosmetics. Not yet twenty-five, she had already climbed several rungs of the corporate ladder at a London merchant bank. And in keeping with her ambition, it was the lure of money as much as a love of art that had brought her to St. Neot's Church in Hoyland.

Sarah picked up the notebook and pencil and copied the inscription that was inlaid into the floor alongside the plaque.

> This brass figure represents Richard Crossly (deceased 1587), habited in full plate armour with a flowing mantle and gauntlets reaching to the middle joint of the fingers. By his side is the figure of Catherine, his wife (deceased 1593), and at their feet are two wild men with clubs. Faithful servants of the House of Tudor.

"Richard Crossly, eh?" she muttered. "Well, meet your new agent, sir. We're going to be famous, you and I. I'll have your picture hanging in every country house from Colchester to California. Just hold still a minute." She unrolled a sheet of paper and spread it over the length and width of the brass. She taped the paper carefully at the edges, smoothing outward from the center each time. The church was cold, and the chill of the stone slabs pierced her bare ankles. Outside the church, dry leaves rustled against the stained glass windows, borne upward by the wind that swirled among the buttresses. Autumn was fast turning to winter. She leaned forward and ran her fingertips over the surface of the paper, testing the stress, affirming the texture. Satisfied, she rocked back onto her heels.

Bare light bulbs hung from the huge fan vault of the nave, casting multiple images of the crucifix onto the center aisle. A chiaroscuro of umbra and penumbra splashed across the iron-gray grid of stone. All was silence and stillness. Sarah tried to concentrate on the task ahead of her. She selected a stick of beeswax and lampblack, reached to the upper-left corner of the paper, and began to rub across the surface with smooth short strokes. "Rub-a-dub-dub, two wild men with clubs," she murmured.

Sarah did not consider herself a religious person, but the rhythm of the rubbing and the tranquility of the church gave her pause to contemplate the potency of religion. All around her was physical evidence of its power—religion as stone and religion as wood and cloth and colored glass—embodiments of an ideology. It wasn't that she believed this weight of evidence proved the existence of God but rather that she doubted God could not exist in the presence of such a sincere preponderance of human endeavor over millennia. It would be a monstrous deceit.

Sarah had always thought of religion in terms of the accumulation of human effort directed toward it—the years of hewing and carving that had gone into all the blocks of stone that were here stacked upward to shape something much more meaningful than its parts; the months of intricate embroidery that had been invested in every piece of tapestry; and the devotion that had cut, leaded, and assembled thousands of fragments of tinted glass into pictorial symbols of faith. Was it all an aberration of the human purpose? Had man created God? And all around her were even more tangible examples of the power of religion: a stone step worn away to nothing by the shuffling feet of worshippers down the ages and a wooden rail polished flawless by the elbows of numberless communicants. A single believer might indeed have no significance—he could be misguided, fearful, or self-serving—but in sum, did it all mean nothing? The icy power of forces beyond her comprehension made her shiver.

"Master Crossly," she said, "if thou wert not such a shining, pretty knight, I'd leave thee to the church mice and hie me to a hostelry." She smiled to herself and wondered if people really did talk like that once upon a time. She resumed rubbing, but her strokes came broader and heavier now.

Here at her fingertips was Richard Crossly, now nothing more than dust and brass, but once flesh and blood sitting in this same church hundreds of years ago. And hundreds of years before that, monks had paid homage to the same God on the same spot with Crossly half a millennium away in the future. Even before the monks, so they say, the ancient Britons had respected the Hoyland hill as a holy place, so what would our descendants think of us? Hopelessly naive? Sadly misguided? She liked to think that her progeny would still journey to this sanctified outpost and carry on the tradition. It would always survive. She was sure of that. Religion would endure until it fulfilled its own prophecies.

She had almost stopped rubbing now. Her fingers held the heel-ball limply. She sat upright, staring at the altar, lost in languid contemplation. That was how religion derived its strength she suddenly realized—infinitely incremented, indefinitely accumulated, a force that would not be denied. As intimations of the divine flooded her mind, a peculiar drowsiness came over her—not sleepiness exactly, more like a detachment from her surroundings, a shifting of focus from the physical world to a spiritual plane. Brass rubbing faded from her thoughts, and the stick of wax slipped from her fingers. She could feel herself lifted out of the present and sent tumbling down the corridors of time.

She heard a sound and stiffened. She listened intently, but the sound did not recur. Then again, this time a scraping sound. Something brushed against the tapestry that hung from the altar. The edges of the cloth were swaying. Were they? The movement stopped, and only the silence of the church echoed around her. As much to give herself time to collect her thoughts as to finish the job, she bent low over the brass and resumed rubbing. But her strokes grew increasingly angular and uneven, and she began to acknowledge that this was destined to be yet another mediocre piece of work.

Then out of the corner of her eye, she saw a flash of silvery light over by the communion rail. She hardly dared raise her eyes from the paper. She was so close to panic. When she did finally look up, the air had taken on a shimmering, opaque quality that disoriented her and made her nauseous. She pressed her fingers against the sides of the plaque for support.

Then there was a low, guttural noise, and something diaphanous began to cut a path toward her through the mist. She froze, petrified. At the last moment, the object swerved to one side, and she felt a chill as it passed by. Pinpricks of ice stung her hands and face. She had no idea what had just happened and sat staring at the altar for several seconds.

The haze slowly began to clear. She leaned forward, intent on packing up her things and leaving, and saw the white paper in front of her splattered with bright-red blood that trailed off the paper and onto her hands and all up her arms and chest. She collapsed sideways into the aisle with a single sharp cry.

A few seconds later, the vicar of Hoyland Church, the Reverend Nigel Applewhite, poked his head out of the vestry and asked Sarah if she needed something. Receiving no reply, he opened the door and walked toward the chancel. When he saw her crumpled body in the aisle, he ran first to her side and then turned and hurried to the front of the church. Brian Kenning, Sarah's boyfriend, was sitting in his red MG sports car outside the church with a crossword puzzle in his lap. His eyes were closed, and he was half-asleep.

"Dr. Kenning! Dr. Kenning!"

When Brian heard the panicky voice of the vicar, he opened his eyes and rolled down the car window. "What's wrong?" he called back.

"Come quickly, Dr. Kenning. It's your girlfriend. She's had an accident." Not aware of how anyone could easily have an accident on the floor of a deserted church, Brian didn't anticipate a serious situation. He got out of the car and walked even-paced toward the vicar. "She's lying on the floor. Do come quickly!"

Brian picked up speed at these words and jogged to the vicar's side. Together, they hurried to where Sarah was now leaning against a pew, breathing heavily. "What's the matter?" Brian asked her.

"I'm not sure. I was doing the brass rubbing and then…" Her voice trailed away. She seemed to be teetering on the edge of consciousness. Brian supported her head. He brushed the hair away from her eyes. Her forehead was damp and cold.

"Did you pass out?" Brian asked.

"Something happened over there." She waved her hand in the direction of the altar.

"Are you feeling faint? Did you eat breakfast this morning?"

"Oh, really, Ms. Harcourt!" the vicar interjected.

"No, no, it's nothing like that," Sarah replied. "Something happened to the air in here. It was like being in a fog—no, underwater. I don't know. And then…" She stopped abruptly and pressed her spine hard against the pew. She plucked at the front of her sweater and stared down at it, puzzled. "The blood," she said. "Where's the blood?"

"Are you hurt? Where?"

"It's gone." The sweater was as spotless as when she first entered the church. She switched her gaze to the unfinished brass rubbing and saw only white paper with the black head of a knight taking shape upon it. "There is no blood," she concluded.

And in a moment, it was over. The two men helped Sarah to her feet and gathered her belongings for her. Brian rolled up the unfinished rubbing. They walked her to the car. Brian thanked Nigel Applewhite for his solicitousness, but the vicar seemed oddly uncomfortable and suddenly anxious for them to leave. Brian started the car and headed for the winding country road that led to the cottage of his aunt and uncle in the nearby village of Bittern Fen. He and Sarah were taking a short vacation from their busy work schedules so that she could do some brass rubbing and he could think through some tough research problems. The remote cottage of his aunt Polly and uncle Will had seemed the ideal getaway, but now this unexpected development in Hoyland Church seemed to threaten their seclusion.

Brian tried to be understanding. He said that she had been working too hard and not eating regular meals. Sarah was uncommunicative. Their relationship was barely three months old and hadn't yet developed the intimacy needed to weather emotional buffetings. His probing of the nature of her experience, terse and awkwardly expressed, was interpreted by her as insensitivity, and she responded curtly. Even at his most eloquent, Brian was unskilled at speaking from the heart.

Brian Kenning was a year older than Sarah and several inches shorter, their physical differences accentuated by his tendencies toward an expanding waistline and a receding hairline. Nevertheless, his features were handsome in a craggy sort of way, and friends said they made an attractive couple. Their commonalities revolved around a powerful determination for advancement. A mutual friend, martini in hand at a loud party, had once declared that they would break the ladder of success by clambering over each other's shoulders. But whereas Sarah's goals were pecuniary, Brian's were intellectual.

He had left this remote part of Lincolnshire nine years previously and had parlayed his incisive mind into an assistant professorship at the University of London in experimental physics. This achievement was grounded on research apprenticeships in three different countries: the University of Strasbourg, Northwestern University in Chicago, and Uppsala University in Sweden. This grand tour had lent him a certain cosmopolitan distinction in matters such as wine and literature, but it had not softened the flinty demeanor fashioned in the wild and windy fenlands. Though he laughed a great deal, it was a gruff sort of reflex action that endeared him to no one.

How had they come together then? The same mutual friend, when posed the same question, had spluttered into his martini and confessed himself damned if he could understand what she could see in him. Conceivably, in matters of the intellect, lucidity held an attraction for people like Sarah, who were cursed with as much turbidity as his lousy martini. On the other hand, he was certain that Brian was as proud as a peacock to have landed such an attractive girl as Sarah. Swirling his drink, the mutual friend had concluded that their relationship just might last.

As they left the village of Hoyland behind them, Brian tried a new tack. "So what do you think happened back there?"

"I'm really not sure. I was trying to do a good job with the rubbing, sort of thinking about God and stuff. I was quite calm and collected. Then I suddenly saw this—"

"You saw something? What?"

"It was over by the altar at first. Then it seemed to move in my direction."

"What did?"

She shook her head. "I looked down, and there was blood all over me."

"And then you fainted, yes? Am I right?" Brian could scarcely suppress his irritation. "You know, Sarah, I've been telling you and telling you. You spend all hours of the day at the bank, then you come home and study till after midnight, and you get up early every morning. You'll wear yourself out, but you won't listen to me." He paused to try to contain his petulance. "You're not eating regular meals, snacking all the time. It doesn't surprise me that—"

"Look, Brian, I know the difference between being overworked and what happened back there. I'm not a complete idiot." She folded her arms and looked out the side window. "I think it was some kind of apparition."

"Oh, that's ridiculous," Brian responded instantly.

"A ghost or something. I don't know."

"That's impossible. You know it is. You just got a bit light-headed."

"I know what I saw."

"A momentary—"

"I know what I saw."

Brian drove the mile or so to Bittern Fen at high speed, frustrated at being unable to empathize with Sarah. He even felt some resentment at the emotional energy her misadventure was draining from him. He knew it was absurd to think that any human being couldn't spare the time to listen to another's problems, but he felt sure she sensed the impatience around the edges of his voice. They circled the topic a couple more times until Sarah suddenly blurted out, "Just drop it!" Brian was chagrined. Their relationship had not been tested like this before. He resolved to try to find more appropriate words for some future occasion, knowing it would require preparation. It was only when he acknowledged how poorly equipped he was to counsel others that she warmed to him a little.

"I truly don't know what happened back there," Sarah confessed, shaking her head.

"Look, Sarah, here's what I'll do. I have a friend in Chicago. His name is Harry Groh. I met him when I was at Northwestern. He's been fooling around with supernatural stuff for years. He might have some ideas, perhaps an explanation even. I'll give him a call." Sarah looked quizzically into Brian's eyes, wondering where that might lead. "Maybe there are such things as ghosts," he conceded.

CHAPTER 4

Joliet
October 2017

Karen Butler sat in the barber's chair with her eyes closed, listening to the scrape of the straight razor across her scalp. It was the second time she had submitted to this indignity in the name of science, but if bald was what Harry wanted, then bald was what he would get. It was early morning, and she needed to be ready soon for a day of experiments at the university. Having nothing else to do while her head was being shaved, she reflected on the changes that were happening in her life.

Since leaving her parents' home in Iowa, she had become bored with the class-study routine of her backwater university. However, the psychology experiments for which she had volunteered had lately injected some excitement into her days. On top of that, she had recently broken up with her boyfriend and resolved to learn to live life on her own terms with all the responsibilities that that entailed. Surprisingly, she had found that she could do it. Even her grades were up. All these things had buoyed her mood considerably, and she felt that her life was finally beginning to turn around.

Karen opened her eyes and stared at the photographs of baseball players that decorated the opposite wall of this quintessentially male institution: the small-town barbershop. "No wonder Harry likes this place," she said out loud.

"Excuse me?" the barber said.

"Harry Groh, my boss, he recommended this place to me. He loves baseball."

"He's that big guy with the beard from the university?"

"Right."

"Yeah, I know him. Dodgers fan, as I recall. Loud."

"Hmm," Karen agreed.

"We're all Cubs fans here."

"Who's that?" she asked, pointing to one of the pictures.

"Ron Santo," the barber replied, looking up.

"And him?"

"Ernie Banks."

"That one?"

"Joey Amalfitano. All Cubs legends."

"Hmm."

"Your boss always gets a charge out of our little gallery. Says he used to see these guys get their butts kicked regularly at Dodger Stadium when he was a kid. Yanks our chains all the time."

"That sounds like Harry. Passion shading to obsession."

"You're done," the barber announced at last, swiveling her chair toward the mirror.

Karen surveyed her gleaming scalp and professed herself satisfied with the job. She hopped out of the chair, paid the barber, and hurried down the street to the campus bus stop. She had just enough time to get to the university and prepare herself for the upcoming experiment.

*****

Tucked away in a corner of the campus of Central Illinois University stood the Illinois Center for Psychological Studies, also known as ICPS, the facility where Karen and her colleagues worked. Its isolation was in keeping with its research specialty: sensory deprivation. The northern perimeter of the site was shielded from the rest of the campus by a stand of Austrian pine, and each of its other sides melted into forest preserve. Deer browsed under the frosted and barred laboratory windows, and a red fox was often to be seen padding down the solitary access road on a summer evening.

The Department of Defense built and operated the facility. At the height of the Cold War, army psychologists had decided that sensory deprivation was a topic worthy of sponsorship. They had wondered if the ability to roam out-of-body, which seemed to be a typical reaction to sensory deprivation, might enable soldiers to tolerate the pain of wounds on the battlefield or withstand interrogation or possibly even access secure enemy facilities. Though the Pentagon's enthusiasm had waned over the years, their dollars continued to flow into research projects. Reactionary students had demonstrated against the facility in its early days, but good public relations work coupled with fees of ten dollars an hour for participating in experiments had restored the area to its former solitude. Few on campus knew what went on inside the building.

Mid-morning that day found Connie Cammaretta attaching coaxial cables to the back of a multichannel pen recorder on a workbench. The control room was small but connected via a wall-length observation window to a much larger laboratory filled with all manner of scientific equipment. Connie flicked a switch and watched seven pen tracks crawl up and down across the chart paper. An eighth pen flatlined. "The parietal lobe is not responding," she said at once. "Shit."

"Goddamn it," said Frank Koslowski, turning from the window to the recorder. "I checked those connections before she went into the tank. They were all fine. Harry's gonna be pissed."

"Can we reset it?"

"We can't pull her out now. She was late getting here, and we're running short on time. We'll just have to go with frontal and occipital. Better than nothing. Harry's gonna be pissed though. Let me know when the alpha pattern's established."

The clock on the wall of the control room said 10:45 a.m. The electronic timer on the control panel read *2:05* minutes after immersion. Frank crossed to the observation window and stared through the dim red light at the figure of Karen Butler floating naked in the tank. A blanket was always stretched across its surface to preserve the modesty of the subject, but Connie, who acted as chaperone to Karen during the experiments, had placed it a little too low down on this occasion, and Frank could see the upper halves of Karen's breasts breaking the surface of the salt solution.

He never ceased to find the scene erotic. He supposed that the pink skull cap—or the nautilus, as the students called it, because of the shell-like noise it produced—should have lent a clinical detachment to the proceedings. But to Frank, it simply heightened the sense of helplessness and vulnerability of the girl. Her head had to be shaved to make the necessary electrical contacts, and for some reason, that also contributed to his arousal. He continued to stare at the swell of her breasts.

"Clear alpha coming in at eight hertz and twelve hertz," Connie said. "Noise is a bit higher than usual. Might be something to do with the bad connection. Scads of beta activity at twenty hertz. She's probably composing a term paper."

"How's her pulse?"

"Slow. Fairly good. She's doing fine."

Frank wondered what it was like to lose total contact with your surroundings, to cast your mind adrift in the ether without compass or rudder. He knew he would go mad in such isolation. He wrenched his eyes off the girl and surveyed the laboratory. The room was dominated by the sensory deprivation tank. The ten-feet-by-five-feet steel canister was filled with magnesium sulfate solution so dense that the human body floated on the surface like a cork. The temperature of the solution was maintained at ninety-three degrees Fahrenheit, the temperature of the skin's surface, so that all aspects of the sense of touch were eliminated.

Frank recalled that the neurophysiologist John Lilly, who had started all this flotation tank stuff, had speculated that the brain opened up under such conditions because it suddenly found its struggle against gravity suspended. It no longer had to devote neural circuitry to maintaining balance and adjusting muscular response. Cerebral RAM was fully available for other tasks.

"Twelve minutes gone and no changes," Connie whispered.

"Good."

Frank turned away from the window and began to fiddle with the spare nautilus cap that lay at the end of the bench. It was skin-tight, eyeless, and perforated throughout to allow body heat to escape. It seemed to him more appropriate to Torquemada's torture chamber. There were two breathing tubes connected to the mouth and the nose, two earphones relaying multispectral audio to each ear, and an array of EEG contacts spaced around the skull to sample electrical responses. All wires and tubes flowed together into a single inch-diameter plastic pipe that led from the top of the subject's head to a control box on the wall of the lab.

In addition to the absence of touch, there was no external stimulus from sight or sound. Frank recalled how in some early experiments, Harry had insisted that the inside of the mouth and the tongue be anesthetized, but this practice had been discontinued after a student had panicked and bitten off the tip of his tongue. Panic was the reaction of all first-timers in the tank, but the good subjects were able to suppress the feelings of disorientation by the third or fourth immersion. The next challenge was to subdue the beta wave response that the scientists associated with conscious thought processes, like mathematical calculation, logical reasoning, and recollection. If everything came together, the alpha response would unfurl like a rose, ushering in the meditative state they were trying to study.

"Beta's cooling down between occipital and frontal," Connie reported. "I think she's got it under control now. Alpha's increasing. She's got it this time." Frank walked back to the chart recorder, and together, they studied the characteristic pattern of the meditative state. Connie adjusted a couple of dials to increase amplification. "Shall I call Harry?" she asked.

"Wait a second." And it was just as well that they waited, because a few seconds later, the alpha wave cooled down too, and they were left with only a jagged, low-frequency delta wave. "She's fallen asleep again!" Frank groaned, turning away from the chart recorder. "I don't believe it. That's the third fucking time this week. I don't believe this girl. She's not getting a goddamn cent for this experiment." Fists clenched, he fought his anger for a moment and then resolved not to waste the session. "Let her sleep for five minutes, no more, then wake her up and start over. And fix that parietal contact!"

Connie cursed him under her breath. Frank stalked off in search of his boss, Harry Groh. He found him in his office with his back to the door, talking to one of his plants. Only Harry, with his domineering physical presence and brash humor, could get away with such ludicrous behavior. Harry Groh stood well over six and a half feet tall with facial hair in profusion. Well-built and clumsy, he had a passion for sport that was in no way grounded in athletic skill. Campus folklore maintained that he should be given a wide berth at intramural events and never ever be drawn into a discussion about baseball because baseball trivia was his first love, and it had to be inflicted daily on the weak and helpless.

Harry Groh's office contained two large rubber plants, one on either side of the window. He talked endearingly to one of these plants throughout the day. This plant he had named Sophie. He did nothing but curse and belittle the other plant, which was named Tex. On occasion, he would give Tex's pot a sharp kick. It was all in the interests of science. "Sophie's blooming," Frank offered, hoping to steer his boss into a good mood.

"There's no statistically significant difference between them," Harry replied. "Sophie may look to be in better shape, but then she has slightly the better of the sunlight. I weigh them every week, and there's no measurable human influence on their growth patterns. Those tree huggers are so full of shit."

"Really?" Frank said with rather too much incredulity to be genuine. "I wouldn't have guessed it just looking at them. Sophie looks in the pink."

Harry turned and stared hard at Frank, searching for a trace of sarcasm, but Frank was guileless and simply blinked back at him. They were not on amicable terms. Harry knew perfectly well what the source of the tension between them was; their relative positions at ICPS upset academic norms. Whereas he had no formal training beyond the master's level, Frank had a doctoral degree from one of the better Midwest schools and three years of postdoctoral experience. Yet through dint of hard work and fund-raising ability, Harry had become group leader while Frank was stuck at the level of staff scientist. Harry could understand why Frank squirmed under this violation of the usual pecking order, but that didn't mean he had to like him.

Frank scratched the back of this neck. He was nervous and uncertain how to report the morning's experiment. Harry towered over him in an unnerving manner and wouldn't allow him to feel at ease. "Karen Butler screwed up again," he blurted out. "She fell asleep for the third time this week. Can you believe it? Dan Patzner's much more reliable. You ought to can the Butler girl."

Harry reflected for a moment on Dan Patzner, the other student they had hired for the experiments. It was true that Dan showed up regularly for the sessions and dutifully did what was asked of him, but it always seemed to Harry that Dan viewed the experiments simply as a source of income. He might just as well have been flipping burgers or delivering newspapers. It was true that Karen did occasionally fall asleep in the tank, but at least she seemed genuinely interested in what they were trying to accomplish. And Harry sometimes had the odd feeling that Karen already knew more about sensory deprivation than any of the scientists did.

"Calm down, Frank. Karen's a good kid. We just need to involve her more. Make her feel like she's fully vested in the project. She's had the longest and deepest alpha state of any of the students we've tried."

"When she's awake."

"Granted. But she's the most promising subject we've got. We can't afford to lose her."

"I told Connie to let her sleep for a while and then try again."

"Sounds good. I'll be over in a minute."

The phone on Harry's desk rang, and Frank took it as a dismissal. Harry picked up the receiver and recognized the voice of Brian Kenning calling long distance. He made some sarcastic gibe in a mock British accent, recalling the origins of their friendship during Brian's year of postdoctoral research at Northwestern University. He had met Brian at an intercollegiate baseball game where he had been a coach and had overheard Brian explaining to a girl how baseball was a degraded form of cricket. Harry had discovered that he and Brian shared the same intellectual curiosity and love of obscure branches of science. They had kept in touch since then.

"How are things across the pond?" Harry asked, flopping into a chair and putting his feet on the desk. "What are you up to?"

"Oh, not too much. Nose to the grindstone. Burrowing into quantum mechanics. You?"

"Keeping the feds off my ass mostly. They'd like nothing better than to cut off my funding and my dick with a single stroke. Ha! They've lost faith in the project, truth to tell. Can't really blame them, I guess. It's always been a bit of a stretch. So what are you calling about?"

"I've got a question for you. And don't laugh when you hear it. What would you think if someone told you they'd seen a ghost?"

"I'm not sure I'm with you, chief."

"I've got a problem, Harry. My girlfriend, Sarah, collapsed in a church last week and returned to the land of the living muttering about having seen a ghost or an apparition or something. It's really bizarre. She's crying out for help, but I can't seem to find the right response. You mess around with things like that, don't you?"

"Not with that sort of thing. All we're doing is trawling the edges of brain function, trying to find out what all that empty attic space is for. We deliberately exclude the outside world."

"I know, but that's what must be happening here, isn't it, a cerebral aberration of some kind? No one believes any of that haunted house stuff. Set up a camera at the bottom of the mansion stairs, and old Lady Gossamer decides to take a long vacation."

"Yeah, I guess. I'm skeptical of the whole ghost thing myself."

"And we're not talking ball lightning or marsh gas or any of that crap, not in an innocuous little English church. It's gotta have something to do with Sarah's mental state." Brian paused for thought. "And I don't relish that possibility at all."

"I guess that is the most likely explanation."

"Don't your students hallucinate in the tank? That's what you once told me. It's probably the same thing. What's the story with hallucinations? What causes them? If I could offer Sarah some reasonable explanation on your authority, I think it might help her."

"Jeez, Brian, I don't know. It's true that our subjects do hallucinate after long periods of sensory deprivation. They say they see all kinds of weird shit. We have a theory about it. We think the brain is compensating for lack of stimulus from its surroundings. We picture the brain as a radio receiver. When the central control system gets no response from its sensors—eyes, ears, fingers, et cetera—it boosts the amplification to find out what's wrong, like you might turn up the volume on a radio.

"Startled, the cerebellum starts to search all frequencies at high gain for any kind of signal. Finding none, it dips into the memory bank along the way and pulls out fragments of past experiences that are readily accessible—anything being better than nothing. But it samples so randomly and with so much distortion that the perception part of the brain thinks the memory fragments are for real and freaks out. That's our working hypothesis anyway."

"How could that happen when the brain's got plenty to occupy itself with?"

"Good question. Normally, it doesn't. What was your girlfriend doing in the church?"

"Brass rubbing."

"What? What the hell's that?" Brian explained as succinctly as he could. "That would require a contemplative mood, wouldn't it?"

"I suppose so."

"Well, perhaps brass rubbing is like our flotation tank in a sense, only drier. Ha! Joke. Any other unusual circumstances?"

"Well, Sarah hadn't eaten any breakfast that morning."

Harry thought about that for a moment, and a clear small bell rang in his head. "No breakfast. Now that is something. By Christ! What if we were to heighten the other sensual cravings: hunger, thirst, even sex! Then we'd have the hypothalamus hunting for stimulus too. Let me talk to Frank about that one."

"But wait a minute. What about my problem? What do I tell Sarah?"

"Oh." Harry rattled his brain for a few seconds. "Tell her it's a well-known phenomenon that crackpot scientists like Harry Groh are on top of. Tell her it's just the brain cruising for action. Tell her no way she's crazy. One day, I'll introduce her to Karen Butler, who's seen snakes crawling out of the heat vents yet still puts her pants on one leg at a time like the rest of us. No need to fret."

"That's a bit cold. Sarah needs sympathy and understanding as much as she needs a rational explanation. With her, it's also an emotional thing."

"Ah, is it? Well, then you need the kind of psychologist who sits behind a 5K mahogany desk rather than in front of a 5K pen plotter. I'm not qualified in that field."

"I know you're not. That's something only I can deal with."

"I don't feel like I've been particularly helpful, Brian. I'm sorry. If we can get together, I'll be happy to discuss it with you some more."

"Yeah, let's try to do that."

"Any chance you can come over here?"

"There is. The American Physical Society is holding its annual meeting in Chicago around Thanksgiving. I'll try to attend. And thanks, Harry. You have been helpful even if only for confirming what I already suspected. Thanks much."

"You're welcome, chief. See you later."

"Cheers."

Harry hung up the phone and finished editing the galley proofs of his latest journal article. Then he leaned back in his chair and sucked his pen. They had eliminated all stimuli to the senses, but the brain was still responding to biochemical signals: Feed me! Water me! Kiss me! Harry jumped up and hurried to the control room, where Frank and Connie were examining long strips of chart paper taped to the benchtop.

"Karen did great the second time, Harry," Frank said as his boss entered the room. "Look at this alpha wave! Nine minutes long. I can't wait to do her exit interview. This is the best she's ever done."

"I told you she is a good subject," Harry replied. "But what's going on here?" He pointed to the tracings in several places. "Your baseline's trending upward. See? Here and here. You must not be calibrated right."

Connie and Frank stared at the places on the chart paper that Harry had indicated, brows furrowed. Sure enough, the alpha wave seemed to be perturbed. They checked scans from a previous experiment but could find nothing similar. "Voltage drift in the plotter?" Connie offered. "Or maybe there's pickup from the audio."

"We did have some problems with the parietal EEG," Frank confessed. "Connie fixed it in between the two sessions, but it could still be interfering with the—"

Harry wasn't listening. "I don't think so. It looks to me like the alpha response is superimposed on a very low frequency pattern. There's undulation in the baseline." He walked to the end of the bench and laid his head on it to view the chart from the side. "It's a modulation wave at just a few tenths of a hertz. See here." He pointed at the chart paper again.

"Could we measure it with this equipment?"

"We'll need to modify the detector to search at frequencies below the delta wave—say, below one hertz. I can build a tuner to do that. Then we can put Karen under again and find out what the frequency is. And tell her next time, no food or drink for twelve hours before the experiment. Better pay her double for this one. Bring Patzner in too. We'll do them both at the same time." Harry studied the pen tracks one last time then walked slowly back to his office, circuit diagrams forming in his head. Connie and Frank prepared for the closeout interview.

Down the hall, Karen Butler showered to remove the salt solution. After being deprived of all sensation for much of the morning, she luxuriated in the feel of the hot water on her skin and the smell of the perfumed soap. It was almost worth being denied such simple pleasures to have them later returned to you. The steamy shower evoked for her the eerie visions she had just witnessed in the tank.

She knew that something different and startling had happened to her this time. Her mind had traveled further than it had ever ventured before. But where had she been? What was that stunning new land she had discovered? A thrill surged through her body at the recollection of it. Did she have the ability and the courage to go there again?

Her friends called her crazy for wanting to subject herself to such mental gymnastics. They said that only a masochist would want to risk the terror of separating mind from body. But she was comfortable with it. It was no worse than wandering through a strange city at night or finding yourself lost in a forest. It was a challenge to see if you had the mental agility to survive.

Even as a little girl back in Iowa, she had liked to stretch her mind. At school, she was never satisfied with getting the right answer to a problem; she would always pester the teacher with what-ifs—some trivial, some perceptive. Now she had been given the opportunity to ask the same kinds of questions of herself.

Karen emerged from the shower into the adjoining locker room, her bald head glistening with water and wreathed in steam. She dried off, dressed, and joined Connie and Frank in the control room. She was annoyed to find Frank staring at her and greeted him brusquely. He was hoping for a flicker of friendship, forgetting that there had been no sharing of her earlier nudity, only his shameful intrusion.

"So?" Frank prodded.

"I don't know where I've been," Karen began, choosing each word carefully yet seeming to find them all inadequate. "I don't know what I've seen."

"Was it different this time?"

"I could feel myself falling out of the void—what you white-coats call the alpha void—but not back into this world. I was drawn to a new and different place, but each time I got close to it, I felt myself being dragged back like I was on an elastic rope. The remnants of my conscious mind didn't want to go there. It was all very vague, but I began to see faces melting into other faces—exquisite porcelain faces like I've never seen before. And unfamiliar trees—conifers with great drooping branches. I got the impression that it was all in the distant past, prehistoric or something. I don't know. The images freshened and then faded over and over again. I don't know where it was, but I've never been any place like it before. It was all indistinct yet somehow vivid. Hard to explain."

Karen could tell that Connie and Frank were disappointed with her ramblings. Just when she felt that real progress was being made, they seemed to think it was all leading nowhere. Frank in particular hastened to be done with the interview, behaving like a spurned lover. Connie became irritated by Frank's impatience and gradually withdrew from the questioning as well. With the distances between the three of them widening minute by minute, Karen struggled to give a coherent account of her experience, but she knew that the scientists couldn't distinguish this event from all the other hallucinatory tales they had heard. Frank put away his pen.

In desperation, Karen searched for some other way to convey to them the special sense of reality she had felt this time. She pulled from her pocket a slim book of poems she had brought with her to the lab for encouragement—the same book that nine months later would be brandished aloft by a Joliet police officer in her empty apartment as a sign of her possible mental instability.

"I've been reading stuff," she said as she paged through the book, "about experiences like this, experiences that other people have had, to try to make sense of it all. What happened today was just like something I've read. It's the closest I can come to describing it." After she had located the right page, she paused a moment to compose herself. "This is what it was like. Use your imagination."

And she read them a quotation from the poet Samuel Taylor Coleridge that immediately erased any lingering sexual thoughts from Frank's mind and replaced them with a dread intimation that the days of whimsical experimentation were drawing to an end and that they were on the verge of a real discovery that would test their dedication to scientific research. Young and small and delicate, Karen suddenly seemed stronger than either Frank or Connie. It was as much the sparkle in her eyes that knew the truth of the words as it was the words themselves.

> What if you slept, and what if in your sleep you
> dreamed, and what if in your dream you went to
> heaven and there plucked a strange and beautiful
> flower, and what if when you awoke you had the
> flower in your hand? Ay, what then?

CHAPTER 5

Joliet
November 2017

"Just one fucking doughnut," Dan Patzner pleaded, reaching across the breakfast table toward the beckoning box of a dozen glazed.

"Not a single doughnut, fucking, or otherwise," his roommate replied, pinning Dan's wrist to the table.

"But I'm dying, man. I haven't eaten a thing in twelve hours."

"No matter. There's sixty bucks in it just to last till noon. Remember what the Grohmeister said."

"It's not possible."

The two students glared across the table at each other. The breakfast table and the two chairs on which they were sitting were the only items of furniture strictly deserving of that appellation in the living room of their cheap apartment. At the other end of the room, four bald tires masqueraded as two armchairs, and stacks of tied-up newspapers covered by an afghan purported to be a couch. A black-and-white television set was perched on a seaman's chest that had been found behind a grocery store by the previous tenant.

"Focus on the money!" Dan's roommate ordered. "This morning's work will set us up for the weekend. We can get through this. Then beer at Nick's on Friday night, a couple of CDs, and party through till Monday morning. Focus!"

"What's all this *we*, White man? I don't see you pushing doughnuts away."

"I'm your conscience, man, your better angel. We're starving your body to stoke your mind. If you won't think of the cash, then think about your duty to mankind. You're gonna go down in history.

I can see the headline now: 'Daniel Patzner, First Man to Cross the Cerebral Cortex.' Or how about this: 'Trepanning for Gold along the Western Pituitary.' They'll name a psych class after you."

"Fuck mankind!" Dan shouted. "I don't give a rat's ass for mankind. I need food." He rubbed the back of his free hand across his lips, made a grab for the juice pitcher, and got his other wrist pinned. "What about my human rights?"

"You volunteered."

"You should've stopped me."

"As I recall," his roommate responded with weighty deliberation, "I tried to. But you wouldn't hear of it. You weren't afraid of anything, remember? This was gonna be easy money for you—ambrosia, no less, because Karen Butler was in it with you. Remember how you were itching to see Karen's tits? Do you? You were beyond reason."

"And I've never seen them yet thanks to that fucking jailer Connie."

"All nude! All bald! The greatest show on earth!"

Dan suddenly realized that he hated his roommate more than he hated hunger. This oily, long-haired medical student was actually enjoying his torment, prodding him deeper into the hot coals. That very afternoon, his motorbike would be out of the kitchen for good. Dan resented the fact that his roommate came from a wealthy North Shore family yet had chosen to exchange his birthright for axle grease and penury. He had money, but he never had any cash. Dan was keenly aware that he, on the other hand, came from poor Polish-Irish stock and was attending college solely to land a decent job at the end of it. His family had never had much money and thought of little else.

"I quit," Dan said.

"No way."

And as they glared at each other one more time, the humor of the situation evaporated. Dan's wrists were released. He didn't retract his arms, however, but simply turned his palms upward in supplication. "How will they know if I ate one lousy doughnut?"

"Don't ask me, man. Blood test, breath test, Sugarscope, the fact that you won't be humping the vending machine for once. You'll find a way to blow it for sure."

"Damn it all to hell," Dan said. "I guess I've got no choice. Let's go get it over with."

They stood up, grabbed their jackets, and walked out the front door. Joliet had sampled its first snowfall of the season: white and demure in the cornfields, gray and violated in the streets of the city. A mere two inches lay everywhere but around the roadside wheels of Dan's Volkswagen, where a snowplow had piled up at least a foot of the stuff.

Dan rocked the car between first and reverse, eventually surging into the street and skidding out of the path of a city bus. He drove recklessly along the wet interstate, his roommate gripping the dashboard like he was ready to take a bite out of it. They took the curve of an off-ramp at speed and slid down five miles of farm-muddied, snow-slicked roads to the campus gates. Dan dropped his roommate off and then drove to the ICPS facility. He parked the car and sloshed his way into the building.

Karen Butler was standing at the far end of the lobby, stamping her feet. She flashed her badge at the security guard and unbuttoned her winter coat. Dan joined her, and together, they removed their hats, unveiling their bald heads like two prized Easter eggs.

"Cueball," Dan said by way of greeting.

"Butthead," Karen acknowledged, bowing slightly. They rubbed the tops of each other's heads in small circles.

"Friendly banter," Dan said.

"Friendly banter," Karen replied.

The security guard glowered down on them from his vantage points of physical superiority and middle-aged complacency and swallowed hard. Their comic ritual seriously irritated him. Where was it written that eccentricity beat out reliability? By way of retribution, he scrutinized Karen's badge carefully, though he had admitted her a hundred times before, then made a show of checking the spelling of Dan's last name. He returned their badges, and the two students took off down the central hallway, checking out the labs that sprouted from either side.

"Eaten anything?" Karen asked.

"Nope. You?"

"No."

"Wanna play some pocket billiards tonight? Wanna carom off the cushions?"

"Not a chance."

"Spoilsport."

As they approached Harry Groh's office, the door opened, and Harry fell into step beside them. "Good morning, subjects A and B," he said with a hint of superciliousness. "No food for the last twelve hours, I hope?"

"Morning, boss," Dan replied. "Lovely morning but for the weather and every other shitty thing in this world. On the positive side of the ledger though, those pancakes and sausage really hit the spot."

"Only a bagel for me, sir," Karen interjected. "I'm the good one, remember?"

"Blood tests first," Harry said, pointing to the health physics lab and feeding off their vanishing smiles. "Oh, and, Dan, I've got a good one for you this morning, one you're sure to know the answer to being a true, red-blooded American boy. Imagine it's the 1920 World Series." His hands constructed a miniature ballpark in the space between them. "Indians against the Dodgers. Fifth inning. Dodgers got men at first and second and no outs. Got the picture?"

"Yeah, but I don't want it."

"Clarence Mitchell slashes a line drive past the pitcher. What happens next?"

"Mickey Mantle whips out his cup and catches the ball in it," Dan replied. Karen giggled, and Harry looked hurt. "I don't give a flying fuck, Harry, and I'm in a lousy mood."

"Think now. Two on and nobody out. What do you think happens?"

"You don't get it, do you? I truly don't give a shit."

"What?" Harry said in mock astonishment as he ushered them across the laboratory floor. "You really don't know? You are a true, red-blooded American boy, aren't you? Let me see that badge. Not one of those screaming foreigners, are we? Not one of those soccer freaks?"

"Fuck off, Harry, sir."

"It'd never happened before in the World Series, Dan, and it's never happened since. Never." Harry thrust out his right hand and pretended to catch a baseball. "Second baseman snags the line drive, steps on second, and tags the runner breaking from first."

"Triple play."

"*Unassisted* triple play," Harry stressed, pushing his face inches from Dan's. "The only time—the only time—it's happened in the World Series. Can you appreciate the significance of that? Of course, you can. Now the big question is this: Who made the play?"

Dan exhaled sharply. He was beginning to think Harry had finally cracked. His intensity was alarming. They bumped up against a lab bench littered with needles, gauze, and glass vials. There was no place to run. Dan shook his head and said, "I don't know."

Harry broke into a broad smile, poked him in the ribs, and said, "Tell you later. Roll up your shirt sleeve, close your eyes, and think of your country." A nurse stepped forward and stuck a needle in Dan's arm. "Let me know if his blood really is red," Harry asked the nurse.

*****

Within thirty minutes, Karen was immersed in the sensory deprivation tank, and Dan was stretched out on an experimental couch in a small lab next to the control room. This couch was intended to simulate conditions in the tank as closely as possible without the inconvenience of immersion. It had special foam padding contoured to the shape of the human body so as to minimize surficial contact. Both subjects wore the nautilus caps.

In the control room, Connie Cammaretta supervised the meters and gauges while Harry and Frank watched Karen Butler through the observation window as she let the reins of the conscious world slip away. The clock on the wall of the control room ticked past ten o'clock while the hand of the timer that registered duration in the deprivation tank swept the seventeenth minute. Harry was examining the pen tracks with Connie, searching for the modulation wave they had detected during the previous experiment, when all hell broke loose.

Without any warning whatsoever, Dan suddenly jackknifed with a single violent spasm and fell off the couch. Harry and Frank heard the loud thud as he hit the floor, and their eyes met for an instant. They raced into the adjacent lab. "Watch the controls!" Harry yelled to Connie over his shoulder. Dan lay motionless on the floor, bent double. Harry wrestled the nautilus mask off his face. He pulled back an eyelid and saw that Dan's pupil had rolled up into the top of the socket and was fluttering rapidly. "He's unconscious," he shouted.

"I'll call the paramedics," Frank replied and ran back into the control room.

Harry administered CPR until Dan finally opened his eyes and began to gasp for breath. "You're gonna be all right, Dan," Harry reassured him. "Just lie still. You'll be fine." Dan stared up at him fearfully but said nothing.

Back in the control room, Connie stared intently at the chart recorder. "Something's happening to Karen's EEG, Frank," she said. "I've never seen anything like this before. Look at it!" She turned to Frank, but he was chattering excitedly into the phone and didn't acknowledge her. As she turned back to the recorder, she glanced through the observation window at the sensory deprivation tank. "Oh my god! Karen!" Connie screamed.

Through the window, she saw Karen's arms thrashing wildly while magnesium sulfate solution slopped over the side of the tank and onto the floor of the lab. Karen's head slid below the surface, and one leg kicked high in the air. The plastic tube that had formerly connected the nautilus mask to the control box on the wall now whipped freely in the air like a snake and slapped against the side of the tank. Karen's head bobbed back to the surface, and her body began to twist from side to side.

"Karen!" Connie screamed again. She jumped to her feet, sending her chair crashing across the room. She ran into the lab, came up behind Karen, and slipped her forearms under Karen's armpits to hold her head and shoulders above the surface of the salt solution. She wedged Karen's body against the wall of the tank with one hand and ripped the mask off her face with the other. The breathing tube, which was bitten completely through, had shattered into several large pieces. There was blood on Karen's swollen lips. Her cheeks were ashen. "Are you okay? What happened?" There was no reply.

Summoning all her strength, Connie dragged Karen's naked body over the side of the tank and laid her gently on the floor of the lab. She grabbed a couple of towels that were on a chair. She wrapped them tightly around Karen's legs and torso and sat her upright. "Are you okay?"

"I'm all right," Karen replied. "I think. Give me a minute." She closed her eyes and vomited magnesium sulfate solution against the side of the tank. "I'm all right," she repeated.

"Oh, Jesus, Karen. Fuck me."

Frank was just about to set down the phone after summoning the paramedics when the door to the outer hallway burst open, and in rushed an Australian scientist by the name of Peter Wilkinson. "You bloody nutcases!" he spluttered, waving a strip of paper in Frank's face. "You've ruined my experiment! I've been calibrating the transmissivity of my new tank all morning. Then you go and send this bloody great spike through the electronics! What the hell are you doing?"

Frank stared at the chart paper, confused. He knew that Wilkinson was conducting experiments on long-range dolphin communication in the suite of labs next to theirs, but he couldn't make the connection. "What are you talking about?" he replied. "Look, there's been—"

"All bloody morning I've been counting," Wilkinson interrupted. "It's a three-hour run! You gotta give the rest of us warning when you—you can't simply…" Just then, Harry walked into the control room with a worried look on his face, clutching the nautilus

46

mask. Frank set the phone down gently. "Christ, Harry, you look shook up," Wilkinson said, rapidly calming down.

"There's been a bad accident," Harry said. "One of my students—"

"Oh, I'm so sorry. I didn't realize."

"Is Dan okay?" Frank asked.

"He seems to be," Harry replied. "I think he's broken his wrist, maybe cracked a rib. I can't tell. Where are the paramedics?"

"They're on their way," Frank replied.

"What kind of an accident?" Wilkinson asked, but they ignored him.

"Where's Connie?" Harry said to Frank.

"I don't know. She ran into the lab."

"Can you keep an eye on the student next door for a minute?" Harry asked Wilkinson.

"Sure thing. You fellers do what you have to do."

Harry and Frank hurried into the lab. It was empty. "They must have gone to the locker room," Harry said, and they ran to it.

Karen was sitting on a bench and wrapped in towels when the two men entered. Connie was next to her, massaging the back of her hand. Karen looked up at Harry and Frank. "You're not allowed in here," she said with a wan smile. "Girls only. I think I chipped a tooth." She put a finger in her mouth and felt her front teeth. "I'm all right, Harry. Get outta here and let me get dressed. Go look after Dan."

*****

There was a big commotion in the hallway when the paramedics arrived. They were escorted by the desk security officer, the head of the facility, and a handful of curious onlookers. Dan and Karen were put on stretchers and transferred to the campus medical center. The director of the facility had a few harsh words for Harry then requested a meeting in his office in half an hour and left in a huff. Harry, Frank, and Connie sat in the control room to compose themselves, each thinking furiously about the events of the last fifteen minutes but saying little.

"I'd better go mop the lab," Connie said.

"You can do that later," Harry replied.

Peter Wilkinson entered the room, the strip of chart paper still in his hand. "Hey, guys, I'm sorry I barged in like that before. I had no idea your kids were in trouble."

"Don't worry about it," Harry replied. "You weren't to know. I think they're both going to be fine. Why did you come in anyway?"

Wilkinson offered him the chart paper. "You sent a big spike through the electronics."

"We did?" Harry said.

"Yeah, a bloody huge one, eight seconds long at a frequency of about three megacycles per second. That's slap-bang in the middle of my measurement range. Take a look for yourselves. Here!"

Harry took the paper from him and examined it. He passed it to Frank. "But we didn't do anything to send out an electronic impulse," he said. "We were just doing our normal monitoring of the kids' brain waves."

"Well, someone did."

*****

Dan emerged from a medication-induced sleep in the university hospital, alone. The walls of his room were pale green and refreshing. Watercolors of barns and cornfields reminded him of home even though he had grown up in a tenement on the west side of Chicago. By contrast with the Stygian forest he had found himself in right before the blow to the solar plexus pitched him off the couch, this was the womb of heaven.

He luxuriated in the starched sheets, the pastels, and the faux butternut trim. He noted that his left wrist was bandaged and immovable. For ten minutes, he lay still, his mind skirting the events of the morning. He spied orange juice on the bedside table and sat up and drank some. It made him ravenous. Unable to locate a call button, he decided he had had enough of indulgence, dragged himself out of bed, and set off in search of food.

In the room next door, he found Karen sitting on the edge of her bed. She looked up nervously when he entered as if they were about to begin a second date and she was ashamed of what had happened on the first one. Noticing that Karen was wearing an identical turquoise gown to his own, Dan made some flip remark about the fashion sense of the hospital administration, but it withered and died on the vine.

"Are you feeling better?" Karen asked him.

"I must have broken something," Dan replied, holding up his splinted and bandaged wrist. "To tell you the truth, I don't remember much about what happened. How about you? You look like you went ten rounds with Mike Tyson."

"Why did you switch it off?" Karen said immediately, and Dan froze. "This time, I was really there. I wasn't dreaming, and it wasn't a hallucination. I was really there."

"What? Where?"

"In that place beyond the alpha state. I don't know what to call it or how to describe it. Didn't you see me?"

Dan felt the skin on the back of his neck tighten. "What do you mean?"

"I was in a forest," Karen continued. "I've been there twice before—well, almost there. But this time, it was for real." She hesitated. "I saw you there."

"What are you talking about? I haven't been anywhere. I was lying on the couch in the lab, and then I got sick. I passed out. I didn't go anywhere."

"You were there for a little while at least, then you switched it off, pulled back into alpha, just like I used to do. But I'm learning to control it now."

Dan stared out the window at the stretch of forest preserve that separated the campus from farmland. The snow had begun to melt in the open fields. The feeble autumn sun had reached its zenith. There was a tight lump in the back of his throat. "This place beyond the alpha state, it's full of those dark-green pine trees? The ones with the funny long branches?"

Karen nodded, her face brightening. "Yeah. I knew it. You were there all right."

"I don't know what happened," Dan said, trying to banish the vestigial images that had preceded his fall. "I was just trying to get Harry's alpha state for him and get the fuck out of there. We were going to get burgers and then go to Best Buy. Then someone punched me in the gut, and I ended up in this candy-striped hellhole. I didn't go anywhere, and I'm not into any of that mystical crap. You didn't see me anywhere, all right?"

Karen swung her legs to and fro and then pointed her toes at the floor. "Okay. Sure. We can talk about it later. Get the nurse to feed you. You look like shit."

Dan stared at her. "Seriously, Karen, why are you so into this stuff? What kind of a kick do you get out of it? Why would you want to shave your head for it? Don't you care about your appearance, for Christ's sake?"

"Don't you?"

"It's different for a guy."

"Is it? Look, vanity is not one of my shortcomings, Dan. Boys chase me no matter what I look like. That's not the point. I just seem to have an aptitude for this mind-bending, and I find it totally fascinating. Don't you?"

"I do it for the money."

"Yeah, I know you do. It's just a game with you."

"It's getting to be a bit more than a game," Dan said, ruefully holding up his bandaged wrist.

"Are you afraid of it? I'm not. These visions, these experiences, they're all a part of me. It would be like being afraid of yourself. Can't you see?"

"I don't know about that, but I do know it's a helluva way to earn a few bucks. I'm gonna find Harry." As he turned to leave the room, he said, "See ya, Cueball."

The back of his hospital gown flapped open as he walked out, and Karen smiled and said, "See ya, Headbutt."

*****

In the hospital lounge, where the pastels began to harden in transition to a sterner world outside, Harry Groh was sitting on a couch, waiting for news of his students. He was very agitated and extremely worried. If either of them should have serious health effects as a result of their misadventures, his job was on the line. "How are you feeling?" he asked when he saw Dan approaching.

"Not too bad," Dan replied, flopping down beside him on the couch. "The wrist hurts a little."

"Wait till the anesthetic wears off. It'll hurt like sin. Look, Dan, I'm really sorry this has happened. I'm also sorry that I came on so strong to you this morning with the baseball quiz. I apologize. I gotta play the game."

"Sure, Harry. I play it too. It's all right. As my roommate keeps reminding me, I wasn't coerced into any of this. I did volunteer." Harry offered him a packet of cheese crackers, and Dan wolfed them down. "Any idea what happened back at the lab?"

"It's a mystery," Harry replied. "Two people knocked silly at the same time can't be a coincidence. There must be some connection, but Lord knows what it is. It'll take a while to decipher the EEG responses. Then we'll have to do exit interviews. We may never know what happened, but one thing's for sure and certain: The Department of Defense is gonna play hell with me when they find out. They'll probably slash my funding to the bone. I might even be outta here."

"Yeah, I suppose so," Dan said, and to break the silence that followed, he added, "So tell me, who was it who made that triple—sorry, that *unassisted* triple—play?"

"What? Oh!" Harry smiled. He stretched his legs out in front of him and folded his arms. He thought for a moment and cast a brief glance at Dan. "I know all you students think I'm crazy." Dan remonstrated with him, but Harry would have none of it. "Yeah, you do. You think I'm nuts. But just bear with me for a minute. Let me explain why I'm into baseball stats." Harry stared at the ceiling and then at the floor. "Let me put it this way. There was a time when the ground beneath our feet was firm, a time when we knew what was true and what was not. In fourteen hundred and ninety-two, Columbus sailed the ocean blue. You know what I'm talking about? But times have changed. National Geographic reveals that the voyage actually occurred in 1493, that Columbus wasn't his real name after all, and that satellite imagery has cast serious doubt on the blueness of the ocean. You can't trust anything anymore."

"You lost me," Dan said.

"Whose version of the past do you prefer? My expert witness versus yours, ten three-minute rounds. You read the newspapers. You know how it is. The DA says the defendant skewers babies in his basement. The defense attorney says the defendant gets referrals from cherubim and seraphim. Then the judge turns to the jury and asks them to create the truth from two contrasting rolls of whole cloth. Stamp it and seal it and put it in the book, and that's the way it happened. Pending appeal.

"But there was a time when the judge could peer meaningfully over his pince-nez, one eyebrow raised, and a member of the public—third row, small mustache—would break down sobbing and confess to the crime. The events of the past were incontrovertible. People knew and respected that. Nowadays, the past is a matter of opinion." Harry shook his head repeatedly from side to side, sorely troubled by this intractable problem, which Dan still failed to grasp.

"Richard III smothered the princes in the Tower of London, right?" Harry asked, turning to Dan for affirmation yet turning away before he could respond. "Not at all. Tucked them up in bed and sang them a lullaby. And all Lizzie Borden was guilty of was a minor infraction of OSHA regulations governing the safe use of sharp-edged tools. Even Rembrandt was out painting the picnic table while his apprentice dashed off *The Night Watch*. It's the same everywhere these days. Nothing can be relied upon. Did I back into your car, or did you drive into my rear end? Flip a coin. Maybe it never happened at all. You want witnesses? Plenty available at a hundred bucks an hour to have seen anything you care to name."

52

Harry ran a hand through his hair and hunched over till it seemed his shirt buttons must explode. "Are you getting the message yet? When you're sliding off a cliff and the ground is slipping away beneath you, what do you grab hold of? A big rock? A small rock? What will be strong enough to save your life? Pebbles? Sand?" Harry Groh, the great bear of a man, clasped his fingers together till the knuckles whitened and the softer flesh turned fireplug red. His mind seemed to be focused on something very small and essential.

"Baseball stats are immutable. Forty thousand witnesses and a mile of videotape. No varnish, no tarnish. They're the undisputed record of actual historical events that touched a million lives—lightly and briefly, I admit, but touched them all the same. They're something you can grab and hold on to for all time to save your life."

Dan was prepared to let him continue and finish his point, but Harry was done. His fingers had uncurled, leaving his palm weighing the essence of that elusive something. But Dan still didn't have the answer he wanted. "So who made the play?"

"Rashomon," Harry answered and chuckled. "Utility infielder for the Yokohama Whales. No, actually, it was Bill Wambsganss."

CHAPTER 6

Bittern Fen, England
November 2017

In the coastal fenlands of Lincolnshire, land and sea keep uneasy company. At low tide, the sea parades its conquered ground, flaunting acres of sandbanks as temptation to the reckless beachcomber. As the tide turns, the sea consumes the sand from all sides, picking off any living thing deceived by its show of benevolence. The waters advance swiftly then under cover of marsh and dyke until they meet their match at high tide in the shell-studded dunes. There are long sieges and sudden incursions—an island gained, a pool lost—but there are no winners.

The natives in these parts are industrious and contented, and only a single dread lurks in their minds: the big flood. For at least the last thousand years, there has been a succession of devastating floods in the fen country. All that is needed is a juxtaposition of high tide and gales from the northeast and the sea is unstoppable. All the concrete walls and sandbags in the world cannot oppose it. Once the defenses are breached, there's nothing to be done. The water settles with deathly silence over the flat ground, reaching five or ten miles inland and swallowing the startled cows, the pop-eyed sheep, and the aged farmer too slow to reach his roof.

The destruction is always frightful and the cause of much alarm to everyone but the fen people themselves, who know the certainty of it and the place, just not the time. Time, however, is of small consequence to a land that is much the same today as it was when the invading Romans discovered a Belgian colony ruling the marshes there two thousand years ago.

On a typical windy November day in these parts, three figures strode along the crest of the dunes. Against a backdrop of thick, scudding clouds, they seemed to tilt drunkenly. Brian Kenning, shorter and stouter than the other two and crowned with wisps of flying hair, was in animated discussion with his aunt, Polly Coleby, a tall, storklike woman in her late sixties with sharp features and a prominent, aquiline nose. The third figure was Brian's younger brother, John, who walked with a swagger, hands in pockets. As one, they paused for a breath, turning instinctively toward the sea. The vast bowl of heaven stretched high above their heads, its bright blue wash spackled with cotton candy.

"Nothing here for the likes of me," Polly said. "Even less for you youngsters, I'd have thought."

"Don't get moody on us, Aunt Polly," Brian responded. "It's a fair old day all things considered, and we're getting fresh air and exercise like you've always told us to. Let's not spoil it."

"I'm not spoiling anything. And it's not that I don't enjoy your company, Brian. It's just that I can think of a hundred better things to do than tramp these dunes."

Brian was surprised by his aunt's melancholy. He was more accustomed to seeing her rock with amusement at one of her husband Will's incautious asides or watching her rule the kitchen with great good humor from beside her blackened stove. The wrinkles flanking her eyes spoke not of worry but of laughter, etched deeper by the harsh winds. For all her rustic ways, she struck Brian as almost aristocratic standing there on the sand hill, surveying the ocean.

"I don't really like it out here either," John added. "I'm too much of a city boy."

"Oh, right!" Brian exclaimed. "A few years in London and you're so cosmopolitan."

Brian had a tendency to belittle his brother. Though John was twenty-three years old and an accomplished graduate student, Brian still pictured him in short pants, clutching a lunch box. John was a scientist like his brother but far less self-assured. He suspected that people saw him as a stick-in-the-mud or a mere caricature of the ambitious researcher. In fact, John was a rather normal young man.

His hair was a little too long, and his shoes were a little too tight, and he had the bravado of most students in their early twenties. When goaded, he was eager to pull pranks that would cause no real offense. He had no ambition that could be explicated. He was leaning toward a career in natural products chemistry because he thought it would help him break into the perfume industry and meet fashion models. He would have laughed at the suggestion that his motives were anything but honorable; however, unlike Brian's explosive guffaw, John's laugh had a lilt that was engaging. People liked him, though John was entirely unaware of it.

"I've adjusted to London life better than you have," John retorted.

"You just think you have. It takes more than a couple of cappuccinos and margaritas to flush the sea salt out of your veins."

"Ah, you're full of it," John exclaimed, kicking up sand.

"Boys, please!" their aunt admonished them. "And don't be so argumentative, Brian!"

Brian strode away from them, clambered down the dunes, and took off across the corrugated beach. At the bottle-green line of foam and seaweed that marked the current waterline, he paused to allow John and Polly to catch up with him. He stood with his back to them, staring out to sea. The water was studded with rough wooden posts, stretching out fifty yards or more to where the waves washed over their algae-covered tops.

"Are those tree stumps?" John asked, pointing to the posts.

"Certainly," his aunt replied. "They say there used to be a whole forest in these parts till the turn of the century. Then the tide came in and gobbled up the lot."

"Is that true?" John pressed her.

"It took a whole village. Sutton le Marsh it was called. Great Granddad's cousins lived there. The tide came in one January night and swallowed the lot: houses, farms, trees—the whole village. The tide came in and never went out."

"How awful."

"Actually," Brian interjected, "this whole area of the North Sea didn't exist ten thousand years ago. Did you know that? It was all land back then. They call it Doggerland. You could walk from here to Amsterdam."

"If there'd been an Amsterdam back then." The hapless tree stumps bore testimony to the power of the sea. Waves still lapped and slapped them like a cat tormenting a dying mouse. "They say you can see the spire of Sutton Church at low tide," Polly continued, "out there somewhere beyond that sandbar. Don't rightly know if it's true or not. Your uncle Will says he's seen it from his boat out there somewhere under the sand."

John thought he glimpsed a spire or a turret far out in the shifting sea, but it vanished at once. He tried to imagine the lost village before and after its inundation, the waters rising steadily through the cottages and shops and churches until all were engulfed. People running away in their nightclothes. He shuddered.

"Time devours all things," Brian said after a long pause, still with his back to them.

"What did you say?" John asked.

"'Tempus edax rerum.' Time, the devourer of all things."

"I've never heard that before."

"It's from Ovid. *Metamorphoses*. Oh, forget it!" He turned and strode south, full of impatience and frustration. John and Polly hurried to catch up with him. Polly tugged at his sleeve.

"What on earth's the matter with you, Brian?" she asked. "You're wound tighter than a watch spring."

"Nothing's the matter," Brian said, then he finally turned to them and relaxed slightly. He looked down at his shoes. "Oh, I don't know. I suppose my job's bothering me a bit—career doubts, lifelong goals receding into the distance, something of that sort. I thought I was all set with the professorship at the university, but it doesn't seem nearly as rewarding as I thought it would be. My research seems so pointless of late. I'm sorry. I didn't mean to take it out on you."

"Why don't you put all that science of yours to some good use," Polly said, "some practical use? Lift your head out of the books and look at the world around you. That's the road to fulfillment."

"What do you mean by practical? I'm not a bloody engineer or a draftsman. I'm a scientist, and that's something completely different. I don't want to build a better mousetrap. I want to know why things are the way they are, but it's so hard to find new frontiers. All of my colleagues are just filling cracks in the masonry built by their predecessors. There's nothing new and exciting going on these days."

"It would seem to me that the right thing to do is to find the mysteries in the world and set about solving them, not to try to find ways to extend the work that's already been done."

"Correct in theory but risky in practice. Nobody wants to fund off-the-wall research. You don't understand how the scientific community works."

"No, I don't, Brian," Polly said forcefully. "But I do know what's meaningful in this world, and I think I know what it takes to be happy. Find yourself a worthy cause, take your courage in both hands, and go after it. Let convention go hang."

Brian was greatly taken by his aunt's forthright attitude and resolved to listen to her advice more closely in the future, but for now, he saw only her steel-gray hair melting into the hue of the dark clouds massing behind her. He pointed out the threat of rain, and they set off briskly away from the sea. Soon, the lapping of the waves was replaced by the pulsing of the wind as they gained height to the sand hills. Storm clouds had gathered to the north and appeared set for a march down the coast. Polly led them on a shortcut away from the dunes. They skirted a beet field that backed onto Bittern Fen Lane, at the top of which stood the cottage that had been home to Polly and Will for forty years.

"I suppose there is something else bothering me," Brian admitted. "It's Sarah. You remember that church you told her about, the one with the beautiful brass knight?"

Polly nodded, breathing heavily. "Hoyland Church, yes?"

"Well, Sarah says it's haunted or something. She says she saw a ghostly figure walking toward her while she was doing the brass rubbing. She's very—I don't know—impressionable. I don't seem to be able to talk to her about it, and it's playing on my mind. I think she's upset with me."

They had just rounded a corner of the field and were passing a tangled mass of bramble bushes when his aunt responded. The first drops of rain were already falling on their path, large and widely spaced. A few cornfields to the north, it was a downpour. Polly glanced up at the menacing sky, then she drove her hands deep into the pockets of her tweed jacket and said to Brian, "She's right."

Brian stopped in his tracks. There were some people from whom responses like that could be greeted with derision; then there were others from whom outrageous statements came so rarely that they demanded to be taken seriously. Before he could collect his thoughts to reply, however, Polly loped off in the direction of the cottage. Brian ran after her.

"What did you say?" he shouted. "What?"

"Sarah's right. I've seen it myself."

John pursued his brother and his aunt through the lashing rain as the storm finally broke over them. He ran hard, his heart jolting with exertion and a rising tide of exhilaration. He caught them by the cottage door, gave a mighty whoop, and tumbled across the threshold.

*****

That evening, as the rain streamed down onto the cottage roof, Brian, John, and their uncle Will toyed with their coffees while Polly retired to the kitchen to wash dishes. Supper was over and had never tasted so good: cured ham and cold chicken, half a veal and egg pie, the last of the summer's tomatoes and beets, and delicious spoonfuls of pickles dredged up from identical little china pots—walnuts, piccalilli, tiny pearl onions, and gherkins. Now replete, the three men sat in front of an open coal fire, cheeks scarlet and brains mulled.

"You can't trust the weather in these parts," Will informed his nephews. "Many's the mornin' I've baited my crab pots on a sea as calm as a millpond and scarce made it back through the breakers by lunchtime. It'll turn on you in a flash. You can't trust it. I told Poll it would turn on you today. The barometer says as much." He nodded to the antique instrument hanging on the wall by the kitchen door as if it held the secret to some arcane knowledge. His face was as brown and wrinkled as the pickled walnuts from supper, and his entire head was encased in salt-and-pepper stubble. He leaned back in his armchair and belched.

Brian stared at his uncle and thought about the simplicity of his life—an endless cycle of rowboats, fields, and firesides. He knew that his uncle had received barely a smattering of education and had left school at thirteen to work as a farmhand. During the course of his seventy-five years, Will had tackled most of the occupations available in the villages of the region and now made a barely adequate living from the sale of garden produce and the contents of his crab pots. Brian wondered if it was better, when all was said and done, to live a simple life like that rather than to struggle for achievement. It held a certain naive charm. Perhaps he should give up the university rat race entirely.

Will tapped the ashes from his pipe into the coal scuttle and filled a new bowl. "Did you lads enjoy your walk on the beach?" he asked. "Brush away the city cobwebs?"

"Yeah. It was great till the weather turned," Brian acknowledged. "We explored some of the shoreline. Talked a bit, you know. Aunt Polly told us how she'd once seen a ghost."

"What was that?" Will spluttered, the quality of his hearing depending greatly on an ability to anticipate questions. Being nearer to his uncle than Brian was, John repeated Brian's last sentence in a loud voice. Will turned his head away from them both, the disgust on his face indicating that he had heard well enough to resent both the volume and the content of the remark.

Brian shrugged his shoulders. "Well, that's what she said."

Will stared into the fire for a long time, deciding how best to comment on what was clearly an uncomfortable topic for him. All he could manage was, "Aye, she's told me as much herself."

"Do you believe her?" John asked. "Were you with her?"

"I was not. Bloody tomfoolery."

"Did she see it in the church?"

"Enough questions!"

Polly returned from the kitchen and walked over to the window to close the tall muslin drapes as if she was embarrassed that the local weather had brought disappointment to her nephews. The polished wooden curtain rings clattered together like dry bones. "It's real wintry," she said, rubbing her elbows with the palms of her hands.

"Somebody walking on your grave," Will said.

"Oh, do be quiet!" Polly replied. She gave the drapes a final shake and then sat down on a straight-backed dining chair by the window, away from the men.

"I was just telling Uncle Will about how you said you'd once seen a ghost," Brian explained to his aunt. She nodded but said nothing. Will was still staring into the fire, and the two brothers waited for him to speak again.

"I saw Hob O' Lantern out on the marsh right enough," he began hesitantly, "when I was a young un. A-callin' me to follow him. But I knew to cover my eyes and lie down on the path till he's gone like my father told me years and years ago. Hob O' Lantern we call him, but some say Will o' the Wisp. He tells you to follow him to his cottage, but he'll only lure you deeper into the bog till there be no way out." John looked across at Brian, who seemed entranced by his uncle's words.

"He turns travelers around with his lantern light, see," Will continued, "till they don't know where they came from or which way to go forward. Then Hob steals them away for his own. I reckon that's what happened to old Jess Lakenham, whose walking stick was found on the path by Friar's Swamp at Hoyland. Ne'er a trace of him seen from that day to this. And that same mornin', the church ringers had tolled the passin' bell by mistake. Old Hob had claimed him, I reckon."

"William Coleby, stop filling those boys' heads with such utter nonsense!" Polly admonished him. "I never did hear such a thing."

"Out there—" he shouted in reply "—out there on the marsh, in the dark, there may *be* ghosts, but not in a church, for God's sake, woman. It's a sacrilegious type thing to even think about. I can't believe you of all people would think such a thing."

"It's not a question of thinking anything. It's what happened."

"It's blather," Will concluded, stirring the fire with such conviction that sparks showered onto the hearthrug. He was clearly not in the mood for further discussion on the subject. He crossed his legs and sucked furiously on his pipe to silence the truth.

"Can you tell us what happened?" Brian asked, turning to his aunt.

"There's not much to tell, really, Brian. A few years ago, I started worshipping at St. Neot's Church over in Hoyland. The vicar here at Bittern Fen had got to be too high church for me. I didn't like him. So anyway, the Hoyland folks roped me onto the church committee. Once a month, I have to see to the flowers of a Friday evening and get things ready for the Sunday services. Usually, I bike over to Hoyland before tea to set them out."

"That's quite a ride," Brian noted.

"Yes, it is—for old legs like mine, anyway. Well, Hoyland's a small enough village, and there's never a soul about the church. Sometimes, the vicar, Mr. Applewhite, looks in last thing at night just to check up. A fine, conscientious man he is too. Much nicer than old Tiffin here at Bittern Fen."

"Applewhite seemed a bit odd to me when we met him last week," Brian said, "sort of distant, distracted. He didn't seem to like us being in his church at all, especially after Sarah fainted. He virtually pushed us out the door."

"That church is his whole life," Polly said. "It has made him a bit withdrawn, I suppose. But deep down, he's a good man."

"I'm sure he is," Brian said. "Go on."

"So anyway, most of the time, I'm just alone in the church, fiddling with the flowers and such, collecting vases, carrying water from the vestry. You can imagine. And that's where I saw the ghost. It is a very old church, you know."

"Yes, I know. You forget that Sarah and I have been there."

"Oh, of course, you have. My poor memory! So—"

"But what did the ghost look like?" Brian persisted. "What exactly happened?"

"The first time I saw it, I was standing by the pulpit, arranging a vase of chrysanths for the Lady Chapel. I'd cut the stems and was nicking the ends when I caught a glimpse of something gliding past the choir stalls. Well, I don't mind telling you, it frightened the life out of me. But what are you going to do in an empty church? Scream? That seemed silly and sort of, well, inappropriate, so I just watched. The thing began to fade after a while, and I assumed it was just my nerves, which have not been too good since that trouble with the shingles."

"Yes, but what did it *look* like?"

"Now that was the strangest part of it, Brian. It didn't look like nothing—no face, no arms, no particular shape, no height to speak of. If I had to compare it with something, I'd say it was more like a sack of potatoes than the figure of a man."

"Damn walkin' tater sack now," Will scoffed. Polly gritted her teeth.

"But you saw it more than once, didn't you?" John said to encourage her. "What about the other times?"

"Oh, I only saw it once or twice. It was always pretty much the same." She gave a sharp cough, stood up, and walked over to the dresser. There, she began to search through knitting patterns but couldn't seem to find the one she wanted. She stacked balls of colored wool and arranged knitting needles. Her fingers were busy, but they trembled slightly. "Best forget all about it," she concluded. She returned to her chair by the window, cracked open the drapes, and stared out at the falling rain and the ragged dusk. "You boys should come with me to the church tomorrow. I have to do the flowers for a funeral. I'd like to show you the true message in St. Neot's, if you'll let me. It's a wonderful, holy place."

"Maybe we'll do that," Brian said.

"I'll come," John said enthusiastically. "I don't think I've ever been to Hoyland Church. It sounds fascinating." He had wanted to say *creepy* or *scary* but had checked himself so as not to offend his aunt or antagonize his uncle. In truth, all he wanted to do was to be able to tell his friends some impressive ghost story when he got back to London.

"You'll get a kick out if it, John," said Brian. "It's really old. The brass that Sarah was working on was of a knight who died in the 1580s. So long ago."

"Oh, the church is much, much older than that, Brian. It dates back to Anglo-Saxon times, they say. Some of the original stonework is still there around the back of the vestry. And after that, it was a Norman abbey till Henry VIII took it upon himself to knock it down. The church that stands there today gets its name from a famous old monk who lived at the abbey way, way back, a thousand years or more."

*****

As John Kenning lay in the back bedroom of the cottage that night, the activity in his brain mastered the fatigue in his limbs, and he didn't fall asleep for a long while. The room itself was chilly, but the goose-down quilt and the soft mattress sandwiched him snugly. His familiar routine of the laboratory and the pub and the bustle of London life seemed far away and to belong to a younger, more carefree soul that he scarcely knew. The events of the day had lifted the familiar backdrops of chalkboards, subway trains, and parties to reveal a dim and distant world of fog and dykes and lanterns. Half-forgotten food. Ghosts and churches. The days of his childhood.

As an occasional car sped past the end of Bittern Fen Lane, its headlights played wonderful games on the ceiling of his bedroom. The glare would be vague at first, concentrated in the far corner of the room, glinting off a china milkmaid on the washstand. With the approach of the car, the light would expand and rise slowly up the wall, turning to cross diagonally by a faded print of Constable's *The Hay Wain*. The patterns seemed to mutate and boil, churning in on themselves, until at the moment the car flashed past the lane end, the lights would collapse into a single gleaming ball that darted across the ceiling as if its life depended on it then vanish.

John lay in the dark with his palms pressed against the mattress. He thought of his uncle's earthy doggedness and his aunt's perseverance. He knew the day was not far off when they would both be dead and the cottage abandoned. He saw Aunt Polly alone in a vast ruined church, searching for phantoms in the walls. He was lost on the salt flats, cut off by the tide. There was seaweed in his hair. A lantern beckoned to him from across the sands, and he followed it. He heard laughter. The light from the lantern fractured into a thousand moonbeams that streamed up into the sky. A pack of dogs chased them across the Milky Way, and he tumbled into the swamp of sleep.

CHAPTER 7

Hoyland Church
November 2017

St. Neot's was not the church of John Kenning's dreams the previous evening. Though it was isolated from the rest of Hoyland village and set well back from the road, there was nothing forbidding about it. It was certainly not the Gothic monstrosity in which he had watched his aunt scour the walls for phantoms. No gargoyles leered at him from atop the cornices. In fact, it gave the appearance of a friendly church and not one to have any truck with ghosts.

John, Brian, and Polly approached by way of a pasture presided over by a sedate Jersey cow. John paused beneath the canopy of the lych-gate and took stock of the view. The church was of good size and mostly built of rough-hewn Northumbrian limestone, but here and there were sections of stone from other times—some older, some newer. The row of colorful stained glass windows along the nave was interrupted in many places by plain leaded panes, a reminder of the decline in both skills and financial resources over the years. Virginia creeper, red and gold in the autumn season, had spread over the vestibule and its adjoining buttresses, lending warmth to the otherwise starkly inanimate presence.

The church had been built on high ground and commanded an excellent view of the surrounding countryside, except to the north, where several magnificent elm trees had grown to the height of the tower. To the west, the ground fell away sharply into a railway cutting, through which ran the now abandoned railway line from Lincoln to Boston. To the east, a line of masonry rubble sloped gently down from the church for more than fifty yards, petering out at the edge of a marsh studded with bulrushes. The grounds were large and contained several derelict outbuildings. It was clear to all that the site had once served a community of far greater numbers and notability than today's meager parish.

The visitors walked up the cinder path from the lych-gate to the vestibule. Along the way, Brian examined the old gravestones that flanked the path. Many had been defaced by the ravages of wind and rain, spiced with sea salt. All were dappled with dark-green moss. From the variety of angles at which they were disposed, Brian wondered if a flood had once struck inland as far as Hoyland. Then he turned his attention to the edifice in front of him.

"Do you know who St. Neot was?"

"He was the monk I told you about yesterday," replied his aunt. "A venerable man, I suppose. See, this was a famous monastery at one time. Hayland Abbey it was called or some such name. Don't ask me to spell it. You can see bits of the old abbey all over the grounds." She swung her arm in a wide arc from tower to marsh. "That line of stones yonder was once the monks' cells, so they say. At the end of it is what they call Friar's Swamp. Very boggy ground it is, stretching almost to the village. Hunt around long enough and you'll find bits of old walls everywhere."

"It must have been an impressive sight in its heyday."

It was only midafternoon, but the lateness of the season and the overcast sky combined to accelerate the arrival of dusk. A bare light bulb twinkled invitingly in the porch, but they shunned it and followed a path round to the back of the church. They turned a corner and were met by the smiling face of Nigel Applewhite pressed up against the vestry window. It was a rather unnerving sight, which caused Polly to momentarily clutch her throat. The smile at the window vanished, and a moment later, the vestry door opened. The vicar folded his wire-framed spectacles and slid them into his vest pocket then greeted his guests.

"Mrs. Coleby, Dr. Kenning, and young Mr. Kenning. Your aunt said you would be coming. Delighted to see you all. Do come in." They followed him through into the vestry.

"Good afternoon, Vicar. Nice to see you again," Brian said and, shunning further pleasantries, added, "And you'll be pleased to hear that Sarah is fully recovered from her mishap, but she still maintains that she saw a ghost by the altar. My aunt tells me that she's seen it too. Any thoughts?"

Applewhite turned away and paced the vestry, trying hard to express himself on the subject, but words didn't come half as easily as did wringing of the hands and adjustment of the clerical collar. "Don't really know what to think, Dr. Kenning. Most uncommon business. I've heard the rumors, of course, but I don't believe a word of them. You say you've seen it too, eh, Mrs. Coleby? Most surprised, I must say. Can't stop you visiting the church, of course, Dr. Kenning. House of God open to all, you know." He smiled feebly for just a moment then took out his spectacles and began to polish the lenses furiously. "Can't imagine what the bishop would say if he found out. A rum business, to be sure." Brian was far from satisfied but said nothing more.

The vicar began to search through a shoebox filled with old sermons crudely typed and severely annotated in red ink. No one moved, so he waved them toward the door to the church. Brian turned the iron ring, pulled open the door, and led them through onto the cold flagstones. It was the first time John had been inside the church, and he was struck by how much larger it seemed from the inside than from the outside. The roof seemed to be half a mile above his head. Light bulbs hung suspended in the body of the nave from long cables that stretched up into the gloom, but their feeble glow only heightened the impression of spaciousness.

They walked over to the center aisle, a clear echo accompanying each footfall. Dividing the nave from the chancel was an old rood screen carved in reticulated Gothic style. The screen had at one time been painted and gilded, but even though a little gilt edging remained in the folds of the tracery, the majority of the paintwork had succumbed to centuries of neglect. On top of the screen, perhaps fifteen feet from the ground, was a life-size crucifix. As the two men arched their backs to look up at it, Polly bent over and pointed to the floor by the pulpit.

"Here's that lovely brass of Richard Crossly and his wife," she said. "We're all extremely proud of it. Your Sarah said it was one of the finest in the county, Brian."

"It's been taken care of, that's why," Brian said, "not like the rest of this place. Look at this wood." He ran his thumb down a post and examined the flecks of paint that adhered to it.

"We're a poor parish. The vicar does the best he can."

They entered the chancel. The choir stalls were arranged in four rows on either side of the aisle. Behind the stalls were ornate screens of the same Gothic fretwork, and beyond those screens were side chapels, buried in darkness. Brian walked up to the communicants' rail and surveyed the sanctuary. The altar was draped in florid red satin, and above it hung a triptych of the Acts of the Apostles. Dimly visible through the screen to the left was the organ, its pipes brooding over everything.

John examined the brighter areas of the chancel, taking care to keep his brother and aunt in view at all times. He was not at all comfortable now that they were inside the church. The antiquity of it all, the staleness, gave him an uneasy sensation. He felt the building must contain many out-of-the-way corners not visited by humanity for centuries, where who knew what spiritual fungus would have had time to germinate. To the right of the altar, about eight feet from the ground, were the remains of some stonework that had been chiseled away and crudely covered over with plaster. Beneath the despoiled work was an inscription that read:

1624

BR MW JW JM FN
Farmers of the Parish
Gloria Patri

"What do you think that means?" John asked his brother, who had strolled to his side.

"It means that five local farmers, whose initials are given in the second line, took it upon themselves to eradicate some offending masonry for the glory of God."

"A change of taste, I suppose," John said. "I wonder what it was they removed."

There was little else of note in the architecture. The chancel was arched across without groins, the arches springing from stone cornices embossed with carved heads. John looked up at the rafters and estimated their height to be two hundred feet, but his perception of distance was again curiously affected by the poor illumination and the absence of reference points. At times, as he tilted his head backward, the roof would appear to recede into deep space; at other times, it seemed suffocatingly close. He had to hold on to a bench to avoid losing his balance.

Polly and John decided to take a stroll round the church while Brian remained to examine the chancel further. They walked to the end of the nave and paused by the font—a hunk of ugly stone devoid of decoration. As they returned down a side aisle, John looked for Brian in the chancel but couldn't see him. Irrational thoughts of ghostly mischief began to buzz in his head. Polly, meanwhile, tried to identify for John the tawdry paintings that hung on the walls under the stained glass windows, but hardly any light from the feeble bulbs reached that far, forcing her to squint and bend close to the canvases.

"Here's *The Stoning of St. Stephen*," she whispered. John peered into a black-and-red wash with many beige faces to the left and a single figure prostrate in the lower right. It seemed plausible. "*The Casting out of the Moneylenders*," she said after a few more strides. She pointed to a dirty blue canvas filled with amorphous red-and-green shapes. There was nothing to positively identify a moneylender, let alone Jesus.

They came to a gap in the sequence of paintings. A Norman archway overhung a tiny door recessed into the stone wall. Two sunken steps led down to the foot of it. "What's on the other side of that door?" John asked.

"I think it goes down to the crypt," his aunt replied.

"What's down there?"

"I don't know. I've never been down there, nor would I want to go."

"Neither would I."

70

John was invited to admire *The Conversion of Saul* and *The Raising of Lazarus*, both of which were as enigmatic as their fellows. In front of him the whole time he dawdled down the aisle was the blackness of the Lady Chapel that adjoined the chancel. Pinpoints of light reflecting off the silver candelabra on the altar were the only visible signs within. At any moment, John expected the ghostly figure of the Virgin to drift out of the darkness. He cursed his fickle imagination. They walked and stopped, walked and stopped. "Yes, Aunt Polly, *The Garden of Gethsemane* is beautiful. Fine composition."

The Lady Chapel was so close now that John could almost reach through the screen and touch the blackness. How would it feel? Soft and silky like satin sheets? As hard as anthracite? How far back did it reach? A few feet or a thousand miles? The last canvas was behind them. They turned and walked along the front of the screen. Did he dare put his hand through it? Would teeth fasten around his wrist? He ran a fingernail along the wood to calm his runaway nerves. What if a claw should reach out from the blackness, hooking at his eyeballs?

"Brian, where are you?" Polly suddenly called out.

"This way," said a voice. "I'm over here."

"Brian?" Polly said. She and John emerged into the light of the chancel, but there was no sign of Brian. He was not by the altar or up in the choir stalls. They stared at each other in bewilderment.

"I'm over *here*," the voice emphasized, and this time, the words clearly came from the vicinity of the organ. Brian suddenly appeared on the other side of the screen and motioned for them to follow him. All three of them squeezed down a narrow passageway between the organ and the chancel screen and emerged in front of the massive east wall of the church. A single dusty bulb shed barely enough light to prevent them from tripping over the uneven flagstones. "Look at this," Brian said, pointing to a section of the wall in deep shadow. All they could make out was a cavity extending back into the stone.

"What on earth is it?" John asked Polly.

"I don't know," she replied. "I didn't know there was anything back here."

"There's an inscription on the wall," Brian said. "It's very old and worn." He leaned forward and began to trace the lettering with his index finger. It took him several minutes to decipher the message: "Sepulchrum Richardi Crossly et Catherinae de Willugby Conjugum. Ista obiit decimo nono Septembris 1587. Ille obiit nono Aprilis 1593."

"Sepulchrum," John noted, wrinkling his brow. "So it's a tomb then?"

"I suppose so," Brian replied. "A tomb or a place where a sarcophagus was kept. But it's a mighty strange place to put one, back here, out of the way. It must predate the organ."

"Richard Crossly," John said. "That's the same name as on the brass plaque in the nave. It must be the same couple. Richard Crossly must have been an important person—at least as far as this church is concerned."

"Yes."

They stood in silence and peered one after the other into the blackness of the hole. They presumed it was empty but could not confirm the fact. Polly suddenly roused herself and declared that she must begin work on the flowers. They returned to the nave, and John and Brian settled themselves on the first row of pews. John felt a little easier with his brother by his side and solid oak at his back. Polly carried vases from the vestry, gathered the flowers that had been deposited in the vestibule by the village florist earlier that afternoon, and began to orchestrate her arrangements on a small table by the pulpit.

Craning his neck, John could just see the friendly strip of light under the vestry door—a door he would have much preferred to be on the other side of. The whole business struck him as pure craziness. There were far more comfortable ways to spend an afternoon. They could have gotten up and left at any time, but they didn't. They watched their aunt arrange flowers. They listened to time passing. They watched for ghosts.

A sharp sound, as of wood splintering, broke the silence. It was followed by a creaking noise that lasted a full second. "Wood settling," Brian said with just a slight query in his voice.

"Deathwatch beetle," John added. He glanced at his watch and was surprised to find that it was already five fifteen. They had been in the church for over an hour. Polly worked away at the flowers, periodically carrying vases to a faucet and placing completed arrangements around the sanctuary. John sat quite still with his hands clasped between his knees for warmth. Out of the corner of his eye, he could see his brother's head moving slowly from side to side, scanning the space beyond the rood screen.

John drifted into ruminations about his future, musing on his chances of graduating the following summer. He began to think he would be better advised to take his chances in the job market after Christmas. He could easily slip away with a master's degree and get on with his life. Maybe that was what he ought to do. But that would mean the torturous interview circuit; he would have to buy a new suit, new shoes. He had have to kowtow to captains of industry. Procrastination did have its virtues. Or maybe he should be more enterprising and ask the pretty barmaid in his local pub to run away with him to France, to Provence, a place he had always dreamed of—good food and sunshine, rough wine, and life at a slower pace. They could be there in less than a day. But was that being more or less realistic?

A shiver yanked him out of his reverie. He was freezing. He looked at his aunt and was startled by what he saw. Her back had begun to undulate slightly in an incomprehensible way. The vases at her side were behaving in the same manner. In a fraction of a second, his eyes darted to the screen, the pillars, and the rest of the church. All were afflicted with the same gentle pitch and roll. He thought he was going to pass out. He closed his eyes and opened them. There was no change. The whole church was lurching through the crests and troughs of an ocean swell.

John turned to his brother. He saw to his surprise that Brian's head was bent backward, and he was staring up at the ceiling. John looked up too. The light bulbs were swaying back and forth in unison in flat arcs of a foot or two. That was what was causing the visual perturbation. "That is so weird," Brian whispered to him.

There was no reason for the lights to be swaying. There was no draft, nor was the church door ajar. John looked again at his aunt. She had stopped arranging the flowers. Her left hand was by her side, wrapped tightly around a single stalk of chrysanthemum, almost as if it was a talisman. She was staring through the screen into the chancel, her face quite serene. As the two brothers watched her, she lifted her right hand and made the sign of the cross on her chest.

"Oh, Jesus Christ," John said, rising to his feet.

"Sit down," Brian hissed, reaching for his brother's arm.

"No, Brian. My god, look!"

The church had grown much darker now. The pillars and walls seemed remote as if layers of smoked glass had descended in front of their eyes. John again felt that he was losing contact with the world and would faint. The ceiling and the rear of the church were no longer visible, and a pale-yellow light bathed the chancel. It was obvious that there was some activity in there visible only to his aunt.

Then John saw it too, a very faint, shimmering light about four feet high. It was so ill-defined that had they not been anticipating its arrival, they would likely have failed to notice it at all. It drifted slowly across the chancel toward the organ, bobbing up and down as it went.

"Can you see it?" John exclaimed.

"Be quiet! I see it."

"What the fuck is it?" Polly heard John's raised voice and turned to him. The object began to fade into the background at once.

"Damn it!" Brian muttered and raced to the chancel steps. The object had vanished completely by the time he arrived. The lights stopped swaying, the illumination returned to its former level, and the icy chill was lifted. It was over as quickly as it had begun.

"Why couldn't you be quiet and just watch?" Brian said sharply to his brother. "Why did you have to jump up yelling like that?"

"I don't know. I'm sorry," John replied. "I was excited. I wasn't sure you could see what was happening. I'm sorry."

"You disturbed Aunt Polly. You brought her out of her reverie. The phenomenon has something to do with her state of mind, just like it was with Sarah. You broke the spell when you shouted out."

"I said I was sorry. I didn't know what we were supposed to do. You didn't tell us."

"All right. It's over now."

"Brian, you can't expect people to—"

"Don't worry about it!"

"Okay." John paused. "So what was that thing? I've never seen anything like it."

"I have no idea. Aunt Polly?"

They both turned to their aunt, who shrugged her shoulders. "That's what I saw before," she said, "the exact same thing."

They all three stood together in silence for a moment, but it was clearly time to leave the church and head for the comfort of the vestry. As they pushed open the door, they were greeted by the sight of the vicar slumped in a chair with his feet on the desk. For one horrible moment, Polly was sure he was dead and rushed to his side, but he awoke with an immense jolt and leaped to his feet. "Most terribly sorry. Must have dozed off. Frightfully dull some of this parish business. Do come in."

He seemed to have totally forgotten what they were doing in his church, so Brian reminded him. "And, Reverend," Brian concluded, "you'll no doubt be surprised to learn that you do indeed have a resident ghost or something closely resembling one. A very peculiar thing happened to us in the church just now. I can't explain it, but—"

"A ghost?" Applewhite took a step away from him. "Surely not. Mind playing tricks in the dark, surely. Mrs. Coleby, what's this all about?"

"I know it's hard to believe, Reverend," Polly said, "and in the church too, but I think it's a fact. I saw it as well, just like the other times."

"Dear me, dear me. Most disagreeable. Whatever shall I do?"

"Don't do anything," Brian said. "It all happened so quickly. We can't really be sure what it was we saw. There's no need for you to do anything."

"An exorcism, perhaps? Oh, whatever will the bishop say?" The vicar plunked himself back down in his chair and pondered his predicament.

"I think it would be best if we left now," Polly said. "The flowers are all done. And we can forget about this other business. We'll be on our way."

Applewhite nodded and murmured, "Puts me in a difficult position, you know."

"Please don't worry about it," Polly tried to reassure him. "The boys know what they're talking about. Just let it be." There was no response, so Polly ushered her nephews outside.

"He looked quite pathetic sitting there," John said. "I hope he'll be all right."

"He's used to the old church," Polly said. "He practically lives in it. He'll be fine."

CHAPTER 8

Heighlendh Abbey
1057

When the devil first came to visit the monk, he put on white robes and slid under the door. It was midnight. The monk was sleeping on his cot, and the first thing he noticed was the stench. It was as if the charnel house had been turned inside out and its contents flung against his door. He opened his eyes just in time to see the devil skitter across the floor and crawl up into a chair by the fire. From there, he hissed at the monk, changing first into a badger and then a large rat. Finally, he slithered back to the floor in the form of some vague, spineless reptile, its saliva fouling the mud floor.

It was well-known that devils visited the abbey. When Guthlac built his first hut on the edge of the marsh in the seventh century, they made contact at once, attempting to engage the holy man in blasphemous conversation. It had happened to many monks since then but never before to him. He was young and untutored in such matters. He sat trembling on his cot, waiting for the coming ordeal. Peat embers glowed in the fireplace, and the devil seemed to warm himself in front of them, his blue breath falling in folds onto the hearth. The monk clapped his hands over his ears when the wheedling and cajoling began.

He began to recite the only prayer he knew, but the devil roared his disapproval and spat tongues of flame. The monk fell silent. He was helpless, calcified, and his faith in the Lord seemed flimsy protection. The devil, meanwhile, continued to drag his tail under the door and arrange his formless bulk on the floor of the cell. The monk saw that his body would be consumed even before his mind could be turned.

After a while, though, the devil seemed to turn in on himself, muttering imprecations under his breath. Seizing the opportunity, the monk leaped from his cot and ran to the door. The devil whirled around, booming a curse so loud that it shot sparks up the chimney and filled the cell with colored smoke. But the monk grasped the door handle and freed himself. He darted out from under the eaves of the dormitory and then stopped abruptly, astonished to see that demons were in possession of much of the abbey grounds, coiling their tails around the trees, sidling up the walls.

The monk's cell was the last in the row of crude stone dwellings comprising the dormitory, for he was the most recent novitiate admitted to the abbey and most lowly in standing of all the brothers. Worst of all, he was as far as he could be from the safety of the abbey. When slimy fingers began to encircle his ankles, he took off running as fast as his habit and sandals would allow. He ran parallel to the dormitory then cut across the sward, his heart pounding with fright and exertion.

He stumbled along the wall of the granary and shouted once up to the window of the loft where Odo the garnerer slept. There was no response to his cry, however, and he was too ashamed to repeat it. He ran to the end of the granary wall and halted at the edge of the main square. There were no demons here; they dared not confront the great facade of the abbey with its thirty-six statues of the saints ranked on high.

He paused for breath. His cowl was wet with sweat, and he shivered in the cold night air. What was he to do? He dared not return to his cell, and all the monks save him were sleeping. What would they think of him, a novitiate, if he woke them for no good reason? They held him in scant regard as it was. He looked up at the sky. From the angle of inclination of the moon, he knew that in an hour or two, the brethren would come yawning from their beds to the peal of the matins bell. He had to act quickly if he was to deliver them all from harm.

He remembered that his friend Adin was inside the abbey at that very moment. Adin had been appointed to guard the tomb of Waltheof and the abbey's treasures, which had been moved from the sacristy during the reconstruction and re-endowment ordered by Leofric, Bishop of Exeter. The monk thought to go to his friend for help, but fast on the heels of that idea came a more beguiling one. He saw how he could use the most powerful relic in all of Mercia to banish the devil from the abbey forever. Would that not earn him the respect of his fellow monks, which he so craved? Oh, but Adin would pay a price! Notwithstanding, a plan began to take shape in his mind. He weighed the consequences for a moment.

Resolved, he left the shadow of the granary and hurried to the main door of the abbey, picking out a path among the blocks of stone and coils of rope that were stacked ready for the building of the transept. He entered the gloomy nave and tiptoed behind the nearest pillar. He could barely make out Waltheof's tomb and the three cases of treasure on the steps of the chancel. Adin was seated beside them, his face buried in his cowl. Perhaps he was sleeping. Perhaps not. The monk picked up a worker's adze that was lying nearby.

It only remained for him to creep up on Adin without rousing him, but how was that to be accomplished? Separating the two of them was a row of statues of abbey luminaries that had been carved for them by Brother Benedict of Rievaulx. The shadows of the statues seemed like stepping-stones to his goal. The monk tightened the knotted rope about his waist and crept forward with the merest glimmer of moonlight to guide him into the shadow of the statue of St. Peter, who held a bunch of keys in one hand and the book of knowledge in the other—"Blessed be the soul of Abbot Engolf, who has had the patience and understanding to try to reveal the faith to such a poor scholar as me, that he will not forswear me for this act"—and into the shadow of the statue of St. Bartholomew, one of the abbey's patron saints, with the knife of his martyrdom pointed at his breast.

"Blessed be the soul of Adin, who alone among the brethren of the abbey has befriended me and who must now be betrayed, that he will not suffer for my transgression," he prayed, continuing into the shadow of the statue of St. Guthlac, the other patron saint and first monk of the abbey, whose sheathed sword signified his conversion. "Blessed be the soul of the departed Abbot Waltheof, who has worked so many miracles for the righteous, that his power will banish the demons this night." He was by the shadow of the statue of St. Thomas with a spear in his right hand and his left hand raised to his chin in doubt. "And may the Lord have mercy on my soul that my own doubts be banished and my memory sanctified by this night's work. Amen."

Taking two steps out of the shadow of the final statue, he raised the adze above Adin's head. His fingers gripped it tightly, but he could not bring it down. The weapon remained poised while his gentle heart explained to his rash mind that such a deed could not be committed. He sobbed inwardly but laid the adze down. He must pray that Adin slept soundly. He removed his sandals and crept forward barefoot.

He opened Waltheof's tomb and tried for several minutes to wrest the holy ring from the finger of the embalmed corpse, the ring that had worked so many miracles in Waltheof's time, but it would not move. He wet the ring with spittle and turned and twisted it against the bone, but it was gripped tightly by the swollen flesh. In desperation, he turned to the largest of the treasure chests, opened it silently, and drew out an obsidian knife. He turned back to the tomb and began to slice through the wrist of the revered prelate. Adin slept on.

Soon, he was hurrying back across the sward with his prize. He kept his head down as he ran so as not to witness the phantom armies of the dead that crossed the sky on nights such as this. He was back in his cell, struggling with the devil, when the matins bell rang at two o'clock to wake the brethren and begin the liturgy. A few minutes later, upon discovering the church violated, the monastery erupted in chaos. When the monks entered his cell, they were shocked to find him brandishing the severed hand of Waltheof in front of his hearth and cursing Satan in a voice that was not his own.

*****

The monk awoke, and it was quiet, daytime. He watched the shadow of the statue of St. Bartholomew drift across his tunnel of vision until it was gone. Another morning had passed of another slow day. The pain in his back was with him constantly now so that sometimes, he could not easily decide if he was in pain or not, and it was only when he shifted his position and felt feathers caressing his spine or something like the coolness of snow upon his loins that he knew it was the pain lifted. He drank water and ate a little bread. He spent the rest of the day as he had spent many days before: scratching a mark into the stone wall with his fingernail at the place he called his *fasti*, or register of days. He paused only in the evening when Abbot Engolf came to pray for him. He, in turn, prayed for Abbot Engolf and asked God for forgiveness. He drank some water and slept.

He awoke to find a brother changing his toilet pan and breaking his bread. For this meal, there was also a square of goat cheese, which he ate first, very slowly. He no longer had any feeling in his right thigh, and his left knee was locked. He dragged himself to a new position and lay still.

He had always considered himself a coward. After Gyrth had passed sentence on him and while waiting for incarceration, he had been terrified to the point of debilitation. He lived for a kind word and a touch on the sleeve and knew loneliness to be intolerable. It was clear to him during the bell-struck hours that preceded his confinement and the drawing of the chalk line across the entrance to his cell that his mind would not remain intact. He believed himself a coward before his imprisonment, and he believed himself one thereafter, but he survived nonetheless.

He scratched a new day on the wall and prayed for the soul of Adin, who had been banished from the abbey the day after the theft of Waltheof's hand for gross dereliction of duty. The monk thought his own crime to be worse than Adin's, but the abbot ruled otherwise. As on every other day, the monk's malefaction—as Gyrth had termed it at his interrogation—hung before him in the entrance to his cell, beyond the chalk line, smelling bad.

The hunger he would embrace and the suffering he could endure in respectful subjugation to the authority of his beloved Engolf. If the abbot had merely asked the same of him, he would have complied. But all this as punishment for a sin? That he questioned. Did not sin involve harm to another for personal gain? He had harmed no one and never would. His actions had been directed solely toward protection of the abbey from the devil. He could not himself see how he had transgressed, but he was told that he most certainly had.

Abbot Engolf talked about the violation of the incorrupt in his prayers, but the monk didn't know what that meant. The relic hung in front of him at that very moment. It was not lost for other men. He supposed that the finer points of the treatment of relics were not known to him, and he was being punished for his ignorance. But could ignorance merit the harsh punishment that had been meted out to him, that he be condemned to dwell in this tiny niche until such time as the suspended hand of the dead abbot should lose enough flesh to permit the sacred ring to fall?

For the first time since his incarceration, he felt anger. He closed his ears to Engolf's prayers that night and fought to banish from his mind a persistent image of Gyrth's eyes bulging from their sockets, his own fingers squeezing the prior's neck.

*****

He thought he smelled honey as he dragged himself from the bowels of a hellish dream—the sweet smell of the meadow where the hives were kept. He thought he swiped his hand across the honey drippings and dipped his tongue into the nectar. A bee stung his thigh. It was just like every fine day since he had come to the abbey, every soft afternoon.

He turned his face to the sun, and the prick of the bee sting mushroomed into such a welt of pain that sweat broke out on his brow. Awaking and remembering, he let out an agonized groan, even as the smell of the honey congealed into the stench of his unnamable malefaction. He fought the pain, pressing both palms against the two opposing walls of his cell and then against floor and ceiling, but the stone was cold and unforgiving in all quadrants of his universe.

They should all be dead by now anyway, all of them. It was written in the holy book. A thousand years had passed, whether marked from the year of Christ's birth or the year of his death. He didn't understand why they were not all dead, and neither did Abbot Engolf. The *pied poudreux* from Rheims had told them of the chronicle of Bishop Otto of Freising that began with the creation and ended with the Last Judgment.

"We who have been placed at the end of time," it began, and several monks had shuddered as the peddler spoke the words. He recalled how the abbot of Fleury had computed that the end would come when the Annunciation fell on a Good Friday. But it was now the year of Our Lord 1057, and the end had not come. This was a mystery. They should all be dead and in heaven by now.

His mind went skipping through the long grass from the meadow where the hives were set to the lower field where the herd idled. He imagined the horrors that might have befallen Gesella and Geneat, his two favorite cows, and their sisters. They were his responsibility. What if Tonsdag should forget to milk them? What if the wolves should come down from the north wold? Remembrance of the lovely wet-earth smell of the pasture broke over him like a slow-rolling wave, and he flung himself from wall to wall and howled like the demon of all demons until the pain cut through his anger and his tears and, finally, his consciousness.

He awoke, and a queer light was playing about the entrance to his cell, lemon colored and diffuse. It was neither the sun at noon nor the candles of vespers, for their patterns he knew well. At first, he thought a monk had come to release him, but it could not be. He watched in fascination as the swirls of light picked out dust motes and played on cracks and bumps in the walls of his cell that he had never seen before. An idea stole upon him that this was an unearthly light, and this idea was fast pursued by the notion that he had died and that this was the light of heaven, a glint from the first rung of Jacob's ladder. But he did not feel dead.

The light dimmed, and he caught sight of two ethereal figures framed by the entrance to his cell. He fell forward before them, his mind spiraling in vertiginous circles at the meaning of this vision.

He looked up, and though he could not clearly see their features, he knew that they must be St. Guthlac and St. Bartholomew, the patron saints of the abbey. Who else would intercede on his behalf? They had surely seen into his heart on the night of his misadventure. The saints had taken on mortal garb and descended from their statues to minister to him. Their voices came from a great distance, high-pitched and fairylike, fluttering down the threads of light.

"He is not without hands," said Bartholomew, and the monk's heart pounded at the remembrance of his transgression.

"He is our companion," Guthlac seemed to reply.

As the monk puzzled over the meaning of these words, a third figure drifted into sight behind the other two, blocking out all but the holy light. The monk knew that this must be Abbot Waltheof, whom he had so innocently violated, and the words meant that Waltheof was sanctified and living on high with the angels. "We are three in God," Waltheof said. A bright light shone from the hand of St. Guthlac onto his own hands, and the voice of Waltheof intoned, "Thy path is blessed."

The monk stared at the beam of light as it moved up to fix on his face. In an instant, it shattered into a million tiny stars that danced around his cell like fireflies. Then the light was extinguished, the angels vanished, and he was plunged back into darkness. Almost at once, however, the darkness that was in his heart also began to collapse, and the hope planted within him blossomed upward and outward until it could no longer be contained and forced its way out of his mouth in the form of a most joyous wailing, the like of which had scarce been heard before on earth. The sound reverberated around the walls of the church, bursting out into the cloister and soaring across the sward to the dormitory and refectory.

Monks came running from all directions. Gyrth was the first to arrive, and others quickly joined him till the cries of the prisoner mingled with the chattering of the monks in a most unholy cacophony. The noise subsided only after Abbot Engolf had been summoned and had forced a path through the agitated brethren. At his command, the prisoner was dragged across the chalk line and deposited on the floor of the church, but it was still many minutes before the wailing ceased entirely and the monk could be persuaded to explain the reason for it. Upon hearing of the monk's vision, Engolf decreed that he should be removed from captivity and refreshed that he might give a fuller recounting of it to abbey officials at a later time.

The attendant monks asked him to walk with them, but after 212 days of living in a tiny niche in the wall of the abbey, Neot could not do so and had to be carried to the washhouse.

*****

In the years following Neot's transgression and punishment, the brethren of Heighlendh Abbey took on a different view of what had happened. They began to venerate Neot's innocence and his good intentions. They came to believe that his vision had been real and that the saintly patrons of the abbey had blessed him. They now spoke highly of him. In addition, the worth of monastic relics began to fade under more pragmatic Norman influence. The embalmed body of Abbot Waltheof was allowed to decay, his severed hand was buried without ceremony in an unremembered spot, and Waltheof's holy ring was appropriated by the Bishop of Lincoln and carried away.

Neot intensified his religious devotion. Within a week or two of being released from confinement, he became a follower of the reforming Benedictine monk Peter Damian of Perugia. In his early tract *de divina omnipitentia*, Damian averred that God could do anything good and that he could not lie, he could act outside time, and he could defeat the devil. Damian was a lover of solitude and devout reflection. Pope Stephen IX appointed him cardinal bishop of Ostia late in the year 1057, and when word of it reached Heighlendh, Abbot Engolf advised Neot that Damian would be an appropriate role model for him. Thus inspired, Neot followed the teachings of Peter Damian for the rest of his life, meditating in solitude and renouncing the practices of sodomy and simony. He also pursued an extreme form of penitence, the flagellation, or *disciplina*, advocated by Damian. Once each day, after compline, Neot would kneel in front of the altar and lash his back with a cattail whip made of bramble stalks.

CHAPTER 9

London
November 2017

"So do you believe me now?" Sarah Harcourt called out to Brian from the kitchen of her tiny Hampstead apartment as she dropped a handful of coffee beans into a grinder. "Do you believe that I saw a ghost?"

Brian, reclining on the couch in her living room, weighed his response carefully. He had reacted too quickly and too casually the last time he had been asked, and he didn't want to make the same mistake again. However, it had been almost two months since she had collapsed in St. Neot's Church, during which time the demands of teaching and research had caused him to set aside his resolution to come up with a sympathetic approach to Sarah's concerns.

With the tips of his fingers, he traced the furrows above his eyebrows. "Honestly, Sarah, it was never a question of believing you or not believing you," he said. "You told me truthfully what you'd experienced, and I never doubted it. It was your explanation that disturbed me. It seemed like you were jumping to conclusions."

"The explanation is what I'm talking about. I really saw a ghost, didn't I? You and John saw it too, and your aunt Polly did."

"We all saw something, yes, or thought we did. But none of us knows what exactly it was that happened. I know I don't. That's all I'm saying. For now, let's just say we each had a similar experience." He knew at once that he had blundered again. He heard the coffee grinder slammed down on the countertop. "Sarah, what I mean is—"

"Brian? Why do you keep trying to put me down like this? What's so hard about accepting the fact that I—"

"Excuse me, but this is not a fact, damn it. I'm sorry, but we're not talking fact at this point. This is called conjecture. Let's try to talk precisely about what happened or not at all."

"Of course, it's a fact. No right-minded individual would keep disputing me the way you do. I can't understand what your motives are for undercutting me all the time. Your PhD doesn't give you a monopoly on truth, you know."

Sarah switched on the coffee grinder to drown out any response, and Brian was forced to listen to its high-pitched whine and to smell the coffee dust as it diffused through the apartment. He should concede the argument right now. He knew he would only lose more by continuing it. He stared out the window at the wet and gloomy afternoon. If it weren't for the rain, he could suggest a walk on Hampstead Heath to air their differences. Rain irritated him. It robbed him of time and sapped his energy. When the grinder stopped, he tried again.

"Sarah, look, I do this kind of thing for a living. Every day, I'm trying to figure out if some new piece of scientific data makes sense or not, trying to see if it fits in with other evidence or with some theory or other. You have to look at these things from every angle before you draw conclusions—inside and outside, upside and downside. That's all I'm saying. What if the vicar was pulling some kind of trick on us? Did you ever think about that? What if there was some unusual transmission of light through the stained glass windows? Huh? I'm just trying to view this thing in a systematic way, but it seems like no one else can spare a second to do the same. Everyone's jumping up and down, waving their preconceptions like...like red underwear."

"And who do you mean by *everyone*?"

"It's not the right way to go about it, Sarah. Listen, I talked to my friend Harry Groh in America. His research team is learning all kinds of new stuff about hallucinations, about—"

"Oh, so does that mean we're still holding open the possibility that I'm crazy?"

"I didn't say that. No one has ever said that."

"Neither has anyone ever said they were on my side, Brian," Sarah observed with a mixture of anger and anxiety in her voice.

"Neither has anyone ever said they'd try to help me understand what happened. Even though you, who say you love me, saw the same bloody thing as I did, you still won't go out of your way to support me."

"I do support you. That's a given. This is insane." She filled the coffeepot with water, switched it on, and returned to the living room with a plate of cookies, which she flung carelessly onto the table. As she sat down, Brian stood up and moved to the window. "I do support you," he repeated with his back to her, "but I can't go out of my way, as you put it, to do so. I can't. That's just the way I am. Of course, you're not crazy. That's not the point."

He stared out the window at one of those unremitting gray rains he had lived with all his life. He remembered sitting as a boy in his aunt's parlor at Bittern Fen, watching a similar rainstorm and begging for it to end so that he could go out to play with the other kids. He remembered how each raindrop on the windowpane had seemed so perfectly round and clear. When the rain had refused to quit, he had been forced to remain indoors and play solitaire with a set of glass marbles as round and as clear as the raindrops themselves. Suddenly, standing there at Sarah's window, he could recall with clarity the unutterable boredom he had felt as a child that day. He wasn't angry at Sarah, he realized. He was simply bored with his life.

He returned and sat down beside her, stretching his arm along the top of the couch. He raised his eyebrows and pursed his lips into a smile that spelled concession. He patted the back of the couch, and she walked over and snuggled against him in the hollow his arm had created.

"I do want to help you," he said. "Really, I do. I'm the one who's crazy—crazy about you."

"You're right. I'm sorry I went off the deep end. It's been a tough week."

"There's no point in us beating each other up over this thing. Can we just explore it a little without getting angry? Deal?"

"Deal."

They sat together quietly. A minute passed before Brian was ready to open up the subject again. "Well, for starters, is it possible you were in some kind of trance while you were doing the brass rubbing?"

"How do you mean?"

"Just some things Harry Groh said, stuff about how sensory deprivation and meditation can cause people to see things. I noticed that Aunt Polly was very relaxed as she was arranging the flowers in the church, almost transcendental."

"I suppose I was out of it a bit. I'd been practicing that Zen relaxation thing to get the fine muscle control needed for good brass rubbing. And I was super hungry as well."

"Harry says that when his students get fully relaxed in the deprivation tank, they see all kinds of things—snakes coming out of the walls, Christ knows what."

"Sounds more like the DT's than what happened to me."

"They think it's a result of feedback in the circuitry of the brain, but I can't for the life of me see any connection with our experiences. Whatever happened in that church definitely seemed to be outside our heads, not inside them."

"I agree."

The coffeepot bubbled fiercely and then expired with a sigh. Sarah got off the couch and returned to the kitchen. Brian mulled over the evidence one more time then relaxed and let his eyes wander around the room. Sarah's apartment was a wonderland. High on every wall of the living room hung her brass rubbings, knights and nobles in their jet-black uniforms. Brian loved the place. It seemed so secure and timeless. He felt he could live there forever in the company of those ancient heroes.

"There is another possibility," Sarah said as she emerged from the kitchen with a steaming pot of coffee and two mugs and sat back down beside him. "It's something I've been thinking about a lot since it happened."

"What's that?"

"Well, while I was doing the brass rubbing of Richard Crossly, I was thinking about religion and what it means to me. I was wondering why it is that so many people believe in God. Do you know what I mean? It's a simple question. I've been living on this planet for more than twenty years, and I've yet to see a shred of evidence for the existence of a supreme being. What's so special about all those people who've been filling the churches every Sunday for a thousand years, two thousand years? What have they experienced? Why are they so sure that God exists?"

"What are you getting at?"

"Well, I began to think, what would it take for me to believe in God?"

"What *would* it take?"

"A sign, I thought, some kind of a sign, any kind."

"A miracle?"

"Maybe. Maybe not quite so dramatic. Just some indication that—"

"Do you believe that's what this was?"

"All I know is I was sitting there on the floor of the church, thinking about how powerful religion is and wondering how you become a believer, when suddenly, there was this light from the altar—"

"And the blood."

"Exactly. The blood. There's always blood associated with miracles and stuff, isn't there? It drips out of the sides of crucifixes. It oozes from the palms of stigmata. A vial of the blood of San Gennaro congeals every year in Naples. You know what I mean. Religion is hemophilic. I saw blood all over my sweater, and the next minute, it was gone. Perhaps that was supposed to be a sign to me." She shook her head and looked down at the floor. "I'm sorry, Brian. I don't know what I'm talking about." Without warning, she cupped her face in her hands and burst into tears.

Brian was taken aback. He watched her for a few seconds and suddenly appreciated for the first time just how deeply the experience had affected her. He raised both arms to embrace her, and she buried her face in his shoulder. She cried harder, one hand falling from her face and clutching him to her. "I don't know what any of it means. I'm so sorry."

He continued to hold her till the crying ceased. Then they rested quietly in each other's arms. He kissed her tenderly on the forehead. He realized that the experience had gotten under her skin and was gnawing away at her. He began to feel angry that she should have to be subjected to such an ordeal and annoyed at himself for being powerless to help her.

He looked over the top of Sarah's head at the wall behind her. His eyes were drawn to a masterpiece of brass rubbing: a medieval man-at-arms with drawn sword and dangling mace. Legs astride, muscular, the knight mocked him. He stared down the centuries at Brian's impotence, his shortness, his flabbiness, and his physical and emotional ineptitude. "My breastplate is thirty pounds of steel," the figure seemed to say. "I killed five men at Bosworth Field. My balls are like canister shot. What do you know of the world?"

What did he know, truly, when you got right down to it? He had done nothing of note with his life. He had never been reckless, never confrontational. He had never stood up for a worthy cause. He had never even taken a journey that wasn't safe and well-planned. The knight was worthy of immortalization; Brian Kenning was a sham.

He raised Sarah's chin and kissed her gently on the lips. She rubbed his forearm to show that she had recovered. Brian then stood up and walked back to the window. Suffused with conflicting sentiments, he tried again to recall the way those raindrops had looked to him all those years ago, but he knew that the magic was only in the first glimpse. Like so many things that happened to you in this world, the memory persisted, but the feeling was irrecoverable.

It struck him that his life was becoming less meaningful as the years went by, even as the time remaining became more precious. The days of charting courses and preserving options ought to be behind him. It was time to fill these valuable years with action. The words with which his aunt had assailed him as they had walked along the beach came ringing back into his ears: "Find yourself a worthy cause. Take your courage in both hands. Let convention go hang." At that precise moment, he knew what his course of action must be.

"Sarah," he said, "I've made a decision. I'm going to find out what this ghost business is all about. Aunt Polly was absolutely right. It's up to people like me to explain the mysteries of the world. That's something I'm good at, and people will benefit from it. I was an idiot not to see it that way before."

"Are you sure?"

"I've never been surer of anything in my life. I can find out if that ghost is real. Certainly, I can. If it's a physical entity, then it's got a molecular presence, and I know enough about molecular physics to be able to detect it. I can settle the issue one way or the other."

"What about your work at the university?"

"It's not that important," he snorted, sweeping it aside with a flick of his hand. "I tell you, Sarah, I can determine for sure whether the ghost is in the church or in our minds. It's no different from measuring the concentration of a trace gas. Get the thing in a spectroscope and it's just like a car exhaust or…or a smoke plume. I tell you, I can crack this. I can put your mind at ease, everyone's minds."

Sarah was unsure how to react—flattered by his offer of help and unwilling to dampen his ardor yet fearful of where his unbridled enthusiasm might lead. She stood up, pulled him from the window, and wrapped her arms around him. "It's gonna be just fine, sweetheart," he said, kissing her hair, "more than fine. It's gonna be great. I gotta phone Harry as soon as possible." He unwound her fingers and, partly with apologies and partly with endearments, hastened to leave. "I need to call him right away."

"Well, all right then. But just remember that science might not solve all your problems," Sarah said. "Don't dismiss religion out of hand. I've talked it over with Richard Crossly, you know. He was worshipping in that church when science was still trying to turn lead into gold. He lived in a world of mud and stink and early death. Science is…is a babe in the arms of religion. Don't presume it can answer all your questions. Are you listening to me?"

"Goodbye, Sarah!" Brian cried as he pulled on his jacket and rushed out the door. "Don't worry!"

"Goodbye! I'll…" But he was gone.

*****

Brian headed for the tube station in the rain, his mind ablaze with plans. He walked at a feverish pace while the rush hour buses growled and crawled alongside him. He had little recollection of the subway ride. Fellow passengers glared at him for staring at them, though in actuality, he was staring through them at a bobbing light crossing a darkened church. He looked at a billboard of a London policeman and saw Richard Crossly in full plate armor, gauntlets reaching to the middle joint of his fingers. He alighted at Clapham South and strode across the common. He peered into a darkened niche in a church wall, and two lovers sheltering under a tree told him to fuck off. He was close to frenzy.

He reached his apartment door and flung it open. Through the door and at a sweeping glance, he redesigned the living room to compete with Sarah's decor. Flinging his coat across a chair, he grabbed a phone book, address book, pencil, and paper. He grabbed his cell phone and called Harry Groh as fast as he could punch in numbers. No answer, so he left a message to say he would be attending the American Physical Society's annual meeting in Chicago.

He called British Airways and made reservations for the flight. He messaged his secretary at the university to make hotel arrangements. A light drifting across the hallway that led to his bedroom and drifting toward the niche in the church wall, he called his aunt Polly. "Please square it with the vicar for our return." He again jabbed his stubby fingers at the phone. "John, you're with me on this, right? Amplifiers, microphones, infrared spectrometers."

The lights of his bedroom were swaying to and fro. Ancient gravestones were jutting out of the floorboards. Trembling a little now, finally, more slowly, he called Sarah. "Thank you, and if necessary, apologies. And if you get a chance, please stop by the British Museum and find out all you can about the history of Hoyland Church." He stared at his bed as the corpse of Richard Crossly rose from it and glided toward him.

CHAPTER 10

Chicago
Thanksgiving 2017

Brian Kenning drank a little too much on the flight from Heathrow to O'Hare, and it seemed no time at all between the plane juddering upward through a coverlet of London fog and dropping gracefully toward Lake Michigan, its wings scooping thick slabs of ice cream cloud. He was drawn from his reverie by the pilot issuing landing instructions. Moments later, he was running a gauntlet of uniforms: immigration officials, customs inspectors and baggage handlers, airline staff and security officers, and skycaps and limo drivers.

He took a taxi to the airport Sheraton, struggling to reacquaint himself with Americana. The cab driver, unperturbed by Brian's English accent, kept up a barrage of conversation on such diverse topics as the Bears, cranberry relish, and construction on the Eisenhower Expressway. Brian was pleasantly surprised to find that he was able to sustain a dialogue on these largely unfamiliar subjects. He admired the driver's sociability and overtipped him when they reached the hotel. His luggage was deposited curbside and spirited away by a red-and-gold uniform, even before the departing cab could envelop him in a cloud of exhaust fumes. He chased his luggage under a sign that read, "Welcome, American Physical Society Members."

Harry Groh burst out of an armchair as Brian crossed the threshold. The two collided in mid lobby like sumo wrestlers and exchanged greetings. Harry escorted Brian to the reception desk and hovered over him while he checked in. They then retired to a lounge scattered with bales of straw, on which were displayed pumpkins and green-and-yellow gourds of all shapes and sizes. Exhausted, Brian collapsed into an armchair. After the customary pleasantries, Harry leaned forward in his chair and took Brian's arm.

"We've had a real breakthrough," Harry said, though it had been Brian who had requested the meeting to discuss his own agenda. "We've discovered a new state of consciousness, Brian. I'm certain of it. This student I've got working with me, Karen Butler, is a dream. You put her in the flotation tank, and she sails off to God knows where. I've told you before how everyone in the field is working on brain wave patterns and the biofeedback stuff that Joe Kamiya discovered at UC Medical Center. It's now well-known that the alpha wave correlates with a higher state of meditation. Do you know what I'm talking about?"

"Not really."

"Well, anyway, we've discovered a new state underlying all the others. It's very low frequency—less than one cycle per second. Commercial detectors don't register in that range, which is probably why no one's seen it before. We're calling it the zeta state because we don't want anyone to discover any others. Ha! That's Frank Koslowski's little joke. Anyway, this zeta state is characterized by intense visual hallucinations according to Karen and a sensation of complete detachment from the real world. Trouble is, she can't sustain it for more than twenty or thirty seconds at a time. She says her mind won't stabilize in the zeta state and keeps retracting back to alpha. But we're all real excited about it anyway. I should have a journal article ready in a week or two."

"That's fascinating," Brian said. "Have any of your other students experienced it?"

"I'm not sure about Dan Patzner. Possibly. He's not so good at communicating with us."

"What about the others?"

"There are no others at the moment, chief." Harry scratched the back of his neck. "Funding was cut last year."

"Sorry to hear that."

"But I'm forgetting the best part," Harry said, inching to the edge of his seat. "One day a couple of weeks ago, we had Karen and Dan in the zeta state simultaneously, and they both freaked out.

Literally. I'm having a helluva time keeping the Pentagon off my ass. I'm thinking this zeta state turns the subject into some kind of giant receiver, picking up electromagnetic signals from God knows where. When you put two subjects close together, the reception goes through the roof. It was too much for them to handle."

"When you talk like this, Harry, I can't help but think of my aunt Polly and my girlfriend, Sarah. When they get into a contemplative state in the church, these ghostly apparitions appear. I keep thinking there might be some connection with your work. Is it possible they're attaining this zeta state too?"

"It's hard to say. Right now, Karen's the only one who truly understands what the zeta state is all about. Maybe we should get Karen to go talk to them."

"Maybe so."

"Now what did you want to talk to me about?" Harry asked, leaning back in his armchair. Brian scratched the stubble that had sprouted on his chin after the long flight. He chose his words carefully knowing how easily Harry would be turned off by an unconvincing thesis. "What do you know about lidar?"

"What?" Harry answered, not quite catching the word.

"It's an acronym for light detection and ranging—lidar."

"Isn't that what those guys used to bounce a laser beam off the moon?"

"Yeah, that was some early work. In the last few years, it's been used for studying all kinds of things: clouds, smoke plumes, volcanic eruptions. You shine an intense beam of light at a diffuse object and then measure either the backscattered radiation or the transmitted radiation. It gives you information about the molecular structure of the irradiated object."

"What part of the spectrum are we talking about?"

"Visible or near-infrared, about one micron. That's where the atmosphere is transparent. There's no absorption by water vapor, oxygen, or carbon dioxide. This region of the spectrum is eye safe as well, so you don't need to shield the light source."

"Do they use lasers?"

"Yeah, ruby or neodymium:YAG and some types of dye lasers. Ruby lasers are probably the best."

Harry nodded at Brian and looked thoughtfully around the room. His eyes lit on a bowl of trail mix on the table next to him. He grabbed it, opened his mouth wide, and tossed a fistful of the mixture at his uvula. He nodded again, this time to himself, and ordered a Coke from a passing waitress. "You wanna use this method to detect the ghost in the church?" he asked, chewing vigorously.

"You got it," Brian replied. "And why not? Lidar's been used to measure concentrations on the order of ten to a hundred molecules per cubic centimeter. If the ghost is a diffuse physical object, we should be able to detect it this way. If the ghost is a trick of the light or merely hallucinatory, then we won't measure any absorption at all."

"How would you set it up?"

"I'd take a ruby laser, see, and I'd place it on one side of the chancel with the detector by its side. On the opposite side of the chancel, I'd place a forty-five-degree mirror to deflect the incident radiation up into the roof of the church, out of the way. When the ghost crosses the beam, we get some backscattered radiation that we can measure. It ought to work, don't you think?"

"Sounds like you're looking for a technician."

"I don't know how strong the signal's going to be, Harry. And there's bound to be a lot of noise from fluctuations in the incident radiation, dark current of the detector, changes in the target geometry, and such like. We'll have to boost the signal-to-noise ratio as high as possible. You've screwed around with electronics for years. Can you help me hook it all up?"

"Do you use photomultiplier tubes for detectors?"

"I think so."

"I've worked with photomultipliers before. I might be able to help with that part."

"And you know about amplifier noise and stuff like that. I'm sure you could do it," Brian said, almost pleading. "And wouldn't you simply like to know the answer?"

Harry didn't reply. It was clear that he was not yet ready to commit. "Do you really think there's a connection between the ghost in the church and our sensory deprivation experiments?"

"I do. The contemplative state seems to be common to both. And these visual hallucinations—or whatever you want to call them—they also seem similar. It's just that you have a much better control of the subject in the immersion tank than we do in the church. It gives a stronger experience."

"I guess it could help to unravel the truth about the zeta state." Harry took a deep breath and folded his arms across his chest. The line of his jaw was as square as the pack of Marlboros jutting from his shirt pocket. "Okay. As regards the scientific measurements, I'm your man. But before we consummate the deal, I need to clue you in on a couple of things. First of all, I'm highly skeptical of the whole damned enterprise. Frankly, I do not believe in ghosts. Period. For me, nature is—has to be—consistent. It must be perfectly random and totally predictable. You sit there and talk to me about ghosts appearing and moving through walls and disappearing and suchlike, but all your sincerity is overwhelmed by the monumental wealth of evidence I've accumulated that says it just ain't so."

"If you don't mind me saying so, that's the way—"

"Second," Harry continued, "you just might find that I'm your own worst enemy. To convince me about this ghost, you're going to have to provide me with a perfect explanation. If I see a single flaw, the merest pinhole of doubt, I'll chip away at it till it's big enough to drive a Mack Truck through. I'll have to, do you see?"

"I see."

"It's like baseball, the perfect game. You pitch eight and two-thirds innings of perfect ball, but one little error, one scratch hit, and it means nothing. There's never been an almost perfect game or an essentially perfect game. It's either a lifetime memory, or it's forgotten with the vendor's hotdog. I once saw Sandy Koufax pitch a perfect game at Dodger Stadium. Every putout is imprinted in my brain, every single one. But one bobble and it wouldn't be worth a couple of spare neurons in the outfield of my memory. That's the way it is with me. I'm gonna hold you to the highest standards of proof, okay?

Frankly, I don't think you'll ever get me to accept the existence of ghosts."

"That's fine, Harry. Honestly, it is. Skeptics are perfectly acceptable. I don't want you to think that we've prejudged the outcome."

Harry's cell phone rang. He pulled it out of his pocket, put it up to his ear, and walked across the lounge, listening. Within a couple of minutes, he came striding back and grabbed Brian's arm. "Let's go! That was Frank. They've picked up some kind of electrical field around the students. Sounds momentous. Come on!"

"Your Coke, sir!" the waitress cried in vain as they strode out the door.

Brian was dragged into the lobby, greatly bemused. He wanted to check his room, unpack, and take a shower, but Harry was running through a door and down a flight of stairs, and Brian had no choice but to follow him. They sprinted across an underground parking garage, jumped into Harry's jeep, and were soon speeding down the tollway at eighty miles an hour.

"Who is Frank again?" Brian asked him when the only excitement left was speed.

"Frank Koslowski, constipated son of a bitch who supervises my labs. He can't stand the sight of me, and the feeling's mutual, but he keeps the experiments ticking over. He's one of those behavioral scientists who ought to be at home studying his own behavior."

"What did he say?"

"I'd asked Pete Wilkinson, this Aussie scientist in the next lab who runs experiments on dolphin communication, to set up his radio frequency receiver near the kids the next time they went zeta. He'd claimed we'd fucked up his experiment that time the kids freaked out. Put a damn great spike on his chart recorder, so he said. I thought it wouldn't hurt to have him try to replicate it. And Frank says Wilkinson's picked up a signal."

"Jesus Christ."

"We gotta get down there and check it out. This could be big. Could be the biggest thing since Ma Bell invented direct dialing."

*****

99

Fifteen minutes later, they swerved off the highway, catapulted through a tollbooth, and merged with the commuter traffic leaving the city on I-55. Harry continued to drive recklessly, and Brian, keeping his eyes on the wing mirrors, was certain they would be pulled over. They raced on for half an hour, their speed increasing as the commuter traffic melted away into the suburbs. Then they were off the main highway and on two-lane blacktops till, finally, they reached the campus and the remote corner of the site where the ICPS building stood. A single car was parked outside, a campus security vehicle, its roof light emitting a solitary rotating beam of red light. Harry blanched when he saw it.

"What's it mean?" Brian asked, looking at him.

"It's a fucking conspiracy of the forces of fucking nature," Harry shouted, slamming the steering wheel with both palms. They jumped out of the jeep, ran up the short flight of steps, and burst through the front door. A security guard in a black leather jacket turned to confront them.

"What's happened?" Harry asked him.

"We've been trying to reach you, Dr. Groh. There's been a disturbance. Come into the office please."

"What kind of a disturbance?" Harry asked as they followed the guard across the atrium. Suddenly, a loud, jarring noise came from within the front office, and all three faltered. There was a crash, and the door flew open. The white-coated figure of Frank Koslowski shot backward through the doorway and landed on its rear end in the middle of the hallway.

"Frank?" Harry said, making a motion toward him. Suddenly, Dan Patzner erupted from the office, hurdled the fallen scientist, and raced across the atrium. The security guard wheeled around and reached for the revolver by his side. "Don't be an idiot!" Harry shouted, quickly reaching for the guard's right hand, which was already gripping the weapon. The guard swallowed hard but permitted Harry's hand to close over his knuckles.

By the outer door, Dan Patzner turned. "I tell you," he said, slowly and deliberately, "that girl is a witch." He pointed at the office door. "That girl is a witch!"

"Freeze right there!" the guard ordered.

"Fuck you!" Dan turned and fled through the double doors into the parking lot. The guard surged forward in pursuit, but Harry wrapped his arms around him and dug in his heels.

"Asshole!" the guard blurted out, his lips curled with rage, but he did not try to escape Harry's grasp. Their eyes followed Dan's figure running into the woodland that led back to the main campus. Then both men became aware of the audience for this astonishing diorama: Brian, pale and silent against a wall, two secretaries frozen like statues in the adjacent hallway, Connie Cammaretta and a second security guard framed in the office doorway, and Frank Koslowski now struggling to his feet.

"Take your fucking hands off me!" the guard ordered. Harry unclasped his hands and held his arms high and submissive. "Let's get that asshole back here." The two leather-jacketed figures ran to their security vehicle and took off at speed.

"What in the name of all that's holy has been going on here, Frank?" Harry spat in a clenched voice at his assistant, who was rubbing the small of his back gingerly with both hands.

"Dan went nuts, Harry. I had to call security to restrain him. He was completely out of control. The guards stiff-armed him over here so we could try to talk some sense into him, but when we brought Karen into the room, he went ballistic again. He wouldn't let her near him. Said she was possessed. Said something about her trying to trap him in the zeta state, reaching for his soul or some crazy shit. Then he pushed me through the damned door. I swear I've broken something."

Connie helped Frank to a chair while Harry ran both hands through his hair several times, brow to nape, struggling to contain his emotions. "What was all that crap about detecting a signal?"

"That part was true, Harry," Frank said. "Wilkinson's got some astonishing readings. It was all going so well. That's the ironic part. He's in his lab, looking over the output now. It was totally exciting for a while. Then this."

Harry could barely speak. His face was a dullish purple behind the tangle of beard, hair, and eyebrows. One lapel on his coat was turned under, and one sleeve was twisted right around. Brian tried hard not to stare at him. The secretaries turned and walked back the way they had come, chattering to each other in low tones. Outside, a sunset was being extinguished to the icy music of a police siren.

Karen Butler appeared at the door of the office, and Brian was galvanized by her unconventional appearance—bald head, Blackhawks jacket with the collar turned up, blue jeans tight across slender thighs, and bare ankles above plain beach shoes. But what struck Brian most of all was her poise. She seemed to know that the real action was not here in the atrium but back in the laboratory and in her mind. He couldn't take his eyes off her.

Karen leaned against the doorframe. She crossed one foot non-chalantly over the other and examined a fingernail. Then she lifted her eyes up to Harry's. "It's not my fault, boss," she explained. "Dan can't handle the zeta state. You'll have to find me someone else."

"I sense," Harry said through clenched teeth, "that we're not going to be doing any more experiments for a while."

Karen shrugged her shoulders in acceptance of that possibility. She turned, and as she did, she caught sight of Brian standing by the wall. For a moment, she thought she recognized him. She gave him a fleeting smile, a smile that said, "You understand, don't you, that this thing is only just beginning?" As she looked further at him, she had a peculiar feeling that she had met him before. In any case, he looked pleasant enough and seemed quite concerned about her, so she gave him a second reassuring smile. Then she stepped back into the office.

"Has Karen been debriefed, Frank?" Harry asked.

"When have I had time to—?"

"Do it now, Frank," Harry said, turning to Brian with a "See what I'm up against?" look. He drew a deep breath. "Let's go talk to Wilkinson."

They walked down the main hallway and turned into a labora-tory festooned with cables and strewn with electronic equipment. A short man with neatly combed hair was sucking orange juice through a straw while studying computer printouts at a workbench. He wore a tight woolen vest, and his shirt sleeves were rolled up to his biceps. He stood up as the two men approached him.

"Peter, this is Brian Kenning, a physics professor from London," Harry said. "And, Brian, this is Peter Wilkinson, a member of our research staff from Australia."

"How d'you do, ya Pommy bastard?" Wilkinson said amiably. "Nice to meet you on neutral turf, so to speak. Who's got the Ashes at the moment?"

"Surprisingly, we do," Brian replied.

Wilkinson smiled and turned to Harry. "So what's with your student? He went nuts when he came out of his trance."

"It's not a trance, Wilkinson. It's a new state of consciousness."

"Too bloody right it is, sport."

"Why do you say that? What happened?"

"Well, just like you asked me to do, I set up my radio receiver halfway between the girl in the tank and that Dan character in the other lab. The two were positioned just like you said they were the day you spiked my experiment. They dozed off, and bingo, I got this clear signal right away, weak but clear. They're not receivers, Harry, old sport. They're bloody transmitters."

"What?"

"They're transmitters. They're sending out electromagnetic waves."

"That doesn't make any sense."

"I didn't say it did."

"What frequency?" Brian interjected.

"I haven't had time to measure it precisely," Wilkinson answered, "but it seems to be about three megacycles per second, which, by the way, explains why I picked it up last time. It's just outside what we call the loran band—the long-range navigation band. That's the part of the radio spectrum reserved for ocean navigation. It's used for finding direction and distance at sea. My research project involves seeing if electromagnetic waves in that region of the spectrum can affect dolphin communication underwater."

"But how the hell can people generate radio waves, for Christ's sake?" Harry pressed.

"Lots of empty attic space," Brian reminded him, eyebrows raised.

"It was a strange sort of signal," Wilkinson continued. "Three megacycles per second corresponds to a wavelength of about a hundred meters. That's about twice as far apart as the students were. I moved the receiver around a bit and found that the signal was strongest at the center, and it dropped off rapidly on either side, which suggests it's highly polarized."

"And what does all that mean?" Harry asked.

"They formed an antenna!" Brian answered in wonder.

"That's right. Hey, you're good!" Wilkinson said. "Somehow, they made a dipole antenna and produced a standing wave of electromagnetic energy in the space between them. Don't ask me how they did it, but that's what I measured. It's heavy stuff."

"I don't understand," Harry said. "All this time, I've been assuming that the kids pick up some kind of cosmic signal when we shut out the world's distractions. Now you're telling me it's the other way around, that they're producing some kind of energy of their own? That's crazy. I don't know what to make of it."

Brian's mind was racing ahead, integrating this new piece of information with what was already known. He became agitated, scratching his chin stubble with a rhythmical motion. He turned to look at Wilkinson's equipment and then walked to the door and back. The possibilities of what could be done with externally projected energy were coming fast and furious, and he also saw another opportunity to link Harry's investigations with his own. He calmed down a little and gave Harry a sidelong glance.

"What to make of it? Perhaps you could make a ghost of it," he said. "Fly back with me to England, Harry, and we'll find out."

CHAPTER 11

Hoyland Church
December 2017

At the end of the pasture, where the cinder path merged with the gravel road from Bittern Fen to Hoyland, the Reverend Nigel Applewhite struggled to put on his bicycle clips with one hand. His other hand was clamped over his straw hat, which a persistent sea breeze fought to dislodge. It was a chill winter's morning, and the vicar shivered as he performed this awkward feat of acrobatics.

Polly Coleby, leaning on her bike and peering into his face, badgered the poor man. "So do you think it's a good idea or not, Reverend? I need to know how you feel about it. Myself, I don't think it's fitting, to be truthful, whatever good might come of it. I mean, it's God's house, not a place for messing about with spirits. But Brian says they only want to come and sit in the church and put a few machines like radios and such in there. So would it really be a desecration or whatever you call it? What do you think?"

"Machines? In my church?" the vicar replied. "Would you turn it into a sideshow?"

"But is what they want to do so terribly bad, Vicar? That's what I need to know."

Applewhite chewed his lower lip. He was dressed in a dirty corduroy jacket that had ridden up while he kneeled, revealing faded gray trousers puckered at the knees by the crimping action of the bicycle clips. His straw hat was unraveled at the brim, and his glasses were askew. Polly found it hard to view him as a figure of authority just at that moment.

"My most sincere belief," the vicar said, "is that the church is as free as the love of God. It can put bonds on no man. On the other hand, this business is so…so very secular." He lifted his bicycle out of the puddle where it had lain and mounted it. He longed to be far away from this conversation.

"But it bothers me greatly, Reverend. Brian's my nephew, and I can stop him coming here if you want me to. You must advise me."

Applewhite's eyes moistened in sympathy. His concerns were the same as hers, but he didn't know what to tell her. He was being drawn into an area so far removed from his expectations of the duties of a country parson that he couldn't judge the correct position to take. Neither dare he ask advice from other church worthies lest he be perceived inadequate for the job. The more he thought about it, the more the awkwardness of the situation seemed to reflect badly on himself. He could do nothing but exclaim, "My wrath, should things ever go amiss in my church, will be like…like a hundred plagues!"

He heard a noise from the road and looked up. A small black car chugged toward them and came to rest by the path. The engine stopped, and a man in a brown suit and trilby hat got out. He was a distinguished-looking man with fluffy white sideburns and a soldierly bearing. His cheeks were country red and blotchy. He approached the vicar, extended his hand, and said, "Reverend Applewhite? I don't think we've met, sir. Not one of your flock, so to speak. Name's Jack Stephens of the *Hoyland and Scardyke Examiner*. I wonder if I might have a word, if you're not too busy." He smiled at Polly, said, "Ma'am," and tipped his hat. The vicar tightened his grip on the handlebars, so Stephens withdrew the proffered hand. "You see, Vicar, news has come to our collective ear of some mysterious goings-on in your church late at night. Yes?"

"What's this all about, Mr.…er? Frightfully busy, you know."

"Yes, of course. But, well, one of your elderly parishioners told us a right old story." He chuckled to himself at the recollection of it and waited for them to rise to the bait. Neither the uncomfortable cleric nor the disinterested bystander moved a muscle. The reporter stroked one of his sideburns. "Well, to cut a long story short, the old lady in question—an unnamed source, as we like to say—fell off her bike right outside your church one night a few weeks ago. Had the fright of her life, so she said. Probably just about here on this very spot." He pointed to the ground, and the vicar looked at it. "She told us about seeing lights and hearing strange noises. Rightly got to believe a respectable old lady if she says so, don't you think, Vicar? Got ghosts in your church, have you, Vicar?"

"Ridiculous," Applewhite muttered and pedaled to the end of the path.

"Well, if you say so. You ought to know, I suppose, spending half your life in the place like you do." Applewhite turned and delivered such a malevolent glare by way of reply that Stephens was momentarily taken aback. Quickly recovering his composure, however, the reporter pursued him. "And then there was that peculiar business with the art student who passed out doing the brass rubbing thing or whatever it is students do these days. We heard about that too. Did that have anything to do with these ridiculous ghosts, Mr. Applewhite?" Applewhite looked both ways and cycled off into the village.

"Funny old stick," the reporter said, watching him recede into the distance. "Hard to read. What's your take on the subject, Mrs. Coleby? I'd heard that your nephew was involved."

Jack Stephens had known Will and Polly Coleby for many years and had an abiding affection for them. They embodied all the traits he loved about the fenland people: strength, perseverance, and good humor. And they were down-to-earth too, not stuck-up like those city folks. They were the kind of people who, to his way of thinking, were most threatened by progress, by the intrusion of the modern world into traditional rural life. As lead reporter for the local newspaper, he saw it as his duty to protect people like the Colebys.

"I've got to get to the post office," Polly mumbled, avoiding eye contact. She mounted her own bicycle and wobbled down the road in pursuit of the vicar.

"Ma'am," he acknowledged, tipping his hat a second time. He stroked his sideburn again and turned to stare up the hill. "And who's going to look after your interests, old girl?" he said to the silent but attentive church.

*****

Meanwhile, in the center of London, an expedition was forming. A week of assembling scientific equipment had boiled down to a crisp December morning in a deserted college parking lot. John, Brian, and Harry loaded two crates into a van borrowed for the occasion. Sarah stood by, stamping her feet and blowing on her fingers. Shortly before ten o'clock, they were ready to leave. Harry and John climbed into the rear seats while Sarah sat next to Brian, who was the appointed driver.

Brian crunched the gear stick into first, let out the clutch abruptly, and bucked through the iron gates of his college quadrangle and into the maelstrom of London traffic. He tried hard to compete with the smooth daring of the city drivers, but after he almost hit a cyclist and a box of ammeters had been thrown to the floor, he slowed down. Half an hour later, they reached the end of the suburban sprawl, and traffic abated. The passengers eased back into their seats. Soon, they were motoring north on a clear highway in good spirits.

"How did you guys get permission to use the church, Brian?" Harry asked. "I'm surprised they'd let you near the place with all this equipment."

"Let's just say we have tacit permission," Brian replied. "I asked my aunt to ask the vicar if he was agreeable. He didn't exactly say no, so she thinks it'll be all right. I want to keep things low-key for the time being. If we make it too official, someone's going to find a reason to stop us."

"Sure. So what's this place like then?"

"The church? Oh, you're gonna love it, Harry. Old and dusty. Spooky as shit. It's about five hundred years old, didn't we decide? My aunt thinks it's even older. Oh, I forgot. Sarah's been doing some homework. What did you find out?"

Sarah delved into a briefcase and pulled out a pad covered with meticulous notes. Clipped to the pad was a brochure of the churches of Lincolnshire. They stared at the rolling fields as she led them through the centuries. "Let's see now. Where to begin? The fenlands. Well, that part of the country was first inhabited by the Belgae, a tribe that crossed to England from what is now Belgium in 300 BC or thereabouts. No one knows for sure. At that time, the whole region was just one huge marsh. When the Romans arrived, they built drainage works and embankments and made the land habitable, though not particularly hospitable. After their departure, the region became part of the Anglo-Saxon kingdom of Mercia. The first sovereign began his reign in—let me see now—580 AD."

Harry gave a low whistle. He wasn't used to such antiquity. He calculated how many centuries ago that was and whistled again. "I know. Hard to believe, isn't it?" Sarah continued. "According to historians, even at that time, Hoyland was a special place. They called it Heighlendh, or the high land. The earliest reference I could find talked about a primitive abbey that existed on the site in 690 AD. It was dedicated to a St. Guthlac, who'd built a reed-and-wattle hut by the side of the hill after rowing across the marsh in a coracle. There are several references to visits by reigning monarchs of Mercia, but I could find nothing concrete until the year 870, when the Viking invasions began.

"You can imagine how vulnerable the area was—flat as a pancake, crisscrossed by navigable rivers, devoid of fortified towns. They pretty much walked in. They ransacked the abbey initially but later restored it when Christianity gained more of a foothold. Next on the scene, of course, was William the Conqueror in 1066. It was the Normans who established a thriving monastery on the site. These new monks were Premonstratensian. I think I pronounced that right. That is to say they followed Augustinian rules but wore white robes instead of black. By the time of the dissolution, an orthodox Augustinian order had been established there."

"The dissolution?" Harry asked. "What was that?"

"Didn't you study any English history in school?" Sarah responded. "When King Henry VIII broke with Rome, he decided to abolish the Catholic monasteries. Hoyland Abbey was one of a number of houses in the north of England to resist. They called it the Lincolnshire Rising there. Farther north, it became the Pilgrimage of Grace. Pissed King Henry off no end.

"There was a violent overthrow of the abbey in 1537. Narratives of the day describe how the monks were forcibly evicted, their relics and other treasures confiscated, and most of the buildings destroyed. However, the main priory building was rebuilt almost immediately as a simple Anglican church. They named it St. Neot's. That's all the history I could find in the British Museum. The church has undergone a number of minor modifications over the last four centuries, but it's basically the same today as it was in the sixteenth century."

"A checkered past," John observed.

"Thirteen hundred years is a helluva long time," Harry said. "A helluva long time. I'm surprised there's anything left at all."

"You need to understand," Sarah explained, "that the locals keep rebuilding on the same spot. The hill holds spiritual significance for them. I'm sure there'll be more history recorded locally—architectural details, saints revered in the area, parish history, things not important enough to make the national archives. For example, I never did discover who St. Neot was. There'll be records of the local dignitaries who are buried there and rolls of the clergy over the years. I'll be able to put a name to the ghost before I've finished." She gave a nervous laugh.

As they sped through the English countryside, the patchwork fields of Bedfordshire and Huntingdonshire slipped by, and the soil in the furrowed fields grew blacker and heavier, signaling the onset of the fen country. The sky began to cloud over. At a nondescript exit, they turned off the main highway and headed east along a narrow two-lane road. They left the rolling hills behind and descended into the flat fenland, which was spread with a delicate quilt of mist. They drove in silence through quaint, deserted villages, giving thanks to the Romans for their insistence on building straight roads.

"The fog's thickening," Sarah said after a while.

"Don't worry, we're only about thirty miles from Bittern Fen."

"Drive carefully please."

Brian leaned forward and peered into the distance, looking for landmarks, but earth and sky had merged into a single veil of haze, and there was little to recognize. He asked Sarah a question: "Do you remember that strange cavity in the east wall of the church? It intrigues me. Two people were buried in it, remember? Husband and wife. Name of Crosby or something. Did you find out anything about them?"

"Crossly, not Crosby. Yes, as a matter of fact, I did. There was a reference to them in McEnally's *Historical Biographies*, and they're also mentioned in this brochure I picked up at the church last time. Their names were Richard Crossly and Catherine Crossly, husband and wife. Richard was born in 1505 and died in 1587. He had the nickname Poing de Fer, which is French for Fist of Iron, supposedly because of his heavy-handed role in the dissolution of Hoyland Abbey, which I'll get to in a moment. His wife died in 1593, but there's no record of her birth. The two of them were interred side by side in a stone sarcophagus that was stored for a century in the east wall of the church."

"In that niche behind the organ," John said, and Brian nodded.

"During the seventeenth century, the sarcophagus was removed."

"What had this Richard Crossly done to deserve such privileged treatment?"

"I think I can explain that. Apparently, Crossly's father, Sir Adam Crossly, was a patron of the abbey all his life. When he died, he bequeathed most of his money and valuables to it. Among the items was a priceless relic given to him by King Charles VIII of France in 1492 for his role in constituting the Treaty of Étaples between France and England. This relic was known as the Sphere of the Planets. It was a representation of the solar system in which the various heavenly bodies were wrought in precious metals and gems—the moon was made of silver, Mars was a ruby, that sort of thing. It was considered one of the finest treasures in all of Europe at the time. It was lost sometime during the dissolution."

"Or stolen by King Henry," John interjected.

"Maybe. Well, anyway, Richard Crossly assumed his father's patronage of the abbey. But later, he fell in with the new ideology of

King Henry. The Crosslys were close friends with Lord Burghley of Stamford, who was one of the leading nobles in the county. When King Henry appointed Thomas Cromwell to reform the English monastic houses, Lord Burghley was given the job of reforming the monasteries of Lincolnshire. Perhaps because of this, Crossly was appointed to the Suppression in 1536. He was only thirty-one then. He'd begun a career as a soldier, so it was natural that he should be assigned the role of implementing the commission's mandates. As fate or the machinations of the king would have it, one of Richard Crossly's first duties was to dissolve Hoyland Abbey, which he and his father had done so much to support in earlier times. The Augustinians were one of several groups to resist. They mobilized the peasantry and instigated the Lincolnshire Rising. They were finally overcome in 1537. The abbot at the time, Gervase, was executed."

"Or murdered," John said.

"Or murdered. You could say that. The dissolution of the monasteries wasn't the amicable transition that many people think. The locals resented King Henry's treatment of the established Catholic church, not to mention the theft of all the valuables that they and their ancestors had invested in the abbey. There was a lot of violence, particularly in Lincolnshire. We can only guess how Crossly with his divided loyalties felt about it."

"He sounds like a treacherous bastard to me."

The fog enfolded them completely now, shutting off the outside world and enhancing the eeriness of Sarah's tale. Ragged haystacks and stark trees loomed up out of the fog and vanished back into it like tableaux built to illustrate the raw sixteenth-century countryside. Shallow dykes shrouded in the thickest of the mist flanked the road like moats of snow. Brian slowed to twenty miles an hour, and on they crawled, straight as an arrow, for the sea.

"Just a minute," John persisted. "If Crossly led the destruction of the abbey, why did they let him be buried in it?"

"Because his service to the king ensured his good standing," Sarah replied. "After reconsecration of the church in the Anglican faith, it was the obvious place to bury him. He'd rescued it from the clutches of papacy."

"Oh, of course. I hadn't thought of it that way."

"Apparently, Crossly had a lot to do with the rebuilding of the church after he played such a big part in pulling it down."

"When did that happen?" Brian asked.

"Reconstruction began in 1550 and has been going on piecemeal ever since."

"And by the look of the place, they've still got a ways to go."

"Crossly was a peculiar character according to contemporary sources," Sarah continued. "After the destruction of Hoyland Abbey, he changed dramatically. He abandoned his military career and shunned a political one. He became religious and spent a lot of time in the church."

"Remorse," Brian suggested. "He was trying to make amends."

"I suppose, but there were other things. In McEnally's book, it says that Crossly studied alchemy and kept company with the leading mystics of the day, people like John Dee, the queen's astrologer. Because he spent so much time in the church, the villagers became suspicious. Rumors spread that he was communing with unearthly powers. Fortunately for him, the villagers could never decide whether he was communing with God or the devil. They didn't know whether to canonize him or burn him. In the end, they let him alone. He died in his bed."

"This may sound stupid," John said, "but suppose he felt such profound regret for what he'd done that his soul can't rest in peace. It periodically rises from his sarcophagus and wanders around the church he once desecrated. It's his guilty conscience, if you like, seeking redemption. What do you think?"

"Sounds like penny dreadful stuff to me," Brian replied. "But then again, if you think about the direction that light was headed—"

"It was headed for the niche where the sarcophagus was stored, I know," John said. "That's what gave me the idea. Perhaps it's revisiting its former place of burial."

"Why would a ghost do that, for Christ's sake?" Harry asked.

"Perhaps he's looking for his wife," Brian replied.

"Yes!"

"They were buried side by side, for crying out loud. How would he have any trouble finding her?" Sarah snapped. "Now can we please change the subject?"

John and his brother exchanged glances in the rearview mirror, then John rested his arm on the window ledge and stared out the side window. He began to get a queasy feeling that they were standing still and that the landscape was crawling past them. Unlike the others, John was not unnerved by the topic of conversation. He felt curiously detached from the journey, as if his real self had remained in the city while a surrogate had been detailed to these supernatural exploits. The fog lapped at the sides of the van, giving way occasionally to a pair of headlights or the brazier of a streetlamp. The roadside cottages had long since been devoured.

"Wasn't that the road to Donington?" John asked, turning to stare over his shoulder at an intersection already swallowed up in the bloodless swirls.

"Was it?" Brian replied, a puzzled expression on his face. "I thought we passed that some time ago."

"I don't think so. I don't think we're that close to Bittern Fen."

"I'm not sure." They pressed on at a snail's pace, Brian hunched over the wheel.

"How do you feel about Aunt Polly's involvement in all of this?" John asked. "She may not want to help us with these experiments anymore."

"She'll come through for us," Brian replied. "We may not need her soon anyway when we learn more about the phenomenon. Maybe we can leave her out of it. I think—"

"That's a callous thing to say," Sarah interrupted. "Your aunt Polly's the reason you were able to start this investigation in the first place. You ought to be more grateful."

"I just meant that we might not need a sensitive agent at all once we understand things better. And if we do, we can always get another one."

"Like whom?"

"Like...maybe like you."

"Now wait a minute," Sarah cautioned him. "I'm not like your aunt. I don't have any of those powers."

"The same thing happened to you as happened to her as far as I can see."

Sarah wanted to dispute him, but he had made a telling point. She didn't like the thought of being a vehicle for conjuring up the dead. She evaded the topic by asking, "Shouldn't we be getting close to Bittern Fen by now?" No one answered. As dusk began to fall, their van became increasingly isolated from the rest of the world. The locals seemed to know better than to drive on such a night.

"That was the Donington road!" Brian cried, peering off to the side.

"Was it?" Sarah asked.

"I don't think so," John replied.

It was just another bridge from nowhere to nowhere. There was no point in looking outside anymore. The road would take them wherever it wanted. John began to wonder if the whole journey was a dream. What was he doing in a crowded van filled with scientific gizmos, heading for a rendezvous with a ghost? That was the stuff of dreams. This whole charade was built around a five-second glimpse of a moving light.

He had thought about those five seconds so many times they had lost all clarity. They blurred in his memory alongside all the aborted schemes and idle longings of his imagination. There was no reality to any of it. There was just a white blanket, a purring engine, and three motionless heads. Sarah finally verbalized the thought that was in every mind: "We're not lost, are we?"

The fog closed further in on John and muffled his brain. His eyelids seemed to be taped open. He saw that there was a man sitting beside him with a pale face he didn't recognize. The man's fingers were long and thin and coiled in his lap like worms. He couldn't remember the man's name. A voice said, "It's this way." The pitch of the engine was instantly modulated.

John thought back to what Harry had told him about the sensory deprivation experiment, about what it was like to float on water, seeing nothing, hearing nothing, no touch, no taste, and no smell, adrift on the surface of the ocean, your mind dripping off the edge of the world. *That's the sound of the sea,* John thought. *We have lost our way. We must be through the village and on the coast road. I should warn the others.*

"This way," said the voice.

But it's the wrong way. We've come too far past the turnoff. The van is slipping down into the dunes. Wheels are churning through deep sand, bouncing off bushes, picking up speed. Tires are running smoothly now across flat sand. I can smell seaweed. These people are all dead. They're trying to kill me. White worms are writhing in the lap of the stranger beside me. There's no escape. I can't move. I can't even blink. I look between the two heads in the front seat. I can see the waves crashing on the shoreline. This is not happening. We must slow down. Closer and closer to the sea. A spire rears up out of the waves. The church of Sutton le Marsh, tall and gleaming, thrashed with spume.

"Come down!"

We are plunging into the spray, sinking beneath the surface of the sea, sliding down the spire of the church. Bubbles are rising from our mouths. Down through the roof of the church, splitting the wooden rafters asunder, down the side of a huge pillar. Sand is in my throat. I am choking, crashing onto the stone floor. The van disintegrates, its parts floating away. I stand up. I have no companions. I am alone in a vast, undersea church.

"This way!"

Figures emerge from behind the pillars—Vikings with blood on their swords, knights in armor, executioners. This is not a dream. If I know that to be true, then it cannot be a dream. Aunt Polly is clutching a bunch of lilies. Brian is walking behind her, one hand glittering like fire. A soldier with a broadsword steps out from behind a pillar. They converge on me, glaring at me. They want me to join them. They want me dead. But I will not die. I will not. Water is in my mouth, my eyes, my nose. I hold my breath until my lungs are bursting. I rise up and glide effortlessly across the church. I am the ghost, and I'm the only one left alive.

"John, can you pass me my purse?" Sarah said. "John?"

"What?" John answered.

"Are you all right?"

"What?"

"We've arrived. We're at the cottage. Did you fall asleep?"

"I suppose I must have." Sarah smiled at him, and he passed her purse forward.

CHAPTER 12

Hoyland Church
December 2017

"Just a nip for the season?" Nigel Applewhite inquired as he scurried among his guests with tumblers of brandy. "Ms. Harcourt?" Sarah smiled and shook her head. "Dr. Kenning? It'll be cold in the church." Brian accepted one. John and Harry also took glasses, but Polly rejected him firmly. The vicar returned to his desk. "Food, anyone?" He gestured to the assembled fare: mince pies, a bowl of frumenty garnished with nutmeg, and sugar cookies that sparkled on red-and-green plates.

No one seemed hungry, but the vicar was nonetheless proud to be a provider. His eyes rose to the decorations with which he had garlanded the vestry that morning: holly and mistletoe around the walls and on the door to the church a wreath of bay leaves, the traditional welcome for elves and fairies.

"Wonderful time of year, don't you think—Christmas?" the vicar enthused. "So much goodwill and brotherhood. The pretty lights in the windows and the darkness outside, the light and the dark, how appropriate for the season! It would make an excellent topic for a sermon." He paused for a moment and adjusted the balance of the spectacles on his nose. Then he cocked his head, let out a sigh of contentment, and darted off in search of paper plates.

This was the first time Sarah had been inside the vestry. She was fascinated by the old photographs of church outings that lined the walls. She walked over to them and gazed deep into the eyes of the nameless parishioners as if searching for the wellspring of the religious faith she couldn't share. The amiable cleric, who sensed an unspoken rapport between himself and Sarah, dating back to her cry for help in his church, drifted to her side. Sarah, sensing no such affinity, welcomed his presence with simple fellow feeling.

"This lady here," he said, pointing to a slip of a girl with prodigious pigtails, "is still a member of the church, a true stalwart in Christ's army. Her name is Doris Hewson. That photograph was taken before the war. You know her, I think, Mrs. Coleby?" Polly affirmed that she did.

"She must be very old by now," Sarah said.

"Over eighty, bless her soul, but never misses a Sunday service. What a treasure!"

"You must preach a good sermon."

Sarah's compliment triggered audacity in the vicar. "I wouldn't be surprised to learn that one of these young minxes is Mrs. Coleby. What about it?" Applewhite winked at the astonished Sarah and cast an impudent glance at Polly.

"Very unlikely," Polly replied. "Mam hardly ever brought us to Hoyland when I were a girl. Perhaps to the bazaar once in a while."

Applewhite laughed heartily and inappropriately. He knew that because of the isolation of his parish and the unpopularity of his occupation, he would most likely remain a bachelor all his life, but he had not abandoned all hope of meeting Ms. Right. Aside from the occasional brandy, flirting was the biggest vice he allowed himself. However, he had indulged in it so infrequently over the years that it had become mannered. His antics struck the other men in the room as amusing and just a little repugnant, like a vulture displaying its plumage. After several more exchanges between Sarah and the vicar, Brian walked by her with a smirk on his face, eliciting an irritated, "What?"

Brian put down his glass and touched the vicar's elbow. "I think we need to get on with this please."

"Warm yourselves some more!" the vicar responded. "The night's young. Another tot!"

"No, thank you. We must press on."

"Well, as you say."

Brian turned to Sarah. "Are you sure you won't come in with us?"

"Please, Brian, I'd rather not."

"It'll be quite safe."

"No. I'll stay and keep Mr. Applewhite company."

This exchange had a remarkable effect on the vicar. "To be sure, quite the best solution," he said with alacrity. "Run along now and get this business over with. Ms. Harcourt and I will get along splendidly. Do run along!" The decision to proceed had been blessed by the church, and there was no turning back. The four who had chosen to participate in the experiment assembled by the door while the two who had opted out gravitated to the warmth of the gas heater. Applewhite was looking forward to a discussion of contemporary ethics with a delightful young woman. Sarah braced herself, not knowing quite what to expect, but suddenly, the terrors of the church did not seem quite so terrible after all. "Call us if you need anything!" the vicar exclaimed with his back to them.

Brian opened the door to the church. A sudden draft made the heater flare up, and the bay wreath clattered its annoyance. They bravely crossed the threshold. John looked back over his shoulder and saw that the vicar had already captured a pithy concept and was throttling it. Sarah was smoothing her skirt over her knees.

The crates containing the scientific equipment had been unloaded earlier in the afternoon and stacked in an adjacent chapel. The men unpacked them, checking for signs of damage. Everything seemed to be in order. Brian took the opportunity to unveil the audio detector he had built, which resembled two megaphones welded onto a knitting machine. "I know it looks bizarre," he said, "but wait till you see its performance. It can hear a moth sneeze at a hundred paces. These two parabolic collectors will be focused on the aisle. I borrowed them from a chap at the BBC. This mike picks up background noise. All the audio signals are digitized so we can filter and discriminate them to our hearts' content. I've got multichannel tape, high-gain audio amplifiers, the works."

They toiled for half an hour to install it all. With minds and hands occupied, they felt little of the apprehension that had plagued their previous visit to the church. Even Polly was in a lighthearted mood as she helped Brian string cables to the antiquated fuse box. Brian set the laser to point across the center aisle, intersecting the expected path of the ghost should it deign to appear.

On the opposite side of the aisle, Harry and John placed the sound system, a video camera, and the temperature sensor. Thermocouples were distributed around the floor of the chancel. Finally, they installed an ammeter/voltmeter circuit in the church's electrical system, which necessitated all the lights being extinguished for possibly the longest minute of their lives. Brian took the meters over to the bench with the laser controls.

Brian surveyed the fruits of their labors and was struck at once by the incongruity of the smooth plastic and shiny metal alongside the rough wood and stone. It seemed intrusive and deceitful, and it became uncomfortably easy to believe that they might be committing sacrilege. Brian suggested they take some test readings. As with all new experiments, things did not function quite as planned. The laser gave the most trouble. At high sensitivity, there were wild power fluctuations, and the intensity could not be stabilized. Brian cursed, manipulated the controls, and cursed some more. With each profanity, Polly cautioned him to remember his surroundings. At length, tired and disappointed, he settled for a lower but more stable sensitivity.

"Shall we begin?" John asked.

"Before we do," Brian said, "I'd like to examine that niche in the wall again to see if we missed anything last time. I've brought a flashlight."

They squeezed down the narrow passageway next to the organ and reassembled in front of the ominous hole in the east wall. By the light of Brian's flashlight, they reread the inscription identifying the *sepulchrum* of Richardi Crossly then inspected the interior. A spider raced for cover. The niche was empty.

"What's that decoration?" Harry asked, pointing to a row of vertical lines that circled the three inner walls.

"Some kind of frieze," Brian replied. "A stonemason's folly."

"I can't see any writing inside," John said, sticking his head into the niche and examining all its surfaces. "Let's go."

They retraced their steps to the chancel and took up predetermined positions. It had been decided, for safety's sake, to bring Polly closer to the chancel than she would have been in her customary flower arranging spot by the pulpit. She was to sit beside the altar in a magnificent gilt chair brocaded in blue and gold satin, which was used by the bishop on the rare occasions when he visited this isolated outpost of his see.

She balked at the thought of her humble person sitting in the bishop's chair, but the men persuaded her that it was the only location where she would be clearly visible to them all. It was safer. She didn't think it seemly but sat down anyway. The thought crossed John's mind, seeing her in profile, that she possessed a dignity the equal of any bishop. With her arm resting on the Eucharistic table and the powerful triptych bearing down on her from above the altar, she looked positively majestic.

With a nod, Brian signaled that all was ready. He flicked a couple of switches, and the dull-red glow from the indicator lights came on. Harry switched on the audio detector and put his headphones on. The digital display of John's temperature sensor glowed comfortingly bright against the dim chancel.

"Everything looks fine," John called to Brian. Polly's eyes closed as she settled back in her chair.

"Take some temperature measurements," Brian said.

"Okay," John replied. He began to read the outputs from the various thermocouples around the chancel. "It's 15.8 degrees, 15.4 degrees, 16.1, 15.5. They're all pretty similar."

"Fine. Keep your readout set on number five, that one in the center of the aisle. Give us a reading every couple of minutes. Remember that when the temperature starts dropping, you must switch to automatic read and store. Two-second intervals over twenty thermocouples will give us a thermal map of the chancel every forty seconds."

"Right. Number 5 is at 15.8 degrees at the moment."

John's preoccupation with the sensors was interrupted by a flash of white light. Polly gave a startled turn toward it, and Brian looked up in anger. "Oops!" Harry exclaimed. "I turned the spotlight on accidentally. Sorry."

"Please don't do that without a warning," Brian muttered. They stared at the shrill light flooding the aisle. The dusty corners of the pews, the dead flies beneath the benches, and the raw cracks in the wood—all were glaringly exposed. The past was not meant to be so harshly revealed. "It's too bright," Brian said. "We'll get no contrast at all. Better to rely on the church lighting. Turn the spotlight off."

"I'm not sure it'll be bright enough for the video camera," Harry replied, acquiescing nonetheless. "What are the power and illumination readings?"

"Voltage is steady at 232 volts," Brian replied. "Current's about half an amp. The illumination at bench level here is—let me see—18 foot-candles. That's, er, about 190 lux if you want SI. That was constant too till you turned on the spotlight. The meter's only just now regaining stability."

"I'm sorry, all right?" Harry said.

"Is the camera ready, John?" Brian asked. "Better shoot some test footage."

"Yes, boss."

John left the temperature sensors and slid down the bench toward the camera. He made some adjustments to focus on the thermocouple in the center of the aisle and then tracked away from it to the rood screen. He panned across the mahogany carving along the top of it. He tracked back to the thermocouple and continued on to get some wide shots of the altar and his aunt. He left the camera pointing at thermocouple number 5 and switched it off.

"It's 234 volts, slight fluctuation, 0.43 amps, 18 foot-candles," Brian intoned.

"Temperature steady, 15.9 degrees."

Polly had relaxed again. Her eyes were closed, and one arm hung limply by the side of the chair. Harry practiced tracking the audio detector across the aisle, just as John had done with the camera. Their eyes met, and Harry nodded confidently. John looked up at the light bulbs, which hung bright and motionless.

"Right," Brian said. "The laser's ready now." He switched it on, and instantly, a red lance cut through the dusty air of the church. The wood assumed a mottled, chocolaty appearance, and the pillars turned a deep, dull crimson. The whole chancel was transformed by scattered radiation, even the air seeming to take on a sickly purple pallor. Reflected off the mirror on the opposite side of the aisle, the beam knifed upward, spreading perceptibly, to be lost in the folds of the ceiling. Brian fumbled with the controls. "The intensity's still fluctuating," he said. "Perhaps it's pulling too much current. We may have to live with it."

The opposite sides of the chancel seemed to John like two islands joined by a red rope. Brian was marooned on one side; he and Harry stranded on the other. John imagined the beam suddenly extinguished, the chancel splitting down the middle, and the two sets of choir stalls drifting apart into the night.

"Keep your eyes open. Watch the church lights." Brian's voice came vigorously across the gap, but he was almost lost from view behind the stack of control boxes.

"It's 15.7 degrees." John's voice cracked—a touch of nervousness. He cleared his throat. "It's 15.7 degrees and steady." Better. He tried to relax and concentrate on the digital readout. He switched on the internal clock of the data storage unit and collected temperature readings. He glanced at his watch. It was six thirty already.

"Everything's stable over here." Brian's head dipped below the level of the bench as he jotted down figures in a spiral notebook.

Fascinated, John and Harry watched wandering dust particles trespass into the beam from the ruby laser and explode in brilliant coruscations. Most hypnotic of all were the whorls projected onto the stone pillars by the scattered radiation. They seemed to twist and curl like living cells, lending a sense of fluidity to the whole building. Some of the laser light seeped through the tracery like slimy river water through a net. Beyond the screen, it mingled with the shadows in the Lady Chapel and swabbed the stained glass windows a dull claret.

"It's 15.5." Brian looked up. "It's 15.4 now."

"The temperature's dropping," Brian said.

John flicked the panel switches to automatic mode. Brian nodded at him from across the aisle. Harry leaned over to see the thermocouple readings for himself. John called out every fifth reading as it popped up on his video display. "Number 1: 15.7. Number 5: 15.4. Number 10: 15.4. Number 15: 15.6. Number 20: 15.5. Back to number 5 again: 15.3."

"Everything's stable here," Brian said. "Is that temperature drop genuine?"

"Seems to be," John replied. He turned to his aunt. She looked so calm and peaceful. Her fingers were moving delicately as if she was rolling stems of flowers between them. Her lips curled into a gentle smile. There seemed to be no cause for concern on her behalf. "Fifteen zero," John said. "It's definitely falling."

"I've still got 234 volts, 0.43 amps, and 18 foot-candles. No change."

John scanned all the readings from the array of thermocouples. "The lowest reading I've got is 14.8 degrees from thermocouple number 7. I'll monitor that one manually. It dropped to 14.6 just while I was looking at it."

There was no sign of anything unusual in the church. Brian and Harry watched intently. Though occupied with his tasks and in the company of family and friends, John began to feel the same irrational pangs of fear he had experienced the last time he had been in the church. His fingers were moist, and the dials felt slick beneath them.

"Where's thermocouple 7?" Harry whispered.

John showed him the sheet of paper with the plan drawn on it. "It's over there." He pointed to the center of the aisle, a little in the direction of the rood screen. Harry, hand on the guide wheel, tracked the sound detectors until they pointed at the spot. "It's now 13.7."

Even as John's eyes moved from the screen to the logbook beside him, he knew something had changed. He wrote down the figures with a tremulous hand and then watched the shadow of his pencil on the book move slowly a fraction of an inch to the left, then back to the center, then off a fraction to the right and then back to the center again. Without raising his head, he peeked up from the book and caught sight of Brian staring up at the swinging light bulbs. "At 13.1. It's starting." John quickly ran through the other thermocouple readings. All were down by a degree or two, but he knew that by the goose bumps on his arms.

"Still no change here," Brian said. "I don't understand that."

"Now 12.8." The swinging lights were gaining amplitude. "And 12.1." John turned to Harry. He had an anxious look on his face, but he nodded when John asked him if he was feeling all right. "Now at 11.9." It was difficult for John to concentrate on documenting the temperature readings. He was fascinated by the orbits of the shadow of his pencil. The columns of figures were blurred and hard to read. He realized then that it was also getting darker.

"Sixteen foot-candles," Brian said. "The lights are going." John and Harry responded by staring up at the light bulbs as they grew progressively dimmer. The figure of Brian at the other end of the flickering ruby bridge faded into shadow. "I've got 10 foot-candles but still 233 volts and 0.43 amps," Brian said. "The illumination has decreased, but the power through the lights is still the same. I don't get it."

"Now 11.7."

"Where is it?" Brian muttered, his voice taut. "Where *is* it?"

"Now 11.5."

The church had assumed a most eerie aspect. The diffuse yellow glow from the swinging light bulbs had melted away to a series of dull-orange pinpoints like stars. The light from the laser beam seemed correspondingly brighter. The whole of the chancel was now bathed in a blood-red glow, made all the more unsettling by the undulation of the shadows.

"At 11.4." John looked over at his aunt and was startled. Her face had reddened, and her hair was a deep mauve, but she also seemed insubstantial. It was as if she was slowly disappearing. It didn't seem possible that the effect was caused solely by the diminution of light. He didn't know whether he should bring it to Brian's attention. Above all, he wanted to remain calm. Gathering his senses, he resolved to remain silent as long as his aunt showed no signs of distress. "It's 11.4," he said. "The temperature's stable now."

"The light intensity's leveling off too," Brian said. "We should be seeing something."

"At 11.4. Thermocouple 5 is…"

John's recitation was interrupted. From his left came a clattering sound. Harry Groh rose to his feet, dragging a voltmeter off the bench. He ripped off his headphones and, trembling violently, wagged a finger in the direction of the aisle in front of them. His mouth moved, but no sound emerged. Then came Brian's excited voice: "There it is! Over there!"

John looked at the aisle but could see nothing. Harry seemed poised to run away. One hand gripped the stall behind him; the other continued to hold some threatening object at bay. "Harry!" John hissed. "Get it together!" He looked once more across the chancel, but this time, his eyes followed the sloping line of Harry's arm and forefinger. No wonder he hadn't seen it the first time; he had been looking too high. For there, lying in the middle of the stone floor, was a human head. At least, John's brain interpreted the shape of the vague, translucent image as a head. He gazed at it for several seconds until he became aware of Brian's voice and glanced down at the digital display. "It's 11.4," he said.

"No, the camera!" Brian said. "Roll the camera!"

John's wits returned. He was about to switch on the camera when he noticed the bewildered expression on Harry's face. He slid three feet to his left and shook Harry's arm. "Harry! Turn the sound on!" Harry stared quizzically at him. "Switch it on!" Harry looked at the array of equipment in front of him as if he had never seen it before. He gaped at the broken glass around his feet. John shook his arm violently. Slowly, Harry's hand moved to turn a dial and flick a switch. He swallowed hard and turned the detector toward the object on the floor.

John returned to the video camera. His fingers fumbled with the focus. He suddenly had no coordination at all. Finally, the camera was running, pointed directly at the object. He heard Brian's voice say, "Keep it rolling." He glanced to his left and watched Harry struggle with the transverse drive mechanism.

"Hurry up, for God's sake!" John ordered, furious they might miss something. "Switch the tape on!" Harry looked at John and then, in painfully slow motion, reached for the tape drive. With a soft click, the drive began to hum, and tape started to feed through. Harry's right hand was clamped over the tracking controls while his left hand hung uselessly by his side as if it had collapsed from the effort of alerting the group to the appearance of the ghostly head. As John checked Harry's instrument panel, he missed a new development.

The object slowly became a figure rising out of the ground. At a height of about four feet, it stopped growing and began to drift in the direction of the altar. Harry and John did their best to track its movement with their detectors. Its motion was ungainly in the extreme. Indeed, the whole aspect of the figure was discordant. The chest was massive and misshapen, and the head was thrust back at an angle, distorted. Though it seemed oblivious to their presence, it was not totally insentient to its surroundings; for as it approached the laser beam, it slowed.

When it was barely an inch from the beam, it stopped completely. Brian reached for the light source and moved it slightly to one side till the beam transfixed the motionless apparition like a pin through a butterfly. Brian manipulated the controls feverishly. He moved to the detector and peered at the CRT display. "I have it!" he yelped after a few seconds. "I've got it!"

The iridescent object hovered before their eyes, impaled on a spear of crimson light. At the confluence of the ghostly material and the laser beam, tiny flashes burst out. For at least ten seconds, the object remained suspended in the beam, during which time Brian took notes from the CRT and Harry and John trained their sights on the pyrotechnics. Then the ghost drifted forward again, out of the beam. Brian groaned.

Recalling the ghost's trajectory from the previous sighting, they expected it would move diagonally across the benches and head for the organ chapel and the niche in the wall. John was steeled for that.

He was not at all prepared for the sudden right-angled turn the ghost made and the quickened motion in his direction.

Harry was on his feet in a flash, clambering over the bench behind him and running to the safety of the side chapel. John thought to follow him but wasn't sure he could make it to the end of the bench in time. He froze, and then it was too late. The ghost turned a little more in his direction, and John saw to his dismay that there would be only a foot or two between them when it passed through the stalls.

His fingers gripped the hard wooden bench, and he kicked at the oak board in front of him. There was no escape. He shuffled down the bench until his progress was halted by the rood screen. He could go no farther, but his palms pressed hard against the bench, driving his back up against the unyielding wood. His mouth opened, and he thought he was going to scream. His tongue slid back along the roof of his mouth. He swallowed awkwardly, nearly choking. He kicked again. His talents did not run to moving through wood, but not so the ghost's. Without hesitation, it moved through the first row of stalls, turning even more toward him.

"Oh my god!" John whispered. The light was terrible now, an obfuscation of reeling shadows. The light bulbs jerked crazily up in the nave. Polly and Brian were no longer visible, and Harry had fled. John was alone with the specter. His fingernails buckled from the pressure he was applying to the bench. Still, the object drifted forward through the second row of stalls, then it stopped.

John was just a few feet from the formless shape that now hovered above the bench. As the shadows of the crucifix crossed and recrossed its outline, it seemed to rotate. In the swiveling outline, John glimpsed a nose, a chin—the vague physiognomy of a face. He knew it had turned to confront him, and he lost control of his bladder.

He didn't know how long he sat in opposition to the ghost, but gradually, he became aware that it had turned back and was drifting away. His left hand was against his face, and the taste of blood was in his mouth. He dropped his hand and looked at it. Pinpricks of blood oozed from the teeth marks he had impressed in it. His legs wouldn't move. He could barely comprehend his surroundings at all. He was hypnotized by the shadows of pillars and crucifix dancing their ponderous dance across the chancel and against the massive east wall. Far away, excited voices were chattering.

"What do you see?"

"I don't know."

"There's something in there!"

"Are you sure?"

"It's glowing."

"What do you mean?"

"Can't you see it?"

"Where, for Christ's sake?"

"There!"

"Give me the flashlight. Pass it here."

"Shut up! Oh god, will you look at that."

"I see it! I see it!"

"Oh, Jesus Christ."

The sound of heavy objects colliding drew John out of his trance. His legs were trembling, and his pants were wet. He had a violent headache. Someone was running. There was a second crash. Putting a hand out to steady himself, John turned and stared in the direction of the organ. He half expected to see the things that were visible in daylight, but instead, he was confronted by a world of dark shapes and shadows.

Where the organ pipes should have been was a black abyss. A slash of yellow light angled across the stone slabs. His eyes lost focus. He gagged. From the depths of the darkness came a scratching sound, claws on stone. John pulled his hand away from the screen. The back of his other hand was again between his teeth. As he inched his way along the bench, a figure struggled to its feet in the darkness in front of him.

"Harry, is that you?" John asked.

A voice murmured, "Holy Jesus." John staggered to the end of the bench. A second figure loomed out of the blackness, bent down to pick up the flashlight, and played it repeatedly over the flagstones so that he and Harry could gather a perspective of the floor. "Hush!"

said the figure, raising a black finger to black lips. "Keep calm, John. Watch your footing and follow me. I need to show you something." As they hesitated, the figure added, "It's me, Brian."

Illuminating the floor in his wake, Brian retreated down the narrow passageway alongside the organ. John mustered all his remaining courage and followed him. Harry brought up the rear. The three men tottered forward, guided only by the torchlight on the flagstones and the feel of the wooden screen against their fingertips. Eventually, they emerged in the space behind the organ. The mysterious niche was in front of them and to their left.

"Do you see it? Why is it green?" Brian said.

This response puzzled John. "What did you say?"

"It's incredible, but why is it green?" John gaped at the shadow that was his brother. "Can't you see it, John?" Brian said.

John shielded his eyes from the glare of the flashlight. He focused on the front of the niche. As his eyes became accustomed to the darkness, he began to see tiny pinpoints of light. He struggled to gain perspective. All at once, the lights melded together, and he knew what he was looking at: a very faint, luminescent hand suspended in the opening of the niche. "Oh, I see it now," he whispered. "I can see it, a hand!"

"That's right," Brian said.

Harry came up behind them and murmured softly, "Amazing."

Then as if they had not endured enough for one evening and the forces of darkness were determined to inflict one final horror on them, a scream ripped through the church. It came from the direction of the altar. Even before they could react, the lights grew brighter, the oscillation of the bulbs diminished, and the mysterious hand vanished. They turned and ran over to the altar.

When they reached the sanctuary, they saw Polly slouched in the bishop's chair, knees splayed. Her hands had fallen from the arms of the chair, and her upturned face had a withered look about it. Brian overtook the others and was the first to her side. She was in a dead faint. He patted her cheek and rubbed the back of her hand. "Aunt Polly? Are you all right? Aunt Polly?" Brian said.

Nigel Applewhite's loping gait brought him quickly to the scene. He seemed to be on the verge of tears. "Mrs. Coleby! Oh, my dear Lord! Whatever's the matter?" They surrounded the chair, and Sarah soon joined them. They whispered encouraging words to Mrs. Coleby while Brian tried to bring her around. Her eyes flickered open. Her hand gripped Brian's with a fearful pressure as if to reassure herself that her companions were of this world and not the next. Her eyes completed the circle of faces.

"It's all right, Aunt Polly," Brian said softly to her. "You're all right. Just sit quietly." Her eyes narrowed to slits and then her brow contracted into deep furrows as if she would cry out. Finally, a look of quiet desperation settled on her face, but still, she could say nothing.

"Please speak to us! Are you recovered?" Applewhite implored.

Polly stared over Brian's shoulder at the wall beside the altar. Her eyes flashed to Brian's then back to the wall. She emitted a croak and swallowed. They were all silent, waiting for her first utterance. And though they had just been through traumatic experiences of their own, they were in no way prepared for the words that finally escaped from her constricted throat. "I saw the devil, the face of the devil! There!"

She pointed shakily over Brian's shoulder, and he turned and shone his flashlight to the wall at the spot she was indicating. Though John and Brian knew the words by heart, they listened with the others while Sarah read the message inscribed in stone:

1624

BR MW JW JM FN

Farmers of the Parish

Gloria Patri

*****

It was some time before they were able to persuade Polly to relinquish the security of the bishop's chair. Then with slow and deliberate steps, they made their way to the vestry door, Brian and John supporting Polly's elbows and Applewhite clearing obstacles from their path. Harry limped behind them, clutching his right knee, which had been injured in a collision with a chair during his panicky flight. Once inside the vestry, it was a long time before anyone spoke, and then it was just a casual remark about the cold. The ghost hunt had grown into something beyond words.

After a sip of brandy, Polly said she was ready to brave the night air. John and Sarah led her outside. Brian supported Harry as he hopped onto the path. Above their heads, the starry sky shone with a rare brilliance. Applewhite extinguished the gas heater and turned off the lights. He locked up, walked to the outhouse, and returned wheeling his bicycle. They all skirted the church and headed for the silhouette of the van parked beyond the lych-gate.

The wind had dropped, leaving that profound silence found only in the countryside at dead of night. The cinder path wound gently down the hill under the sheen of starlight. The gravestones on either side jutted up from the grass like crooked teeth, though the grass, it seemed, had tried hard to conceal the ancient dead by smoothing its linen over the grave humps. Harry stumbled, and Brian felt his entire weight transferred to his shoulder. They paused while he regained equilibrium. In the distance, a foxhunter's beagle barked.

Outside the lych-gate, Applewhite mounted his bicycle. "Dr. Kenning, I must speak to you tomorrow at two o'clock in the vestry, if you please." Brian nodded. The vicar leaned on a pedal and cycled off into the silvery night. The others clambered into the van, and Brian drove back to Bittern Fen and the Coleby cottage.

*****

As they pulled alongside the garden gate, the front door opened, and Will stepped onto the porch. His hands were deep in his pockets, and a pipe hung from the corner of his mouth. Out all around him streamed the light and the warmth and the welcoming ambience of home. Polly made her way cautiously up the slippery path with Sarah's help, her plight communicating itself to Will. First, one hand and then the other left the warmth of his pockets till both were outstretched to guide her over the threshold. "Polly, my love?" he said anxiously.

They entered the parlor, Polly's arm in Will's hand, his arm around her waist. She murmured repeatedly that she was all right, but Will didn't seem convinced. Brian followed, helping Harry up the steps. John hung back by the garden gate, though Sarah beckoned for him to come inside. Something didn't feel right. After what had happened, he didn't know how he could face his aunt and uncle in the intimacy of their own home. All the explanations he could think of were woefully inadequate, and the value of their experiments suddenly seemed much inflated compared with the damage they had done.

The strain of the evening began to shake John apart. He put a hand on the gatepost and planted his feet firmly on the ground. Without further warning, his stomach contracted, and he bent over and vomited onto the garden. He wiped tears from his eyes and heaved a couple more times. Sarah came to his side. He spat the remaining vomit from his mouth, wiped his lips, and blew his nose. Finally, he lifted his head and sucked in the raw night air.

"Come on inside, John," Sarah said. They joined the others in the parlor. Polly was sitting on the edge of an armchair in front of the fire, delicate as eggshell porcelain, hands clasped in her lap. Will was kneeling beside her, lightly touching the small of her back. Passivity glazed her eyes where earlier the alertness of terror had flashed. She seemed, if nothing else, soothed by the familiarity of her surroundings. Will murmured words of comfort to her then fell silent. "I think she'll be all right," Sarah said after a long pause. "Honestly." She glared at Brian, mutely asking what else she could say and why he wasn't the one saying it.

Polly pinched the bridge of her nose and screwed up her eyes. "I tell you straight. It was the face of the devil I saw up there on the wall. What does it mean?"

Will turned around and said with powerful simplicity, "What have you done, m'lad?" Brian couldn't reply. His lips were welded shut.

Sarah looked hard at him and then realized it was again going to fall to her, a familial outsider, to offer an explanation. "I'm sorry, Mr. Coleby. We all are. We don't know what happened in the church tonight. I'm sure Mrs. Coleby will be all right, though. She's just a bit shaken up. We're all…so deeply sorry." She faltered, but neither John nor Brian could rescue her.

Will transferred his gaze to Harry, who was sitting in the other armchair, massaging his knee. "What's the matter wi' 'im?" he asked.

"I busted my knee," Harry responded.

Will turned his back on them all and began to stroke Polly's hair. They wanted to speak to her themselves, to comfort her, but Will stood between them like a sentry.

*****

The cottage was dark and quiet. Brian rose from the couch and tiptoed to the guest room where Sarah was in bed. He cracked open the door and asked if she was sleeping. She said she wasn't. He opened the door and entered the room.

"Brian, this is neither the time nor the place—"

"I need to talk to you."

"Brian, there are people—"

"Please, Sarah, just talk. I promise." She didn't respond. He walked over to the bed, drew back the covers, and laid down beside her. She made no motion toward him. He felt the warmth of her body, but it didn't stir him. "Do you think I should quit this ghost business?" he began. "Am I in too deep?"

"It's been a long day, Brian. Why don't you think about it in the morning?"

"I've been searching for a mission like this for years, but now that I'm on to something, I'm terribly afraid people are going to get hurt. Should I stop or go on?"

"I can't tell you what to do. If I say stop, you'll hold it against me for the rest of your life. If I say go on, I might be condoning something dreadful. I don't know where your zeal will lead you, to be honest, and I'm not sure that I trust your judgment. I'm sorry to

135

have to say that, Brian, but I really don't trust your judgment right now. You'll just have to do what you think is best."

"After tonight, I'm not sure that I know what is best."

"I know you say you started this business to help me and Aunt Polly, but I suspect the real motivation is inside yourself. You're the ambitious scientist. You're the one who wants to blaze new trails. Tough decisions come with the territory."

"That is true."

They lay together quietly, Brian disappointed that he had received no guidance and very little sympathy. Eventually, Sarah sat up and reached for her purse by the side of the bed. She delved inside it and pulled out a small box. She opened it and took out a gold ring. "I've been carrying this around with me for weeks, waiting for the right moment to give it to you. It was my grandmother's. After what happened this evening, I think I'd better give it to you now. I'm suddenly very uncertain about the future, especially your future, but I think the time is right. I think you need to know how I fit into the puzzle. I want you to know that I'm faithful to you and supportive for as long as you need me." She took hold of his right hand and slipped the ring over his finger.

"It's an engagement ring?"

"If you want to call it that or just a symbol of my commitment. I need you to know that you're not alone. You have a future with me if you want it. You don't have to drive yourself to destruction for my sake. Remember that. And I do love you, you know."

"Thank you," Brian said, leaning to kiss her cheek. "Of course, I also—"

But she put her fingers to his lips, forbidding response. "Now go to sleep."

He thought he ought to say more to her, to reciprocate, but he didn't seem able to do so. And the more he thought about Sarah and their relationship, the more his thoughts slipped in another direction, toward another girl, a girl in a red-and-black hockey jacket leaning against a doorframe, examining her nails, a girl with big blue eyes and a winning smile and a mind that knew no limits and a bald head. Crazy, crazy, crazy.

They lay side by side in the dark, staring up at the ceiling. *We're just like Richard and Catherine Crossly in their sarcophagus,* Brian thought. *Richard and Catherine. Brian and Sarah. Two bodies decayed. Two hearts still beating. Did Richard love Catherine? Does Brian love Sarah? Can anyone truly know the answers to such questions, whether it be five hundred years ago or today? Richard and Catherine Crossly—they're the clue to solving this mystery. But it all happened so long ago. How much can I possibly hope to discover about them?*

He cast his mind back to the darkness of the church and that ghastly, disembodied hand. He could see it now, twinkling at the edge of the niche, a greeting from the Middle Ages. What could it be? And then there was that other thing. When he played his flashlight on the suspended hand, what were those two points of light reflected from deep inside the cavity? Whose eyes were staring back at him?

CHAPTER 13

Hoyland Church
December 2017

"Dr. Kenning, I must tell you how disappointed I am. I permitted you to use my church in good faith as a privilege, and you have let me down." The Reverend Applewhite directed a cockatrice glance at Brian, John, and Sarah, arrayed in front of his desk, looking guilty. "When your aunt asked me if you could use the church, I agreed charitably, but not without reservation. She had faith in you, and I had faith in her. And see how you have repaid us both!"

"But we were not the cause of what happened," John ventured. "We're not to blame."

"It's not a matter of cause, don't you see? It's not a matter of blame. It's a question of trust betrayed, of confidence undermined."

"I'm afraid I don't understand this at all," Brian interjected rather too casually. "We didn't force anyone into this experiment. It was a brief excursion into the supernatural that went a little astray. No one got hurt and—"

"Don't make your position any worse than it already is!" the vicar barked. "Trying to evade responsibility. Good heavens, what went on in my church last night was precious close to blasphemy. You don't seem to appreciate that at all. Seeing the devil indeed. And have you no shame for the pain you inflicted on your poor aunt?"

"Please, Mr. Applewhite," Sarah intervened, "let's try to keep this thing in perspective. Brian and John were just as surprised and upset by what happened as you and I were. Try to bear that in mind."

"And I'm sure there's a perfectly sensible explanation for what happened," Brian added. "There is no devil involved. You can be sure of that."

The vicar turned away, removed his spectacles, and began to polish the lenses vigorously. The conversation was drifting onto unfamiliar and unwelcome ground. His specialty was ethics, not heterodoxy. Moreover, the determination he had honed for confrontation was beginning to lose its edge, and the very last thing he wanted to do was to argue with Sarah. "Let us not dwell too much on Lucifer. This is a bad business for us all. And those other things, the lights, I'll have to get an electrician in."

"There's nothing wrong with the lights." Brian's unblinking stare conveyed a blend of superiority and impatience, and the vicar was forcefully reminded of his own inadequacy. He averted his eyes.

"Well, there seemed to be last night."

"I hope you know that we're sorry for all the trouble we've caused you," Sarah offered.

"You're very understanding, Ms. Harcourt," Applewhite replied with a wan smile.

Brian sensed that the vicar's ardor was all but extinguished, and he moved to the wall of photographs, his mind wrestling with a number of unresolved issues. "In order to help Mrs. Coleby understand what happened to her, we need to know more about the history of this church, if that's not too much of an imposition." Brian knew he was pushing his luck, but he had correctly surmised that the fight had gone out of his opponent. "Do you have any literature on the history of St. Neot's Church?"

"There are a few pamphlets and things in that cupboard over there. A thesis by one of the seminary students. See what you can find."

The accompanying wave of the vicar's hand signified more a resignation to Brian's persistence than the precise location of the documents in question, so Brian asked John to search the cupboards one by one till the pertinent literature was found. "May we borrow these?" Brian asked.

"If it's to comfort your aunt, you may," Applewhite responded.

Brian handed the papers to Sarah. "And if it's all right with you, Vicar, we'll go out through the church, remove our equipment, and tidy up any mess we made. We won't bother you further."

As they headed for the door, Applewhite raised a finger to attract their attention. "Er, before you go, one thing I ought to mention, a reporter was here this morning."

"What?"

"That man from the *Examiner* was here again—Stephens his name is or something like that. Wanted to know what happened here last night."

"How on earth did he find out?"

"Apparently, he was driving past the church and saw the flickering lights. He said he also heard Mrs. Coleby scream."

"Did he know that we were doing an experiment?"

"I suppose I might have mentioned your proposed visit to one or two of our parishioners. Didn't see any harm in it at the time. Nothing specific."

"The last thing we want is the press involved."

"For once," the vicar said, "I agree with you."

"So what did you tell him?"

"I told him it was the organist practicing late. The power for the organ does sometimes cause the lights to dim and flicker. I said the scream was probably a cat."

"Good."

"No, Dr. Kenning, it is not good. The last thing I wanted to do was to lie to him. I simply couldn't force myself to tell the truth. I'm not at all proud of the falsehood."

"Was he happy with your explanation?"

"He seemed to be. He didn't stay long."

"If he returns, give him any excuse you like, but don't tell him what actually happened."

The vicar reared up at this instruction, eyes glittering. "Really, Dr. Kenning, I believe you have no integrity whatsoever!"

"Now look here!" Brian said, taking umbrage at the remark and poking a finger at the indignant cleric. "I can only take so much of this. I don't know who you think you are, but you obviously haven't the slightest notion of the importance of what we are doing in this church—"

"Are doing in this church?" The vicar's cheeks reddened. "*Are* doing? *Were* doing, you mean. This whole affair is over, my boy."

"I am not your boy, nor would I want to be. And you may think this affair is over, but I can assure you that it's not. There's something happening in this church of such monumental importance that it makes your pathetic little concerns pale to nothing, and I intend to find out what it is. You don't know what forces are locked up in this place."

"Absolute rubbish!"

"It's not rubbish. I'll go over your head if I have to."

"Why, you impertinent little—"

"Don't you talk to me like that, I—"

"Stop it," Sarah begged, stepping between them, "both of you. It's ridiculous, grown men arguing like this."

"Oh, I'm tired of talking to him," Brian snapped and marched quickly out of the vestry and into the church. John thought it best to follow him, and Sarah was again left to sew up the loose ends.

"I can only repeat that we're sorry for the trouble we've caused," she said.

"Not half as sorry as I am." He was crestfallen by the exchange with Brian, and his gaunt frame trembled visibly. The weight of the modern world and the impulsiveness of youth were more than he could bear. He slumped down in his chair and looked pathetically to Sarah for some kind of support.

"Don't take it to heart, Mr. Applewhite," Sarah said. "Brian's just letting off steam. He'll get over it."

"Why did this have to happen in my church?" Applewhite groaned, holding his head in his hands. "Why me?" Sarah had no answer to that. She turned and headed for the door. Applewhite looked up. "Goodbye, Ms. Harcourt—Sarah."

*****

141

In the chancel, the scientific equipment stood abandoned and intrusive. Telltale signs of disorder reminded them of the previous evening's ordeal—an upturned chair by the organ, scattered hymnals, and the shattered voltmeter in the choir stalls. John and Brian tidied up and boxed the equipment while Sarah sat on a pew, reading the pamphlets loaned by the vicar. Their unspoken thoughts were of Polly's outburst the previous evening.

"What do you think that inscription means?" Sarah asked Brian, pointing to the plasterwork slapped on so crudely by the farmers of the seventeenth century.

"I'd assumed it meant that a group of locals was celebrating some masonry work they'd commissioned. You see signs and plaques like that in every church."

"I wonder if I can find out anything about it," she said and began to leaf through the documents in her lap. "Let's see. The date was...1624."

Brian walked to the bench where his notebook lay. He picked up the book and flipped to the page where he had copied spectra from the CRT display. He examined his annotations and made some mental calculations. He called John over. "You know, John, the ghost really does exist. It's going to be a tragedy if this project has to be abandoned. The object was in the laser beam for a good twelve seconds, and I was able to get a clear reflected signal off it. That means it was a real physical object made of real molecules. Electronics don't hallucinate. I may even be able to calculate its density and infer its chemical composition from the spectrum. And it seemed to be a conscious entity too. Did you notice how it faltered as it approached the beam? It was as if it could see that something was stretched across its path."

"Yes, I noticed that," John replied. "It was incredible. Do you have any idea yet what it all means?"

Brian shook his head. John walked off and packed up the video and audio tapes in a box for future analysis. Finally, the two brothers transferred the two crates to the van. When they returned, Sarah rushed to meet them, her head buried in a manuscript. "Listen to this, guys!" she cried excitedly. "You won't believe it. It's from a dissertation by someone called Gabriel Lennox for the degree of Doctor of Divinity at Keele University. It has to do with the church architecture."

"What does it say?"

"Listen. 'From the east wall of the original structure of the chancelry,'" Sarah read, "'a series of stone figureheads once projected. Abbot Gervase, in his account of the church architecture of the early sixteenth century (which copy preserved since 1788 in the library of Lincoln Cathedral), describes a number of these figures as portraying seraphs and infant cherubs. Sometime after the reconstruction of the east front, probably in the early seventeenth century, these carvings were removed to the church vestibule (constructed circa 1590), where they can be seen today, though considerably worn by the effects of pollution and weather.'

"'One heteroclitic piece was among those removed. This carving was described by Abbot Gervase as a singularly grotesque projection known as the Devil with a Dark Lanthorn. The occasional insertion of antithetical subjects in a series of sacred carvings is well-known in masonry of the late Anglo-Saxon and early Norman periods (see Richardson, 1960, and DeVere, 1949).'

"'Richardson attributes this practice to the desire to illustrate for the congregation the power of the church to capture and imprison evil. DeVere, on the other hand, attributes it to mere mischief on the part of the stonemason. The piece in question is known to have been removed and destroyed circa 1624 by a body of the parishioners who objected to its presence alongside the high altar. The episode is recorded by historian Charles Wellesley and commemorated in the form of an inscription left by the workmen.'" Sarah shook the papers in Brian's face. "That's what your Aunt Polly saw, the Devil with a Dark Lanthorn."

Brian grabbed the manuscript from her hands and read it for himself. "That's it! I can't believe you found this!" He paused and screwed up his eyes. "What's a lanthorn?"

"See the footnote?" She pointed to the bottom of the page. "It's an old word for *lantern*."

"That'll be it. That's what she saw."

"But how could that be?" John asked with a cynical snort. "It was destroyed in 1624. How could Aunt Polly possibly see a stone head that hasn't been in existence for almost four hundred years? Talk sense."

"But that has to be the explanation." Almost immediately, Brian smacked the palm of his hand with his fist and exclaimed, "I've got it!"

"Got what?"

"Don't you understand what's happening here? We've not just summoned up a ghost from the past. We've summoned up the entire past. We've reproduced the church exactly as it was when the ghost originally walked. That's why Aunt Polly saw the ancient stone head."

"But that's not possible," Sarah scoffed. "How can you create stone out of thin air?"

"How can you create flesh and blood? From a scientific viewpoint, there's no difference."

"But how could stone materialize? It doesn't make any sense."

"All I'm saying is that it makes as much sense for a molecule of stone to become visible as it does for a molecule of human tissue."

"Let me try to understand this," John said. "Are you suggesting that the whole of the ancient church is somehow materializing?"

"Yes," Brian continued, "but dilutely. It's as if only a fraction of the molecules from the past appear in our world and time."

"And assuming there is a center for the manifestation—"

"Where the cold spot occurs—"

"Then the phenomenon decreases as you move away from the center."

"Exactly. Imagine one molecule in a million at the center, one in a billion ten feet away, and one in a trillion twenty feet away. A hundred feet away, there's nothing to be seen."

"From the outside, the church is normal. I get it."

"We're seeing dilute, hence transparent, materialization of objects from another time."

"Well then, shouldn't we see other things from the old church too, things like the floor and the roof?"

"Don't you get it yet? We do see the roof but indirectly. What we observe is that the lights in the nave dim. The present-day lights are located above the level of the medieval ceiling. When the ancient ceiling begins to manifest itself, it blocks out some of the light from the bulbs. It's so simple. The illumination at floor level is decreased, even though the power through the church's lighting circuit never changes. The lights are shining as brightly as ever twenty feet above a ghostly ceiling."

"And the original floor is lower than the present one," John continued. "Succeeding floors have been built on top of earlier ones. That's why the ghost seems to be so short. It's walking on an ancient floor a foot or two below the level of the modern one."

"That's right! When the ghost kneels to pray, you can scarcely see it at all. Only its head protrudes above the level of the present-day floor. It all fits. We haven't just brought a ghost into the twenty-first century. We've conjured up the entire past—flesh, stone, warts and all. Unbelievable." They stared at one another and at the enigmatic church surrounding them, each one of them wondering if such a thing could have really happened.

"So what about that hand you saw?" Sarah asked. "The green hand?"

"Well, I suppose the hand must have been real at some time in the past too," Brian replied. "Perhaps your history books can tell us." He tapped the pile of papers Sarah was holding. "Perhaps John and Harry have the answer on tape. John, we need to get those tapes into the lab as quickly as possible and analyze them."

"Yeah, I know, but let's think about this a minute," John persisted. "Richard Crossly destroyed the abbey in 1537 and died fifty years later. Right? The stone head was removed in 1624, so it was still around when Crossly was rebuilding the church—in the 1560s, say. It could be his ghost praying for forgiveness. The chronology's right."

"But the head was probably Anglo-Saxon or Norman, remember? That's what Sarah said. It could have been there for hundreds of years before the farmers removed it. All we know for sure is that it was carved prior to 1624."

"You're right. I'm getting ahead of myself."

Buoyed by these revelations, they walked to the church door and stepped outside into one of the most beautiful winter afternoons any of them could remember. The sky was a brilliant cobalt blue with barely a wisp of cloud on the horizon. The amber sun glowed like a Christmas ornament, and a chaffinch twittered from the branches of an oak tree. A wave of excitement broke over them, leaving even Sarah breathless. It seemed like an answer might be found to the riddle after all. John kicked up some cinders as he walked, and Sarah giggled and kicked some back at him.

"You know why the light bulbs sway, don't you?" Brian said.

"Why?"

"You know how windy it can be on top of this hill."

CHAPTER 14

Hoyland
December 2017

Jack Stephens waggled the stem of an unlit pipe between his front teeth, making a sound like dice being shaken. He stared at the center of his desk—at a London phone number scribbled on the cover of a matchbook—and grimaced. To call or not to call? The grimace widened with the ache of indecision. Then the rattling stopped, and the subsequent clatter of pipe on desk was the sound of dice tossed propitiously. Jack snatched up the phone and dialed the number. To the sound of distant ringing, he stroked his sideburns into shape and loaded an opening salvo. "Aim high, for starters," he said to himself.

A faint voice at the other end of the line said, "Hello?"

"Dr. Brian Kenning, is it?" Jack asked.

"Speaking."

"Good morning to you, sir. Jack Stephens from the *Hoyland and Scardyke Examiner*. Hope I didn't catch you at a bad time. You see, the thing is, I'm writing a little piece on the superstitions of Lincolnshire, and I'm looking for a spot of help. Expert opinion, you might say. Might I ask if you believe in the supernatural yourself?"

"What name did you say?"

"Stephens, sir, Jack Stephens."

"Oh yes, I know who you are. You're the reporter who's been hounding Mr. Applewhite. I'm sorry, but I've no desire to speak with you on that subject—or on any other subject, for that matter."

"Now, now, sir, no call for that attitude. It's just that I'd heard you were some kind of an authority on things of that nature. Haven't you been conducting some investigations of your own in Hoyland Church?"

"I told you, Mr. Stephens, I've nothing to say."

"Well, Mrs. Coleby says—"

"Look, would you please stop harassing us? Particularly my aunt. You don't know what you're talking about."

"Oh, don't I, indeed." *You hold the moral high ground, Jack. Lower your sights a little.* "Then how about you share some of your superior knowledge with me, Dr. Kenning? I'm sure it would be most enlightening. And by the way, I've known your aunt a lot longer than you have, and I dare say I know her just about as well as you do too."

The line went dead, and Stephens glared at the receiver angrily. *The trouble with those city types,* he reflected with some bitterness, *is that they think we've all got wool between our ears. They think you take a man out of the fields and show him some dirt and soot and it sharpens his wits. Strikes me as it'd be the other way 'round. I can't abide them coming down here and patronizing us. It makes my blood boil. And we can't rely on that daft parson to keep them at bay. No, it's the duty of the press to protect the interests of the village.*

Jack sat down, grabbed the matchbook, and lit his pipe. He sucked on it furiously for a minute or more, wondering just exactly what it was that this Kenning person and his brother were doing in the church. He leaned back expansively in his tiny editorial office, which had once been the ticket office of Hoyland Railway Station; the *Examiner* had moved its operation into what was left of the station after the government took away the tracks in the interests of a more efficient service. The back of his chair grated against the ticket window. A carbonaceous haze spread over the proceedings.

There's no telling what they're up to. Black magic or something. They've probably turned the Women's Institute into a coven. Got them dancing naked as babies every Tuesday and Thursday nights. Fancy the vicar telling me the lights were flickering because the organist was practicing. Does he think a reporter can't check facts? Old Jed Matthews has been down in Norfolk with his sick old dad for two weeks. He wasn't even in the county that night. And no cat as I know of ever screamed like that.

He rattled the pipe between his front teeth again, this time with a touch of regret. *I should've stopped the car right then and there and gone up to the church for a confrontation. If it hadn't been getting late on in the evening, I would've done too. I might've spared poor Mrs. Coleby some suffering. She deserves more respectful treatment. When you're in the newspaper business, you've got to steel your nerve sometimes. Steel your nerve—that's the way to get the cream off the milk. Yes, them Kenning boys are up to no good in our church, and I don't intend to sit around and let them get away with it. Be buggered if I will!*

As Jack's personal rancor began to subside, it was replaced by righteous indignation on behalf of the community. He saw the Kennings' interference as yet another example of the too-clever-by-half modern world insinuating itself into simple rural life and destroying it. Jack had anointed himself protector of Hoyland heritage, and no aspect of it more so than the old days of steam. Fascinated since boyhood with the locomotive, Jack conducted his daily journalistic business in the old ticket office while in his imagination, he was punching tickets, setting signals, and switching the mail train through.

He recalled those glorious times when there were five mainline trains a day between Lincoln and Boston, when countless railway tracks laced the county, linking vibrant villages, holding together families and friends, not petering out in nettle beds and rust. He was the archivist of Lincolnshire railways, mapping the lost lines, preserving those sepia memories. He loved nothing better than to spend a solitary weekend walking the vanished rails with his Ordinance Survey maps and a plug of good tobacco. He had turned a hobby into a crusade. To Jack's way of thinking, the *thump-thump* of a powerful steam locomotive represented the best of the old rural ways. And what had replaced it? The automobile! The tipsy sons of gentlefolk throwing BMWs designed for autobahns into tight corners built for horse and cart. Try again. It was people like the Kennings who had intellectualized the countryside out of existence.

He stood up and shouted, "Go see if first edition's run off yet!" A young lad in the hallway ran into what was once the station's waiting room, where a rickety printing press was immortalizing local gossip. Jack stepped to the hearth and piled more coal on the fire in the corner of the room. "The only bloody thing the government left that was worth having is the coal pile in the station yard," he said out loud. "And they'd have taken that away too if they could've shifted it." He held the palms of his hands to the flames and blew tobacco smoke up the chimney.

The boy entered with a copy of the newspaper. Jack snatched it from his grasp, turned to the inside front page, and let his watery eyes savor columns three and four.

Psychic Forces at Work?

It has been brought to our attention that a number of mysterious incidents have occurred of late in the parish church of St. Neot in Hoyland, writes your correspondent Jack Stephens.

He read aloud the details of his interviews with the vicar and parishioners. He relished the sarcastic description of how he had seen flickering lights and heard a scream. "What do you think?" he asked the boy, cheering up at the knowledge that the derision was well-targeted, richly deserved, and all his own work.

"It's very clever, Mr. Stephens," the boy replied.

"Perhaps I should've named names. But libel's always in the back of your mind when you don't have much to go on. Maybe next time. I'm following up on this one, Sammy, lad. I'm going to get my own story and sell it to the Sunday Supplements with my own byline." He stepped to the boy's side and put an arm round his shoulders. The boy didn't care for his breath or the smell of his waistcoat, but he didn't resist. "I'm going to be famous, son. One day, you'll be glad you knew me. Run along now. It's lunchtime. Time for me to ride the rails."

Jack Stephens strolled out of his office and onto what used to be the platform and climbed down to where the rails once lay. He set off between the shafts of the platform toward the derelict signal box in the distance. The ruts of the old tracks were still visible beneath his feet. They curved beyond the signal box for a quarter of a mile toward the cutting alongside St. Neot's Church, but he didn't intend to walk nearly that far today.

He pretended he was a tightrope walker, stepping out on the steel rail. He spread his arms wide and feigned losing his balance. Preoccupied with the thought that there might still be undiscovered railway memorabilia lying in some forgotten corner of the signal box, he walked on for a few yards and then stopped. In his mind, the Boston-to-Lincoln mail train came hurtling around the bend ahead of him. He closed his eyes. He could hear the pistons driving, smell the coal smoke, see the cotton candy puffs of steam, and remember what it used to be like in the good old days. Ah, that England of old was something worth fighting for!

CHAPTER 15

London
December 2017

Brian, John, and Harry spent the best part of two hours closeted in the Visual Aids Department of Brian's college at London University, examining the spoils brought back from Lincolnshire. The movie, in which they had invested such high hopes, turned out to be an utter failure. Though the test footage was sharp and clear, the crucial minutes of the ghost's appearance and traverse of the sanctuary were indecipherable. The three men sat in the projection room watching a screen that was only fractionally lighter than the darkened room. All that could be seen was a gray background broken by swirls of yellow haze and slashes of maroon laser light.

"I told you know-it-alls we should have used spotlights," Harry reminded them. "When the church lights faded, it was too dark for the camera."

Brian gave a rueful nod and agreed. The audio tape, however, was something of a success. Harry worked on it alone in the recording studio for half an hour and then subjected the others to a barrage of static through the loudspeakers. "That's the raw, unadulterated recording," Harry said. "Now listen to it after I combined and amplified the channels, eliminated some of the background, and enhanced the signal-to-noise ratio. Kudos to Brian." He replaced the tape with a fresh one. There was a five-second delay and then a faint stream of static, but this time, there was something superimposed on it.

Brian and John craned their necks toward the loudspeaker as if proximity was necessary for comprehension, but they soon realized that comprehension was going to be impossible. The sounds had the timbre of the human voice in an upper register, but there was nothing else human about them. The vocal inflections were jarring and punctuated with alien whoops and caws. Occasionally, a burst of discordant cadences came to the fore.

When it was over, John shook Brian's hand. "Congratulations," he said. "You woke up the Devil with a Dark Lanthorn."

"What the hell was that?" Brian said.

"That was your ghost speaking," Harry replied.

"But it was nothing like a human voice."

"Nevertheless, chief, that was what your audio detector picked up." They listened to the recording again. John winced at the harsh glottal stops but supposed, at second hearing, that it could possibly be human. It was just terribly distorted, like the physical appearance of the ghost.

"I'll tell you one thing, Brian," Harry said. "This recording is consistent with the ghost being a dilute entity, as you described it. The audio intensity was extremely low. A normal mike would never have picked it up. And it was only by some digital magic that I was able to get you this much to work with."

"So what shall we do with it?" John asked Brian.

"Well, I'll tell you what I'd planned to do with it if something interesting showed up. I'd intended to give it to someone in the Linguistics Department here to see if they could make sense of the words. Should we do it anyway? What do you think?"

John and Harry had no reaction. Brian shrugged and reached for the college directory. He fingered the name of Jerome Rix, professor of medieval linguistics. Fifteen minutes later, they were outside his office. The elderly professor was putting on his raincoat prior to departing for a lunchtime seminar.

"Ah, good morning, Professor Rix," Brian began. "Please excuse us. My name's Brian Kenning. I'm a professor here in the Physics Department. This is my brother, John Kenning, a graduate student in the Chemistry Department, and this is Harry Groh from Central Illinois University in the United States."

"Physics? Chemistry?" Professor Rix said with surprise. "What can you possibly want with me?" Across his mind flashed a vision of himself as a high school student drowning in caustic seas, slashed to the bone by splintered glassware. To him, physics and chemistry were invented solely for the purpose of shortening one's life span.

"I'm sorry if we caught you at a bad time," Brian continued, "but we have a tape recording we'd like you to listen to. We heard you were one of the leading authorities on medieval English, so naturally, we came here first."

"Is it from a play or something?" he asked, warming to them. "I get a lot of actors striving for authenticity."

"Something like that. Elizabethan, perhaps. It's whatever you can make of it."

"Very well. Leave it on my desk with your phone number. I'll call you later today." He declined to take the tape from Brian's hands as if he believed it might be contaminated with some subtle toxin. He strode past them and headed off down the hall. They left the tape on his desk with a note. Throughout the afternoon, they sat in Brian's lab, drinking coffee and chatting idly. The remarkable sounds on the tape were uppermost in their minds, but there was no basis yet for speculation.

At four thirty, the phone rang, and Brian answered it with, "This is Brian Kenning."

"Yes, Dr. Kenning, and let me preface my remarks by saying that if I'd been on the committee that awarded you tenure at this university, you could as well have whistled for it. Hoaxes by students are barely tolerable, but hoaxes by faculty members are unforgivable."

"But Professor Rix—"

"Never in my long career has anyone had the audacity to perpetrate such a deception on me. Whether this is a misguided charity stunt or the result of an alcohol-induced wager, I neither know nor care. Be warned, however, that at the drop of a hat, I would call your head of department instanter. What do you say to that?"

"Really, sir, I gave you that tape in good faith—"

"Good faith be damned! That recording is nothing but electronic gibberish. How dare you waste my time with—"

"But, sir, it must mean something. It was—"

"It's of no consequence what you believe. I can assure you that that cacophony, recorded no doubt with some elaborate gadgetry that cost more than the budget of my entire department, has nothing remotely to do with language. It's gibberish, I repeat."

"But we recorded it—"

"Good day, Dr. Kenning. My time is clearly more precious than yours."

Professor Rix hung up, and Brian turned in exasperation to John and Harry. "What a jerk," Brian said.

"Well, he only heard what we heard," John said to mollify his brother. "You can't be terribly surprised that he could make nothing of it."

"He didn't have to chew my head off."

It was appropriate that they retire to the local pub. They had reached an impasse, and Harry was due to return to Chicago the next day. As the evening wore on, though, alcohol slowly gained mastery over their frustrations and brought with it renewed optimism. They had truly seen a ghost, and no one could take that away from them. Fame and fortune were within their grasp. The ridicule of the Rixes and the Applewhites and the Stephenses of the world would soon be exposed as narrow-mindedness. The unbelievers would pay a medieval price. The rack was prescribed for the professor and thumbscrews for the cleric; Jack Stephens was consigned to hot coals.

The scotch and the rhetoric flowed freely. Brian did battle with the word *apparition* three times before admitting defeat and picking on its little brother *ghost*. Harry set fire to a napkin inadvertently and doused the flames with ginger ale. John smoked a cigar for the first time in his life. The stream of liquor flowed on, but the rhetoric eventually faltered. Suffused with camaraderie, they wanted the experience to last forever, but patrons came and went, and the clock on the wall ticked briskly toward closing time. John tried his best to preserve the evening, but it slowly crumpled into a ball of noise and smoke and vanished into a ringing blackness.

*****

Two blocks away, Professor Rix was hard at work in his office, preparing an article on vowel development in the Middle Ages. The writing was not going well, though, for he was distracted by thoughts of that idiotic tape. He felt a little guilty about his impulsive reaction to it and his needlessly acerbic call to Dr. Kenning. But there was also something puzzling about it. It was almost too outlandish to be a fake. Pranksters would surely have left an obscene calling card.

He found himself beating time against his desk in some half-remembered rhythm. Irritated by the distraction, he walked to his recorder and played the tape again. It was dark outside his office, and the eerie sounds echoed around the walls and reverberated from the deserted alley beneath his window. The utterances mocked both his failure to interpret them and his inability to put them out of his mind.

He stopped the tape after hearing a sound that was vaguely familiar. He replayed it and listened intently to what sounded to him like the word *nam*—perhaps an old dialectical form of the word *name*. He picked up a pad of paper and scribbled the word at the top of the page. He played the passage again, drumming all the while on the table. He wrote the words "AELC CHRISTEN MANN" in large letters across the page and underneath them scrawled, "EACH CHRISTIAN MAN." He walked once around the room and returned to the recorder. He lifted the spools off the deck, held the exposed tape up to the light, and examined it. He inspected the spools, top and bottom. With a shake of the head, he remounted the spools and fast-forwarded to the end of the tape.

*****

John awoke with a cramp in his calf muscle. He sat up and massaged his tender leg. The room was cold and unfamiliar, and he had no recollection of arriving in it. He was lying on a mattress on a dismal, dusty floor. Someone was snoring on a couch at the opposite end of the room. He felt thirsty, and then he felt nauseous. He laid back down and closed his eyes for a minute.

When he stirred the second time, sunshine was slanting through open drapes, and the room was warmer. He rolled onto his side, cracking an eye at his watch, but the hands made no sense. He pulled what looked like a shabby raincoat over his shoulders and began to doze off. Almost at once, a figure lumbered into the room, bringing with it light, noise, and vibration of the floorboards in equally distasteful proportions. The figure on the couch emitted an immense water buffalo groan.

"Rise and shine, you lazy sods!" Brian shouted.

John attempted to insert his head into the sleeve of the raincoat. "Miserable bastard. Fucking freezing."

"Harry, you're gonna miss your flight if you don't move it," Brian said.

"Sweet Jesus," groaned the figure on the couch. "What time is it?"

"Almost eight o'clock. I made some coffee."

John sat up. He realized that they were in Brian's apartment. He flung back the raincoat and stared at his bare chest, wondering what had happened to his shirt. He climbed gingerly to his feet and located his clothes. The three of them shuffled into the tiny kitchen and spent the next half hour clutching coffee mugs and trying to banish the tastes and smells of the previous evening. Brian offered breakfast, and John threw the salt cellar at him. Brian's phone rang, and he took the call in the kitchen. With a jolt of recognition, he suddenly brightened and said, "Oh, Professor Rix."

"I had another bout with that tape of yours last night," Rix began. "Finally made some sense of it."

"You did? How on earth did you manage that?"

"A modicum of skill, my dear boy. I corrected an error of yours."

"That's fantastic. What did you make of it?"

"All in good time. My apologies, first, for the high-handed behavior yesterday. No call for it at all. It's been a long term, you know, and what with Christmas looming—"

"Understood. No hard feelings. So what about the tape?"

"Yes, a most interesting recording. May I ask again its provenance?"

"Well, it was a…a rehearsal, like you said, for a play."

"Then I'm afraid you'll have to rewrite extensively. If you're trying for authentic Elizabethan pronunciation, that is. This is way off."

"Really?"

"I've studied the recording closely. It consists of a fragment of a monastic chant. It has similarities to certain Gregorian chants, but it isn't one."

"A monastic chant?"

"But, of course, you know all this."

"Yes. Please go on."

"The tone sequences are sometimes familiar to me and sometimes not. However, the words I've been able to decipher are extremely interesting. I particularly noticed the use of the word *husl*. This is an Old English word of Saxon or Mercian origin meaning *communion*. In those days, chants were usually in Latin, of course, so this appears to be an improvised litany in the common language of the day. We would call it a melismata. It is most interesting to me that the voiced fricative in *husl* is stressed."

"What does that mean?"

"It dates the piece as prior to the thirteenth century."

"Are you sure?"

"Indubitably. But let me continue. The word for *seen* is monophthongized. I do not hear the typical Old English diphthong *seon*. This suggests something in the 1100s, early Middle English. Also, we have vocalization of the velar fricative in the word for *bow*. I hear *bowe*, not *boga*, which would be the Old English form. The piece could be from around the time of the Norman Conquest due to the presence of several words of French origin—*abbot* and *sacrament*, to name just two. But then again, I hear the word *lige* for *falsehood*, which is inconsistent."

"I'm sorry, Professor. I can't follow all this technical stuff. Could you just date the piece for me as best you can?"

"Well, it would appear to be a dialect typical of Northern England at, say, the juncture of the Old and the Middle English periods. I'd plump for the end of the eleventh century or early twelfth, something like that, certainly not the sixteenth. Is that helpful?"

"What? Yes, yes, excellent work."

"Of course, it's not for me to say that the piece is an authentic record of eleventh-century speech. We really know very little about that period. Nevertheless, I can say with confidence that certain words, certain pronunciations, are characteristic of that particular period and no other."

"Thank you, sir. You've been extremely helpful."

"Might I ask who coached you on the handling of this script? Was it one of our university colleagues? Mooney, perhaps?"

"No, not him."

"You don't wish to divulge your source. I understand. We live in a competitive world. Anyway, I congratulate your instructor on a very passable imitation of eleventh-century speech, except for that *lige*, which is definitely anachronistic. You should check on that."

"Thank you, Professor. I will."

"My pleasure. Good luck with the play."

"The what?"

"The play. Good luck with it. You may pick up the tape from my office at your convenience."

"Yes. Thank you." Brian returned from the kitchen and looked at John and Harry. "The ghost isn't Richard Crossly after all."

CHAPTER 16

Joliet
December 2017

Karen Butler and Connie Cammaretta met for pizza on a cold Friday evening right before Christmas. The restaurant was a familiar sanctuary for them, warm and pungent, and they often used it to relax and share lab gossip. On this occasion, however, they exchanged only perfunctory remarks as they ate. Their thoughts were on the debacle at the center during Thanksgiving week. Harry had left with Brian for England shortly after Dan Patzner's outburst, leaving everyone nonplussed, and it was generally agreed that the topic would be shunned until Harry returned to straighten things out.

By the time the pizza had dwindled down to the last slice, Connie was unable to contain her curiosity. She toyed with a crust and ventured a gambit. "Have you talked to Dan since—"

"Since he dumped Frank on his ass and fled the scene?"

"Yeah."

"Not a word." Karen swirled the ice in her drink. "I don't feel like it's up to me to make the first move, Connie. It wasn't me that dynamited the program. Anyway, what do you say to a guy who thinks you're trying to steal his soul? Huh? He's like one of those New Guinea natives who won't let you photograph them. What do I say to him? 'Hey, Dan. Let me come over and explain, and I'm gonna bring along a friend with a tail and a pitchfork as a convincer'? Nothing's gonna sit well with him at this point."

"Why does he think like that? What did you do to him, for Christ's sake?"

"I already told you. He's scared shitless of the zeta state. I didn't do anything." Karen took a long drink and then cupped the glass between her hands. She leaned forward, checked adjacent tables for people she might know, and whispered what had been suppressed for nearly a month. "That last time, Connie, it was so bizarre. You can't imagine. When we entered the zeta state, Dan and I were tossed into the same mysterious forest as before. I could see him sitting right across from me. We were like the Babes in the Wood. Then suddenly, other figures appeared all around us, vague shapes—incorporeal, you might say—sitting in a circle and staring at us. Can you believe that? People from the zeta world, I guess."

"People? What kind of people?"

"I don't know. I couldn't see their features. They were just out-lines—silhouettes almost. I don't know how to describe them. I didn't know what the fuck was happening."

"And Dan?"

"Oh, I could tell that Dan was about to freak out. You could see it on his face. But I couldn't let him break the spell, Connie. It was the wildest thing I'd ever experienced, and it wasn't like we were in any danger or anything. I tried to make a sign to him, like, 'Hang on! Don't lose it!' I just had to see more."

"Weren't you scared?"

"*Scared*'s not the right word." Karen pursed her lips and tried to think how best to describe the sensation. "Apprehensive, maybe, a bit. Fascinated more than anything. I really wanted to know who these zeta guys were and why they were looking at us, but Dan would have none of it. He quickly pulled back into alpha, and the whole scene faded. Next thing I knew, he's up and raving at me like a luna-tic. The rest is ICPS history."

"I know he blames you for what happened."

"He thinks I engineered some big sorcery thing. He thinks I'm a fucking witch and I brought my coven along to convert him, real Salem stuff. He reads too many tabloids."

Connie leaned back in her chair and chased pizza crumbs around her plate with a fork. The jukebox sprang to life with an old Supremes number. She stared at the circular stains on the table as if they were tiny crop circles. "I don't suppose there's any chance Dan will call you."

"I don't think so. It's a shame. He was getting good at it. I don't know where I'll find a replacement."

"The program's probably dead anyway, Harry says. He doesn't think the Pentagon will tolerate shenanigans like that. He thinks they'll pull the plug." Karen nodded and stared out the window at the nondescript parking lot dotted with beat-up student cars. The gunmetal facade of a strip mall framed the view, ice streaking the ledges and sidewalks and dripping from the gutters like squalid gray stalactites. A bus stopped in front of the neighboring gas station and disgorged two laughing students into the slush. Connie cinched her face and stared into Karen's eyes. "Why are you so into this Ouija board stuff, Karen? That's what I really don't understand."

"I guess you'd have to be raised on a farm in Iowa to know the answer to that."

"I've never even seen a farm but from the highway."

"Reinbeck," Karen declared, thumping her chest with a fist. "My heart's in Reinbeck, Iowa." She paused. "Unfortunately, it's trapped there and can't escape. You have to understand, Connie, that everything in Iowa is so"—she made shapes in the air with her fingers—"so *rectangular*. That's the only word I can think of. The fields, the corn rows, the poky little towns with their gridded streets, even the farms that squat there like so many playing cards—all that space fenced in and packaged. You were brought up in the city. You can't possibly understand."

"Try me."

"I'm not good at explaining this, but to me, this geometrical order is reflected in the minds of the people. The folks in my hometown understand just a few simple concepts: church, school, taxes, food, and more church. Do you know what I mean? They've got everything compartmentalized like those tiny drawers in an old bureau. You can't muss anything up, or they're lost."

"Structured."

"Right, perpendiculars everywhere. It's in the genealogy too. I often think about all the family trees in Reinbeck with their neat verticals and horizontals. There's not a single hillbilly diagonal anywhere."

"But you don't hate it, do you?"

"No, no, I don't. It's a fine way to perpetuate a wholesome existence. It's just that it circumscribes your life. I'm never going to hike to China or fly to Brazil to save rain forests. I wouldn't know where to begin. When you're in a tight-knit, multigenerational gridlock, you can't do those kinds of things. Chicago is like the far side of the moon to my family. And all these rectangles fold into one big origami maze that leads back to the beginning, back home."

"Your family holds you back."

"Don't get me wrong, Connie, I love my folks dearly. I'll be home for Christmas no matter what. But you know how it is. The town has me marrying the boy next door. Literally. They want us to carve out a little square in between my folks' big square and his folks' big square and shuttle apple pie to and fro till we all crumble into dust. I can't do that, Connie. The human race would never get anywhere if we just turned into replicas of our parents."

Connie used her fork to tap out the last few bars of the Supremes song then pushed her plate away and downed the rest of her Coke. "What do your folks do?" Connie asked.

"My dad's a farmer," Karen replied, "all bone and sinew. My mom cooks and eats."

"Sounds fine to me. So why does all this drive you into the tank?"

"It is fine, Connie. That's the biggest part of the problem. I'm trapped in the bosom of my family"—she struck her chest again— "just like my heart's trapped in my rib cage. But up here"—she tapped herself on the side of the head—"up here, the gate swings free, and it opens up to a lot more than Chicago or China. It's deep space, Connie, new worlds, places I can go to without ever leaving the farm."

"It'd creep me out."

"I really don't see why it should be frightening. And that's where Dan and I differ. I don't see myself as a victim. I'm the leader of an expedition."

"Being immersed in the tank doesn't scare you? Not at all?"

"Not anymore. In some ways, it reminds me of the blackness and the stillness I remember from sitting on the porch back home, looking up at the night sky. Do you know how many stars you can see on a clear night out in the boonies, Connie? Millions and millions. You've no idea. Galaxies, nebulas, planets, the Milky Way. I used to know the names of all the constellations. When I first came to the city, I wondered where they'd all gone. I love that big, pregnant sky. In fact, I carry it around with me. You should see how I fixed my bedroom ceiling. I painted it black and hung stars from it that Mom crocheted for me. Reminds me of home."

"Sounds a bit depressing."

"You think so?"

"It would be to me."

"Floating in the tank is just like gazing up at the stars."

"And going zeta?"

"Going zeta is like traveling to the stars."

Connie clicked her tongue against her teeth. She had a great deal of admiration for Karen's bravery, but she couldn't understand why such a pretty girl would want to mess around with her own mind like that. She decided to change the subject. "I've seen you talking to that Aussie at work, the dolphin guy."

"Pete?"

"Yeah, Pete Wilkinson. Are you going out with him?"

"Gimme a break! With that bow tie and the prissy little mustache? No way. I just like to talk with him about what's happening to me. He's so smart. He knows so much physics. He can come up with all kinds of explanations."

"He discovered that you were sending out some kind of waves, didn't he?"

"That's what he thinks. Did you ever take any physics courses? Electromagnetism?"

"A long time ago. Easy in, easy out."

"Well, Pete believes that the two of us, Dan and I, set up some kind of energy transmitter when we enter the zeta state, an antenna or something, the same kind of thing a radio station uses to transmit signals."

"Well, I could understand if you both had braces—"

"Be serious, Connie. This isn't easy to explain. Pete talks about phases and modulation and damping and shit like that, none of which I understand. But whatever it is that happens inside our heads seems to create a...an energy field that Pete can detect with the electronic equipment in his lab."

"Some kind of brain waves?"

"I guess. I've been reading about the brain in my spare time. Did you know that there are big chunks of it that have no known purpose? Pete thinks that Dan and I might have found a way to organize the electrical circuits in these mysterious parts of the brain. He thinks we've dusted off and retooled some primitive neural networks that are dormant in modern man. By exercising this circuitry, we're learning what these parts of the brain were originally intended for."

"There's a special part of the brain dedicated to the zeta state?"

"Maybe. Pete likes to think of the brain as a huge city threaded with all different kinds of intersecting networks: the phone lines, the electric lines, the gas pipes, the subway. Each system is organized to fulfill a special purpose in the most efficient way. He thinks this unexplored part of the brain is like a neighborhood that's in total darkness. No one goes there anymore. No one even knows it exists. But Dan and I have stumbled across this forgotten part of the city, and we've been playing around in it. We discovered a switch box and some circuit diagrams. We spliced a couple of wires together, and on came a streetlight. We replaced a fuse and powered up the traffic signals."

"That does make some sense."

"But it's more than that, Connie. It's like we're learning how to synchronize the lights at each intersection. We can time the switching so that it's possible to speed right through without catching a red light."

"Right through to Zetaville."

"You got it. And when all the neurons fire correctly, that's when we get to see who lives in Zetaville."

"So why can't you sustain it?"

"That's the problem for me at the moment. I seem to get things just right, but then something pops up and destroys the synchronization—a mouse chews through some insulation, a drunk pees on a power line. There's a crackle, a few sparks, and the streets are dark again."

"What does Harry think?"

"Harry thinks the answer is biochemical. He's been talking to a professor at Northwestern University called Lieshman, who specializes in mind-altering drugs. Harry's coined the term protective adaptation, the ability of the human body to evolve over many generations to protect itself from harmful influences. He thinks that early man discovered that the zeta state was bad for it in some way and developed a physiological response to counteract it. Personally, I don't think he knows what he's talking about."

"Just between you and me, I think Harry's beginning to lose it," Connie said, warming to the subject. "Have you heard him talk to those potted plants in his office? Have you heard what he says to them? Such language! And he won't let anyone near them. When he went on vacation last summer, he left water in a graduated flask for Frank to give them. Can you believe that? Measured out to the nearest milliliter! I really do think he's cracked." Karen shrugged her shoulders and hunched over the remains of her drink. "So what about Frank, Karen?" Connie asked. "Is he still, you know, interested in you?"

"Let's not talk about Frank. I can't stand him anywhere near me."

"He won't take no for an answer, huh?"

"He needs a Berlitz course in body language. I can't believe he's still pestering me after all the rebuffs I've given him."

"They say some men just see that as an invitation to try harder."

"Every time I turn a corner, he's there, staring at me with those sunken Baltic eyes of his. And that stubble! I swear to God, he extrudes it by force of will alone. What a creep."

"Pray he's only a creep," Connie said, and Karen winced. "So are you going out with anyone right now?"

"Well, there's always someone, isn't there? But no one special."

"What did you think of that English prof Harry brought over? What was his name?"

"Brian something. Canning or something like that. I thought he was kinda interesting."

"I guess so, in a Papa Bear sort of way."

Karen stared off into the distance and cocked her head to one side. "When I first saw him in the atrium, right after Dan had run out of the building, I thought I recognized him. I thought I'd met him before. But I was obviously mistaken. We live thousands of miles apart."

"Didn't you love his accent? So Michael Caine. But he was a bit chubby for me. And those clothes. Donate them to the Salvation Army!" They both laughed.

"I thought he had a certain air about him," Karen continued, "a quiet confidence. I kinda like that in a guy. And I'll bet he doesn't converse with his office plants." They laughed again. "Harry says this Brian guy is really interested in the zeta state. He thinks it's got some connection with ghosts in Merrie Olde England. That's what Harry's doing over there, you know, ghost hunting. It gets weirder and weirder."

"Maybe the fir trees and the people you see in the zeta state are ghosts."

"Maybe. What the hell, I'll probably never find out now."

Their waitress approached. They resisted her offer of dessert but allowed their glasses to be refilled. The waitress dropped the check on the table. Neither of them had the desire to turn it over and look at it. Karen, in particular, seemed distant, regretful that something valuable had been lost.

"I'm still seeing Paul," Connie said sheepishly after a long pause.

"What? Oh, I'm sorry, Connie. I forgot to ask."

"That's all right. Things are going pretty well. The two of us have an understanding. If we're still together on New Year's Eve, we're going to get officially engaged."

"That's great. Anticipatory congratulations."

"Thanks. It'll be two years on December 31. We met at the New Year's Eve party, remember?"

Karen nodded. "Sure."

"Are you coming to the party this year?"

"I've got no date."

"That doesn't matter. Lots of the students come stag. It's gonna be a riot. I'm on the committee, as usual, and we've decided to go the whole nine yards this year—big tree and a DJ, a gazillion balloons. You gotta come."

"I guess I will. I know most of the grad students, and not all of them have tried to hit on me. I'll probably come."

"I could always get Frank to invite you," Connie said with a grin.

"Don't joke about it, please. I watch *America's Most Wanted*."

"Oh, Frank's not that bad. He's just got a hyperactive libido."

"I don't care for any of the guys I know right now, Connie, I tell you. They're so far from what I'm looking for. I sometimes think I'll never find…" She pushed her drink away. "Are you ready?" Connie nodded. "I'll pay," Karen said. She turned over the check and dropped some bills on the table, and they left.

CHAPTER 17

Joliet
New Year's Eve, 2017

"Party animal! Woof, woof!" Karen looked up and saw Connie's face beaming at her from the middle of a throng of students in the CIU faculty club. Matted black hair slanted across Connie's forehead from under a purple hat dusted with sequins. Her cheeks were red enough to stop traffic. As she pushed her way closer to Karen's table, the tightness of her bright print dress sent a momentary jolt of embarrassment through Karen. Connie was rounded in all the right and the wrong places. Music thumped the air. "Come and dance!" Connie panted, holding out her hands.

"Later," Karen replied.

"No. Now!" Connie insisted.

"Go find your boyfriend."

"I've misplaced him!"

Karen smiled and waved Connie back onto the floor. Connie blew her a kiss goodbye and plunged back into the sea of dancers. Karen looked across her table at the half-dozen students lounging around it. She wondered how she looked in the blue silk blouse and new jeans bought the day before. Her hair was growing back in now that the experiments were stalled, and it looked like corn stubble with a morning light behind it. She guessed she looked okay. Then she wondered why it mattered how she looked if she really didn't care, and her fellow students didn't seem to either. *I shouldn't have come.*

She looked around the room for the other members of Harry's research group, and her eyes fell first on Frank Koslowski. He was dressed in an old-fashioned brown sport coat that clashed with the gray along his jawline and in the hollows of his cheeks. His long black hair was slicked back behind the ears. Frank didn't socialize with his research colleagues, preferring to slouch at the bar with a group of technicians from other departments. He eyed the table of students repeatedly, and Karen could see that there was much taunting and snickering going on. She guessed that she was the focus of it. She resolved not to look in that direction for the remainder of the evening.

Harry Groh was by the opposite wall, sitting at a table with another faculty member and his wife. He had returned from England just before Christmas, still limping from the torn knee ligament sustained in Hoyland Church. A story was circulating that he had fled from an angry ghost, and a playful postdoc who had taunted him about his encounter with Casper, the priest with a sheet over his head, had received a verbal roasting.

Dan Patzner was the one member of Harry's group who didn't show. Karen was nervous that he might even though a mutual friend had informed her that he had chosen a different party to attend. Rumor had it that Dan was flunking out and wouldn't be around next semester. Karen knew he had been suspended from campus for one month for his infraction at the center, but the suspension had ended a couple of days ago. A confrontation was bound to come eventually, and Karen knew it would be awkward. Even as she kept a watchful eye on the door for any sign of Dan, Frank kept a watchful eye on her.

*****

Several hours into the party, as she was returning from the bathroom, Harry took her elbow and led her to a side table with a conspiratorial air. "What's up?" she asked him.

"Can we talk business for a minute?"

"Oh, Dr. Groh, please, not here, not now."

"But we haven't had a proper chance to talk since I got back from England. Unbelievable things happened over there, Karen. You wouldn't believe me if I told you. My mind's in a whirl. I just need to ask you a couple of questions."

"Well, all right then, but keep it brief. This is a party."

"Well, first, Brian Kenning and I are both struck by the similarities between the zeta state and the trance that Mrs. Coleby, Brian's aunt, enters right before the ghost appears. I've been rereading the transcripts of your sessions since I got back. You say that you see vivid images when the zeta state comes upon you—porcelain faces, fir trees. I forget the exact words. The important question is this: Are you seeing these things only in your mind's eye, or are they really there, such that someone else could see them?"

"I don't know. There's no way for me to tell."

"No, of course, there isn't. And we don't know either. We've always denied access to the laboratory during the experiments because you're naked in the tank. That might have been a mistake. We don't know what happens to your surroundings when you go zeta. Maybe your faces and trees are real, just like the ghost created by Mrs. Coleby. Measurements with Brian's spectrometer suggest that the ghost in the church is an actual physical entity made of actual physical molecules."

"Really? That's wild. All this time, I've been thinking that zeta is a spiritual experience."

"I don't think it is. I think that somehow—God only knows how—you're influencing the physical world outside your head, transmitting something. You know what Wilkinson thinks. It's a crazy possibility, but the pieces are starting to fall into place."

"I guess that would explain why Dan and I see each other when we go under."

"It would. Exactly."

It was a quarter to twelve. Several of the students were hauling a giant ball covered with aluminum foil up to the ceiling. The feat required a ladder, a rope, a pulley, and coordination, and the students were giggling and jostling one another in a way Karen knew she had outgrown. She watched their performance but listened intently to Harry.

"The other thing I wanted to ask you about," Harry continued, "is your description of being pulled back from the edge of the zeta state. You say in the transcripts that you feel yourself crossing over from alpha to zeta, but your physical body resists, and you can only hold it for a short while."

"That's right. I bet I haven't been in the zeta state for more than twenty seconds or so in any of the tests. Though I'm not consciously scared, my body pulls my mind back. Or that's what it feels like. It's involuntary. I feel like I'm on a piece of elastic."

"Like I said before, I think that's a defense mechanism. I've recently been reading up on chemical secretions that protect the body from pain. Some years ago, two Scottish scientists discovered these morphine-like chemicals called endorphins that are produced by the body to counteract pain. Have you heard of them? Endorphins?"

"Vaguely."

"When you put a person under stress, the concentration of beta endorphin in the body rises. So what if there was a trigger mechanism that flooded your system with a protective chemical every time you went zeta because, somehow, the body knows that the zeta state is perilous?" Karen nodded. It seemed to her that this explanation could be consistent with what she had experienced. Harry took hold of her wrist and squeezed it. "We need to get to the bottom of this, Karen. Let's try an experiment of our own tomorrow evening."

"I thought the project was shut down."

"Only unofficially. The director's still waiting for the DOD report on the Patzner incident. Look, tomorrow is New Year's Day. The center's closed, but I've got a key to the lab. Let's do a little experiment. You get into the zeta state, and I'll take blood samples while you're under. I'll send them off to Northwestern University for analysis. Professor Lieshman's got a biochemical lab that can do a full peptide and amino acid screening for us. We'll see if they can find any unusual secretions in your blood when you hit zeta. What do you say?"

"Could we get in trouble?"

"I'll take full responsibility. Don't worry. Come at six o'clock in the evening. There'll be no one in the building. I guarantee it. Let's start the New Year off with something prodigious!"

"Will Dan be there?" Karen asked apprehensively.

"No, no. We're done with Dan. This was always just about you. You can do this yourself, Karen. I know it."

"Do you know how to draw blood?"

"Sure."

While Karen was considering Harry's request, Connie rushed up to her, grabbed her arm, and pulled her to her feet. "It's time!" she squealed. A young professor climbed onto a chair and shouted, "Wait! Wait! Ten. Nine. Eight..." The students slackened the rope, and the aluminum-covered ball inched its way down from the ceiling, spraying sparkles of colored light around the room.

Karen looked back at Harry and mouthed, "Six o'clock?" He nodded. She shrugged her shoulders and nodded back to him. "Okay."

"Two. One. Zero! Happy New Year, everyone! Happy New Year!" The dance floor erupted. Balloons popped, ribbons flew through the air, and someone began to spray a soda siphon. Karen laughed, her eyes bright from reflected glitter and the momentary joy of celebration. She made her way onto the dance floor. She struggled through the throng of students and faculty, hugging her close friends and smiling at her casual acquaintances. Suddenly, startlingly, Frank Koslowski was in her face. He offered his lips, his eyes impaling hers. She stepped aside at the last moment, and he kissed air. Firecrackers crumpled outside the building.

The revelry continued, but Frank stood alone amid the chaos of embraces, glaring at the floor as if this failure was symptomatic of some larger misfortune. Karen was shaken and a little frightened, but before she could react, Connie grabbed her hand again and whisked her away into a conga line. Frank shoved his way through the line of dancers and stumbled back to the bar. Anxiously, Karen looked for Harry at the table where she had last seen him, but he was gone.

She left the party an hour later in the company of fellow students. It was bitterly cold, and the car's heater failed to master the icy drafts intruding at every seam. She huddled for warmth against the bodies of her classmates, listening to their braggadocios and salacious chitchat, but she felt alienated. She was different from them, different from just about everyone else on the planet, it seemed. She had learned something that the rest of the world had forgotten.

*****

Back in her apartment, Karen Butler's mind would not be still. Worries about her troubled relationships with Dan and Frank nagged her, but she was eventually able to push them aside and concentrate on the ideas implanted by Harry. She fixed herself a mug of green tea and collapsed on the couch among the mass of books she had accumulated during her own search for an answer to the zeta mystery. She had become fascinated with the great seers and visionaries of the past. Could they have experienced the same thing as she? What were their explanations?

She hunted for an old book by H. G. Wells that she had recently bought at a local antique shop. A passage from it kept running through her mind. She opened the crusty blue boards and thumbed through the pages. Eventually, she found the passage she was looking for.

> One figures great towns red with destruction while giant airships darken the sky, one pictures the crash of mighty ironclads, the bursting of tremendous shells fired from beyond the range of sight into unprotected cities... There is a vision of interrupted communications, of wrecked food trains and sunken food ships, of vast masses of people thrown out of employment and darkly tumultuous in the streets, of famine and famine-driven rioters.

She turned to the front of the book and checked the publication date: 1908. Wells must surely have seen the two world wars that

THE TIME QUANTUM

came years later. Those were descriptions of saturation bombing, V-2 rockets, and the German U-boat blockade. But what exactly did he mean by the words *figures*, *pictures*, and *vision*? They weren't explicit enough. Was it merely creative writing fueled by a fertile imagination, or had he actually seen these events in some way? Had he visited the future? Had the future visited him?

She sipped her tea, the tiny hairs on her arms standing straight up. Then there was Coleridge, her favorite poet. She had always felt something of that kind about him too. She looked him up in Wikipedia. She already knew that he had been a sickly man and an opium addict. The description of his poetry reinforced her views about his art: "A movement…toward the natural world of sights, sounds and tangibles, suggested with piercing clarity." That was how it seemed to her, piercing clarity, just like when she tipped over the rim of the zeta state into the world of forests and faces. Coleridge had gone zeta. She was certain of it.

She picked up her anthology of Coleridge's poems and shuffled into the bedroom, yawning. It was past three o'clock. She slipped off her clothes, put on a nightgown, and slid between the coolness of the sheets. She turned to "Kubla Khan" and read once more the evocative tale of Xanadu. She felt a kinship with Coleridge, the kind one might develop while traveling with a close companion on some long and hazardous journey. As she came to the famous last lines, she was convinced they applied as much to the poet himself as to Kubla Khan: "For he on honey-dew hath fed and drunk the milk of Paradise."

She instantly felt deep inside her that if she pursued and perfected the zeta state, one day, she would dine just as royally. Her mind was made up. She would meet with Harry the following evening. She would listen to his explanations and try her best to understand them. She would learn how to counteract her body's natural defenses. She would attain zeta and stabilize it and explore it till all its mysteries were revealed.

She stared up at the black ceiling of her bedroom and the crocheted stars hanging from it. They were close enough to touch. She thought of that big Iowa sky and how many stars could be seen from the porch at midnight. She remembered how it felt to let her mind

175

worm its way between the galaxies, to explore the beauty of deep space. Then just for a moment, the joy of solitude tripped over into the fear of loneliness. She suddenly wished she had a sister to confide in or a lover, but for now, there were only Connie Cammaretta and Samuel Taylor Coleridge. Still, she thought, courage was a skill like any other. It just needed practice. Someday, she, too, would drink the milk of paradise.

*****

Fourteen hours later, Karen lay on the sensory deprivation couch in the laboratory of the ICPS facility. The building was as dark and silent as the grave. Harry leaned over her and shaved two circles the size of quarters in the hair on either side of her head. He applied dabs of petroleum jelly to her scalp and then affixed suction cups. He reeled out connecting wires and clipped the ends of them to the contacts on the cups and to the chart recorder on the floor. The room was cold and dimly lit.

"I'm going to use just one set of EEG connections," Harry said, "so that I can tell the onset of the zeta state. I don't want to do a Dracula number on you."

"I hope this'll work," Karen whispered. "It would be easier if Dan was here."

"You'll do just fine." Harry switched on the chart recorder, and the irregular tracings began.

"Coleridge took opium, you know," Karen said.

"Who did?"

"Samuel Taylor Coleridge, the poet. Is it possible he took opium to reach the zeta state?"

Harry was carrying a rack of glass vials from the bench to the chair. He set them down carefully and removed the first one, which he placed next to a syringe. He paused for a moment and stared at the wall. "Opium is like beta endorphin. It's a suppressor. If anything, he took it to make the visions go away."

Karen nodded and closed her eyes. "Either way," she murmured.

"Just relax," Harry said softly. "Do your thing. I'll be right here beside you."

Karen let her limbs go limp and her mind flow out of her body. After about five minutes, the pen jerked upward and then swooped into a deep trough. Harry reached for a piece of cotton and took hold of Karen's arm. He swabbed it gently with a topical anesthetic and inserted the needle into a vein. She made no motion. He adjusted the suction until blood dripped slowly into the first vial. He collected about two cubic centimeters of blood and then switched to the second vial.

When he had the sampling technique perfected, he took a moment to glance at the chart recorder. The alpha wave was beautifully defined, but he had three vials filled before he was convinced she was entering the zeta phase. He slowed down the rate of flow of blood and began to time the fill period. When he switched to the sixth vial, he became aware that the lab was darker than it had been moments before.

Anxiety began to creep over him, just as it had in Hoyland Church. He needed only enough time to take blood samples and leave; this was not intended to be another supernatural confrontation. He trembled slightly as he placed the seventh vial in the rack and drew out another. There was a large dark mass beginning to appear a few feet to his left. He closed his eyes tightly, but it was still there when he opened them. He tried to clear his head by shaking it vigorously from side to side. He fumbled as he attached the vial to the syringe. A drop of blood escaped and splashed onto the floor.

Harry stared at the drop of blood, struggling to muster fortitude. He refused to be a coward this time. In order to maintain harmony in his mind—perhaps even sanity—it was necessary to establish either the veracity or the falsity of these experiences no matter how many sacrifices it entailed, and the first sacrifice must be his fear. This was his laboratory, his student, and his idea. He would not be intimidated. He raised his head and gazed up at the array of ghostly trees that now filled the laboratory. The eighth vial was filling fast, and his shaking fingers could barely control the pressure on the syringe.

He reached out a hand to the tree by his side. He touched a finger against what he could clearly see to be bark, but it penetrated the surface without contact. He withdrew his hand with a sharp exhalation. Awestruck, he stared up at the tree. The branches were perfectly defined. He could clearly see gnarled ridges running vertically along the trunk. He could even make out a fir cone. So this was Karen's forest! He touched the bark again, and this time, he became aware of a very slight tingling in his fingertips—almost imperceptible but not quite.

The vial was full. He jerked it from the syringe, and it slipped out of his fingers. It hit the floor and rolled under a chair, smearing blood in its wake. Harry swore softly and reached for the next vial, but Karen stirred, and the trees began to fade. He was only able to take one more vial of blood before her brow wrinkled, and she started to cough. He removed the needle from her arm and pressed a cotton swab against the pinprick, followed by a Band-Aid.

She roused herself. She seemed to be in a little pain and slightly disoriented, but she smiled nonetheless, because she knew she had succeeded. Harry squeezed her hand in a moment of mutual reassurance then took the vials over to a refrigerator—half of them empty, half filled with Karen's blood. He left the room.

Karen checked her arm then got up and went to wash her hands in the sink. She splashed water on her face. She locked the door of the laboratory behind her and walked down the darkened hallway toward Harry's office. As she approached, she heard his voice. Puzzled, she slowed down and halted in the open doorway. Harry was standing by the window with his back to her. He was facing one of his rubber plants and speaking to it in a soft, clenched voice.

"You can die now, you son of a bitch. Do you hear me? I thought I knew what this fucking world was all about, but I didn't know jack shit. I've seen things these last few weeks that'd make your roots spin. The spoon benders and the tarot readers were right all along. They knew it, and you knew it as well, didn't you, you son of a bitch? You just stayed alive to keep me guessing. Well, I'm a believer now, Tex, so you can quit fooling with me. You can die now." He gave the pot a sharp kick then grabbed one of the branches and shook it vigorously.

"Harry? Are you all right?" Karen said.

He turned to her. "What? Yeah, I'm all right."

"What's the matter?"

He looked out the window but saw only his own reflection silhouetted against the black fields. "Actually, I'm having a hard time with all of this. Karen, I—it's all so impossible! I had this secure foundation for my life, and now it's crumbling, and I can't see anything underneath it. Have you ever tried to grab a handful of sand to stop yourself from falling?"

CHAPTER 18

London
January 2018

In the days before Christmas, Brian had become increasingly intro-spective. The mystery of the ghost in Hoyland Church held him by the scruff of the neck and shook him and shook him and would not let him go. How was it possible that ancient people and ancient struc-tures could become visible—no, could materialize—in our modern world? Didn't that violate the laws of physics?

In the solitude of his apartment, he pondered the impossible. He set down equations about the quantum states of matter on a lined pad with a sharp pencil then balled up the sheets of paper and filled a wastebasket with them. He listened to Beethoven, imagining mol-ecules moving through time. He dived into the works of Eddington and Einstein and came up dry. The answer was always the same. There was simply no way it could happen.

As the intractable problem wore him down and his preoccupa-tion bred a sense of isolation, he became more and more repelled by the thought of Christmas. When Sarah invited him to spend the hol-idays with her family, he accepted at first out of politeness then called to decline. He simply couldn't face the social niceties of the season, and he was forced to admit to himself that he really didn't want to be with Sarah at this time. He was afraid of what he might be induced to say to her under the soft glow of Christmas lights, what he might be obliged to listen to her say to him, and where it all might lead.

Then when his own family called and begged him to come to Lincolnshire for the holidays, he declined again, saying there was a Christmas party at work, a journal article to be written, carol singers at the door right now—gotta go! And in the end, he did go. He fled. He packed a suitcase and left for Edinburgh, where he hibernated for two weeks with a dour bachelor colleague who also had no time for celebration. The year turned over without fuss. Sarah called him two days before he was due to return and insisted on meeting him off the train at King's Cross. She said she had unearthed some startling new material.

The day of Brian's return to the city was miserable. It had rained from dawn to dusk, and Sarah had been forced to take a taxi to the station after work. With ten minutes to spare, she located the arrival platform. It was cold and damp, and its open superstructure did little to impede the squalls. She waited with her collar turned up, shivering. The train duly arrived, and Brian emerged from a crowd of passengers, clutching a suitcase. They hugged and walked arm in arm away from the platform. As they chatted about the holidays, Sarah diverted him from the taxi rank and the subway entrance and pushed him through the door of a drab station cafeteria.

"Can it be that urgent?" Brian asked, smiling.

"It can't wait. It's more important than railway cuisine."

They entered the self-service line and emerged with two coffees. Brian chose a corner table. They sat down. Sarah hunted through her purse and withdrew several photocopied sheets of paper, which she unfolded and slapped down on the table. "J. Edwin Cook's *Saints and Relics of East Anglia*," she said. "A limited edition of five hundred copies printed in 1906."

"What does it say?"

"It says what you've been waiting to hear. Pages 45 to 48." She pulled her chair closer to the table and began to quote from the extract. "'Neot: birth year unknown; died in 1088, canonized Saxon of the eleventh century. See also Heighlendh Abbey; Hoyland Abbey; St. Neot's Church, Hoyland; St. Neot's Church, Simpringham; Mission of St. Neot, Burstoft.' Are you ready for his story?"

Brian nodded. "Fire away." He put sugar in his coffee and began to stir it slowly.

"'Neot was an apprentice Saxon monk in the Norman abbey of Heighlendh at the time of Abbot Ingulphus, Latinized from the

Anglo-Saxon Engolf. During his early monastic life, Neot's principal duties were to tend cattle in the wapentake of Elloe. Ingulphus describes him as an ingenuous fellow of greater kinship with his herd than with our Saviour. Rebuilding of the monastery began in the year 1057, and it was found necessary to move the tomb of Waltheof, the holy Mercian abbot, in order to enlarge the transept. This tomb was sacred to the monks of Heighlendh, as well as to the peasants of the surrounding countryside. It had, as Ingulphus recounts, been the scene of many miracles.'"

"What date did you say?" Brian asked. "It could be important."

"In 1057," Sarah replied, "a few years before the Norman Conquest—1066 and all that. Anyway, to continue Cook's account: 'While the tomb was being moved, the seal broke open. Within, to the amazement of all present, the body was found to be sweet-smelling and incorrupt. Ingulphus handled the body and declared, "Ecce odor filii mei." The attending monks were struck with awe. Two days after the tomb had been moved, it was discovered by Audin, a monk who had been on guard over the tomb, that the right hand of the body had been entirely ripped away during the night and was not to be found. Audin denied any knowledge of the sacrilege. Notwithstanding, for dereliction of his duties, Audin was immediately banished from the abbey.'

"'The hand of Waltheof was discovered the following morning in the cell of Neot, who confessed that he had severed it during the night. His motive unclear, the young Neot admitted only a great reverence for Waltheof's holy ring, which he had been unable to pry from the hand. Neot was condemned to death by Gyrth, the prior, but because of his previous good nature, the sentence was commuted by the abbot, and the monk was permitted to perform a penance.'

"'The unhappy soul was confined to a cavity in the east wall of Heighlendh Abbey that he might atone fully for his wrongdoing. The length of the sentence was determined in uncommon fashion. The hand of Waltheof was suspended in the mouth of the niche, and Neot was denied release until the flesh would become sufficiently corrupt as to permit the ring to fall off the finger. Ingulphus prayed nightly for the salvation of Neot's soul.'"

"Prayed," Brian murmured, "on his knees in the chancel."

"'Upon the 212th night of his incarceration, Neot summoned the monks of the abbey with fantastic cries. He described a vision that had come to him in which he had witnessed the figures of St. Guthlac, St. Bartholomew, and Abbot Waltheof arrayed before him in the guise of the heavenly host. A celestial light had shined upon him, commanding him to some holy purpose. Ingulphus was sorely troubled as to the meaning of this vision and ordered Neot released until its import could be determined.'

"'When Neot was removed from the niche, he was a changed man in both body and spirit. His legs were so crippled from the confinement that he could no longer stand upright, nor did he ever walk unaided again. But his spirit was accordingly blessed, and he worked many miracles from that day forth. Following the teachings of Peter Damian, he became a flagellant. His death in 1088 was mourned throughout the county. In 1210, Neot was canonized. And twenty years later, the monastery was dedicated to him. Today, Neot is one of the most famous saints in all of Lincolnshire.'"

Brian stared at his cracked coffee cup and the stained tabletop, his heart beating a tattoo against his ribs. "So what we witnessed in the church was much, much older than Richard Crossly and the dissolution of the abbey. The hand we saw in the niche was a holy Anglo-Saxon relic, the hand of Waltheof."

"It would seem so. But why would it be glowing green?"

Brian continued to stir his coffee, catching the thick liquid in his spoon and then letting it drip slowly away. "Green? That could be chemiluminescence, cold light. The hand had been preserved for years in an airtight tomb. The flesh smelled sweet when the tomb was opened. Putrefaction would set in quickly once it was exposed to air and moisture. Decaying fish emit chemiluminescence. That's what caused the green light."

"And Neot was stuck with it under his nose for 212 days."

Brian laid his spoon in the saucer. He took one sip of the coffee and set the cup down with a grimace. "Bloody lousy coffee."

"The ghost you saw must have been Abbot Ingulphus," said Sarah. "He prayed in front of the altar, and then he walked over and prayed in front of the niche where Neot was incarcerated."

"Yes, and that means that Professor Rix was right about the time period. He'd said it was around the end of the eleventh century. It was 1057 or thereabouts. My audio detector picked up a litany chanted by the abbot for the salvation of Neot's soul. Fantastic." Brian's mind was racing in many directions now. *And the ghost that Sarah saw,* he thought, *was Neot, hobbling away from the transept after his daily flagellation, blood from his shoulders splattering onto her brass rubbing. And the eyes that had stared back at him from the depths of the niche were the eyes of the imprisoned Neot.*

"But why on earth would we tune in, so to speak, to an uneventful evening of prayers in 1057?" Sarah asked him. "Wouldn't you expect to see a Viking massacre or an execution or something equally dramatic? There was nothing exceptional about the events you witnessed."

"Hmm, yes, I can't see any significance to that particular time period. We now know what we saw, but we're no closer to understanding why or how we saw it. And why the misshapen appearance of the ghost and the distorted voice? Abbot Ingulphus wasn't some kind of a freak, was he? A hunchback?"

Sarah shook her head, recalling no mention of anything unusual about his physique or speech. "Poor Neot," she muttered, "shut up in a tiny hole like that for almost a year. No wonder he couldn't walk normally when he came out. What do you do to stop yourself going insane?"

"Not much you can do—meditate, pray, carve on the"—he paused—"on the walls! You carve on the walls! You make a calendar of how many days you've been in there! Remember what Harry saw in the niche? A frieze of vertical lines running around the interior walls. I'll bet you a pound to a penny there are 212 lines!"

A mournful Pakistani waiter sidled up to them and attempted to remove their coffee cups, the implication being that they had occupied the table longer than the value of their purchases warranted.

Brian shielded his undrunk, unwanted coffee with one hand and waved the man away with the other.

"They're trying to get rid of us," Sarah said.

"Don't worry about it."

"So what do you think about Neot's ability to work miracles after his confinement? Do you think that's possible?"

"Miracles? Who knows? In those days, truth was so mixed up with superstition and hearsay. Maybe he was just a good physiotherapist. Maybe he'd always had that innate ability, and his incarceration brought it into the open."

"What about the vision of the holy men? Could that have given him the power?"

"I don't believe in divine intervention. He was probably hallucinating after being shut up for so long. He believed he saw something and turned it into a profitable career."

"You're so cynical, Brian. You never miss a chance to knock religion on the head."

Brian shrugged his shoulders. That was a topic on which they had long since agreed to disagree. Sarah finished her coffee. The lugubrious busboy circled their table like a hawk, his eyes fixed on Sarah's empty cup. "Let's go," Brian said. He dragged his suitcase from under the table, and they walked out of the cafeteria. As they headed for the entrance to the subway, they paused briefly by the station exit to watch the January rain slice across the city. Brian was pensive. "I wonder what London was like on a wet Friday in 1057."

CHAPTER 19

Hoyland Abbey
1088

When the devil visited Neot for the last time, he coiled himself around the tongue of a boy from Burstoft, who had been brought to the abbey to receive unction. The devil drew from the boy's mouth obscenities so execrable that they were unfamiliar to both mother and prior, and a dairyman who happened to be collecting milk churns from the abbey had to be called inside to interpret.

The boy and his mother had walked five miles across the fields for a moment of the prior's time. They had then waited until midafternoon with other afflicted souls behind the chapter house. They were the very last in line, and when their turn came, the woman was so overcome with exhaustion and trepidation that she fell to her knees and could not be drawn to reveal the boy's condition. Only after a little wine and the prior's encouragement could she speak. Her son, she explained, was taken with seizures of the blood when his pulse would race and petechiae erupt on the skin of his face and neck. It was during these seizures that his breath would come rapidly, laced with the devil's abominations. The woman requested a palliative for her son's suffering.

Neot drew the lad aside and spoke to him in soothing tones. He explained that when man fought the devil alone, he would rarely win; but when God and man fought together, they could not be vanquished. If he would accept God as his companion-in-arms, his affliction would be cured. Did he understand? The boy nodded. The prior sent a message to the kitchen to bring twelve *glofa* cakes.

These had been baked from unbolted flour and pulverized foxglove leaves that had been dried inside the kitchen chimney. The foxglove leaves he had picked himself, as legend demanded, with the left hand from the north side of the hedge. He instructed the woman to feed the boy one cake stirred in milk whenever the fit came upon him. She sobbed her thanks and pressed two small coins into the prior's palm, but he would accept no payment, telling her to give alms instead to the poor of her own parish. Clutching the sack of cakes, she led her son away.

His day's work done, Neot prayed briefly and stretched his arms. His fifty years weighed heavily on his shoulders. He called for the novitiate who attended him and asked how long to vespers. One hour, he was told. Though it had often subjected him to great agony, he had not missed any of the seven canonical hours on any day since his blessed vision of the saints thirty-one years earlier. He would not miss vespers that day, though the pain and fatigue were strong.

He gazed at the woman and her son as they hurried away across the sward. It was a wondrous thing that people should hold him in such awe. He told the novitiate that he felt himself the most fortunate man who had ever lived. For an ignorant cow minder to rise to be prior and chief obedientiary in one of the kingdom's greatest houses was unheard of. Indeed, he could have been abbot of Hoyland—for the name of Neot was better known than that of any other cleric in Lincolnshire—had he possessed the temperament for administration and been willing to learn the art of bookkeeping.

But he preferred ministering to the bodies and minds of the people. While he was most famous for his medicinal skills, education was his passion. Having been made so painfully aware of his own ignorance in his youth, he sought now to rectify the misguided view of the day that teaching belonged only in the monastic enclaves and the nurseries of the nobility.

When he had been young, there had been no education for any child of the village. Each was indentured to either the field or the scullery. But by the time of his death, thanks to his own energy, twenty itinerant teachers were employed by the monastery to visit the villages of south Lincolnshire so that each child might receive at least a rudimentary education. He himself took pride in instructing the oblates, those children given up by their parents to become monks.

Through the window of his dayroom, he gazed out over the grounds of the monastery, even as far as the last cell in the dormitory, that dank small room in which he had lived out the first few years of his apprenticeship. From there, he had crept every morning before daybreak to fill the sacristan's warming pan with sea coal; and from there, he had trudged every afternoon to tend the herd or clean the swine runs. And on wet summer nights, that pitiful dwelling on the fringe of the bulrushes had been the first port of call for the vile gases creeping up from the swamp beyond. It had taken him years to realize that the devil was not to be found in swirls of marsh gas, nor was God to be found in sacred relics, for that matter. Those two eternal antagonists contested within the minds of the villagers. And in the wisdom of his advancing years, he became convinced that it was education more than religion that set God on the surest road to victory.

He asked to be carried to the fields for the hour until vespers. The attendant stepped outside and returned with a companion. They inserted poles through the arms of the prior's chair and lifted him waist-high. They carried him down into the fields and set him under his favorite apple tree. He noted the row of new beehives against the abbey wall and the grass neatly scythed around them—a far cry from the ragged appearance of the monastery grounds in Abbot Engolf's time.

The spring sun slanted through the boughs of the apple tree, and a lean wind scattered blossom into the hedgerow. In the lower pasture, a solitary boy prodded a heifer with a stick, reminding him of the days of his own apprenticeship. How was it that he had been able to rise from cow minder to prior? The source of his powers and the fame they had brought him was a puzzle. True, he had suffered and been rewarded by a vision of the three blessed saints. His companions interpreted this as a gift of miraculous powers, the kind that Jesus had used to heal the sick and raise the dead. Whispers had carried such words around the county till a thousand throats had kneaded them into veneration.

But he did not see it that way. He believed that Waltheof had bestowed on him his earthly powers from the realm of the angelic host, but the gift seemed to him more like the gift of patience than of magic—the patience to listen and to learn, the patience to transcend physical pain. He did not have the second sight of men born at twilight; he could not read the witches' signs. He knew that foxglove leaves were remedial for the circulatory system not because of divine revelation but because he had listened to the older monks when he was young and had tried and tested his remedies over many years.

He called to the boy who was minding the cows to come join him. He took delight in any company these days, for mostly, he was friendless. There was no one left of the brothers he had known in his youth. Adin, who had been his best friend and had been banished from the monastery, had not been seen since that day. Tonsdag had done well for himself and became a scribe at Guisborough. Odo had died of the dropsy. His old mentor, Abbot Engolf—or Ingulphus, as the Cluniacs would have it—had passed away ten years ago. There was no one now to whom he could turn for friendship, yet the kind word and the touch on the sleeve meant as much to him as ever.

The boy ran up to the prior and wished him good day. The prior returned the same. He recognized the boy. "You are the son of Adin."

"One of five sons," the boy answered politely. "My name is Algar. It means 'elf spear.'"

"Algar, yes. Did you know that your father was once my best friend? When I was a novitiate. But I have not seen him for thirty years or more."

The boy looked off to the side. "My father will not go to the abbey anymore. He will not go to mass or to any services of the church."

"I know. It is because of me."

The boy paused and then looked the prior full in the face. "Is he damned to hell?"

"I think he is not. I have prayed for his soul ten times over. He will go to heaven." The boy smiled and seemed greatly reassured.

Then Neot related how he, as a young man, had minded the cows in that same field. The boy scoffed, doubting that a prior could have had such humble beginnings. Wryly, the boy asked if he, too, might one day be raised to such eminence. With the grace of God, he might, replied Neot, and with the learning of the schoolmaster.

"But must I attend the school every day?"

"If you will."

"And read the marks that are scratched on paper?"

"Indeed. But hearken to this also: You will find lessons in the fields that cannot be found in books. Nature will teach you things that you will never hear from the mouth of the schoolmaster. Honey can be drawn from the rock, oil from the hardest stone."

"Such words," said the boy, shaking his head.

"Then hold only this thought in your mind, Algar, and the gates of the abbey, even as the gates of heaven, will be open to you: Love in the heart and truth on the lips. I learned that from my mother long before I knew aught of God or devil. It is enough."

"I thank you, sir, and truly will I think on it. I would stay and hear more, but I must roust the cattle home, and you must be away to...to...v-vespers." Neot smiled at the boy's halting pronunciation of the last word. "I learned the names of the hours from the schoolmaster." The boy laughed, and he turned and ran down the hill as fast as his legs would carry him.

Strong young legs like I once had. The spring sun shone cold. A bee crawled across the back of the prior's hand. He watched it nuzzle the hairs on his wrist. Without provocation, it stung him. The pain raced up his arm and tossed him back into his prison cell once again. He saw himself twisting and howling and pounding on stone walls. He saw the hand of Waltheof suspended before his eyes and smelled the odor of rotting flesh. He closed his eyes. The memory faded. He was so very tired.

The shining faces of St. Guthlac, St. Bartholomew, and Abbot Waltheof floated out of the apple blossom and beckoned him to join them. He breathed shallowly. The bell in the church tower began to toll for vespers. Neot turned his face to the sun in the western sky and died.

CHAPTER 20

London
January 2018

One week after his brother returned to the city, John Kenning crossed swords with his supervisor in the hallway of their building as he was arriving for work. Spurred on by lustful visions of postgraduate romance, John made a case for a shortcut in his research, something that might bring forward the date of his departure from academia. His professor listened politely and then rebuffed him. "You can't change course at this late hour, John. You need to buckle down and demonstrate that you possess the kind of brain that can overcome research obstacles, the kind of intellect that is worthy of a doctoral degree. Try an ether extraction of the terpenoid isomers. Forget that other stuff." The professor turned and walked away.

John's stomach flipped. He loathed ether. In fact, he was afraid of it. An ether fire was an ever-present danger in an organic chemistry lab. Once, as an undergraduate, John had seen ether jump out from some tiny crevice in his apparatus with a fierce detonation and a steel-blue flash crisped with vermilion. He had blinked a couple of times and surged into action to prevent something that was already over. A twist of smoke grinned at him and vanished. Wondering how that particular genie could have escaped its bottle, he had inventoried the damage. The chemical that had taken him weeks to prepare was caramelized, but luckily, he got to keep his eyebrows. It was an experience not easily forgotten.

John was well aware that an ether distillation was a rite of passage for the dedicated chemist, something to be lived through and bragged about in the bar at the end of the day. But to dilettantes like himself, who never thought they would ever have to perform a dangerous procedure by themselves, it was a bowel-twisting ordeal calling for the dexterity of bomb disposal. But at least nitroglycerin stayed in one place; it didn't creep out of its container and wander off in search of ignition like ether did. John truly loathed the stuff.

He repaired reluctantly to his lab and began to assemble a distillation column while the treacherous bottle of diethyl ether lurked in an adjacent fume hood. Another graduate student was synthesizing citronellol, which filled the laboratory with the fragrance of geranium, but John sensed nothing pleasant. The pent-up anger from his recent confrontation oozed out in audible curses and complaints. His fingers had a tremor that made assembling glassware difficult.

Trapped in a tunnel of physical danger and emotional torment with nothing but the dim candle of graduation at the end of it, John could suddenly find nothing right with the world. Even his long hair, which had seemed so stylish at a nurse's party the previous evening, now seemed merely an affectation in the cold mirror of the distillation flask.

As he filled the water bath, he wondered why on earth he allowed himself to be manipulated by people like his brother and his professor. Had he no backbone? Could he not determine his own path through life? What the hell was it that made him so servile? He dragged a Claisen still head off a shelf, connected it to the slender condenser, and attached rubber hoses to each end of the condenser. One hose he clamped to the faucet; the other he placed in the sink. He moved like an automaton. "Damn the buggers," he said.

He tried to concentrate, but soon, that seductive genie inside his head started up again, advising him to stop here and now and walk directly to the pub and ask the barmaid to run away with him. No certificate of academic prowess was worth this agony, the voice said, but all the while, his fingers tightened clamps and greased joints. He pulled his safety goggles out of a drawer and tossed them on the benchtop so he wouldn't forget. His cell phone rang. "Jesus Christ!" John moaned. He answered it.

"John, this is Brian. Great news!" Brian recounted the essence of Sarah's revelation about St. Neot and then requested a favor. "I was wondering if you could go over to Rix's office and retrieve the tape. I'd like to listen to it again and see if I can follow his explanation."

"I'm busy, Brian. I'm about to start an ether extraction. Can't you go?"

"I've got a lecture to give. And I'm off to Manchester tonight. Please?"

John's inner malcontent observed that the ordeal by ether could easily be postponed. "All right. I'll go over there now and do the experiment this afternoon."

"Thanks a lot, John. I owe you one. If Rix is in, ask him how on earth he was able to turn water into wine. You remember how unintelligible the tape sounded to us."

"Okay."

*****

John walked over to the Linguistics Department before lunch and entered Rix's outer office with a keen regret that Brian was not with him to blunt the professor's sarcasm. "Could I have a word with Professor Rix please?" John offered up to the secretary's saccharine smile. "If it's convenient."

"What name shall I say?"

"John Kenning." A manicured fingernail poked the intercom. John's name was whispered into the machine, and after a brief delay, he was cleared for entry. The secretary pointed to the inner sanctum. He knocked on the door.

"Come!"

John stepped into a spacious office, the walls of which were lined from floor to ceiling with bookshelves that sagged under the weight of the literary detritus of forty years of research. Professor Rix was scarcely visible. He was seated at a desk by the window with a red pen in his hand, proofreading the text of his latest journal article. His eyes scanned backward and forward furiously while his pen traversed a narrow gorge between two cliffs of books and journals. His elbows were pressed against his ribs. There was simply no room for them on the desk.

"Yes?" he drawled, making no effort to slow the proofreading.

"I've come to pick up the tape."

Rix stopped reading and looked up at John. "Ah, yes, the brother. It's over on the coffee table." He resumed work for a moment then put down his pen and stared across the room. "Fascinating, that recording. A delight, in fact, and a very professional job. I'd like to know how it was made, but I'm sure it's none of my business. I'd swear Mooney had a hand in it or Norman Glass at Oxford. Still, eleventh century, to be sure."

"It's 1057."

"Really? Earlier than I would have expected, but perhaps—hey, wait a minute. You can't possibly justify that degree of accuracy! I thought scientists were renowned for their attention to such matters. Huh! Just goes to show."

John stood stiffly by the door. "Well, that's what my brother says."

"Turn of the eleventh and twelfth centuries. Take my word for it." Rix shuffled the papers in front of him and squared his jaw in preparation for resuming work. John didn't move. "Something else?"

"There is one thing. We were wondering how you managed to make sense of the recording. You thought it was a hoax when you first heard it. Remember?"

The professor cleared his throat and looked solemnly at John. It was the first time he had shared a moment of real human contact with any of them. His lips were tight and slightly curled at one corner. The incipient words were clearly unfamiliar to him. "I made a mistake the first time."

"A mistake?" John had not intended emphasis, but the professor bristled.

"The same one you all made, I suspect."

"What mistake was that?"

Rix leaned back in his chair and pinched his nostrils. A meaningful silence hung in the air. At last, Rix decided that he could risk looking foolish on this one occasion and replied, "I was listening to the tape backward."

"What?"

"Somehow, the tape had gotten wound the wrong way. Another of your mistakes, in all probability. I was listening to it backward the first time. I realized the problem later in the day, rewound the tape, and everything was fine. The tape is in the correct configuration now. It just needed a trained ear." John could make no sense of this disclosure. He had helped Harry unload the tape in the church and mount it on the recorder in the studio. How could such a mistake have occurred?

"Will there be anything else? This article, you know."

"Sorry. I was miles away. Do you think I could just listen to the tape on your recorder before I go? It won't take a moment."

"If you must." John walked over to the recorder, which was on a coffee table at the far end of the room. He mounted the tape, switched it on, and turned up the volume. Nothing. He fast-forwarded a short way and listened again. Nothing. "It's at the end of the tape," Professor Rix informed him. John fast-forwarded till he was close to the end of the tape and hit the play button, and there it was, finally, unmistakably, the faint sounds of a monastic chant crackling across the centuries, the rusty rhythms of Abbot Ingulphus praying for the soul of Neot. John understood none of the words but knew well the significance of their imprint on tape. "And now I really must get on," Rix complained, one hand waving in the air.

John swept up the tape and walked out of the office quickly, bowing his thanks. He left the building in a daze and retraced the journey to his laboratory, trying desperately to understand what this revelation meant. He began by recalling the handling of the tape in the church—how Harry had unwrapped a fresh spool and mounted it on the machine and how the tape had looked when mounted. He could recall everything—how much tape had been wound on each spool, how the tapes had been removed in the church, and how they had been stored and remounted in the lab. He cast his memory back to the studio, where he had watched Harry play and replay that unintelligible drone. He recalled the positioning of the labels on each spool. By the time he reached the subway entrance, he was convinced that there had been no mistake. The tape had not been loaded backward. The sound must have been recorded backward at the source.

Did that mean that Ingulphus was chanting backward? Was that even plausible? He vaguely remembered reading something about the backward recitation of holy words. Wasn't that what the devil worshippers did? But that just meant reciting words in reverse order; nobody could speak individual words backward, surely. He thought about it as he walked, his brain in turmoil. If the sound was recorded backward and the monk wasn't reciting backward, then the events they witnessed must have happened backward, in reverse time.

He recalled his impressions of the ghost of Ingulphus as it crossed the aisle of the church and swerved toward him. *Not walking forward,* he thought, *but walking backward. Not rising up from the floor but kneeling down on it. Not walking toward the niche but walking away from it.* He tried to recollect the distorted appearance of the phantom. *If walking backward, not forward, then it was not his face but the back of his head, not his chin but the nape of the neck.* The misshapen head restructured itself in his mind. *Not staring up at the roof but bowing the head in prayer. Not a protruding chest but normal shoulder blades.* The malformed torso rearranged itself. That was the answer!

He entered the building and took the stairs two at a time. He called Brian but found that he had left for lunch. After placing the tape in his desk drawer, he walked three times around the laboratory, marshaling the evidence a final time. He could reach no other conclusion but that the ghostly events they had witnessed had been happening in reverse time. He was stunned by the implausibility of this, the only logical explanation.

He returned to the bench and reviewed his morning's handiwork. Everything seemed to be in order, and procrastination had been exhausted. He dissolved his sample in ether and transferred it to the distillation flask, which he placed in the bath and connected to the still head. He switched on the heating mantle, adjusted the thermostat, and placed an acetate sheet between himself and the apparatus for protection. He turned on the cooling water and put on his goggles.

He was five feet away, hunting for his notebook, when the fire began. A sheet of flame appeared above the benchtop for just an instant. Then it split in two, sending an orange tongue in the direction of a nearby hot plate and an incandescent flash toward the distillation column. When the flash reached the glassware, it formed a ring of cobalt flame that, for a brief moment, circled the leaky joint between the still head and the condenser.

It seemed to John that he saw first the single sheet of flame and then the two diverging forks of fire, but before they registered in his mind as distinct events, the flask burst asunder, and the whole apparatus was engulfed in a single conflagration. The sound of detonation reached his ears an instant later, and at some juncture, his nose detected the sickly sweet smell of ether underlying the perfumes of geranium.

He ran for the fire extinguisher and put out the fire before it could sneak into the fume hood and ignite the full bottle of ether. Slowly he regained his composure. He had been lucky even though his precious terpenoid was lost. He sat down on a stool, breathing hard. He saw again the two flames racing in opposite directions from their unified beginning, and something brought the tape recording back into his mind. "Two thousand and seventeen running forward. Ten hundred and fifty-seven running backward," he said out loud. "But forward and backward from what?"

CHAPTER 21

London
January 2018

John's discovery that time was running backward in the ghostly world of Neot and Ingulphus provided the key to unlock a remarkable and previously unsuspected truth about the workings of time. Brian summoned John to his apartment barely three days after John's interpretation of Professor Rix's error of the tape had been disclosed to him. Brian's living room was cold when John entered. The shades were drawn, and the lights were low. The only sound was a vague but insistent throbbing of rock music from a neighboring apartment. The two brothers sat opposite each other in worn leather armchairs. Brian began the discussion softly, almost seductively. "How do you view the concept of time, John? How do you visualize it?"

"What? Time? I don't know. By association with events, I suppose."

"You see it as a tapestry with all the events of your life up to now recorded on it in chronological order?"

"I suppose so. What are you getting at?"

"But can you also imagine events outside your own experience? Do you have any reason to doubt, for example, that there existed a period of time in June of 1815 during which the Battle of Waterloo was fought?"

"Of course not."

"There's no mind now in existence that witnessed it firsthand. No one can corroborate it."

"That doesn't matter. I know it happened."

"Okay. And what about the future? Can the human mind also perceive future times to some extent? Though the event is inaccessible to the eye today, the rising of the sun tomorrow morning can be perceived by the human mind, can it not? And by the day after tomorrow, this future event will have gelled into a past event no different from the Battle of Waterloo. Even if tomorrow's sunrise should fail to occur, God forbid, one would be unwise to doubt the existence of the period of future time that it failed to occupy."

"It's a bit more of a stretch, but yes, it's essentially the same thing."

"So time can be thought of as a very long tapestry and a very wide tapestry writ with the past and future events of all human lives."

"That's pretty much the picture that comes into my mind. In fact, it's an extremely long tapestry, maybe infinitely long, stretching from the beginning of the universe to the end, enfolding all human life and much more."

"Right. Okay. But can't we also think of time in another way? It seems to me that the human mind also perceives time as an endless series of nows that descend upon it from a veiled future and depart from it into a naked past instantly. Though we may occasionally think we can discern discrete nows—the first glimpse of a Van Gogh, say, or the pain of a pinprick—our experience surely suggests that now is merely an infinitesimally small dam between the future and the past as the one streams remorselessly into the other. Ever thought of it that way?"

"Not really, but it makes some sense."

"I've been reading some of Einstein's works, John. He once wrote this: 'The sense experiences seem to form a series, namely the time series indicated by earlier and later. The experience series is thought of as a one-dimensional continuum.'"

"Yes, time sometimes does seem to work that way. I know what you mean—or what Einstein meant."

"Einstein is saying that time has no discrete states, not even nows. But does it have to be that way? Think about the duration of now. Couldn't we consider the macroscopic events of our experience to be progressively subdivided until a minimum discernible is reached? Can we not imagine an indivisible quantum of time? I've been absorbed by this idea for several days. As far as I can see, the philosophical problems posed by this notion are no greater than those posed by the energy quantum. The only reason that a time quantum hasn't been postulated before now is that there's never been a shred of evidence to suggest that time is anything but a continuum."

"And you think you know better? You think we have evidence that time is not a continuum?"

"I do." Brian said it so matter-of-factly. The two words flowed slowly and smoothly out of his mouth and seemed to sink through the cold air of the shuttered room and spread themselves across the threadbare carpet. After a moment, he repeated himself. "Yes, John, I do. Think about quantum mechanics for a minute. Think back to your physical chemistry textbooks. What if time were quantized, came in very small packets? If that were true, it would open up possibilities for interaction between different time periods."

"Ways in which we might see ghosts from other time periods."

"Right. First and foremost, our research suggests that past events are not inaccessible to the conscious observer. And by extension, neither are future events, though the evidence for that is more tenuous at present. I believe that the phenomenon by which past and future events become accessible has long been known to mankind, but it has always been rejected by conventional science—on spurious grounds, in my opinion. The phenomenon I'm talking about is the appearance of ghosts. The explanation of the appearance of ghosts requires, I believe, a quantized view of time."

"Go on."

"It all started to come together for me when you said that time appeared to be going backward in 1057. That's the key. Throughout history, ghosts have been associated with dead people and ancient places, and I think that ghosts are, indeed, remnants of past events. In fact, I think that an empirical theory of the manifestation of ghosts implies the existence of a quantized structure of time and suggests that the temporal quantum is as much a molecular phenomenon as its energy analog.

"Just as the energy quantum was discovered not by an ad hoc philosophical investigation but as an explanation of observed physical effects, so the concept of the time quantum seems to be the most appropriate construct to explain our experimental observations. Indeed, it seems to me that, as with the energy quantum, it's at the molecular level that the hypothesis of the time quantum is on firmest ground."

"I need a simple example, Brian."

Brian leaned back in his armchair. He tapped the knuckle of his right thumb against his lower lip, searching for a way to illustrate his idea. Then he got up and walked to the window and drew the drapes tight together, further enclosing them from the world, shielding them from Eddington's arrows. He could not, however, exclude the persistent bass rhythm that reverberated through the wall like some divine metronome meant to frustrate his attempt to conquer time. He returned via his desk, bringing with him a pad of paper and a pencil. He sat down and scribbled some timelines and energy level diagrams, then he drew several pictures of trees positioned in a row along a straight line.

"Okay, John. Consider, if you will, a tree. Through eons of time, there are no molecules of this particular tree in existence. It is correlated with a future time period. Nevertheless, just as in quantum field theory, a vacuum has potentialities for the creation of elementary particles, so certain locations in space have temporal potentialities for occupation by molecules of the tree. Comes the planter, and in due course, the tree exists in a particular frame of time and space. Comes the woodcutter, and the tree is gone forever. At different times, therefore, there is no tree, tree, and no tree again in a particular set of spatial coordinates. The molecules of the tree exist in one particular set of time coordinates and no others."

"The tapestry of time has a picture of a tree on it in one particular swatch. Nowhere else."

"If you like, but must this inevitably be the case? Think about the energy of a molecule, John. A molecule possesses many discrete energy states, corresponding to rotational, vibrational, and electronic quanta. The molecule will remain in its lowest or ground state in the absence of external stimulus. But if the correct stimulus is applied, the molecule can make transitions to states of higher energy for short periods of time prior to relaxation back to the ground state. In other words, the normal energy state of a molecule can be perturbed such that it transfers to another energy state in accordance with strict quantum mechanical selection rules."

"That much I know."

"I'm suggesting that the time at which a molecule exists is a similar property to the energy it possesses. Normally, a molecule exists in its ground temporal state, in the absence of external influence—the now state, if you will. Under the correct stimulus, however, a brief transition can be made to another temporal state, forming a ghost molecule in that other state. In aggregate, a complete ghost object may be formed in the alternate time frame."

"Are you saying that molecules can jump into another time frame?"

"That's right. No problems are then encountered with the notion of ghosts moving through solid objects. The ghost molecules materialize and dematerialize in interstitial locations within real objects in the other time frame. Presumably, the intrusive molecules are prohibited by selection rules from materializing in a spatial location that's already occupied. The problem of one molecular array moving through another is avoided. Moreover, the transitions must be completely reversible to prevent permanent transfer of material from one time frame to the other. Do you see?"

"I'm beginning to." The rock music abruptly ceased. The brothers looked up at each other as the sudden silence rang in the air around them, a silence that seemed like the roar of nows streaming over the dam of time. John's nerves were shaky, so he went to the kitchen to get a glass of water. When he returned, he asked Brian, "But you need energy to move molecules from one quantum state to another. What do you think causes molecules to move from one temporal state to another?"

"I think the energy necessary to transfer molecules from one time frame to another is obtained in an unusual way. The sensitive subjects in whose presence the phenomenon occurs—particularly,

Karen Butler and Dan Patzner—appear to generate an energy field of approximately three megacycles per second over a range of fifty meters or so. Remember what I told you about the observations of that Aussie scientist Wilkinson in the CIU lab? I think this special energy field induces thermal energy to be extracted from the air and utilized to promote the molecular transfer between temporal states. You measured a temperature drop of seven degrees in the church the night the ghost appeared, remember?"

"You're right, I did. That makes sense. Do you have any thoughts about how many molecules make the leap at any given time?"

"I looked again at the spectrum I took in the church and made a rough calculation of the transition probability by calculating the infrared reflectance properties of the ghost. I estimate that the population of ghost molecules in the alternate time frame is approximately 10^{-7}. That is to say, approximately one ten-millionth of the molecules are in the alternate temporal state at any given instant. Although this number may seem too low for the object to be visible, it's possible that the random materialization leads to some kind of an ordered, pseudo-crystalline structure for the ghost object, which would enhance its reflective properties. That would be consistent with our observation that the ghost is a translucent, transparent object."

"A kind of gaseous prism."

"That's a good way to put it. I think we've been observing a process of temporal transitions between two relatively insignificant time frames, 2017 and 1057." He grabbed his pencil and wrote t (sub n) = 2017 next to the lower temporal state on his diagram and t (sub −n) = 1057 against the upper one. "And if time is moving forward in the present, 2017, and backward in the alternate state, 1057, then it seems to me that these must be mirrorlike, temporal quantum states split out from a base state." He wrote t (sub b) in between the other two states.

"To preserve symmetry, just like energy transitions, what would that base state be?"

Brian handed John the pencil and paper. "Write down the number 2017, and underneath it, write 1057."

"Okay. Now what?"

"Add them up, and divide by 2. What answer do you get?"

"Er, 1537. That's the midpoint in time between them. Why is that year familiar to me, 1537?"

"You've forgotten what Sarah told us in the van. That was the precise year in which the violent dissolution of Hoyland Abbey took place." He took back the pencil and paper and amended his previous note to read $t_b = 1537$.

"That's right!"

"Something incredible must have happened in 1537—almost certainly something to do with the destruction of the abbey—that ripped up the fabric of time and created virtual temporal states cascading away from it into both the past and the future: time moving forward in our world and backward in Neot's world to preserve symmetry. That enabled us in 2017 to link up with the world of 1057, the world of Neot and Ingulphus. A tiny fraction of the molecules that rightfully belonged in Anglo-Saxon times was transferred to our time frame. The Karen Butlers and Aunt Pollys of this world—and I suppose my Sarah too—have the ability to bring about this molecular transference. Other people have been able to do it throughout history. It could explain all so-called supernatural occurrences."

"My god, Brian."

"It's this zeta field that fuels the phenomenon." Brian scrawled the term ζ-*field* in between the temporal states and circled it several times. "And I think it might also be possible to bring about molecular transitions between our present time frame and the base state of 1537. The configuration of the energy field may well be different, but I have reason to think that, if the correct conditions are achieved, a stronger linkage—analogous to a molecular resonance—might be created, leading to a higher population of the Tudor molecules in our present time frame." This time, he wrote down $t_n \Leftrightarrow t_b$. "It might be possible in this way to probe the nature of the event in 1537 that caused all this to happen."

"Brian, this is truly amazing. Did you think it all out yourself?"

"I've been alone here for three days straight, thinking of nothing else." He looked John in the eye. "I think I might have discovered one of the most important laws of matter. Can you believe that?"

Brian gave a short, sharp laugh—almost hysterical, John thought—then lapsed into silence and stared at the floor.

John was overwhelmed by what he had heard. Everything Brian had told him made sense and would explain what they had witnessed, but whether it was true or not, he couldn't say. It was certainly an impressive tour de force by his brother to construct such a theory. John looked hard at Brian. Was he really a genius? Was it possible that he had a brother destined for greatness? Or was Brian perhaps just dangerously self-deluded, inching blindfold toward the end of a plank above shark-infested waters? John couldn't tell. Whichever it was, it was clear that events had returned them to the world of the mysterious Richard Crossly.

CHAPTER 22

Tattershall Castle
1537

Tattershall Castle reared up out of the western edge of the Lincolnshire fens like some fabulous beast. Built in the 1430s by Ralph Cromwell, Lord Treasurer of England, it emulated the whimsical French castles of that period, which were illustrated so finely in the book *Très Riches Heures du Duc de Berry*. Its checkerboard brickwork was rouged with ocher and ornamented with mottoes and rebuses, and each of its many turrets was capped by a fussy little spire made of wood wrapped in lead. Like a unicorn in a farmyard, it did not belong among the severe stone dwellings that dotted the fields around it. Six-storied, the tallest building for twenty miles around, the Great Tower of Tattershall Castle kept an authoritarian, if somewhat wall-eyed, watch on the superstition and asceticism that lay between it and the sea.

In 1536, the monasteries of Lincolnshire and the supporting peasantry had led a rebellion—the so-called Lincolnshire Rising that presaged the wider Pilgrimage of Grace—against King Henry's reformation of the church, and Tattershall Castle had been pressed into service as a base of operations against the Catholic rebels. Consequently, as a great wind flogged the castle walls one chilly spring evening of the following year, several high-ranking agents of the king waited within for an assignment from the king's architect of suppression, Thomas Cromwell, unrelated to the family that had built the castle a hundred years before, insofar as anyone knew.

Charles Brandon, Duke of Suffolk, stretched his legs toward the immense fire of split oak logs in the hearth and looked about him at his noble companions. In April of that year, he had been granted ownership of the castle by King Henry in tail-male, along with the surrounding lands and a ferry across the River Witham, as advance payment for subduing the Lincolnshire Rising and continuing the closure of local monasteries. He was fifty-three years old and a military leader and courtier of high renown. Square-jawed, corpulent, and full-bearded, he appraised his colleagues, who, thanks to his best Trent ale, were now well in their cups and low in ribaldry.

On the other side of the hearth, in mirror image to Brandon, sat Sir Richard Rich, chancellor of the Court of Augmentations, present only to sign the warrant for their impending actions and wishing to be gone in haste. Next to Rich, on a solid oak bench, sat Sir Richard Cecil—otherwise Master of Burghley—and his seventeen-year-old son William Cecil, who would later become the renowned Lord Burghley. Sir Richard had nominated his teenage son to command the force that he would contribute from his own estates and villages. Arrayed between Brandon and the Burghleys in a tight semicircle of armchairs were Edward Fiennes de Clinton, later to become the first Earl of Lincoln; Sir Christopher Willoughby; and Richard Crossly, the man appointed by Charles Brandon as suppressor-in-chief for Lincolnshire. All told, these seven men were arguably the most influential persons in the county at that particular moment.

All but one wore the traditional finery of Tudor nobles: doublets with flounced sleeves, bonnets and hose, and tunics draped over the shoulder. Their clothes were dyed bright shades of wine red, saffron, and Lincoln green, and glass beads were hand sewn upon them for ornamentation. Only Richard Crossly was dressed simply—in the buff-colored jacket of the English common soldier stitched with cord down the front and bearing the plain red cross of St. George on the chest. Crossly was different from his companions in more ways than dress. He was stockier and more muscular than they with tight black curls atop the jack's protective collar. He also sat apart from the others, drinking more and laughing less—perhaps because he was the only one present of common birth, perhaps because he was the bloody hands of their corporate body. Of the seven, he alone appeared ready for action.

The group was ensconced in the second-floor audience chamber of the Great Tower of Tattershall Castle, awaiting word from the king. None of them, least of all Crossly, had any enthusiasm for the coming excursion against the upstart monks and peasants. By the fire, it was warm and jovial; but by the shuttered, ill-fitting windows, the draperies billowed outward, and the wainscoting groaned. In the dank high corners of the room, moss grew. Out on the fens, death lurked.

The only sounds for some time were the spitting of logs in the hearth and the thrashing of flames in the torchères. Then wishing to break the silence with an inoffensive remark, Willoughby asked of Rich, "How doth the queen, Sir Richard? She is several months with child, is she not?"

"Queen Jane is in good health, I believe," Sir Richard Rich replied. "She leads a quiet life these days. Only the royal physicians and the best of midwives attend her. She must have quails to eat every day, and the king has them sent from Calais."

"The king dotes on her, I have heard."

"Like the rarest jewel," Rich responded. "Though with the plague thick in London at present, few may see her."

"'Tis well for the country and for all our heads that Jane is with child," Charles Brandon interjected, reminding them of the fickleness of the king's heart and the frailty of their own necks. To a man, the group affirmed the truth of the remark and examined the depths of their ale mugs.

Emboldened, Sir Richard Cecil inquired of the Duke of Suffolk, "Wert thou in London last June when their marriage was proclaimed, my lord?"

"I was indeed, and what a time it was! What celebrations! The flags and the bunting and the petticoats waving in the street were a sight to behold. I myself was at the steelyard when the Hanseatic merchants lit a hundred torches and passed free ale and wine to the citizenry. Bonfires burned through the night at every street corner. And the dancing! Oh, that a king might marry every day!" He immediately regretted the last remark, as it reminded them all of the fates of Katherine of Aragon and Anne Boleyn.

"They say the pickpockets and thieves were thicker than lice that day, being assured of the king's pardon on his wedding day. 'Tis true?"

"Verily. Many a townsman awoke in the gutter with a hammering head and no purse."

"E'en so, a day that will live in the heart a lifetime." The rural nobles nodded and wished they had been there.

Crossly stirred. "Sir Richard, where is Cromwell's man, dost thou think?"

"He will be here anon. The stormy weather slows him."

"Whatever business be set for us, I would as soon be on it. I have little taste for revelry this night and none for quarreling with monks the morrow. I would rather be in my four-poster at Ketteringham Lodge, if the messenger has taken to some tavern cot."

"Patience, Crossly. The messenger will come. This rebellion that thy county folk have undertaken is a chancre on the king's manhood. It must be cut out well and deep even if some healthy flesh be excised along with it. Thou surely knowest the probity of it." Crossly agreed, though with a tone so bitter that none present could say if he spoke true.

At the age of thirty-two, Richard Crossly was a self-made man of a self-made family. His father had amassed land and wealth by dint of service to the crown, both as chief quartermaster of the army and as political adviser to the court. The elder Crossly had been rewarded with his own coat of arms and an open invitation to counsel the king at his pleasure. Richard had inherited all but the invitation yet took no profit from any of it, preferring to seek his own path through life in the army. However, with no foreign campaigns since the siege of Boulogne before he was born, he had been forced to settle for idle skirmishes with the Scots on the Northumberland border.

Having served there with distinction, he was now appointed to lead the king's forces against farmers and shopkeepers and monks of all people! It was a dispiriting assignment for an ambitious young man, and a level of frustration had crept into his life of late. The empty gossip of the court only made his sword hand itch.

Crossly turned suddenly and said to young William Cecil, "Sirrah, though this company be cordial, our men below see nothing of firelight. What say we attend our charges?"

The young man turned to look at his father, who nodded, and then turned back to Crossly. "By all means. Lead on, Crossly," he said, rising.

The two men walked to the door and descended the stone staircase that spiraled inside the corner turret. In the ground-floor parlor, in parody of their masters, the lower-ranking officers sat around a table with members of Brandon's household. The two men proceeded on down the staircase and toward the basement of the Great Tower, where the common soldiers were lodged.

"William, a word, if I may make so bold," Crossly said as they descended. "A word thy father might speak if he were here with us. If thou wilt, thou mayest drink all night with yon jack-puddings upstairs and earn naught but a sore head for breakfast. And thou mayest also, if it pleases thee, let slip the tittle-tattle heard at court and garner death or fame for thy intrigue—I know not which. But if thou art inclined to be a soldier, take heed. On the field, thou wilt see no hair of the Duke of Suffolk or Sir Richard Rich. Only the white-coats will be there to guard thy back. Pray they think well of thee then. Strive now to earn their fealty."

"I know my duty to my men, I believe," William said haughtily but with the offhand air of a man who had learned the words but had no experience of the deed.

They reached the basement, which was crowded with soldiers. Some talked in low tones conspiratorially. Many slept on sacks of grain. A scarred man threw dice onto an upturned fruit basket while others watched the roll. There were no windows and no fireplaces, and the air was rank. The largest group of soldiers circled an enormous barrel of beer, though none of them seemed merry. No one paid any attention to the arrival of their commanders.

"How many doth thy father bring?" Crossly asked William, surveying the men.

"He could spare only a company of billmen and twenty Landsknecht pike."

"No bows or arquebuses?"

"He felt they would not be needed against peasants."

"Armor?"

"Only jacks."

"Thou hast not seen a Lincolnshire poacher loose an arrow. Even Sir Edward Stanley's archers would be jealous."

"It will not come to that, I am certain." Crossly folded his arms across his chest, sizing the worth of the men. "And what doth the county provide?" William asked.

"From Clinton, a company—half billmen, half bowmen. Willoughby, precious few."

"Horsemen?"

"None save thy retainers and mine and a few squires in search of the king's favor."

"In sum?"

"Not three hundred men." They mused on that figure and tried to reckon the size of the opposition. Crossly shouted to one of the men seated around the fruit basket, "What thinkest thou of the rebels, white-coat?"

"Pope-holy all of them," the man returned. "I will gladly smite their costards for the king." The two smiled at each other in the common bond of soldiery, and a ripple of laughter spread around the room.

"And what thinkest thou of the rebels, Crossly?" William Cecil turned and asked.

"Of their cause, I think not at all. Their religion is their own affair, though for me, I would as soon put Peter's pence back in the pockets of honest Englishmen. As for their worth as men, I hold them no worse than the king, who wants only an apple and a fair wench to dally with. Thou hast thy tales of the king's jesting, and I have mine. I have heard it said that—while still married to Queen Anne, mark thee—he spied a young girl while riding near Eltham, sprang off his horse forthwith, and ravished her under a tree while his retainers played at shuttlecock. And she not fifteen years of age, they say.

"Is such a man a better judge of paradise than the Abbot of Whalley Abbey whose bowels he put out, a better judge than More and Fisher? Those are my thoughts on this bad business. E'en so, do I serve the king honorably." William at once felt ashamed of his prattle in the audience chamber. Crossly's talk was treason, but it registered with him as bravery and conviction.

The door to the stairwell opened, and Sir Richard Rich entered in the company of a dirty man in leather leggings and a skullcap. The four converged, and a half circle of soldiers gathered at a respectful distance to learn their fate. Rich held out a sheaf of papers, the first page of which was emblazoned with a seal of red wax, from which hung a wide red ribbon. "Word hath come," he said. "It is to be Hoyland. My secretary hath inscribed the name of the abbey in the warrant. The rest is common to all. By my signature, the plan hath become an order of the Court of Augmentations."

Crossly took the papers from Rich but looked at neither. Rather, he stared across the room at a recumbent soldier, twitching in his sleep, as if he already fought the battle of tomorrow. *We are but puppeteers banging together the heads of innocent Englishmen,* Crossly thought. *They quarrel only in our script.*

Seeing that Crossly did not examine the warrant, Rich proceeded to give him a synopsis of its contents: "All gold, silver, and jewels to be expropriated and carried with Burghley's men to the Tower of London. The roof of the abbey to be burned, and the lead therefrom melted down and carried by the same to the Tower of London. The abbot Gervase to be apprehended and delivered by the same to Newgate Prison. Any landowner resisting the king's warrant to be summoned to the next assizes at Lincoln Castle to argue against confiscation of his land. Any commoner resisting the king's warrant to serve sixty days in gaol.

"The monks of Hoyland to be turned out of the abbey grounds with whatever possessions they can carry, their lodgings burned, and the gates of the abbey chained. Clinton's men to remain on guard for thirty days. A full report with a listing of the names of the dead and the valuables expropriated to be presented by thy good self before the Court of Augmentations within thirty days. Is the warrant plain?"

"It is plain," Crossly replied. "We march at dawn. If the rebel force is strong when we reach Hoyland, we will camp the night and engage them the next day. If the rebels disperse—as is my belief and my earnest wish—thou wilt see the conflagration from the top of the Great Tower the morrow night."

"Alas not, sirrah. My secretary and I depart for Nottingham by noon." Crossly transferred his gaze from the sleeping soldier on the far side of the room to the smirk on Sir Richard's face. Their eyes fought a brief battle for supremacy, then Rich turned away, and he and the messenger departed.

"What opposition may we expect?" William asked.

"Thou canst be certain," Crossly replied, "that word already races ahead that the king marches on Hoyland Abbey. Many of the county and not a few in this room think little of the king's policies. Lincolnshire and Norfolk gentlemen have hunted for years with the abbot and supped his fine Cluny wines. They see nothing righteous in King Henry's break with Rome. Whether they will fight, I do not know. The rabble may bully the trained bands, but I doubt they have the stomach to fight regular soldiers. We shall see."

"Abbot Gervase is a powerful man?"

"I knew him years ago. My father, my brother, and I took sacrament at the abbey each Sunday. He is a holy man with a will of iron. Rich and poor alike look to him for salvation and the surety of eternal life. He will protect his church, and his followers will protect him. In many ways, he is a formidable foe."

"I saw a shadow cross thy face when Sir Richard named the quarry. I think thou hast some special love for the place."

"Hoyland Abbey hath been the spiritual home of my family since before the Crusades. At this very moment, it holds my father's heritage of jewels. His prized possession, an artifact known as the Sphere of the Planets, sits in a glass case by the altar. My god, William, it was given to him by the king of France! It will turn my stomach to have to deliver it to King Henry under this warrant. I pray the monks see fit to magic the Sphere away before we arrive."

"I see bitter work ahead for thee, Richard. I will try to sweeten the lemons."

"Stay close to me the morrow. I would not have thee sacrificed for naught." Crossly touched him on the shoulder then ushered him back up to the audience chamber. Barely ten minutes thereafter, a chambermaid carried ale to her brother, who was standing watch in the guardhouse on the Middle Ward. He, in turn, strolled to the outer moat and passed time with a carter delivering rations to the granary. Thus, scarcely one hour after the king's messenger had brought the word into Tattershall Castle of the march on Hoyland Abbey, that same word left the castle and was carried on horseback eastward into the fenlands.

CHAPTER 23

London
February 2018

To test the waters, Brian decided to place a short article about his
theory in an esoteric periodical called the *Journal of Paranormal
Phenomena*. He expected an enthusiastic response, but as momentous as his discovery seemed to the group, it caused little impact on
the outside world. Rather recklessly, he appended his email address,
and a slow trickle of messages from readers of the journal was the
only sign of recognition in the weeks following publication. Some
of them offered supporting evidence, some contradictory. A few
passionate eccentrics volunteered theories of their own. There was
nothing sufficiently convincing to influence the hypothesis one way
or another. The tabloids didn't pick up on the article. Though had a
smell of it wafted the way of Jack Stephens, he would've been on the
phone to a national daily at once.

One message, however, caught Brian's attention. It was from
a lady who said she had experienced something similar and would
be willing to participate in further investigations. She sounded sincere. Her offer was attractive to Brian, because he was already plan-
ning a follow-up set of experiments to probe the events of 1537. He
called her, and they agreed to meet at a café on Brompton Road one
Saturday afternoon in the middle of February.

The volunteer was a Scottish lady, hailing originally from a
crofter's cottage on the Isle of Mull, though lately residing in a small
flat off Fulham Road. Her name was Florence McDaniel Gibson,
the last to bear the name of the Gibsons of Mull, for she was the
only child of a withered branch of the family tree and in her late

fifties. Physically, she was a substantial person—not fat, as near as Brian could tell, and not muscular, just substantial. She wore several layers of woolen cardigans and an austere tweed jacket, all of which contributed to the impression of bulk. Her fair, slightly reddish hair curled outward from each side of her head like the ringlets atop a Greek pillar.

Florrie Gibson's qualifications for joining the team rested on an experience she once had on the Hebridean island of Iona. In the company of other ladies from Mull, she had taken a trip to the Iona Community, a religious order established to follow the teachings of St. Columba. On the first evening of her stay there, Florrie had spent an hour in prayer with a friend in the Church of St. Mary, part of the island's abbey.

According to her account, after an hour or so, the church grew "colder than a butt hoop on Boxing Day," and the women began to observe wraithlike figures drifting across the nave in front of them. They broke their vigil and hurried from the church grounds, never to return. However, they did mention their experience to the leader of the community before they left the island. Intrigued by their story, he had contacted Ms. Gibson two years later with an incredible anecdote that appeared to substantiate their account.

A roadway of red granite had been discovered by an archeological excavation running from the abbey to a field on a headland overlooking Martyr's Bay. This was the Sraid nam Marbh, or Street of the Dead, known to have been constructed in the fourteenth century to carry plague victims away from the church for burial in an isolated spot. The roadway ran directly to an unknown doorway in the apse of St. Mary's, long since bricked up and plastered over. The leader of the community noted that the roadway and the door were collinear with the path taken across the church by the ghosts in Florrie Gibson's vision.

"Does that not sound more than a wee bit similar to your own spirits, Dr. Kenning?" Florrie asked Brian in between sips of hot tea.

"I'd say it does indeed."

"I have a gentleman friend in the Fulham Spiritualist Church." She leaned forward and whispered in confidence, "It's purely plutonic." Brian smiled at both the malaprop and the rectitude of her motives. "He reads all the literature on the subject, and he told me about your writings in yon journal. He advised me to call ye, in the hopes that I would find some peace of mind and lay off the pestering of him with my stories."

"I think it's fortunate for us that he did. Your experience sounds very similar to ours."

"That's why I'm here. I've seen 'em too, and the beasties didna' lay a finger on me."

"Would you be willing to help us in one of our experiments?"

"With the good Lord to protect me, aye, I will."

"We'll pay your expenses, of course."

"I knew ye would, laddie."

Brian returned to his apartment and called Harry to ask if he would be willing to come back to England for a new round of experiments and bring with him the students who knew how to reach the zeta state. Harry said he thought Karen might be willing but ruled out Dan Patzner. Frank Koslowski would come along too. Harry grumbled about how he could afford to come up with airfares for all of them, but Brian sensed he would find a way to sponsor the drive for truth that mattered so much to him.

On impulse, Brian composed a formal letter to the Bishop of Lincoln requesting approval to spend time with his colleagues in St. Neot's Church, pursuing, as he put it, a religious phenomenon of the greatest importance to mankind. He enclosed a copy of his article and his resumé. Much to his surprise, he received a reply within a week. To his even greater surprise, he was granted permission to conduct a limited number of trials in the church, provided a representative of the bishop was present at all times. This was to be one of the bishop's acolytes from Lincoln, a canon by the name of James Hastings.

Brian was invited to suggest a date for the experiment. With a calendar in front of him and a little thought, he opted for a Thursday in late April. It was far enough past Easter to fall during a lull in the church calendar yet close enough to it that the academics in the group could spend time away without disrupting their teaching commitments. He talked with Canon Hastings by phone, and the date was confirmed. Brian was instructed not to contact Mr. Applewhite. That would be the church's responsibility.

Brian called John with the news and received a tentative agreement for his participation. He arranged a meeting with Sarah to broach the same subject. After a lengthy discussion, she agreed to take the place of his aunt in the next experiment to spare her any further torment. There was no equipment to be built, no paper to be written, and no historical evidence to be gathered. There was nothing for them to do with the intervening weeks but pretend that their normal, everyday lives were what really mattered.

CHAPTER 24

Tattershall Castle
1537

On the morning appointed for their assault on Hoyland Abbey, the soldiers of Richard Crossly's punitive force awoke to dry weather, clouds scudding fast to the east. Those who had not drunk ale to excess the previous night were in fine spirits. They preferred to march with the wind at their backs, especially if it blew them up against ploughboys rather than the French cavalry. By contrast, the drunkards had to be dragged from their beds, oblivious to the weather, ignorant of the enemy, unfit for marching or fighting.

Soldiers began to gather in the Inner Ward before dawn. The grass was dewy and cold. Magpies, rousted too early, screeched their disapproval from the oak trees under the castle walls. Bowmen lined up in front of the quartermaster's wagon to fill their quivers while Brandon's cook ladled bowls of hot milk mixed with fat bacon and bread from a cauldron under the eaves of the kitchen.

At seven o'clock, the men assembled in front of the door to the Great Tower to listen to an inspirational speech by the Duke of Suffolk, who promptly turned tail at its conclusion and went back to bed. The portcullis was raised. The men filed across the double moats and mustered on the hard-packed dirt road that led to Boston and the sea. After some debate over marching order, the soldiers formed up and set off.

At the head of the column rode Richard Crossly. Alongside him was his steward, bearing the standard of the king, lest anyone be in doubt under whose authority they marched. The distinctive flag of King Henry featured a red dragon statant on a green-and-white field sprinkled with gold fleurs-de-lis, red tongues of flame, and Tudor roses. Held aloft, it united the disparate companies of men into a single force with a common purpose.

Behind the two leaders rode five standard-bearers in line abreast, carrying the pennants of the Duke of Suffolk and the families of Burghley, Clinton, Willoughby, and Crossly. It was Crossly's younger brother who bore the family crest of the sun and the planets embroidered in gold and crimson on a turquoise field.

Burghley's men marched in the van in five lines of twenty men each, their bills at the slope, young William Cecil leading them. They wore parti-colored coats of green and white with brown leggings. Expecting a show of force rather than combat, they had left their chest armor in Stamford, which some were later to regret. Their heads were protected by steel helmets, their halberds slender and shiny and imported from Italy. A single-edged sword hung from each waist.

In the center of the column, in the customary fashion of medieval armies, rode the nobles, followed by the local squires. Supporting them were the men of Clinton and Willoughby, five abreast and thirty deep, bowmen in front and billmen behind. The common soldiers wore simple cotton tunics and padded jackets with the cross of St. George emblazoned on the chest. They carried no swords, only rondel daggers for use in hand-to-hand combat. Their lines were more ragged than Burghley's men, their conversations bawdy.

Bringing up the rear were three supply wagons followed by a horse-drawn cart that carried two blacksmiths, an anvil, and a sleeping surgeon. In the fields beyond the dykes, the German mercenaries—the Landsknecht pikemen—marched in single file ten paces apart, their vicious twelve-foot-long pikes intended to deter attack from the flanks. Reed buntings took wing as the pikemen approached and mewled aloft.

All told, they were a colorful, confident band. This was a soft assignment for the troops, and they had not failed to note the paymaster's wagon waiting in the castle yard for their return. They covered ground quickly. Along the road, they encountered not a soul, for word of their approach had been broadcast during the night. Only the occasional field hand stared slack-jawed at their passage, distracted from his tilling. By early afternoon, they had reached the out-skirts of Hoyland. The clouds broke, and slabs of blue sky appeared. Rumor filtered down the lines that there would be no fighting.

A mile west of the town, young William Cecil cantered to the front of the column and engaged Richard Crossly in conversation. "Tell me, sirrah, why is it that the commoners of Lincolnshire think so highly of the abbey that they would rebel against the throne to protect it? Thou hast their ear, Crossly. I do not."

"A sharp question, William," Crossly replied. "'Tis certain that many trust to the abbey for their livelihood. Still more trust to the landlords that dine at the abbot's table. They see this not as servitude, mark thee, but rather as guarantee of food for this world and the next. In truth, their lives are entwined with the church. It hath been thus for untold generations. Yet I think this is not the greatest part of it. Remember, we are far from the king's palace here. We are among an independent-minded race. These are descendants of the Iceni, who alone among the Britons withstood Julius Caesar. They are proud people and do not like to be tickled by the long arm of the king."

"Yet have they not the wits to see how they are stroked by the longer, silkier fingers of the Farnese? 'Tis a mystery to me how the monks command such respect. They are idolaters, all of them. They worship their relics as if each were the Lord Jesus himself—a splinter of the true cross, a branch from the bush of Moses. They have collected the bones of a dozen Magi."

"True enough. Their inquisitive genius hath even set them to rummaging in the Virgin's toilet box. No less than three of her chemises are venerated in France. While traveling with my father, I saw one at Aix-la-Chapelle that had the cut of an alb sewn for a giant. The Holy Mother might have pitched tent in it. Yet have I seen the Dominican friars carry it through the town in pomp stuck on the end of a pole."

"'Tis idolatry of the worst kind. I cannot fathom it. Yet thou knowest as well as I that the roads to the shrines are the busiest in Christendom, each pilgrim carrying his rarest offering. We must sweep these Rome-runners into the sea that they carry no more English silver to the Farnese."

Crossly nodded but tempered his ridicule with the words, "Not all so bad, perhaps. Thou wouldst grant that the Ursulines do much good, teaching the children and caring for the sick."

"Some of them perhaps, but I have heard John Calvin remark..." He stopped in midsentence. He looked over Crossly's shoulder at the steward, who had suddenly sat back in his saddle as if pushed in the chest with the flat of a hand. At the same time, the man raised his flag high in what William thought an unnecessarily flamboyant gesture.

Then clutching the reins so tightly to his chest that his horse reared up in fright, the steward toppled backward out of the saddle, and William saw an arrow sticking out of the man's side. Even as he recalled hearing the swish of the arrow's flight a moment earlier, like the sound of a falcon swooping on a vole, he heard the same sound twice more, closely followed by two thwacks, and saw two soldiers in the front rank fall, one gurgling in agony with a bolt through his neck.

"Down! Down!" Crossly shouted. Men began to drop to the dirt. In a swirl of hooves, the standard-bearers dismounted. Two of them planted their flags firmly in the ground, knelt, and prayed for their lives. Willoughby's man threw his pennant aside and rolled into a ditch. Crossly dismounted and attended to his steward, who lay ashen-faced in the roadway, breathing shallowly through a punctured lung.

Several more arrows were loosed at them. A tall, red-haired man from the Burghley household took one full in the chest and expired at once. A second billman was hit in the thigh and collapsed screaming. The men were more mobile now, though, and many arrows flew wide of their mark.

"Where be the archers?" Crossly shouted to Edward Clinton.

"Up ahead or in the woods." He pointed. "I know not."

"My lord, twenty of thy best men at full speed across this field!"

Clinton turned and barked, "James Macklemore, to foot! Gather thy men and seek out the murtherers!" Most men in the front ranks were prostrate, staring at the impaled soldier who gasped and writhed beside them, clutching both ends of the arrow that had pierced his neck. "At once!"

A dozen soldiers jumped to their feet and sprinted, ducking and weaving across the field, bills at the ready. Others rushed ahead to secure the road. The impaled man squirmed to one side, and the arrow snapped in two. He kicked both legs out in front of him and lay still, his tunic soaked with blood. Crossly mounted up, spurred his horse, and galloped down the line, reassuring his men. Willoughby helped comfort Crossly's wounded steward, taking care to keep his horse between the woods and himself. The surgeon came running at a crouch from the rear of the column.

In the fields, the German pikemen were unmoved. They were veterans and had learned that a cool head saved many a life, even as the young bloods bounded into the arms of death. They knelt on one knee and scanned the tree line. They knew they had a chance to dodge an arrow at that range if they could pick up its flight quickly.

The rain of arrows ceased, and the billmen came walking back. "The brush is thick," said the first to return. "They have melted into it." The men began to stand up and dust themselves off. Crossly's steward struggled for a last breath and then gave up the fight. Crossly returned to learn that the culprits had not been apprehended. He stared from his horse at the disorder in the front ranks, and anger flashed in his eyes—anger at the unnecessary injuries, anger at the abbot, and anger at the king.

"Four dead," said the surgeon. "Five stuck but lightly."

"Into the wagons with them. We march in ten minutes."

The column was on the move again, and this time, the men needed no urging. Now that the danger had passed, they embraced Crossly's rage and vowed vengeance. A faceless enemy had taken its toll and would have to pay the price. A faceless enemy was easy to hate.

Soon, the first stone cottages of Hoyland came into view. As they drew closer, the men observed that the main street of the village was blocked by a barricade made of wagon wheels, tree stumps, rocks, straw bales, and old gable beams—almost anything that came to hand, it seemed. When the column was a mere fifty paces from the wall, flames began to lick around the straw. Two young men raced away into the town, and as with the archers in the wood, there was no catching them. The barricade was rapidly engulfed.

Crossly called for the column to skirt the village, leaving the wagons behind with a small force to protect them. The ground was very boggy in places, and the movement was slow and noisome. But half an hour later, they were back on the road and nearing the abbey. They saw from afar that an agitated crowd, several hundred strong, was ranged in front of the abbey gates. Yells and curses carried to the soldiers' ears. As his force drew closer, Crossly saw that the peasants were armed with a hodgepodge of weapons: scythes, sharpened staves, axes, old swords and lances that were relics from earlier wars, and plenty of bows. A few sported homemade shields.

Despite their show of defiance, Crossly judged them a tentative band. Without a second thought, he formed up the German pikemen and Burghley's halberdiers and sent them at a trot against the rabble, who, still yelling their scorn, fell back along the abbey walls. Crossly then brought up his bowmen and had them draw arrows to hold the peasants at bay. With the gates now unprotected, he approached the abbey, escorted by a handful of his most trustworthy soldiers. On the other side of the locked gates, a dozen monks waited patiently. They were backed by a score of abbey retainers, each with an ax or a pitchfork in his hands. Crossly advanced and shouted, "Which one among ye be Abbot Gervase?"

CHAPTER 25

Hoyland Church
April 2018

On the morning appointed by Brian Kenning for his grand séance in St. Neot's Church, a veil of mist enveloped the sleepy village of Hoyland. The sun rose, and the mist twinkled fitfully before beginning to dissipate. As the last wisps of vapor were fading away among the gravestones in the churchyard, Florrie Gibson strode up to the vestry door. She knocked repeatedly until persuaded there was no one within. She pondered her situation, examining the church from every angle as if searching for alternative means of entry. Eventually, she sat down on the stone wall that flanked the path and pulled a book from her pocket. *The Oracles Speak* proclaimed its cover in loud Gothic script. She began to read, becoming quickly engrossed in a lurid exposé of astrology. Ten minutes later, she was startled to see two figures bending over her.

"Nigel Applewhite," the vicar said, extending his hand. "I'm the vicar of St. Neot's. This is Mrs. Coleby, a parishioner. And you are?"

"Florence McDaniel Gibson," she replied, rising. "But ye can call me Florrie. Your crenelation's crumbling."

"I beg your pardon?"

"Your crenelation," she repeated, pointing to the church roof. "It's crumbling." Nigel Applewhite and Polly stared up at the roofline. "Ye'd be liable, do ye not know, if the stones fell on anyone. A personal damage suit could drain your wallet—coffers, I suppose I should say—if they should fall on a vindictive soul."

"Pardon me, but who are you?" the vicar asked.

She pulled a business card from her purse and handed it to him: Meredith, James, and Tyler. Solicitors at Law. Bayswater Road, Fulham. "Call us if an action should be brought against the church."

"Which one are you?"

"None of 'em. I already told ye, my name's Florrie Gibson. I work part-time for, well, the Unholy Trinity, as we calls 'em." She laughed, and the vicar stared at her blankly. "Messrs. Meredith, James, and Tyler, the Unholy Trinity. Well, anyway, I know the law, yes, sir. When I was a lassie, the Gibsons of Mull were the only purveyors of law on the island. My father was the solicitor, my mother was the recorder of deeds, and my brother and I tied the ribbons around the writs. I've learned more about the law than is healthy for me, I dare say. In this particular, I know ye'd be liable." She glanced back up at the stonework while the vicar stared at her face in bewilderment.

"Are you selling insurance?"

"What? Nay, laddie. I'm here for the conjuring of the spirits. Dr. Kenning of your acquaintance advised me of the time and place. You're here for the same purpose, no doubt."

"I'm here to host the wretched affair, if that's what you mean. Not privy to anything more than that. I suppose you'd better come inside." He extracted a large brass key from his pocket and unlocked the vestry door.

"Dr. Kenning's nay here then?"

"I gather not."

"Ach, and me awa' from my bed these five hours."

They entered the vestry and awaited the arrival of the others. Fifteen minutes later, Brian's car crunched to a halt on the gravel strip, and he, John, and Sarah got out. The first thing John could clearly remember about that day was setting foot in the vestry and being astonished to find his aunt smiling at him. Her presence was not what Brian had led him to expect. The second thing was the look of anger that Sarah directed at Brian.

"Aunt Polly, what on earth—" Brian began before being interrupted by Sarah.

"Brian, don't tell me, after all you promised, that you—"

"No. I had no idea. I swear. I never said a thing to her."

"It's all right, loves," Polly said. "Don't get yourselves in a lather. I'm here at my own urgings. Mr. Applewhite let me know you were coming today, and despite my upset last time, I'm still curious about the meaning of it all. And the bishop's coming too, you know."

"Not the bishop, dear lady," Applewhite corrected her. "Not the bishop at all. I told you before, a canon from Lincoln Cathedral. Here to superintend your nephews or something. Not at all necessary in my opinion."

"As you say, Vicar, but a high dignitary of the church, to be sure."

"Well, I don't know what to say, Aunt Polly," Brian muttered, shaking his head in disbelief. "After all you've been through. You're a real trooper."

"Don't get me wrong, Brian," Polly said. "There'll be no more ghost hunting for me. I've lost the thrill of the chase. You can dabble in it all you want, but you must dabble without me. I just thought I'd come along and observe the proceedings to see if you could explain my little ghost. And I've brought lunch for us all."

There were two sharp raps on the door, and Applewhite went to open it. A tall man with an unruly black beard and tortoiseshell spectacles stood in the porch. In his right hand was a shiny valise, and under his left arm was a rolled up copy of the *Christian Science Monitor*. On his face was that glaze of superiority often cultivated by black-bearded men of the cloth who wore tortoiseshell spectacles. He coughed and drew the lapels of his coat together at the throat.

"Canon Hastings?" Applewhite inquired.

The visitor made no reply, and though it must have been patently obvious that he had arrived at the correct destination, he drew a slip of paper from his pocket and read from it. "St. Neot's Church? The Reverend Nigel Applewhite?"

"Yes, indeed. Do come in, sir. Most honored."

A hand was offered, and the vicar shook it. It had the consistency of a beached flounder. The newcomer sidled past the vicar, approached the rest of the party, consulted his notes once more, and said, "Dr. Brian Kenning?"

"That's me," Brian said.

"Dr. Kenning, I am Canon James Hastings from Lincoln Cathedral. No doubt you were expecting me. I'm here under the authority of the Very Reverend Michael Symm-Horton, Bishop of Lincoln, to supervise these studies of yours into certain, shall we say, spiritual phenomena. My instructions are to ensure that no infractions of a sacrilegious nature occur. You are required to adhere at all times to the letter of the ecclesiastical ruling on such matters, as conveyed to you by myself. Any deviation from my instructions and I shall be obliged to terminate the proceedings and refer back to Lincoln."

"Oh boy," John muttered sotto voce.

"Should your experiments endanger any of the participants, then I am again instructed to halt the proceedings and refer back to Lincoln. Should you at any time require the rite of exorcism, I—"

"Good Lord, no," Brian said. "What exactly do you think we're trying to do here?"

"Should you at any time require the rite of exorcism, I am instructed to perform certain rituals prescribed by the bishop and—"

"Yes, yes. Look, is all this rigmarole really necessary?"

"In the event that your activities are compliant, I am instructed to act as official observer on behalf of the Church of England. I am to take notes on the purpose, practice, and results of all tests for the further edification of the Church Commissioners." He drew a cream-colored document from his valise and presented it to Brian. "My brief from the bishop. The Reverend Applewhite is to take no part in the proceedings. All business concerning the use of the church of St. Neot in relation to your studies must be conducted through me."

"Oh, I say!" Applewhite exclaimed, taking a step forward. "My church after all."

"No, my dear sir," Hastings interjected, turning toward him with a condescending smile. "You are to remain detached, both physically and spiritually, from the proceedings. The bishop's decision, you understand, not mine."

"Of course. Bishop's decision, as you say. Not entirely in agreement, though. Certain diocesan rights, you know." He lapsed into sulky mutterings.

"Is everything clear?"

"Crystal," Brian replied.

Canon Hastings shunned further introductions. The other members of the party were below his need-to-know threshold. He removed his coat and laid it across the back of a chair then took off his gloves and placed them on the table. He smoothed his hair with both hands and sat down. Finally, he produced a notebook and proceeded to make entries in a precise but crabbed hand.

"He's going to be trouble," John said musically, not moving his lips.

"You may begin at your convenience, Dr. Kenning," Hastings said. "But please remember that it is forbidden for you to use the church without my presence."

"Oh, come on! Is that really necessary?"

"Adhere to the letter of my ruling, remember? To the letter."

"Or you'll have to refer back to Lincoln. Right. My memory's very good."

"Precisely. Shall we begin?"

"Actually, we're waiting for three more participants—Professor Harry Groh, Karen Butler, and Dr. Frank Koslowski, scientists from America. They've come over to help us. They've been holed up in Lincoln for two days and should be here shortly. We can take a look around the church if you like."

"Let's wait till the party is fully assembled."

Brian hesitated for a moment. Then as if he suddenly considered it of paramount importance to establish that he, not the canon, would be the one to dictate the course of events, he strode across the vestry floor and entered the church. The others seemed unsure whether to follow him or heed the canon's words. Hastings didn't lift his face from his notebook.

Brian was back in the vast mausoleum. Walking down the transept toward the nave, he was startled to see Karen Butler leaning against the rood screen. She was staring alternately up at the roof of the church and down the long aisle that led to the back of the nave, like a surveyor gauging dimensions. She wore thick cord jeans, white sneakers, and a dark-blue jacket. Her hair was longer now and drawn tightly back to the stub of a ponytail. Brian had seen her only once before, on the day Dan Patzner had lost his nerve and fled with security guards at his heels, but she had trespassed on his thoughts a number of times since then. There was a connection he could not fathom. Dan had called her a witch, and Harry had called her a mind traveler, but Brian saw only the same magnetic presence he had briefly glimpsed in Illinois five months before.

Karen lounged against the screen, hands in pockets, grinding gum. It was an attitude that his aunt and the vicar would never dream of adopting in church and would strongly disapprove of, but somehow, the pose didn't strike Brian as disrespectful, not even slovenly. To his way of thinking, it was the hidebound churchgoers who were often disrespectful by clinging to ritual out of habit and accepting dogma without question. Karen seemed to him to represent a limber spirit of inquiry, an intellect that acknowledged the trappings of religion but transcended them.

Then Harry lurched from a side chapel, followed by Frank Koslowski, and threw himself upon Brian. "Brian, great to see you again! How are you doing?"

"Fine, Harry, fine. How are you? How's the leg?"

"Full range of motion again. Can't wait for the softball season." He swung at an imaginary ball and drove it high into the nave. Karen pushed off from the screen with the sole of her shoe and joined them.

"What are you all doing in here?" Brian asked. "We've been waiting for you in the vestry. How long have you been here?"

"We just arrived. Maybe ten minutes ago. We came in through the front door. I didn't know about the, er, whatever you just called it."

"The vestry."

"The vestry, right. We came up the path. We left the rental car by the roadside. I was just showing Frank the hole in the wall where that saint was incarcerated. Makes Stateville prison in Joliet look like the Hilton."

"Oh, right. Did you have a good flight?"

"Yeah, fine," Harry said, scratching his beard. "Fucking expensive—excuse me, Lord—but fine. I sure hope the DOD accountants think these ghosts have a military application."

"Are you going to have a problem?" Brian asked. "I said I would try to find—"

"Don't worry about it, chief. My call."

"Did you get the results of Ms. Butler's blood tests?"

"Sure did, Brian, a couple of weeks ago. Zilch."

"Nothing?"

"Nothing special in the blood when entering the zeta state or while in the zeta state. But I talked some more to Andy Lieshman at Northwestern about it, and he wasn't surprised. He said that any neurologically active chemicals would probably only be found in the brain cells, not in the blood. He asked if we had any brain sections he could examine."

"Our subjects would have to be dead before we could get brain samples."

"I think he was joking, Brian." Harry gave a nervous laugh and then struck Brian sharply on the forearm. "Let's talk about that later. Have you got all your guys together?"

"Yes, we're all set. Let me go and get them." Brian returned to the vestry and led John, Sarah, Florrie, and Canon Hastings over to the nave. Introductions were brief and tentative.

As the group broke up and reformed into English and American contingents, Karen came over to greet Brian. "Dr. Kenning," she said, "I read your paper on the plane. I thought it was amazing. How could you come up with such a theory?" She smiled and held out her hand. He clasped it gently.

"Ms. Butler," he said.

"Karen."

"Karen, right. The last time I saw you was in the ICPS lobby."

"Yeah, I remember you were there. Not one of my better performances."

"It seemed like everyone had their hands full that day."

"Yeah, everyone was so wired."

"Except for you, I think. You seemed very—I don't know—very self-possessed."

"Really? You think so? Well, you were too, as I recall."

"Me? I was petrified. I thought someone was going to get shot!"

They both laughed and exchanged one of those special glances that lasted just a hair longer than strictly necessary. Brian read Karen's eyes, and they seemed to say, "Yes, there will be another time, if that's what you want, to explore this thing more thoroughly." Karen read Brian's eyes, and they said, "I need your help. I've almost reached the biggest prize of all, but there's no hand to grab if I should fall." Then Brian suddenly became aware that Sarah was observing this exchange, and he turned back to the group with slightly flushed cheeks. They were all assembled. They were ready.

CHAPTER 26

Hoyland Abbey
1537

When Richard Crossly called out the name of the abbot, a monk stepped forward from among the assembled clerics, unruffled, smiling. He said, "My name is Gervase." He was a taller man than Crossly, slender at the shoulders but with a fleshy large face. He was dressed in a woolen habit overlaid with a black scapular tied at the waist. The cowl was drawn back, laying bare his monastic tonsure: a dome of baldness circled by a ragged gray fringe. He was no longer a young man, and as he smiled, his face creased around the eyes and cheeks. If more weathered than pale and in other garb, he might have been taken for a pensioned-off gamekeeper, muscle rendered to fat. His bearing was powerful, nonetheless, and his voice rang full and deep as he added, "And who art thou?"

"I am Richard Crossly on the king's business."

The abbot looked him in the eye for a moment and then touched his forefinger to his lips. "Would that be the son of Sir Adam Crossly who cherished this abbey more than his own home, Sir Adam Crossly who vouchsafed his greatest possession to our keeping?" He gestured to a monk at his side, who drew forth the Sphere of the Planets from the folds of his habit and held it out in front of him like a talisman against their assault. Crossly held his anger in check as the abbot continued. "Would that be the young Richard Crossly who took the sacrament from my own hands for ten years and more? Forgive me, but I have not seen thee kneel in a long time, and my age withers the memory of faces." He added with a sly smile, "Perhaps I am mistaken."

233

"Thou knowest it be true, brother abbot, but it signifies naught."

Gervase renewed eye contact. Crossly reached into a pocket in his jack and pulled out the papers given him by Sir Richard Rich. He stepped forward and held them up to the bars of the abbey gate. He turned them around so that the abbot might read them. "This is a king's warrant signed by the chancellor of the Court of Augmentations. It is sanctioned by the Act for the Dissolution of the Lesser Monasteries. Submit to its terms under the Law of England and the authority of King Henry Tudor. Gloria Patri. Accept the warrant!"

Gervase dropped his gaze once more and studied the ground beneath his feet. With the toe of his sandal, he formed a cross in the dirt. "Seest thou this dust in which the cross is drawn? It hath been ploughed by monks and sifted by monks and trod flat by the sandals of monks since e'er St. Guthlac plucked it from the waves before time began. King Henry Tudor holds no majesty over this dust. It belongs only to Pope Paul of Rome, holy father of all the church in these isles. Depart from this holy ground, I say, lest thou chance damnation by defiling it."

"Look again, abbot. The dust on thy side of the gate is no different from the dust beneath mine own feet." Crossly kicked the ground by way of illustration. "See that it be so! It is English dust, and King Henry holds sway over every acre of it."

"King Henry is a heretic!" Abbot Gervase shot back.

"Nay, nay, King Henry is not that. Did he not defend the church against the writings of Martin Luther? Did not Pope Leo confer on him the title Defender of the Faith? What idle vices occupy thy time that thou hast not read King Henry's book *The Defense of the Seven Sacraments*? Thy view of these times is cockeyed. Thou and thy brethren long since plaited the true faith into a most ungodly knot, and King Henry seeks only to unravel it. Heresy lies in thine own iniquities. Submit to the warrant!" Crossly thrust the papers through the bars, but Gervase refused to accept them.

"Thou hast no authority here, I repeat. Observe that the will of the people is against thee." He gestured toward the angry sounds swelling outside the abbey walls. "Make violence against my broth-

234

ers, and the townsmen will cut thee down. Depart from this holy ground, I say again!"

"Take care, Gervase. Thou art sailing in a sieve. I have five hundred of the king's troop at my back. Not thou or thy pope or any country rabble shall swerve me."

"King Henry is a fornicator," Gervase continued, softly now but with the strike of a viper. "Wouldst deny he hath broken with Rome to feed his lust? Wouldst deny he blasphemed the Holy Father that he might lie with the six-fingered witch Boleyn? All England knoweth it be true, yet few will admit it. My belly is not as yellow as thine."

"And Alexander Farnese that took the name Paul hath three bastard sons. It is the common talk of Italy. It is all of no consequence."

Gervase grasped the iron railings with both hands and spat, "King Henry is an adulterer and a fornicator!" Incensed at this defamation of the king, a young halberdier lunged forward and thrust his bill through the bars. It ripped the abbot's habit and scraped his side.

"Hold, sirrah!" Crossly shouted, grabbing the weapon and yanking it back.

"But they are the vilest of knaves," the soldier responded in anguish. "I say we crush their thieving fingers in the pilliwinks!" Cries of agreement spread behind Crossly's back. "Stuff his lying gob with a choke pear and melt the key!" The soldiers cheered. A rock was thrown, striking a monk behind Gervase.

"Hold, I say!" Crossly doubted that his men could be contained under such provocation, but he proceeded in a measured voice, praying for a peaceful outcome yet. "Thou wilt not be harmed, sirrah, if thou accept the terms of the king's warrant. Thou wilt be taken to the Tower of London under my protection and at some later date asked cause by the king."

"I will not answer to that man."

"Thy brethren will be free to leave the grounds with all their possessions. No harm need befall a single man here present. What sayest thou?"

"I say I will *not* answer to that man." Gervase, his spirit roused, gripped the bars tightly. He confronted Crossly and his men, matching determination with determination, bile with bile. "King Henry is like only unto King Ahab that did sell himself to work wickedness in the sight of the Lord and to follow idols." A strand of saliva dripped from the corner of his mouth.

"Take care, Gervase. Thou art sailing in a sieve, I tell thee."

"He hath gone to serve Baal! Like King Ahab, he hath done more to provoke the Lord God of Israel to anger than all the kings that were before him!" The soldiers surrounding Crossly began to shout the abbot down. "Mark the scriptures that I taught thee as a boy, Master Crossly!" Gervase declared.

"I mark them well," Crossly shouted back. "And I say thou art not Elijah the Tishbite to speak so of the king!"

"And the king did act abominably in following false idols!"

The scene was close to uproar. Some monks had stepped forward to side with Gervase, shouting their agreement, while others had fallen back in fear. The retainers, to a man, were mortified and could no more have lifted a pitchfork in anger than leap to the top of the church tower. The soldiers jostled their commander, shaking their fists at the monks, and Crossly spread his arms wide to hold them back.

Gervase continued to slap them with the first book of Kings: "Thus saith the Lord, in the place where the dogs licked the blood of Naboth shall dogs lick the blood of the king."

At this slander, Crossly knew the men were beyond his control. A dagger flew by his shoulder and bounced off a stanchion. Two men began to shin up the gates. "Thou art lost, Gervase," Crossly said. "I cannot save thee."

The abbot's face unwound, and the smile returned. Quietly now and seemingly to Crossly alone, he said, "These knees have not bent before Baal, and this mouth hath not kissed him. I am pure in the sight of the Lord. He shall save me."

Crossly suddenly formed the impression that the abbot had deliberately provoked his men and actually desired a violent resolution of the confrontation. He could not discern the abbot's true motive, however, and stared at him with a puzzled expression. His bewilderment soon turned to anger, though, at the thought of the lives that would be lost in consequence. He slapped the warrant against the abbot's chest and watched it flutter to the ground.

"The dogs shall lick King Henry's blood!" Gervase repeated then turned and strode away. Soldiers swarmed over the gates like insects. The monks retreated into the abbey and barred the door behind them. The retainers fled. A soldier unlocked the abbey gates from the inside, and angry billmen poured through them. Running hard, Crossly was the second man to reach the door of the abbey. He picked up an ax, pushed aside the soldier in front of him, and broke down the door with broad, powerful strokes.

CHAPTER 27

Hoyland Church
April 2018

Brian sat on the chancel steps and communed with the church. It seemed to brood on top of the hill like some sad and ancient philosopher, wise beyond its years and ready for death. Witness to a thousand years of humanity's scratching and prattling, it seemed aware now only of the passing of its own usefulness. Its tapestries hung limp and threadbare. Its pillars seemed brittle. Helpless to prevent the coming drama, the church spread its wormy rafters over the eight adventurers and held its breath.

Brian decided it was time to brief Sarah, Karen, and Florrie Gibson. "Fifteen thirty-seven," he said, drawing gravity from the numbers. "That's the key to this mystery. Something of great significance occurred in this church at the time of its destruction by Crossly's force. Whatever it was, it ripped up the fabric of time and sent ripples backward to 1057 and forward to the present, enabling us to witness Abbot Ingulphus praying for the soul of Neot. It must have been something monumental—monstrous, perhaps. We simply don't know. But I'm confident that the three of you can resonate with that time period and discover the truth. Think 1537!"

Brian positioned Karen, Florrie, and Sarah on the front row of the choir stalls. Harry and John slid into the back row next to the Lady Chapel. Canon Hastings followed them but sat down at the opposite end of the row. Frank clambered into the pulpit with a video camera. Their mood was uniformly somber.

"I'm going to stand up here," Brian declared, moving to the bench in the chancel reserved for the vicar, parallel to the rood screen with its back up against it. He climbed onto the bench and looked full circle around him. He glanced at Hastings, who gave him the nod to proceed.

Throughout the morning, they sat in silence. Every ten minutes or so, Brian roused the three women and repositioned them—sometimes in a line on the same side of the aisle, sometimes in a triangle; now close together, now far apart. But they had no success. The participants grew bored and were glad when Brian called a halt and permitted them to take a break. The cold wood and marble had stiffened many a joint.

They returned to the vestry, where the vicar exchanged small talk with Sarah and felt reassured. They ate the lunch that Aunt Polly had brought, sipped on her elderberry wine, and then returned to their task. According to John's notebook, it was at 2:18 p.m. that the strange noises began.

The observers became aware of a rhythmical pulsation in the chancel. John looked sideways at Harry, and his nods indicated that he could hear it too. He leaned forward and cocked his head to one side. The throbbing intensified a little, modulated to a barely audible mixture of sounds then resumed. The lights were not swaying, but John sensed that it had turned colder. He rubbed his bare forearms.

Brian whispered, "Florrie." She looked up. He motioned her to move to one side, which she did, but nothing changed. He moved her a little to the other side, and the noises faded away. Sarah shuffled her feet and opened her eyes. Brian stepped down into the chancel and said, "I think we're getting somewhere. The separation's about right, but we don't seem to be able to create a strong enough zeta field. It's very frustrating."

"What do you think we should do?" Sarah asked.

"The field seems to be strongest when you're in a triangular configuration. I'm wondering what would happen if there were four of you together in a square so that the wave patterns at the center of the square reinforce each other."

"What do you mean by 'four of you'?" Sarah asked suspiciously.

"I was thinking that if we had Aunt Polly here too—"

"No, Brian, you're not to ask your aunt. Brian, no!"

"I really don't want to. I've taken advantage of her enough. I know that."

"It's just not fair."

"But we're not getting results here." He turned and walked into the vestry with Sarah in hot pursuit. He approached his aunt, rubbing the side of his head. "Aunt Polly," he began, "we don't have a strong enough zeta field. We're starting to make contact, but it's just too weak. We've got to—"

"Brian," Sarah interjected, "listen to me! You told me there would be no need for Aunt Polly to get involved. You promised me! That's the only reason I'm sitting out there in the church, freezing to death. You promised me that you wouldn't impose on her again."

"But we're so close," Brian pleaded, focusing his petition on his aunt. "We can hear sounds, but we need a stronger energy field. What do you say? We've got Canon Hastings in there with us. It's all for the benefit of the church."

Polly was torn. "This is not to my liking at all. You know that, Brian. I've been scared out of my wits once before. But if the bishop approves, then I suppose I'm sort of obliged to do what I can to…" She gripped the armrests of her chair and began to rise, but Sarah placed a hand on her shoulder.

"You're not obliged to do anything of the sort, Aunt Polly," Sarah said. "This is just Brian's way of manipulating the situation. We'll do the best we can without you."

"The best is not going to be good enough, Sarah," Brian said pointedly. "You don't want to have to sit in the church for a week, do you? With one more experienced subject, we'll be able to make contact in no time. I'm sure of it. And if we can't, then there's no harm done."

Polly remained poised on the edge of her chair for a second and then rose against Sarah's restraining hand. "I do appreciate your thoughtfulness, Ms. Harcourt. You're a very considerate girl. But this whole business has sort of wormed its way under my skin. We're like two peas in a pod, me and Brian, I'm almost sorry to say. And I'm not as feeble as I look, dear. Thank you for your concern, but I'll do what I can to help." She patted Sarah's hand and walked to the door.

"Oh, Brian, how could you?" Sarah said. "Do you think of no one but yourself?"

"No, dear," Polly intervened. "Don't say that."

Back in the chancel, Brian positioned the four women in a square, two pairs on opposite sides of the aisle. He waited for their heads to droop and then resumed his watch from the bench. Within five minutes, the throbbing sounds returned. Sarah's head rose for a minute as if she had left some complaint unregistered, then her chin lolled back onto her chest. Hastings began to fidget, looking around him for the source of the draft that was chilling his legs.

The noise changed from an ethereal throbbing to a string of low, guttural phonemes. It seemed as if the long and short *a* vowel sounds were being continuously repeated. John formed the unsettling opinion that some long-dead entity was muttering "Payback! Payback! Payback!" at the group. *Nothing to pay us back for,* he thought. *We haven't done anything.* The chant melted away and was replaced by a medley of unrecognizable sounds located, it seemed, throughout the church. It was as if they were each being whispered to by their own personal, ghostly confidant.

"I think we should—I don't..." Hastings said, half rising to his feet, but John and Harry gave him such withering looks from the other end of the row that he sat down again and muttered, "This is not at all what one expected." Powerfully, insistently, the sounds returned. They seemed to come from the direction of the altar, and yet there were other noises—a high-pitched whimpering and crackling, scratching sounds—coming from the Lady Chapel. A vague mist descended over the proceedings. "We should stop this now," Hastings said. "Dr. Kenning, the terms of reference I was..." He cast a despairing look to Brian, then his interjection faded away of its own accord.

The chanting ceased abruptly, leaving only the clamor from the Lady Chapel. The air shimmered and seemed poised to reveal something new. Each observer held his breath during the hiatus. The mist concentrated in certain parts of the church and began to condense into opaque clusters. These clusters then began to take on distinctive form. The shapes became thicker and denser and slowly coagulated into nebulous human figures. They were everywhere! There were people everywhere, ducking under the arches, huddling by the altar, gesticulating from the side chapels.

Hastings turned to Brian. "This business must stop forthwith, Dr. Kenning!"

"Shut up!" Brian hissed. "This is why we're here. Shut up and put it in your damned notebook!" Hastings covered his eyes with the palms of his hands and lay sideways on the bench. The pulsation returned as a vibrant chant from human voices, and John realized he had misheard the word. It wasn't *payback!* It was more like…

"Ahab! Ahab! Ahab!" The mist gave a last delicate flutter and was gone, leaving a whole new montage draped across the church. The figures were still faint and translucent but now clean-edged and well-defined. In the center of the chancel stood a soldier. In his right hand was a sword, and from his waist hung a dagger. He wore a tunic with a red cross on the chest. He pointed and shouted, seeming to be an officer of some kind. On either side of him were soldiers, similarly dressed and armed.

In the sanctuary were monks, at least a dozen of them, dressed in dark-colored habits. Some of them faced the three soldiers; some were turned to the altar, praying. The chanting came from them: "Ahab! Ahab! Ahab!" It was mixed with archaic supplications and the most abominable high-pitched wailing. John pointed out to Harry a monk holding aloft a translucent object that radiated red light in a curiously penetrating beam. The object twinkled—now blue, now green, and now red again. The monk held it in front of him like a warning to the soldiers. It was the Sphere of the Planets.

"Oh god. Oh, Jesus," Harry gasped. A bright light shone from above and behind them, and John turned to look for the source. The light was moving and falling and being replaced by more light. It put him in mind of a waterfall, but then the crackling sounds he had heard earlier intensified and brought a different thought to mind: *The church is on fire!*

With the blade of his sword, the soldier motioned to the monks who cowered in the sanctuary. They fell back, draping themselves across the altar, several falling to their knees. One grabbed the silver cross and clutched it to his breast like a shield. The soldier slapped one of them with the flat of his sword, demanding that he move.

There was a crash, and the vestry door burst open. All inside was aflame. Great tongues of fire licked up the walls, and showers of sparks fell from the ceiling. Framed in the doorway was a figure, frozen like a fawn in headlights. Brian stood on tiptoes, staring at the inferno. "Applewhite!" he shouted, but the vicar stood spellbound. "Get away!"

Hastings rose from his recumbent position, sobbing like a child. He saw the commotion by the vestry and stood up. Suddenly protective of his colleague, he broke from the stall and ran across the aisle. He darted between the ghostly soldiers and the throng of monks. The leading soldier, broadsword at his side, stood frozen to the spot, his head slowly turning. *I swear to God,* John thought, *the soldier can see him!*

Hastings ran toward the organ chapel and the vestry, but he was too late. Something exploded in the topmost part of the roof and ejected a massive ball of fire. Brian shouted again, "Get away!" Applewhite seemed to sense danger but see none. Brian waved his arm to one side, motioning the vicar to move. Applewhite screamed, and his face jerked upward, eyes flinching at the prospect of a blow. He raised a forearm above his head and seemed to be on the point of running clear when the fiery globe crashed down on him. The ball of fire and the hapless vicar were dashed to the ground in a seething, incandescent mass.

Hastings pulled up midway between his fallen colleague and the startled soldiers. He looked first at one and then at the others. He glanced upward at the conflagration above his head and, terrified, backed away. His eyes lost their focus and stared into the back of the church. He bumped up against the keyboard of the organ. His hands reached behind him, clutching for support, fingers spreading across the ivory keys.

His mouth opened wide, molding a silent scream. He leaned back on the keyboard, and his fingers drew a hideous chord from the pipes. He jerked his hands away and collapsed. The soldiers watched him. *As if he were a ghost,* John realized. Some in the chapel moved toward him but then stopped. Another fireball fell onto the motion-less vicar by the vestry door. Hastings's eyes flashed swiftly to it and then slowly closed.

Several more swordsmen entered the chancel, summoned by the others, it seemed, and joined the onlookers. The first three pointed out to the new arrivals the figure of Hastings in front of the organ. They stared at him in silence. One of the soldiers turned and ges-tured to where Sarah was slumped in the choir stalls. He took a step in her direction and faltered. The men closed into a tight circle in the center of the chancel, all staring now at Sarah, while the officer pointed his sword at her and made mock thrusts. *They're as scared as we are.*

The quivering sword remained leveled at Sarah's throat while the man holding it gabbled in a faint and unfamiliar dialect. The soldiers began to look about them while still more men arrived from the body of the church. A tall halberdier with a chain mail skullcap pointed at Karen and waggled his wrist in consternation. John felt he should run away at once, or he would never get out, but a stronger impulse held him statuesque in hope of escaping detection.

A monk broke from the ranks of his brethren by the altar and ran down the aisle, his eyes bright with the reflection of the flames. The soldiers made no move to stop him. John could see he was headed for Brian, who was still standing on the bench by the chancel screen. The monk fell to his knees in the center of the aisle, barely ten feet from Brian, who seemed bewildered by this new development.

The monk ripped the cowl away from his head, revealing an amazing sight. His eyes bulged like saucers, and the tendons in his neck and temples stood out in high relief. His bald head was deep purple, and the veins on his scalp pulsed. He stretched up his hands in supplication. *He can see Brian,* John thought. *He can see him!*

A soldier off to the side of the main group also spotted Brian's outline against the screen. His face twisted into a mask of terror, and he spat an oath that attracted the attention of his fellows. One by one, they turned to look in Brian's direction. They began to squint and shift their angle of sight, not certain what they were looking at. One of them made the sign of the cross on his chest. Another dropped to his knees in prayer. A third turned away and threw his sword to the ground. John saw Brian standing wide-eyed against the screen and realized what was happening. *They see him as Jesus Christ!*

The officer took a couple of steps in Brian's direction and stared intently at this new image while the others held back and waited on his lead. The supplicant monk continued to mutter and hold his arms outstretched. All remained motionless for a moment, frozen in some terrible Victorian tableau, then the officer's mouth flew open, and John heard his cry, weak but distinct, above the general tumult. It was full of anger and hate and seemed to breach the dam of a lifetime's frustration. Stealthily, in a crouched position, the officer inched his way toward the monk and Brian. He waggled his sword threateningly at the pair of them, again making mock thrusts. Brian seemed to sense the onset of some violent resolution of the drama and extended his arms in front of him, pleading against the inevitable.

Still kneeling, eyes fixed on Brian's face, the monk began to levitate off the floor toward Brian's inviting arms. The veins on his neck stood out like whipcord. John could taste electricity in the air. Instantly, the hair surrounding the monk's tonsure spiked out in all directions. Brian's notepapers flew off the bench and began to whirl in tight vortices on the floor of the church. The monk continued to rise above the floor—six inches, a foot.

"No, no, no!" Brian implored, holding his palms downward to prevent the monk's ghastly approach. The monk's habit began to undulate from ankle to neck. Blood dripped from his nose and ears. A maelstrom of papers swirled under his feet, blue sparks crackling between them.

The approaching officer held his ground a yard or two away, watching but unafraid. He grasped his sword in both hands and raised it above his head, the blade flashing bright red with the reflection of the surrounding flames. His biceps tightened as he firmed up his grip. Brian held out his hands and shouted, "No, don't!"

The officer took one step forward. The sword whirled in a smooth arc through the chancel smoke. John saw the juddering impact against the monk's neck, and as John's eyelids started to close, he glimpsed the blade completing its circle, glinting now a deeper, duller red. He did not see the monk's head strike the floor.

When he opened his eyes, gasping for air, John saw the monk's torso jerking on the stone slabs, arteries and tendons smeared across the cowl. Blood was everywhere. The severed head rolled to a stop against a bench. A swatch of black cloth remained stuck to the officer's sword. With a single motion, he used it to wipe the blade clean.

Brian's arms remained outstretched, begging now for the killing not to have happened, pleading to ears that had not heard for four centuries. The officer stared up at him. He gave a single shout of defiance, drew the sword back with one hand, and hurled it up at Brian with all his might. The sword cartwheeled through the air, sliced through Brian's left hand, and embedded itself in the screen behind him. John yelped, but the sound was drowned out by Brian's harsh cry of pain. Brian clutched his wrist in horror.

The officer turned to his men triumphantly. He pushed one in the chest and gave orders to the others with newfound confidence. Three soldiers marched into the sanctuary and began to manhandle the monks cowering by the altar. The monk holding the Sphere of the Planets ran off to the side, and a soldier caught him a vicious blow on the back of the head as he passed. The monk staggered against the chancel screen then ran through into the Lady Chapel. Harry turned and watched. The monk got but a few yards before two arrows whistled through the air, fired from the far end of the church. One embedded itself in the monk's shoulder; the other caught him full in the stomach.

The monk stumbled and fell headlong into the side wall. The precious artifact flew from his grasp, bounced a couple of times, and slid under a chair. Almost at once, the wall buckled inward, and the whole outer half of the Lady Chapel gave way in an avalanche of stone and glass. The roof caved in, and burning spars were added to the debris. In a matter of seconds, the whole area became a red-hot mass of smoking rubble five or six feet deep, entombing the monk and a screaming halberdier.

Back in the chancel, John saw that the soldiers were dispersing and heading toward each member of their team. A timid soldier in a blue-and-gold tunic stepped over the torso of the decapitated monk and headed for Sarah. Two soldiers converged on Hastings, who still lay in shock by the organ. And to John's utter horror, a pikeman drove his lance through Polly's chest. Her eyes lost their glassy stare and sparkled brilliantly for a moment, then the glaze returned, and she fell back against the bench, a pike handle sticking out of her chest.

A burly soldier drew his sword from its scabbard and headed in John's direction. In a flash, John was up on the bench, looking for a means of escape. There was a wall of fire behind him and a piece of blazing timber blocking the entrance to the stalls. He was trapped. He vaulted down one row, but that only brought him closer to the soldier and didn't reveal an escape route. He took two steps to the side, but the soldier veered also and maintained his line of approach.

John let out a howl of despair as he realized there was no means of escape. His knees buckled, and his legs crumpled. He fell awkwardly onto the seat, one foot bent under him. His head cracked against a pew. He lay in shock and watched the ghostly soldier clamber over the remaining two rows of benches. Towering over John, the soldier raised his sword vertically and prepared to skewer him. It was all over. John screwed his eyes shut and drew one knee up to protect his midsection. He shielded his head in his arms and sobbed. And nothing happened. He gasped for breath, curled into a tight ball, and waved an arm wildly in front of him. But nothing happened.

When time again had meaning for him and he could mark off its passage against the world outside his skull, he opened his eyes. He watched a wisp of smoke slither along the top of the chancel arch. It licked obscenely around the legs of the crucifix and sneaked away into the darkness of the nave. From under his nostrils, the acrid smoke had cleared. John sucked in a refreshing gulp of air. The soldiers and the monks were gone. The fire, gone! He put out a hand to steady himself and rose from his fetal position. Harry, big as he was, was wedged under the pew beside him, rocking backward and forward, fingers spread across his face. John reached out a hand and touched his shoulder.

"No!" Harry groaned, and John saw his face stiffen behind clawlike fingers. He let his hand drop to Harry's arm, but terrified, Harry tore it away. John whispered words of reassurance and then jumped into action as the memory of a pike handle protruding from Polly's chest flashed through his mind. He raced across the aisle to join Brian and Florrie by her side. The weapon had vanished, and Polly was gazing serenely across the chancel. Strands of gray hair hung about her face like steel wool. Her cheeks, though, were pale and drained.

"Are you all right, Aunt Polly?" John asked.

"She's dead," Brian replied.

John looked at his aunt's chest. There was no sign of injury. "The weapon wasn't real, Brian. There's no blood anywhere."

"Nonetheless."

Florrie began to cry, and John stared at her. How could his aunt be dead? Nothing had been real. The soldiers were ghosts. The pike was a ghostly pike. It couldn't have left a permanent mark on her. They had merely been observers of a world long gone. How could it—how dare it—have such an impact on the real world? John was both shocked and angry.

"I don't know what happened," Brian said, his voice cracking. "Maybe a heart attack." He sobbed as he laid her body down on the bench. "Oh my god, I don't believe this has happened. Oh god."

"We must call somebody," Sarah said. "The police."

With the mention of the police, it suddenly all became real to John. It was ten minutes past three on a slow April afternoon in the country. The sun was slanting through the stained glass windows, splashing rainbows across the flagstones. Soon, it would be teatime. Soon, it would be summer. It was all real, and his aunt Polly would see no more of it. John's face cracked into tears. The women turned to him and whispered small words of consolation.

Brian was left alone with the body of his aunt. A terrible panic swept over him and set his fingers trembling. "What have I done?" he mumbled. "This is all my fault."

"Over here!" Hastings shouted from the vestry door. "Help me!" He was crouched over the motionless form of the vicar, patting his hand.

Brian looked up. He looked back at his aunt's ashen face then tore himself away and ran over to the canon's side. "Is he alive?" Brian asked him.

"Yes. At least, I think so. But I can't bring him around. And yet he's scarcely burned at all. There's just a little redness on the skin. See here. I don't understand it. I saw him in the middle of all that fire."

"We'll call an ambulance," Brian replied.

"What happened to the fire?" Hastings asked, looking at Brian with great bewilderment. Brian ignored him and ran into the vestry to call for help.

CHAPTER 28

Hoyland Church
April 2018

The aftermath was soul-destroying. They were all summoned back to the church the next day to meet with the local constabulary. Detective Inspector Bob Jamieson, a career detective in his early fifties, took charge of the investigation. He was professional in his approach and considerate of all involved but clearly baffled by the bizarre circumstances. His assistant was a young detective named Walter Carling, who seemed to appreciate nothing but a driving need to "get to the bottom of things," as he put it several times. He was lean and bossy and pretty certain that some kind of serious crime had been committed. His search for the fundament was so insensitive, however, that no one felt inclined to help him find it.

The detectives interviewed each member of the team at length. They searched the floor near the vestry door for evidence of the falling fire that Canon Hastings described to them but to no avail. They looked for the medieval weapons that Hastings had seen but were likewise frustrated. While the policemen pondered these baffling circumstances, Brian took hold of John's arm and drew him into the shadow of the pulpit.

"John, do you feel like talking about what happened yesterday?"

"No," John replied.

"Did you see the leader of the soldiers throw his sword at me?"

"Not now please."

"Did you see it?"

"Yes. I saw it. It hit your arm. But it wasn't real, right? Your arm's fine."

"Yes, but I *felt* it, John. I felt a pain in my wrist as the sword sliced through it. There's no sign of a wound, though"—he showed John his unmarked wrist—"not a cut or a bruise or anything. But that's easy to explain. It was a sword of extremely low molecular density that momentarily intersected my flesh. The materializing steel molecules stimulated nerve endings before they vanished. It felt like a mild electric shock. It hurt, but it didn't cause any damage."

"Whatever you say. I don't much care at the moment."

"Let me show you something else," Brian whispered, dragging John over to the screen where he had been standing during the experiment. He pointed to the rail. "Look here." John reluctantly studied the wooden edge. "Touch it!" Brian ordered him.

John ran his fingers across the uneven surface and traced the indentation of a worn fissure in the wood. "Are you trying to tell me that the sword caused this?"

"It did."

"That's ridiculous! The sword was of low molecular density, like you said. There couldn't possibly have been enough molecules to cause this much damage. The ghostly sword could no more cut into the wood than it could cut through your wrist."

"No, John, you don't understand. It didn't cut it yesterday. That's where the sword struck the wood four hundred and eighty years ago, in 1537. This cut is ancient." Sarah and Harry looked over at them as Brian's voice rose. "You do understand this thing, don't you, John? There was a miscibility of our two worlds. Just as we saw the past superimposed on our present, the monks and the soldiers saw the future superimposed on their present. In 1537, the commander of the soldiers saw a ghost from the future—me—and threw his sword at it, striking the wooden screen. The resulting cleft in the wood has survived through the ages. It actually happened in their time."

"At the time of the dissolution of Hoyland Abbey?"

"Yes. This thing is a reciprocal phenomenon, John. I hadn't fully appreciated that till now. I'd been so fixated on how the ghosts materialized in our world that I'd never given a thought to what was happening in their world. But the phenomenon works both ways. I see that now. As a matter of fact, I think it follows directly from the quantum field equations. There has to be symmetry."

"Look, Brian," John said, "I don't mean to throw cold water on your enthusiasm, but Aunt Polly died as a result of this latest experiment only yesterday. She died! How can you talk about equations? We need to give this thing a rest."

"No, John, we don't," Brian said calmly. "If we walk away from it, Aunt Polly will have died in vain. I started this thing to help Sarah and to help Aunt Polly. Now it's even more imperative that we persevere. I owe it to Aunt Polly."

"Oh man! I can't believe you. Not under the circumstances."

Brian nodded and put a hand on his brother's shoulder. "I do know how you feel," he said. "I'm not asking for anything from you." Then he turned and looked away, but he continued speaking calmly and clearly to John as if the past and the present had become one to him. "It was Crossly, you know. It was Richard Crossly who threw the sword at me. I've no doubt of it. He was the leader of King Henry's force. It was he who executed the monk. No wonder they called him Ironfist. What a savage!"

"Was Abbot Gervase the monk he killed?" John asked.

"The historical record would suggest that."

"The monk seemed to levitate. Did you see that? And what was all that static electricity about?"

"It was some kind of religious ecstasy, I suppose."

"You were the cause of it, Brian. Gervase thought you were the Savior. He thought that he was rising up into the arms of Christ—Christ who had come to save him from his enemies."

"I realize that."

As the two brothers ruminated on the implications of that thought, Sarah walked over to them from the nave of the church. "Brian, you have to tell the police to let us leave," she said. "I can't stand being in this place a moment longer. I'm going to go crazy." When Brian didn't immediately respond, she turned on her heels and went to talk to the two detectives. John followed her. "And you'll never see me inside this church again," she added for Brian's benefit.

"I recommend that you do leave now," Detective Jamieson told her when she returned, "all of you. But you mustn't go back to London yet. We'll put you up at the Red Lion in Hoyland for a few days. There'll be more questions tomorrow and then the inquest in a day or two. You'll each be called as a witness to Mrs. Coleby's death."

The prospect of recapitulation made John's stomach burn. However, he agreed that they should leave and called Brian over. When Brian didn't respond and couldn't be seen, John went to the chancel to get him. As he turned the corner of the screen, he saw Brian on his hands and knees by the choir stalls. John watched him scrabbling on the floor for a moment and then called his name again.

"Coming," Brian replied, furtively placing something in his pocket.

"What are you up to?" John asked.

"Nothing. Let's go."

"What were you doing over there?" Detective Carling asked after they rejoined the group. "What were you looking for?"

"Nothing," Brian repeated.

The detective was suspicious but let it pass. The whole group then walked back to the vestry. In the doorway, they unexpectedly came face-to-face with Jack Stephens. He immediately lunged at Brian, but Detective Carling wrapped an arm around his waist and said, "Easy there, Jack!"

"You'll not get away with this sort of thing, Kenning!" spat the agitated reporter. "I know all about what's going on here. Done to death one of our most respected villagers you have, and you'll not get away with it, not this time. You've no respect for decent folk like Polly Coleby. She's your own flesh and blood!"

"That'll be enough out of you, Stephens," Detective Jamieson said. They knew each other well. Journalism and the law were forever colliding in the tiny streets of Hoyland. "Back to your ticket office!"

"If we had found out about this little charade in advance, Kenning," Stephens continued, "we'd have put a quick stop to it, that we would. We'll teach you city slickers not to mess around with our village."

"Oh, pipe down!" Brian said sharply.

"Why, you little bugger!" Stephens exclaimed, surging toward him, but Carling's arms clasped his waist and held him fast.

"Cool down, Jack," Detective Jamieson advised him. "You'll get your chance in print. Pen is mightier than the sword."

"Aye, that it is. Take a look in next week's *Examiner*, Kenning, if you want to get burned some more!" He laughed contemptuously. Brian turned, seemingly ready to accept the physical challenge, but Detective Carling was already dragging Stephens off to the front door of the church. "We'll be ready next time!" Stephens yelled as he was manhandled down the aisle. "We'll be ready! Murderer!"

Brian could barely contain his rage. "Can't you do anything to stop him harassing us like that?" he asked Detective Jamieson.

"Er, no, actually, I can't," Jamieson replied, and Brian got the distinct impression that he really wanted to use the word *won't*, not *can't*.

Brian turned away with a deep sigh. He was almost hamstrung by the remorse he felt at his aunt's death, but he knew that if he allowed himself to become incapacitated, then everything would fall apart, and the past few months would dissolve into nothing more than a huge, needless tragedy. The added intrusion of outsiders' vindictiveness and the grueling police interrogation was almost more than he could bear. For the time being, he could only stay focused on his mission with the fillip of anger.

John, on the other hand, did not feel any force driving him to rise above his grief and guilt. The death of his aunt had knocked all the stuffing out of him. His mind was tormented by memories of the happy times spent in her company and the dread of having to live out a life in which he was partly responsible for her death.

CHAPTER 29

Hoyland Church
May 2018

Polly's funeral service took place in the nave of the church she had loved so much. With the Reverend Applewhite still in hospital, a vicar from a neighboring parish was brought in to do the honors. John, wedged between his brother and his uncle, was forced to sit and be reminded of the reality of Polly's death, in all its many ecclesiastical variations, out of the mouth of the dry and dispassionate cleric. As the service wore on, John gradually escaped from the stench of shame and the icy grip of a future that horrified him and escaped into a past that still had value. How he did this and why, he didn't know at the time; but later, he looked back on it and thought he must have been practicing, preparing himself for what was to come.

"The Lord is merciful and gracious, slow to anger, and plenteous in mercy." John became mesmerized by the vicar's hypnotic voice. The lilt seemed to erase any real content and turned the oration into nothing more than broad ripples of sound, undulations that stretched through the void of the church. John closed his eyes, and the vicar's words washed down from the pulpit and bathed his temples with balm. He felt as if he was floating on some limitless ocean, each syllable of the vicar's words a gentle wave beneath him.

Aunt Polly had a terrific sense of humor—at least, she did when I was a boy. You could get her to laugh at almost anything. She would hunch up her shoulders and chuckle and chuckle till nothing could stop her. The tears would roll down her cheeks, and her eyes would squint to narrow slits until she could barely see you laughing back at her. If she could see you laughing back at her, it only made matters worse. Other people's pleasure was a delight to her. You could even get her to laugh in church if the mood was right.

"He will not always chide. Neither will he keep his anger forever."

I remember one Easter when I really set her off. It wasn't in this church, though. It must have been in that corrugated apology for a church at Bittern Fen. But it did look nice that day. There were daffodils all over the place. I never thought there was such a yellow in God's palette. It was Palm Sunday, and I couldn't have been more than eight years old.

Aunt Polly took me to a children's service. She held my hand all the way from the cottage to the church, even when the village girls started calling me names. Of course, I didn't know what love was at that age. I just knew that being with Aunt Polly was pleasant and worth a few taunts. Mother was sick, I remember, and couldn't go. I don't recall where Brian was—too old and too wise for church even then, I suppose. It was just Aunt Polly and me.

They gave the children little crosses made of straw. I clutched mine in my fist till Aunt Polly told me to slip it between the pages of my prayer book to keep it flat. Her hair was black then and shiny as coal. Wherever the prayer book is now, the cross is probably still inside it. It's been so many years since I opened that book, so long since I prayed.

"He hath not dealt with us after our sins or rewarded us according to our iniquities. For as the heaven is high above the earth, so great is his mercy toward them that fear him."

They asked the children to kneel and recite a little prayer. I did my best, but many of the words were unfamiliar to me. When it was over and I was sitting on the pew next to Aunt Polly, I turned to her and said, "I don't like that prayer."

"Why ever not?"

"I don't like mice. They're horrible."

She told me not to worry. She said there were no mice in the church. She said the vicar chases them out with his broom if they try to come in. I nodded. We sat obediently, listening to the vicar's sermon, then she turned and whispered in my ear, "Why did you ask about mice?"

"That prayer was about mice."

"The prayer?"

"It said, 'Pity mice implicitly.'" I stumbled over the last word, but I knew it fitted the context. "Why should we pity them? They're nasty little things. They're all over the barn, and I hate them. Uncle Will sets traps for them. I don't pity them at all."

She turned and stared hard at me. "Not mice," she said. "'Pity my simplicity.' My simplicity. See? Nothing to do with mice at all. Silly boy."

"As far as the east is from the west, so far hath he removed our transgressions from us."

I tried to stifle it, but it came welling up from deep inside me. It was like a tidal wave that began in my feet and demanded exit through my mouth or my nose. I had to let out a snicker, or I would have exploded. I knew I had to behave, but the vicar was babbling on about some ancient nonsense, and it fed the feeling. Actually, I think I would have been fine, but Aunt Polly turned to look at me, and there was a telltale crease in her cheek. I giggled into my palm until the next wave passed. When I looked up, her head was bowed, and there was a broad smile on her face.

That was it! Suddenly, there were mice all over the church—mice dressed as choirboys squeaking the hymns, mice bumping into candles and setting their tails alight, and an elderly hamster bent over the organ, pounding out an anthem to cheese. And yes, there he was, reading the sermon, a big rat with soaped whiskers. I turned red and spluttered into my handkerchief. Aunt Polly's shoulders began to shake, her eyes searching for a sober sight to cling to. An elderly spinster turned to glower at us, and the minister stumbled over an awkward phrase.

"Like as a father pitieth his children, so the Lord pitieth them that fear him."

We simply had to leave. There was no other option. Aunt Polly grabbed my hand, and we scurried down the aisle—like mice!—our flushed faces in stark contrast to the pale cheeks of the indignant congregation. Outside, we sat on a bench by the church door and roared with laughter. Aunt Polly slapped her knees and rocked back and forth, gasping with delight, till I feared she would pass out from lack of oxygen. Her pleasure fed off mine and mine off hers. In the end, like a tired bonfire, our laughter burned itself out, and we were left glowing among the embers. She took hold of my hand again as the spring sunshine bathed *us in a cleansing light. I was probably only seven or eight years old at the time.*

"For he knoweth our frame. He remembereth that we are dust."

The memory of that day kept me warm through many traumatic years, and it snuffed out my need of religion for good. Nowadays, whenever I see those pale faces filing into church, I just want to yell at them to quit wasting time and go sit in the sunshine with someone they love.

"As for man, his days are as grass. As a flower of the field, so he flourisheth. For the wind passeth over it, and it is gone, and the place thereof shall know it no more."

John wiped his eyes with the back of his hand. He gazed at his aunt's coffin with the single white lily on it and felt utterly desolate. His own weakness had caused this to happen. When his aunt had walked the dunes with them last September, she had been fit and fearless. And he had just stood by in the intervening months and let all this happen. Truly, he was an accomplice in her death. When he was a little boy, she had protected him and loved him—and when he should have returned that protection and love, he'd failed her. He would have given the world for his hand in hers again.

"But the mercy of the Lord is from everlasting to everlasting upon them that fear him and his righteousness unto children's children—to such as keep his covenant and to those that remember his commandments to do them." The vicar closed the Bible and descended from the pulpit. The congregation rose, filed out of the church, and reassembled by the fresh-dug grave. The pallbearers arrived with the coffin and lowered it into the grave to the accompaniment of the vicar's eulogy.

Uncle Will kicked dirt onto the box with the toe of his boot. The mourners walked back to the church and dispersed to their cars and their homes. Will turned his back on the grave and faltered, not knowing where he was supposed to go. Brian and John came to his aid and led him to the lych-gate. They all drove back to the cottage. Will trudged to the front door and then stepped to one side, as he always did, to let Polly go first. When he realized she was not behind him, he sat down on the doorstep and wept.

*****

Later that evening, John walked into the kitchen and found Sarah washing the dishes and crying. "You don't have to do that," he said. "A woman's coming from the village tomorrow."

"I don't mind," she sobbed. "I need to keep busy. You know, it's funny, John. I swore several times that I'd never set foot in that church again, never ever. And I broke each of those promises. I can't do anything right. Nothing ever really changes, does it? We all just stumble on."

"Don't talk like that."

"These last few days have been more than I can stand, John— the inquest, the police, the funeral, that horrible newspaperman. When will it all be over?"

"Soon, I'm sure. And there's no need for you to get so wrapped up in it. It's a family thing, Sarah, first and foremost."

"I suppose I'm doing it for Brian's sake, whether he appreciates it or not."

John picked up a cloth and began to dry the stacked dishes. "How are things between you and Brian?" He had wondered for some time if the changes he had seen in Brian might have damaged their relationship. The tension between the two of them was certainly obvious to all. "Do the tears have anything to do with him?"

"Maybe. He's changed so much over the last few months that I don't know where I stand anymore. It's not that I've stopped caring for him or that he's stopped caring for me as near as I can tell. I don't suppose I'd be standing here washing these dishes if I thought differently. It's just that recent events have driven a wedge between us. It's a big wedge, John, and it's driving us apart. Brian's made these experiments bigger than our relationship. I don't think I can hold us together. Perhaps it's all for the best."

"Don't say that, Sarah. I've got you marked down for a sister-in-law. When all this has blown over, things will return to normal. You'll see. You can pick up where you left off."

"We can't go back to the way things were before your aunt's death. That will always loom over us."

"I know, but…"

She stopped washing dishes and stood with her forearms in the dirty water, staring out the kitchen window, at the nondescript fenland. "I knew your brother was driven from the moment I met him. His passion was appealing somehow back then. I had a vision of the two of us blazing trails together—me with my business and art, him with his science. I wouldn't have minded that kind of a life. But the way I saw it, we'd be holding hands along the way. Do you know what I mean? We'd be celebrating our accomplishments together and solving our problems together."

She glanced down at the dishwater and swirled it abstractedly. "But his trail's veered away from mine. I can see him receding into the distance. I've become nothing more than an extra in one of his productions. And now he's caused the death of that sweet, gentle old woman, and…" She started to cry again.

"Don't talk like that, Sarah, please," John said. "You're just upset about Aunt Polly."

"I am, I know. That's the main reason for the tears. But something else happened in the church. When Brian and that Karen Butler girl met, they—I'm not sure—well, there was a certain look exchanged between the two of them. Did you notice it?"

"No."

"A certain kind of knowing look. Is there something going on between them, John? Would you tell me if there was?"

"I'm sure you're imagining it. They've had no opportunity—well, very little opportunity. And yes, I will tell you if I hear anything."

"I'm so stressed out," Sarah said. "I could've imagined it, I suppose."

"Maybe you and Brian could make plans for a vacation together or something after the police have finished with us in a couple of weeks, get your relationship back on track."

She shrugged. "I can't allow myself to make plans, John. It's up to your brother now. He started this ghost business, and it's up to him to stop it if he wants our relationship to survive. If I pull him away from it now, he'll only make me regret it for the rest of my life. I know what he's like. He has to make the conciliatory move. I love him, John, but I'm helpless." She emptied the water out of the bowl and spluttered a sharp laugh through her tears. "I'm sorry. I didn't mean to drag you into this. You've suffered too, I know. Pass me the towel, will you?" She dried her hands and wiped her eyes.

"So where's Brian been these last two days?" John asked. "I haven't seen hide or hair of him. He's out of the house before breakfast. Do you know what's going on?"

"You don't want to know. He's been at the coroner's office with Harry. He mentioned something about brain cultures and things like that. It was so ghoulish I didn't pay attention."

"Aunt Polly's?" John asked incredulously.

"Shut up, John, please! I can't take any more."

Together, they cleaned up the kitchen and returned to the parlor. The fire had gone out, and the room was cold. Will was perched on the edge of a chair like a piece of sculpture made of thick copper wire—strong against deformation but easy to topple. Dried saliva whitened the corners of his mouth. He would rub his chin with the palm of his hand, mutter a few words, and then repeat the process. His words seemed to orbit some private truth about the purpose of life. When he started talking about boats and the need to ship oars, Sarah got worried.

"Ebb tide's strong in May," he said, "like a mother's pull on her children. When the ebb tide runs, it's almost more 'n you can do to row back to shore, if 'n' you had something to row back for."

*****

Brian woke John early the next morning and dragged him out of the cottage before breakfast. He seemed compelled to retrace the autumn walk they had taken with their aunt, and so the two brothers followed the same curving path atop the foothills. Down to their left, the rippling sand stretched away to the sea; to their right, the wet fallows sported the first fuzz of spring crops. Against a chill wind, they trod the thin line between soil and sand, organic and inorganic, the living and the dead.

A bird broke from a dyke and weaved across the muddy field, heading toward the coast road. "That was a snipe," John said. "Did you see it?" He pointed to the field, but Brian was looking the other way. Admittedly, the view was more inspiring in that direction. The sand had been sculpted by the nimble tide into patterns far more exotic than the plough could hope to fashion from clay, and the sea was a prettier backdrop than the deserted roadway and the tangled bushes that lined it. But at least the fields held the promise of life.

"There's Uncle Will's rowing boat," Brian said, pointing to a small craft beached on the sands. "He took me out in it once."

"He won't use it again. He's turned right in on himself since the funeral. He hasn't been out of the house. Aunt Polly meant everything to him."

"Oh, I think he'll use it again, at least once."

"What do you mean?" John asked, but Brian didn't elaborate. His sullenness irritated John. "Brian, you can't keep this bottled up forever. Aunt Polly's dead. How do you feel about that? You haven't said a word to anyone. Can we talk about it?"

"How do I feel?" Brian responded with venom. "How do you think I feel? However you twist the facts, the truth remains that if it weren't for me, Aunt Polly would be walking beside us today, just like she did last autumn. I'll have to carry that burden for the rest of my life. You and Sarah think I'm cruel and egotistical. I know that. You think I don't care what happens to people, but you're wrong. I'm as compassionate as the next man. I've got a path to follow, though. I committed myself to it months ago. I can't let what happened to Aunt Polly incapacitate me. Do you understand that?" He paused for a moment, staring at his shoes as he walked. "I'm devastated. I'm guilt-ridden. I press on."

"It's hard to sympathize with you, Brian, when you talk like that. You say you're compassionate, yet you sound so cold when you say it."

"If I give up now, Aunt Polly will have died for nothing. Sarah will never know what happened to her in the church. Thousands of Florrie Gibsons all over the world will sit and fret about strange experiences they've had, never knowing why. I feel like I have a responsibility to them. I don't mean to sound arrogant, John, but I'm on the verge of uncovering something truly momentous. It's all within my reach."

"Sarah says she doesn't know you anymore."

"I'm rediscovering myself every day."

They came to a patch of coarse grass growing on the path. Amazingly, a cluster of buttercups struggled for survival in that bleak outpost. John stooped to pick one but decided their fortitude deserved better reward. The wind bent them against the back of his hand in gratitude.

"All that talk about goals and choosing doors was literally true, John," Brian continued. "Aunt Polly's death doesn't alter any of that. She would've understood, believe me. Those doors only swing one way. Once you've crossed the threshold, you have to move on to the next one. That's what life is all about. There's no starting over. And there's no glory in expiation."

"Am I supposed to interpret all that to mean you refuse to drop this ghost business even now, after all that's happened?" Brian shrugged his shoulders. John ground his teeth in anger, feeling grains of sand grate between them. He spat into the bushes.

"Applewhite died last night," Brian said.

It was like a slap in the face. "Died?"

"There was a phone call while you were asleep. He lapsed into a coma two days ago, and he died about eight thirty last night."

"Died of what?"

"I've been in touch with the hospital all week. In fact, I told the doctors what to look for. They found a high concentration of lead in his system—throughout his whole body, in fact. Can you guess where it came from?" John shook his head.

"Do you remember when we saw Applewhite run out of the vestry? Do you remember how he was engulfed in all that fire? That was molten lead falling from the burning roof. A huge piece went right through him and knocked him to the ground. Several more pieces smashed onto him as he lay there. It was the shock that rendered him unconscious, but it was the trail of lead left in his body that killed him. He died of acute lead poisoning."

"How could that be?"

"That last contact was much stronger, John. Remember how much more distinct the images were? It was a really powerful resonance. My guess is that the molecular concentration in our world was several orders of magnitude greater than before, maybe 10^{-5} or even 10^{-4}."

"Yes, I'd agree with that."

"And let me ask you something else. Did you see me bending over in the chancel while we were waiting for the police? Did you think I was acting mysteriously, trying to conceal something?"

"Yes, I did. What were you doing?"

"I'd noticed something unusual in the choir stalls."

"What?"

"Dust."

"Pardon me?"

"Dust. You obviously didn't see it, but there was a thin layer of dust all over the chancel when the experiment was over. There was no dust before we started. Applewhite kept the place spotless."

"So what? Our escapade probably dislodged some dust from the tops of the screens. There must be lots of inaccessible ledges high up in the church. I don't think that's very significant."

"I gathered up some of the dust in my handkerchief and shipped it to the college lab for analysis. I got the results on Friday. It wasn't the kind of dust you'd expect if it had merely wafted down from high up in the church. That would have been mostly stone with perhaps traces of wood from the rafters. No, this dust was different. It contained high levels of metals—copper, iron, gold, silver, lots of lead. There was also fibrous material, like hair and fabric, and there were even traces of human tissue and bone. The analytical chemist said he'd never seen anything like it. He called it molecular soup."

"So what does that mean?"

"He did a radiocarbon dating of the organic compounds in the dust, the wood and such. The age profile of the material was astonishing. It fell into two distinct groups, one considerably older than the other. And the age difference was—can you guess?"

"I'm lost," John confessed, shaking his head.

"About five hundred years. Everything points to the fact that the temporal mixing during the last experiment was not completely reversible. We've had some material permanently transferred from 1537 to the present. A tiny fraction of the molecules that rightfully belong in 1537—bits of the church, the swords, the clothing, even the people themselves—remained in our present time frame after the resonance was over. Some of the temporal transitions must have penetrated a barrier, like you find with quantum mechanical tunneling. Some molecules were unable to relax back to their own time frame and became marooned in our world. It was the lead residue in Applewhite's body that caused his death."

"That's stupid, Brian. Radiocarbon dating is notoriously unreliable. The sample was probably too small, and the technician gave you the answer you wanted to hear. You've worked with those spectrometric devices. You know how temperamental they can be with messy samples. You've no grounds for making a rash conjecture like that."

"You haven't seen the spectrogram. There are two distinct peaks."

"Forget it, Brian," John pleaded. "It doesn't matter anymore."

"On the contrary, it matters a great deal."

"No, it doesn't. It's just a piquant diversion from your proper work, and now it's turned dangerous, deadly. I know that your research at the university seems banal to you sometimes. Mine does too. But it's all we've got. It's time to get back to the real world and try to repair the damage we've caused. Get back with Sarah and get on with your life."

"Sarah's already cast me adrift."

"No, she hasn't, Brian. Truly, she hasn't. I talked with her last night. She just wants you to communicate more with her. She wants you to share your thoughts with her, share your life. She's not given up on you."

"She no longer believes in my cause."

"That's a silly reason to abandon someone."

"Then maybe she no longer believes in me."

"I know that's not true. I heard it from her own mouth."

Brian stared at John and said, "Then I guess it must be me," as if it had just dawned on him.

John thought that now was a good time to raise one of Sarah's other concerns. "She asked me if there was anything going on between you and Karen Butler. Is there?"

"That's a private matter, John."

"Is there, Brian? Sarah's in bad enough shape as it is without the additional blow of unfaithfulness."

"Then no," Brian said.

They crossed the dunes and struck out across the sand toward Will's boat. The wind battered them fiercely, raising a flush of blood to John's cheeks. They came to one of the wooden groins that sliced the beach into rectangular slabs to prevent tidal erosion. The wood was green with age, and algae hung from the iron ring that had once secured the boats of local fishermen. John stepped onto the cross-lot strut and held the slimy post to steady himself. The tide had sucked sand from the other side of the groin, so he was faced with a leap over a crab-flecked pool. He jumped and caught his heel in the water. He cursed and strode on. Brian struggled to keep up. They watched the brown-and-gray sandpipers chase the water's edge in search of food and then be chased away by it.

The dilapidated condition of Will's boat became apparent to them as they drew closer. Fifteen feet from it, they came across a split oar and observed that a slat was missing from just above the water-line. Ten feet away, they were startled by the eruption of a seagull from the bottom of the boat in a cloud of feathers and fish scales. Their noses led them the rest of the way to a half-eaten herring in the prow.

"It's in a terrible state, isn't it?" John observed. "It looks like it hasn't been used in months. See how that green stuff is taking over?"

Brian picked up a rusty knife that lay under the seat and volunteered to return it to Will. "There are some funny hooks and things here too," he said, reaching under the seat. "I don't think the boat's worth a damn." He collected the rest of the fishing tackle, stuffed it into a battered lunch box, and wedged it under the seat. He tied down a length of rope that the wind was whipping against the hull and then stood quietly for a moment, staring into the bottom of the boat.

"John, do you remember the story of Neot? I don't have it all memorized, but Sarah said something about Neot describing a vision that had come to him on the two hundred and twelfth—whatever—night of his imprisonment. He said that he'd witnessed the figures of St. Guthlac, St. Bartholomew, and Abbot Waltheof arrayed before him in the guise of the heavenly host. I do remember that bit. The three spirits commanded him to some holy purpose, and a celestial light shined upon him."

"So?"

"Three figures?" John shook his head. "A celestial light? What do you think that was, pixie dust?"

"You can't take those historical accounts literally, Brian. There are many—"

"It was a flashlight."

"What?"

"It was my flashlight as I explored the corners of the niche. It wasn't Bartholomew, Guthlac, and Waltheof. It was Brian, John, and Harry."

"Neot could see us staring in on him. We were ghosts from the future. Of course."

"Reciprocity again."

"So all that talk about miraculous powers entrusted to him was pure hokum."

"A hyperactive imagination under stressful conditions."

"What about the miracles he was able to perform after his release? The healing and such?"

"His innate ability, I guess. Before the vision, he had no learning, no confidence, no willpower. In the blink of an eye, he was given a special gift: the healing powers of Abbot Waltheof. But it wasn't true. He did it all himself." The wind lashed the sides of the boat. Brian dropped into the shelter of the hull. John sat down by his side and hugged his knees. Their differences seemed tempered in the more tranquil conditions. They both gazed out to sea.

"So where do you go from here?" John asked.

"Back to the stone circle," Brian replied in a measured voice. "Back to the campfire."

"Meaning?"

"That's what this is all about, John. I understand now. We all knew how to do this stuff once upon a time. When we were scared or we needed help, when the crops failed or the plague came calling, we'd get the family together at the holy place, smoke a little dope, slip into the zeta state, and commune with our ancestors, seek their advice, feel better about things, and move on. The primitive peoples of the world still retain a memory of how to do it.

"The Australian aborigines, the Yoruba of Western Africa, the Haitian voodoo dancers—they each have their own way of speaking to their forebears from times gone by. That is to say, they have their own way of entering the zeta state. They remember how to do it. But the rest of us got civilized. We learned that reaching out of our own time was dangerous, and we developed an autonomic response to prevent it happening. Sarah, Karen, Aunt Polly—there's nothing special about them. They've just learned a forgotten art." He turned and looked John in the eye. "I can learn it too."

"You? You're crazy."

"No, no. I'm deadly serious. I'm going to do it, and I'm going to do it better than any of them. I'm going to cut through millennia of neurochemical defenses and get to the primal response."

"You'll get more problems than you can handle."

"Someone's got to find out where the frontier is." He dug a razor shell out of the wet sand and began to polish it against the sleeve of his jacket. "Abbot Gervase is at the root of it all. It was his religious ecstasy that initiated everything. He generated the quantized temporal states. Remember the levitation and the vibration of his body, the electrical energy? God knows what forces were unleashed. I have to learn more about what happened that day."

"Well, I'll tell you right now, Brian, I want no part of it. And you won't find anyone else willing to help you either. Sarah certainly won't. You've overstepped the mark. And I don't want any more lives to be lost or ruined because of your fanaticism. If necessary, I'll have to stop you."

"You must do what you have to, John. My path is clear to me now, and if I have to go it alone, then so be it. Try not to think badly of me."

CHAPTER 30

Three days after Polly Coleby's funeral, the group was given permission to return to London. Frank Koslowski was immediately dispatched to Chicago with a mysterious dry ice cooler. A week later, Harry placed a call to Northwestern University from Brian's office. The recipient was Andy Lieshman, chairman of the Department of Neurobiology.

"Andy, is that you?" Harry shouted down the line.

"Harry? Good to hear from you again. I've got Dr. Koslowski here with me. We have you on speaker phone."

"Hi, Frank. How did the specimens travel?"

"Fine. I had a little trouble getting them through customs at O'Hare. I guess they're suspicious about medical samples. But no big deal."

"Good. Thanks a lot for carrying them, Frank. So, Andy, what news do you have for me?"

"The good kind, I guess, though it didn't help that the brain tissue was so crudely cut. Did you have the local butcher slice it for you? We had a real hard time reconciling the sections with the autopsy notes. Nevertheless, the news is good."

"I'm sorry about the quality of the samples, Andy. The coroner's people over here had never done this kind of thing before. Dr. Kenning and I worked with them to meet your specs, but they didn't have the right tools, and as I say, they don't claim to be experts."

"There's so much smearing and variation of thickness that I doubt we'll be able to pinpoint any neuroactive sites, but perhaps that's not important to you. Anyway, there was enough tissue to do the gross physical and chemical characterizations. That's all finished."

"Did you find something?"

"Yes, actually we did. We isolated the same neuropeptide from several of the samples. We've determined its molecular weight, and we've done the amino acid sequencing. There are a couple of wrinkles still to iron out on the chemical structure, but GC/MS should have that by the end of the day."

"What's the substance?"

"Like I said, it's a neuropeptide, a new one to us. Let me think how best to describe it to you." He paused for a moment to organize his response. "You probably know that there are two kinds of peptides active in the nervous system. There are the big ones, like beta-endorphin, which have twenty or thirty amino acids in the string, and then there are smaller ones, the enkephalins, which have only five or six. Are you with me so far?"

"I learned a little bit of that in biochem."

"Your neuropeptide has seven amino acids. The sequence, if this stuff means anything to you at all, is TYR-GLY-GLY-PHE-MET-THR-SER. And there's an extra amine group tossed in there somewhere. This sequence is part of the beta-endorphin chain, so we're pretty sure we're correct. All of these opioid peptides derive ultimately from lipotropin, Harry, so it's relatively easy to spot the sequences."

"Opioids did you say?"

"Yeah. Those are the pain-killing type of neuropeptides."

"You say you haven't come across this one before?"

"Nope. It's definitely a new one. It doesn't have a name. We've taken the liberty of christening it seriphin, an endorphin-like substance terminating in the serine amino acid. Do you approve of the name? Almost angelic, isn't it, to be corny?"

"Seriphin. Okay. So where does this stuff come from?"

"It's synthesized by the brain, Harry. These kinds of chemicals interfere with the electrical integrity of the synapse. They're produced within the cell body, transported through the vesicles, and launched out from the presynaptic neuron. After crossing the synapse, they bind to certain receptor sites on the postsynaptic neuron. Each peptide has its characteristic docking site, so to speak, and elicits a characteristic electrochemical response. Because seriphin is similar in size and structure to the enkephalins, my guess is, it suppresses calcium channels."

"Shuts down electrical circuits do you mean?"

"Yes, that's generally how the opioids work. They block the normal conducting channels and reduce electrical activity. That's why compounds like morphine have pain-killing properties. Think of the analogy of a sprinkler system. You start a fire, you produce smoke, the smoke is sensed by a detector, the detector closes an electronic circuit in the sprinkler system, water is released, and the fire is quenched. It's an automatic deadening response."

"Is it possible to tell in which part of the brain this seriphin stuff is being released?"

"That's not easy from these specimens. The concentration in the cerebellum seems to be particularly high, but I don't know why that would be. Usually, these neuropeptides are found near the core of the brain—in the hypothalamus or the septal area. I don't know any that prefer the cerebellum, and I can't imagine what function seriphin would serve there. I'm sure you know, Harry, that the cerebellum is the least understood part of the brain. It's a huge, convoluted sheet of cells, maybe a hundred billion of them, more than the rest of the nervous system combined."

"The dark side of the city."

"What was that?"

"Oh, that's just an expression we've been using here."

"Okay. Well, anyway, the cerebellum has a very complex fibrous structure with extensive branching and divergence. It clearly has sophisticated interneuron connectivity, appropriate for a control mechanism."

"Would it be capable of synchronized neuron firing? Could it set up large-scale electrical circuits within the brain?"

"I'm not familiar with all the literature, Harry. Traditionally, the cerebellum is identified with motor control—musculature and balance and stuff like that. But we're not totally sure."

"The things that are not needed when you're floating in a sensory deprivation tank."

"I guess not."

"I think the primary function of the cerebellum is something entirely different."

"You do? And what would that be?"

"I think it's designed for external transmission of energy."

"Oh no. No way!"

"I think it is, Andy. That's why the cerebellum is so large in humans and contains such intricate circuitry. It's a transmitter of zeta energy, and this seriphin stuff is a biochemical off switch."

"Oh, excuse me, Harry, but no way! I'm the professor of neurobiology here, not you. That's a wild-ass theory, if I've ever heard one. Fibers from the spinal cord ascend—"

"Okay, Andy, okay, maybe I'm off base on that one. Let's move on. What can you tell me about the functional effect of seriphin? Any clues as to the nature of its influence?"

"Well, each neuropeptide binds to a particular type of postsynaptic receptor and elicits a particular type of response. For example, morphine binds to something called the mu receptor site that's linked to pathways of pain transmission. The delta site binds enkephalins in limbic parts of the brain that have something to do with emotional response. There's a sigma site that binds the hallucinogen phencyclidine, and finally, there's beta-endorphin itself, which mediates behavioral response in the hypothalamus. Shoot an animal up with beta-endorphin and it'll often go into complete akinesia."

"Say again?"

"Akinesia. The animal refuses to move."

"A protective response to danger."

"In the extreme."

"So seriphin binds to some other receptor site. Maybe also as a protection from danger?"

"That's conceivable, I guess."

"It's binding to the neurons that produce the zeta effect. It's flooding the circuitry and knocking out power. Karen Butler even described it that way."

"That's what Frank's been telling me. He wants to name it the zeta receptor site. He seems to have a thing about the end of the alphabet." He chuckled nervously.

"Andy, listen. Brian Kenning and I have the perfect explanation for all of this. Whatever this zeta thing is, it involves the production of electrical currents in the cerebellum. In turn, these currents generate a special kind of energy field surrounding the body. This field can extend for tens of meters. We've measured it, for Christ's sake, Andy! But the brain as a whole, in its role of protecting and controlling the body, has developed a response mechanism. It secretes seriphin into the vesicles of the cerebellum and jerks our subjects out of the zeta state."

"I don't know about that, Harry. You'll have to speculate alone on that one."

"Let me ask you one more thing. Supposing we wanted to counteract the process, would there be any way to stop the production of seriphin?"

"Well, it might be possible to limit it by behavior modification, biofeedback. Some people seem to be able to control their own body chemistry to a certain extent. From what Frank has told me, this Karen Butler girl might have developed some ability in that direction. But there may be another way, a chemical way, not to eliminate seriphin production but to block its neurological effects. You need to find an antagonist."

"What's that?"

"An antagonist is a chemical substance that will bind to the same receptor site as the neuropeptide but not interfere with the synaptic currents. In other words, it won't close down the conductance channels. The classic antagonist is a substance called naloxone. Some years ago, it was discovered that naloxone will compete with morphine for the mu receptor site. If you introduce naloxone into the presynaptic ventricles, the pain-killing effects of morphine disappear. In essence, the naloxone molecules hijack all the docking sites and leave no room for the morphine molecules. The electrical currents flow unabated. The pain persists."

"They have stereochemical similarities but not neurological similarities?"

"Precisely. Think back to the analogy of a sprinkler system. In the case of naloxone, it works something like this. You start a fire, the detector senses smoke, it activates an electronic circuit, and the control system switches on the dishwasher."

"Wrong response."

"The house burns down." There was a long pause at each end of the transatlantic phone line as the potentially critical implications of the last remark were assimilated by each of them.

"Naloxone," Harry repeated.

"That's only one of the opiate antagonists we're working with. We've synthesized a number of them. We're learning the significance of stereochemical structure—if you like, the molecular shapes and functional groups that fit particular docking sites on the postsynaptic neuron. It turns into a jigsaw puzzle after a while. I don't know if any of them would be specific to seriphin."

"Could you send some samples back with Frank?"

"Jesus, Harry, have you any idea how much time and money it takes to synthesize these compounds?"

"I'm sure it takes a lot, but look, Andy, you're a part of something big here. You've discovered a radically new neuropeptide. This is cutting-edge research. It'll get you to the top of the ladder."

"I'm already at the top."

"Well then, maybe there's cash in it somewhere, perhaps a Nobel. We'll help you with the last piece of the puzzle: characterization of the neurological effects of seriphin. Send Frank back with some samples, whatever you can rustle up. Please."

"Okay, okay. Give me till the end of the week to prepare some possible seriphin antagonists. There won't be huge quantities, mind, just a few milliliters of each. You'll have to use them sparingly. I'll put them on a plane with Frank."

"Great. We'll test them all and let you know which ones work. Well, Andy, I think that about wraps it up. No, wait, one final thing. How do we introduce the antagonist into the body?"

"You'll need to do a cerebrospinal injection. The medics call it an intrathecal. You can't do a normal injection, or the drug will be stopped by the blood-brain barrier. It's not dangerous if properly performed. I'll send some literature over with Frank. Anything else I can do for you?"

"No, I think that's everything. Thanks a million, Andy. You've been a terrific help. Brian's going to be overjoyed when I explain all this to him. It's a giant leap forward."

"My pleasure, Harry. We'll talk again. Bye for now."

"So long, both of you. See you next week, Frank." Harry replaced the receiver and looked at Brian. "How far are you prepared to go with this thing?"

Brian rocked his head from side to side and said, "Tell me what I have to do."

CHAPTER 31

London
May 2018

Karen was sleeping late in her tiny hotel room off High Holborn. The grand tour of London had been completed earlier in the week. She had fed the pigeons in Trafalgar Square and whispered into the dome of St. Paul's. She had gawked like a chimp through the gates of Buckingham Palace. A bobby had tipped his helmet at her, a bus driver had cursed her for not tendering exact fare, and at midnight in Soho, she had watched a punk with a purple mohawk kick in the window of a wine shop. There didn't seem to be much left to do.

The jangle of the bedside telephone woke her. She fumbled with the receiver, her head abuzz with the remnants of an interrupted dream. The voice on the line was unfamiliar at first, then she realized it was Brian Kenning, asking if she was up for a day's sightseeing. She looked around the room, listened to his voice, and felt suddenly awake and refreshed.

"Somewhere you haven't been yet," Brian was saying. "How about Greenwich?"

"What's at Greenwich?"

"Zero degrees longitude and a magnificent view of the city."

"What time is it now?"

"It's about nine thirty. Can you be ready in an hour?"

"No problem."

By ten thirty, she was standing on the Victoria Embankment, looking at the River Thames with her hands in her pockets. Under her Blackhawks jacket, she wore a new Union Jack T-shirt bought earlier in the week. Her hair hung limp and wet from a hurried shower, but the weather was fine for May, and her occasional shivers reflected excitement as much as the cold. Brian arrived within five minutes, carrying a bag with a blanket and a picnic lunch.

"I hope you haven't been waiting long," he said.

"No."

"That's good. Great." They smiled nervously at each other. "The train was so slow this morning," Brian said.

"Mine too, but I didn't have far to come." She stretched her arms and rubbed her eyes. "So what prompted you to call me?"

"I don't know. I thought you might like a guide for the day, and possibly a translator."

"I could sure use that." She laughed. "Those bus drivers are impossible to understand. What exactly is a wanker? I've been told that I am one."

"It's what your typical London bus driver is. Don't worry about it. Shall we get started?"

"Sure. Lead on."

They walked to the dock from where shallow craft worked the tourist trade up and down river. They bought tickets to Greenwich and took seats in the front of the boat. Only half a dozen passengers were on board when the pilot cast off and steered the boat into the center of the Thames. The breeze picked up, and Karen shook her damp hair into the wind, combing it with her fingers. The boat slipped smoothly under the arches of Blackfriars Bridge, then Southwark Bridge. The morning mist that hugged the pillars of the bridges swirled into the boat and brought with it the odors of dead fish and motor oil.

"I hope you didn't have other plans," Brian said, "and were just being nice to spare my feelings."

"No, no. I hadn't decided what to do today—a museum, I thought, or maybe a park, something unstructured. I'm quite happy to spend the day with you."

"Oh, good. It's just that I've about worn myself out with this ghost business and then the arrangements for my aunt's funeral. I needed to get away for a day."

Karen pointed to the north shore. "Isn't that the Tower of London?" she remarked as they emerged from the shelter of London Bridge and spotted the familiar turreted outline on the north bank.

"That's right. See that old gate just above the waterline? That's called Traitors' Gate. It's where they used to deliver condemned men and women for execution. The river served as a highway in the old days. It was so much easier to navigate than the narrow, crowded streets."

Karen shielded her eyes and stared at the walls and battlements of the Tower as the boat drew closer to it. Brian took in the view also, though it held no novelty for him. "You wouldn't believe the number of famous heads that have toppled onto Tower Hill. Let me see, there was King Henry VI, Lady Jane Grey, Anne Boleyn, Sir Thomas More, and another wife of Henry VIII—I forget which one. Oh, and the nephews of Richard III were smothered to death in there supposedly. The last man to be imprisoned in the Tower was Rudolf Hess, the Nazi."

"Really? That's fascinating."

"And I seem to remember reading somewhere that Richard Crossly brought the treasures of Hoyland Abbey to the Tower of London after the dissolution. Some of them may still be inside those walls. Perhaps that precious relic of Crossly's father, the Sphere of the Planets, is lying in some ancient, forgotten strong room."

"It's amazing how history comes alive in London. Just seeing the Tower of London in front of you brings home the story of Richard Crossly so powerfully."

"And it makes it so much more believable. I know what you mean."

"It was lucky for Crossly that he didn't have to take that last boat ride to Traitors' Gate."

"Yes. I suspect he kept on King Henry's good side. Those uncomplicated types who reasoned with their fists often survived longer than the intriguers. But King Henry was so mercurial. I bet there were many who breathed sighs of relief when he died."

"Many necks were spared, huh?"

"Right. You know, King Henry used to take this same boat trip we're taking. He kept his lady friends lodged at Greenwich Palace."

"To await the king's pleasure, I suppose."

"Philandering bastard."

"How did King Henry die? Did someone give him a taste of his own medicine?"

"Natural causes, I think. Wasn't it syphilis or the gout or something?" Brian couldn't recall the diagnosis but was sure his demise was the result of a surfeit of some vice or other. "Do you want to know something creepy about his death? They carried his coffin to a chapel on the way to burial. The coffin was made of lead and was extremely heavy. It got damaged by the motion of the carriage. During the night, it split open on the floor of the chapel. Blood and other bodily fluids seeped out, and a dog that came with workmen the next morning licked them up."

"Yuck."

"It's true. Apparently, a monk had prophesied that this exact thing would happen to the king if he married Anne Boleyn illegally. It's a biblical reference to an evil king: 'And the dogs shall lick his blood.' It was told about King Ahab. Everyone was shook up when the prophecy came true."

Soon, their boat veered away from the center of the river and drew alongside the pier at Greenwich. They climbed the hill to the observatory and perused the collection of old telescopes and chronometers. Brian took a photograph of Karen straddling the prime meridian. He nudged her elbow, laughing, and suggested that time began here and now for her. She looked quizzically at him and said that she didn't think it did. They wandered through the National Maritime Museum, which they both found uninteresting, and took some photographs of the Cutty Sark.

At midafternoon, they found a quiet spot on the grass with an excellent view back to the city and sat down on the blanket. Brian pulled from his bag French bread, cheese, and two apples. "No wine, unfortunately," he said, setting down two cans of soda.

Karen broke off a hunk of bread, ate it, and laid down on the blanket, hands cupped underneath her head. She smiled at the old dowager city, already tinted pink from the sun's descent into the western counties. "What a wonderful view."

"In a way, I can relate to Richard Crossly," Brian said, settling down by her side, leaning on one elbow. "He was a man thrust out in front, you know, given the power of life and death over people, having to weigh moral issues he'd scarcely even thought about before, trying to keep things in perspective and juggle his responsibilities. I'm having such a hard time with all of that. I'm glad he died quietly in his bed. There's hope for me yet."

"You know, Brian, I never realized you were such a determined person. When I first saw you at the center that day, I thought you were—"

"What?"

"Well, a bit stuffy, if you'll forgive me. Cuddly and harmless, slippers and a pipe, that kind of a man. But from what I've seen these last couple of weeks, I know I was mistaken."

"I'm glad you see it as determination. Everyone else calls it obsession. They all think I've gone too far. They want me to stop, even my brother. There's no one left to help me but Harry, and he has a tendency to panic when the action gets hot and heavy."

"Harry's the one who's obsessive, if you ask me. He's on the verge of losing it. All this supernatural stuff has unbalanced him. He's starting to believe all kinds of kooky things. He even believes that plants can sense human emotions. Can you imagine that? I've heard him yelling and screaming at the rubber plants in his office. I wouldn't rely on Harry too much if I were you." She held quiet counsel with herself for a moment, her thoughts drifting out over the roofs of the city. She settled herself into a more comfortable position on the blanket. "No, you're not like that. I think I know where you're coming from. I feel the same way about my zeta ability. It's something so special it would be a crime to set it aside. I feel like I've just scratched the surface of my potential."

"Yeah, that's the way I feel. Everything's starting to come together for me. But it's so hard. Every day is a torment."

"Determination is an admirable thing. We're a lot alike in that respect." She turned and smiled at him.

Brian clicked his tongue against the roof of his mouth, trying to decide how much he could confide in her. He stared at the distant river. "I was thinking about Bernadette Soubirous yesterday."

"Who's she?"

"Bernadette of Lourdes."

"Oh, right."

"She was the girl who first saw the Virgin Mary in the grotto. I was thinking that perhaps she went into some kind of religious ecstasy like Abbot Gervase. Maybe it screwed up the temporal states, just like in Hoyland Church. Now every once in a while, when the devout get together and pray, some of them enter the zeta state and catch a glimpse of figures from the past who walked the holy site. At Hoyland, we call them ghosts. At Lourdes, they call them the Virgin Mary."

"That never occurred to me."

"I've been thinking that many so-called miraculous visions could be the same thing—soldiers in the First World War seeing the Angel of Mons, old ladies seeing Marie Antoinette in Le Petit Trianon at Versailles. I bet it's all one and the same."

"But why do these alternate time states come into being? Why do we see anything at all?"

"I think it's something like the Biefeld-Brown effect."

"Never heard of it."

"This guy Thomas Brown claimed that electrodes could ionize air molecules somehow, generate an ionic wind. That would explain all the sparks and corona effects we observed in the church. Somehow, the abbot was so energized that he generated the effect himself. Also, Brown has claimed that the effect generates a force that could be utilized to lift objects up into the air. He called it electrogravitics and filed several patents on it."

"Levitation."

"Right, like what happened to Abbot Gervase. Did you ever see that movie *The Philadelphia Experiment*?"

"I did. A ship disappeared or something, right?"

"The USS *Eldridge* it was called. It was about research to make the ship invisible, but the film involved time travel as well. It was supposedly based on secret military research in World War 2."

"Yes, that's right. I remember now."

"All that stuff was premised on the Biefeld-Brown effect. So I think that just every once in a while, a person gets so emotionally energized—by a religious experience or whatever—that they initiate the effect by themselves, and it disrupts the normal flow of time, creates all these quantized temporal states that can later be populated. It couldn't possibly get more rapturous for a monk than to see the welcoming arms of Jesus Christ outstretched toward him."

"Heavy," Karen murmured.

Brian's eyes moved from the river to Karen's face. "So what do you think the zeta state might be?"

"I've come at it from a totally different direction. I've been reading about the fantasies of poets like Coleridge and seers like H. G. Wells and Nostradamus. I believe they wrote down what they saw in their zeta trances. I get goose bumps every time I read Coleridge's poem 'Kubla Khan.' It's so familiar to me."

"I hadn't thought of it that way."

"How would you interpret the visions that Dan and I had back at the center? The fir trees and the circle of faces?"

Brian looked back to the river and the dusky horizon. "There were no old churches for you to connect to. You were connecting with some past time when a coniferous forest covered that part of Illinois. The figures were Native Americans in a circle round a campfire—shamans, probably. They thought they were summoning up their ancestors, but they were seeing ghostly images of you and Dan from the future. I think I've got that part of the mystery figured out."

"Huh. I'd wondered if it might be something like that."

Brian began to chew on an apple, but after several bites, he tossed it under a tree. A squirrel darted down the trunk and retrieved it. Brian laid down by Karen's side on the blanket, growing bolder. "Frank's bringing back a whole lot of chemicals from Northwestern that might intensify the zeta state. Would you be willing to test them with me?"

"Are they safe?"

"I really have no idea. Professor Lieshman thinks so. I'm going to test them on myself."

"You?" She chuckled. "You don't know how to achieve zeta."

"Not yet, no, but I can learn. The ability is inside all of us. I'm convinced of that."

"Do you think so? I'd be surprised if it is. It's not easy at all. It takes a lot of practice."

"I know. You're out there in front of the rest of us. But would you be willing to help me?"

"I'll have to think about it. It sounds risky."

"Okay. I understand."

"I guess this means you're going to keep going? Even after your aunt's death?"

"I haven't much further to go. I'd like to know more about how Abbot Gervase's religious ecstasy created the time distortion, so I need to repeat the resonance with 1537. And I'd like to see how far the zeta state can be pushed. It might be a bit dangerous, but I try to think of the positives." He adopted a self-mocking voice and made quotation marks in the air as he said, "The benefits to mankind." He grew serious again. "Beyond that, I don't know."

Then without thinking and without knowing why, Brian suddenly said, "Karen, when I saw you that first time at the center in Joliet, I thought you were the most...intriguing girl I'd ever seen, intriguing and...and pretty." He turned to look at her, but her eyes slid away. He studied the soft line of her jawbone, nestling into fine blond hair around her ears. "When you smile, your face is so lovely. Your cheeks almost have dimples, but not quite. Did you know that? It's like they have the promise of dimples, which is so much more delightful."

"That's not very professorial," she said, still looking away. He touched his knuckles very lightly against her rib cage, and this she didn't resist. "What about you and Sarah? You're engaged to her, aren't you? I see the ring on your finger."

"She gave a ring to me. I didn't give one to her."

"That doesn't excuse such talk."

"I suppose not. Sorry."

He laid back on the blanket, but his fingers still touched her side very lightly. The sun was dropping closer toward the dome of St. Paul's, turning it into a luscious big orange. Haze drifted off the river and hid the smaller buildings from view. A child skipped down the hill below them, singing, and Brian's heart was in his throat. "When do you go back to Chicago?"

"Next Wednesday."

"Harry and Frank have promised to return in a couple of weeks and help me test the drugs. Will you come with them?"

"I might."

"Can I see you again tomorrow?" He turned to look at her, and this time, she returned his gaze. She stared into his eyes, looking for a glimpse of the future. There was depth and mystery but no guidance.

And all should cry, Beware! Beware!
His flashing eyes, his floating hair!
Weave a circle round him thrice,
And close your eyes with holy dread,
For he on honey-dew hath fed
And drunk the milk of Paradise.

Without knowing why, she leaned forward and kissed him on the cheek.

CHAPTER 3 2

London
May 2018

"I forgot my umbrella," Karen said the next morning.

"You'll need one today," Brian responded, pointing to the overcast sky.

"I'll go get it."

"I'll come with you."

They turned back into the lobby of Karen's hotel, which they had just left, and took the stairs up to her room. She unlocked the door and walked over to the tiny desk by the window. She slung her purse across the back of a chair. "I've got a guidebook here too," she said, "somewhere." She fumbled with the magazines and other papers that littered the desk's surface. "Oh, and here's my camera. I'd forget my head if it…"

When Brian kissed the back of her neck, she flinched. His hands gripped her shoulders to steady her. She looked up to the ceiling and thought, *I'm not ready for this. I'm not ready.* He turned her shoulders toward him and kissed her forehead. Instinctively, she recoiled again. "Brian, I don't think this is a good idea." *It was only yesterday,* she thought, *only yesterday that it began. And this is not the place, not this dismal hotel, this foreign city.* Then she asked herself, *Did you forget your umbrella on purpose?*

He said simply, "Karen." There was an instantaneous casting of horoscopes in her mind. *What will the day bring? How will this day affect the rest of the week, the year, my lifetime? Are the omens propitious?* She didn't see love in the cards, though she knew that love was little more than a cipher to her like so many other things—wealth, fame, and security—an icon for a state with which she had no familiarity whatsoever. Karen's unblinking sky-blue gaze settled on Brian's trust-worthy smile, and neither would be dislodged. He drew her closer to him till their bodies touched. *Oh god*, she thought. *Oh my god, this is going to be it. He's going to be the one.* After that, she had no more thoughts.

*****

Later, as they lay side by side, staring at the ceiling, Brian remarked with a wry smile on his face, "What on earth do you see in me?"

"In you? That's putting me on the spot." She stared at the window as she responded. "Well, I certainly have a great deal of admiration for you. You're the opposite of all that irritates me in this world, all that smallness, you know—counting calories, saving coupons, miles to the gallon. Don't you feel it, Brian, the pulse of pettiness beating mercilessly and draining the spirit out of us? You're not that way. Neither of us is that way."

"I never thought of myself as being the opposite of something," he said.

"You're a watcher of the big picture, someone who can transcend all that triviality and focus on the important things, the things that stand the test of time. You're the first man I've met who has that kind of vision. I like it. I know it takes tremendous courage to keep your eyes on the horizon. So what do you see in me?" Karen asked, smiling and propping herself on one elbow to look at him. "To turn the tables."

"Well, I do think you're pretty. Oh, I'm sorry. That's so corny." He was embarrassed for a moment. "I'm afraid I'm not very good at these kinds of conversations, if you want to know the truth. I wasn't brought up with sisters or other girls around me. I've had to learn rather late in life how to be comfortable in the company of women. And I guess I'm still learning. I hope you'll understand if I sometimes appear to be a bit inconsiderate or insensitive. Chalk it up to immaturity. I promise to work at it. I think I need a teacher."

"That's all right," Karen replied, squeezing his arm. "Not being chased at all is just about the same as being chased all the time. I'm actually not very experienced myself at dealing with the opposite sex."

Brian was gradually becoming more comfortable in her presence and gaining confidence. He could even look at her unbelievably beautiful body without his heart palpitating. And a new fluency was being drawn out of him by the powerful honesty of her conversation. He could speak words and sentences that would have stuck in his throat just yesterday, and he could think thoughts that used to be anathema to him.

"Well, you are very beautiful to me," he continued. "I can't deny it. And I think you possess a life force that positively glows. It's like an aura. Everyone sees it." She blushed and looked down. "I've never met anyone like you, Karen. To tell you the truth, I've never even seen women the way I see you. They were always something to be pursued and acquired in a rather materialistic way. Do you know what I mean? I wanted to be a professor, and I became one. I wanted a sports car, and I bought one. I wanted a girlfriend, and I found Sarah. Not really choices, just accumulation of possessions. That sounds horrible, I know. But since I've met you, I've suddenly lost interest in those kinds of things. I think I could give up everything else as long as I have you."

"Brian, we've only been in this relationship a couple of days!"

"Yes, but somehow, I seem to have seen all this coming. You've been influencing me ever since that very first day at the center. Every decision I've made since then has had you in mind to some degree. I don't know quite how to explain it."

"To be honest, I've had a similar feeling. I seem to think that we've—how to put it? It seems like we already knew each other before we met or that some kind of destiny is drawing us together. Very strange."

"I know it."

"But, Brian, look, I'm not promising you anything. Do you understand? I can't at this point. There are things I must do in my life. Living alone for a while is one of them, becoming self-reliant. Exploring the zeta force is another. It took me a long time to gather the strength to do these things. Just breaking the stranglehold of my family took years. And turning loneliness into solitude, well, I'm still battling that one. Gaining inner strength has set me on a path I can't easily change, won't easily change. Please try to understand. It's important to me. But these things aren't related to my feelings for you, and they aren't exclusive. I like you a lot."

"You don't have to explain yourself, not today. It's enough for me that you're here."

He reached for her shoulders to embrace her, but she held him at arm's length for a moment. "No, I need to establish the ground rules. It's important that there be no misunderstandings."

"Well, I've got my crusade too, so that's something else we have in common."

"True."

Time soon lost all meaning. The wheel of intimacy turned around and around, drawing up for both of them, as from some deep well, experiences and emotions that had floated unrecognized in the cold depths for years, drawing them up and splashing them out into the sunlight of mutual delight. The hours slipped away unnoticed. Shadows pulled themselves off the floor on one side of the room and laid down to rest on the other side. Long drafts of water, small pieces of sliced mango, cleansing showers, and soft towels.

"Do you want to go out and do something?"

"No."

Night became day and dissolved into night again, the diurnal cycle measured not by sun and moon but by aural prompts from the world below their window. Morning sounds were first—the staccato chatter of commuters, taxis, buses, coffee and egg, and the impatient sounds. In the middle of the day, a more leisurely libretto—house-wifey, spacious, touristy, ice cream sucking and pop-top flipping, directions to the lost visitor, bicycles, and sharp laughter. Then the evening sounds, jagged and random—motorcycles gunning, cats at courtship, dogs criticizing, drunks approaching and retreating, running feet, and derisive laughter. Deep in the night, lost kabuki souls stabbing at their cocoon.

"We really should get up and do something."

"No."

Early one morning, probably, Brian awoke and turned to his hopelessly entwined partner to deliver yet another token of endearment and reassurance. He placed a tender kiss on her forearm. She sighed in her sleep and reached behind her to make sure his protective body was still there. He felt the kiss returned. It was many moments later, when his drowsiness had lifted sufficiently, that he realized he had kissed his own arm. He tightened his grip on her body and drifted back to that small place beyond the world and people where he couldn't be found.

On Sunday, the streets were quiet. There was a faint aroma of garlic and coffee. "I feel so safe here," she said. "I want to stay like this forever." He buried his nose in her hair to remember the scent and the texture of it. They laughed. They stared at each other. They talked. They said nothing. They slept and they woke.

"I have to go home tomorrow," Karen said one evening.

"Don't go. Stay."

"I can't. I have to go home."

"All right. But please come back with Harry and Frank. Please?" She didn't reply, and when the shadows pulled themselves off the floor the next time, she dressed and packed her suitcase and left.

Brian shimmered at first, elated that he had begun a relationship with such a fantastic girl, such a beautiful, intelligent, motivated woman. He, Brian Kenning, small-town academic, in love with Karen Butler, blond American student. He laid flat on his back, hands locked under his head, and dreamed of the wonderful future ahead of him. Perhaps they would marry, he mused, and travel the world, build a floating Anglo-American mansion in the middle of the Atlantic, have wise and beautiful children. Each boy would be proficient at both baseball and cricket; each girl would wear red, white, and blue ribbons in their hair. On Guy Fawkes Day and the Fourth of July, children's faces would be laughing up at fireworks.

Quite suddenly, the faces vanished. A sudden terror gripped him. Reality swept in under the door and squatted on the stained plastic leaves of the fake plastic plant on the dresser. This was not the beginning, it said, but the end. Karen was gone—gone back to her home country, to another life, to other boyfriends, girlfriends, replacements for him. What they had shared was over. He saw a wall being built between them, bricks remorselessly stacked and mortared, time shrugging its apologies and drawing a veil between them, time devouring even this most precious of things. Time devoured all things, he thought, *all* things. There was no picking and choosing. He turned over and gripped her pillow tightly.

*****

Love was not in the cards, Karen reminded herself as she sat in the lounge at Heathrow Airport, waiting for her plane. It was not in the cards. Brian was just a bright new star in a firmament that already glittered. He would not be the dominant force. She would not let that happen, no supernova. But the memories kept flooding back no matter how hard she tried to rationalize them away. She closed her eyes and was in his arms again.

As she walked onto the plane, her thoughts changed. Love might not have been in the cards six days ago, but now perhaps love had been born, bloody and raw, not calculating, not complaining, just quietly taking stock of the marvelous new world around it and breathing.

CHAPTER 33

London
July 2018

John refused to contact his brother after their walk on the beach. If reason would not persuade Brian to abandon his destructive quest, then perhaps a cold shoulder would. He decided it was time to begin to write his dissertation. He set up his laptop in the bedroom of his apartment and commenced the laborious process. There were many long days at the computer, trying to make firm ground out of a morass of squishy data. As a diversion from the mental effort, he decided to paint the walls of his apartment at the same time. He purchased several cans of orange and gray paint and a big brush and fell into a stultifying routine: three hours of word processing to half an hour of painting. The tasks began to cycle smoothly, and his thoughts turned away from Brian and ghosts.

Late one evening, when he had set aside both the computer and the paintbrush and was lying on the couch, watching television, his phone rang.

"John? It's Sarah."

"What's up?"

"Have you talked to Brian recently? Say, in the last couple of weeks?"

"Me? No. I've been keeping out of his way. I don't know if he told you, but after Aunt Polly's funeral, we had a big argument. I tried to get him to go back to work, but all he wanted to do was bounce new ghost theories off me. He made me so angry that I decided to ignore him for a while. We haven't been in touch since. Why do you ask?"

"Because I don't know what's going on. I've been calling him for days. Either his phone's switched off, or my calls go quickly to voice mail, and he never calls me back."

"Have you called him at work?"

"He hasn't been to work. They say he phoned in a vacation request."

"He's gone on holiday?"

"No, John, you don't understand. I've been to the flat twice. He's in there, all right. In fact, there are several people in there. I can hear voices, but as soon as I knock on the door, it goes quiet. He doesn't want to see anyone."

"You must be mistaken."

"I'm not, John, believe me. Can you come over with me tomorrow? I've got to find out what's going on for my own peace of mind. We may have to force the door."

"Force the door? Sarah, I'm not into the strong-arm stuff. Why not call the police?"

"I don't want to do that. There's no cause—well, not enough cause. We just need to make him talk to us. Will you come with me? Please?"

"Oh, all right. I'll meet you outside his apartment at ten o'clock tomorrow morning. Is that what you want?"

"Yes. That'd be terrific. Thanks a million, John. I'm really worried this time."

John sat back on the couch and recalled the harsh words he and Brian had exchanged as they parted. A fool, John had called him, a conceited, heartless fool to want to bring grief to his family and friends. A coward, Brian had responded, a gutless coward who would shirk his duty to humanity and the memory of Aunt Polly. John had been depressed for the rest of that morning and then caught the afternoon train back to London in a huff. He suddenly realized that that was all of six weeks ago.

On impulse, he took out his phone and dialed Brian's number. After five rings, someone answered. "Brian, is that you?" Silence at the other end of the line. "Brian, listen to me. It's John. Don't hang up!" With a soft click, the phone went dead. John held it in the air for a few seconds, musing on what his brother could be doing, then replaced it gently in his pocket.

*****

The next day, John met Sarah outside the shabby row house in Clapham where Brian lived. Sarah produced a key and unlocked the front door. They made their way upstairs to Brian's apartment. John touched his lips with a forefinger, requesting silence. They tip-toed to the door and listened. Sure enough, John could hear muffled voices from within, but he couldn't make out any words. He looked at Sarah. She looked back, intimating that he must take the lead.

He rapped hard on the door and shouted, "Brian, this is John." The conversation within ceased abruptly. He knocked again, louder. "Brian, come on now. Open up!" Nothing. He banged as hard as he could. After a lengthy wait, he motioned Sarah to stay where she was then turned and marched down the stairs. He opened the front door, slammed it shut from the inside, and then raced back on tiptoes to join Sarah beside the apartment door. Again, he signaled for silence.

They waited in the dirty, unlit passageway. John's eyes settled first on a graveyard of empty milk bottles that had accumulated in a corner. He began to count them. Eighty-four dead men were laid to rest. Then he looked up at the ornate plaster ceiling, once the pride of some upper-class family but now sullied with soot and festooned with spiderwebs. No one cared about common spaces anymore.

The door handle began to turn. John leaned forward. The door creaked open. Frank Koslowski's head poked out and looked down the hallway. When he saw John standing there, Frank jumped back into the room, but John was too quick for him. He took one step forward and kicked the door open. Frank fell back, and John secured entry by charging in and holding the door open. Sarah stepped into the space he had vacated, and the two of them stared into the room.

"Jesus Christ!" Sarah exclaimed at once. Most of the furniture had been pushed into the corners of the living room. In the center was a long couch, on which sat Brian and Karen. They were facing each other, and Brian had a bandage on the middle of his naked back. Both were dressed in blue jeans, and Karen had on a skimpy T-shirt. Brian was wearing the nautilus headgear. Electrical cables snaked from it to a coffee table, on which stood an EEG machine. Brian was thin and unshaven, having shed at least ten pounds since last John had seen him. His face was gaunt, the sunken cheeks shaded all the way to the corners of his mouth.

Seated on a chair by the EEG table, Harry Groh pored over stacks of chart paper. On an adjacent table lay various chemical para-phernalia—a thermos with Northwestern University stenciled on it; a test tube rack filled with sealed vials; and assorted beakers, pipettes, and other glassware. Two syringes and a scalpel rested on a gauze pad. There were also various electronic measuring devices positioned around the room with wires leading back to Harry's table. The floor was littered with books, scientific journals, coffee cups, food wrappers, and discarded articles of clothing. A single bare light bulb hung from the center of the ceiling, casting a garish brilliance over the proceedings. The odor of antiseptic seared the air. White fog drifted out of the top of a dry ice container and drooped down onto the floor. Karen's and Brian's eyes were closed, and their hands were tightly clasped.

"What the fuck is going on here?" John asked.

Harry rose from his chair. "Come on, guys," he said, motioning them to leave the room. "Let's not start anything."

"What do you mean?" Sarah shot back. "Get out of my way!"

"They're in deep zeta. We shouldn't mess with them. It could be dangerous." Harry attempted to insinuate himself between John and Sarah and the couch, raising his palms up to them.

"Don't try any of that stuff with me!" Sarah warned. "Brian?" The two prone figures began to stir. "Brian, just what the hell do you think you're doing?" Though at least eight inches shorter than Harry and a hundred pounds lighter, Sarah shoved him aside and confronted the couple. Karen was first to rouse herself, then Brian slowly opened his eyes and became aware of his surroundings.

"Sarah?" Brian said softly. "What are you doing here?"

"Me? What am I doing here? What the hell are *you* doing here? And what's she doing here with you? Is she the reason you've been avoiding me? And what on earth's the matter with your back? John, call an ambulance."

"Just go, Sarah," Brian responded. "Please. You don't know what's going on, and it would take forever to explain. Just leave and forget all about this business."

"What are you talking about?" Her voice was very shaky, and she turned to Karen with an inquisitorial look. Karen's sole response was to squeeze Brian's hand.

"We've discovered"—Brian began then rolled his eyes—"a lot about each other."

"What does that mean? Are you saying you're having an affair with her?"

"I'm talking about mutual discovery, a journey. I mean, yes."

"Yes, what? Yes, you're having an affair? Jesus, Brian, what the hell is this all about? Can someone please explain?" She looked at everyone in the room in turn. "And all this...this..." She swept her arm above all the scientific equipment.

"Let me try," Harry ventured. "The experiments have been taken several steps further, Sarah. Brian has now learned how to attain zeta, and Brian and Karen together have formed an unbelievable partnership, incredibly deep zeta, and strong energy production. Hunger has intensified it. On top of that, we've discovered an effective antagonist to the body's natural defenses. It's called anoxyseriphin. When you inject it into the cerebellum, it stabilizes the zeta state. We're on the threshold of some truly fantastic discoveries. You should see these charts." He gestured to the coffee table but knew neither John nor Sarah was interested.

"Brian, I just can't believe this," Sarah said, tears welling up in her eyes. "After all the damned support I've given you, after all the damned sacrifices. You're a fucking bastard!" She stormed to the door and then stopped, torn between abandoning everything in disgust and fighting to hold on to her dreams.

John gravitated to her side. "You're such an idiot, Brian," he said to his brother, more in despair than anger.

"You really gotta leave," Harry responded.

John and Sarah stormed out of the apartment. As John rounded the corner of the hallway, he stumbled over a milk bottle and sent it tumbling down the stairs to shatter on the tiles below. "Eighty-fucking-three then!" he shouted.

At the sound of breaking glass, Sarah began to cry so badly that John decided she should not be left alone. He took her back to his place, and by early afternoon, she had dropped into a deep sleep on his couch. He worked for fifteen minutes at his computer then took up the paintbrush and slashed the kitchen walls, inflicting livid orange wounds. He became so angry that he threw the brush down, walked into the bedroom, and picked up the phone.

He called the police. He gave them Brian's address and reported that he had reason to believe there was drug use at the apartment. He said it was possible someone had taken an overdose. He gave them his phone number. Half an hour later, his phone rang. Startled, Sarah woke up just as John began to talk to the head of the Clapham constabulary. Had he given them the correct address? It was repeated and confirmed. The policeman politely explained that the apartment was empty when they arrived. There was no evidence of drug use, just a few sticks of furniture and a ton of litter.

"They've decamped," John said to Sarah.

*****

Brian drove his sports car fast out of the city with Karen by his side. The back of the car was crammed with hastily packed boxes hidden under armfuls of clothing. Both Brian and Karen stared into the middle distance, preoccupied and anxious. There was no conversation till they were well clear of London traffic.

"I hope Harry and Frank catch the right train," Brian said.

"They'll be fine," Karen replied.

"They have to change trains at Peterborough, I think, or somewhere. Then they'll need to get a taxi to Hoyland."

"Don't worry." She patted his knee. "They're big boys. They can handle it."

"I didn't see any option at the time. There's so little space in these two-seaters—"

"Don't worry."

He accelerated past a convoy of trucks and then pulled in front of them. He slowed down. "Are you ready for this?" he asked.

"As ready as I'll ever be."

"It may well be dangerous."

"I've thought about the risks. I'm not afraid. You'll be with me."

"I hope that'll be enough."

Brian spoke in a flat, emotionless voice. Both flippancy, which had flourished in his youth as a shield against social ineptitude, and harshness, which had grown out of his fear of time passing and purpose unrecognized, had faded away in the last few weeks. He had risen above those cheap traits on the pilasters of wonder that a woman had given herself to him utterly for 120 consecutive hours and still sought his company. So the lack of modulation in his voice partly reflected a vanishing of tentativeness, but with it had departed also, though he didn't know why, the wonderful buoyancy of their forever weekend. Only a grim determination now propelled him forward.

"I'm no longer sure if I'm up to the task," he said. "I'm suddenly very apprehensive."

"Why? Don't be."

"I've always been a rational person, Karen. I've relied on reason to see me through the crises. But I now think that reason may be inadequate for what lies ahead. Reason is actually a pretty weak animal, don't you think? It cowers in the corner of the room when passion and cruelty and hatred are let loose. If we come up against Crossly again—"

"Now you sound like Harry."

"No, Harry's in even worse shape than I am. He has no weapons at all to fight visceral emotion. All Harry has is a blueprint of the way the world works, a big engineering drawing that took him years to construct, endless erasures and countless footnotes. But it's static. It has no mechanism for assimilating new paradigms. He's very vulnerable. At least I have one weapon even though it's a feeble one. But I see now that people like you and Aunt Polly are much more robust than us rational types. Your weapons were forged in the heat of emotional turmoil. They're dynamic. You welcome combat as a means to hone and strengthen, whereas Harry and I see combat as a threat to stability. No, you're much better suited to these experiments than I am."

"Perhaps. We'll see." They drove northward, the sky sultry and overcast.

"Do you love me?" Brian asked. "I love you."

Karen's reaction was instantaneous. "Please don't ask me that." It was as if she had seen the question rising up out of the ardor of the last few weeks and out of the drift of his soliloquy—almost, in fact, as if it had sprung fully formed out of the concrete highway, rushing toward them and sliding up the hood of the car to perch, inquisitorially, on the dashboard.

"I don't know what those words mean when they come out of your mouth. And I don't know what the answer to them would mean coming out of my mouth. I only know that the words are too important to be treated lightly. You can be so free and easy with such words, Brian. Most people are like that, I guess. It's just that I can't judge the strength of the feeling behind them. And when you hear my answer, what expectations will it build? How will you know the motives behind it? I have no context, no yardstick." Brian stared ahead and said nothing.

"I'd rather not speak those words, if you don't mind," Karen continued. "I'd rather show you my feelings and demonstrate them to myself at the same time. I need to be tested, Brian. I need to be given an easy option to renounce you or a painful way to accept you, something that will show us both beyond words, beyond any nuance of guile or subterfuge, what my true feelings are. Then you'll know, and you'll never have to ask me again. And I'll know too. Perhaps it will happen soon. Perhaps today." Brian's fingers stretched around the leather cover of the steering wheel. His question was to go unanswered. He must face the coming ordeal without that strongest of crutches.

As the car hurtled in the direction of whatever it was that fate had ordained for them in St. Neot's Church, he suddenly felt detached from the body of the driver, floating above the scene. He saw the hands of a professor from London clutching the wheel. He saw the short fair hair of a student from Iowa discoursing on the perils of intimacy. The man and his lover, side by side—Brian Kenning and Karen Butler; Richard Crossly and Catherine, his wife. At least the pairings were now correct.

In the vee between the thumb and forefinger of the driver's left hand, he saw a small vein throbbing, a pulsation he had never noticed before. Blood drove remorselessly through tissue, animating that bizarre, corporeal mystery that was himself. And as he stared at it, he was pulled back into his body with the stunning force of a slingshot, thinking, *For a long time, I was not. And soon, perhaps, not once again and forevermore. But today, I am alive. Alive. I'm alive.*

CHAPTER 34

The sun hung high above the Lincolnshire fields like the bright copper bowl of a warming pan. The sky was pregnant with fat little clouds, and the whole slow day seemed ripe for drama. As Jack Stephens followed the lost railway tracks on his customary lunchtime ramble, the edges of nature were blurred by a haze of feathery buds and shoots, and this lack of focus drained from his mind all constructive thought. Pan's pipes were discordant today, though. The poppies that speckled the banks of the railway cutting reminded him of drops of congealed blood. Strange insects gathered by the wayside and rubbed their legs together menacingly, and tiny, seedy things floated upward in the hot air and stuck to his moist eyebrows.

Without warning, three RAF jets from a local airfield shot across the sky in rapid succession, locked in a mock dogfight. The lead pilot did a barrel roll and peeled off to the right, pursued by the others. Jack shielded his eyes from the sun and watched the planes till they were out of sight, making childish machine gun noises in the back of his throat. Grinning, he jogged the rest of the way to the ladder of the abandoned and derelict signal box.

He took the iron rungs two at a time, pushed open the door, and threw himself down in the old signalman's chair overlooking the Lincoln-to-Boston line. This was his throne! From here, he could relive the lost joys of the old steam railway. He opened his lunch box and wolfed down three banana sandwiches. He ate an apple and threw the core out the window, snorting as it carried with it one of the few remaining shards of glass that clung to the edges of the frame.

Then with a bottle of lemonade to his lips, he stood up and began to search the abandoned structure for railway memorabilia.

This day, he was lucky. He discovered an old railway timetable wedged under a rotting cupboard. He pulled it out and pored over the yellowed pages, chuckling occasionally to himself at a particularly adroit scheduling of connections or the unearthly hour of departure of a milk train. It was more valuable to him than a Shakespeare folio. He crammed the papers into a pocket of his jacket and climbed down the ladder.

Though perspiring heavily, he was in such a good mood that he decided to walk farther down the line than he had ever ventured before. He had an idea that there might be a switching shed up where the main line curved around Friar's Swamp. After only a short distance, though, the cutting narrowed, and the path became overgrown. He was stung by nettles and startled by a water rat.

But gradually, the banks of the cutting fell away, and he emerged onto level ground. To his right loomed the Hoyland hill with St. Neot's Church perched on top of it; in front of him stretched the flat marsh, dense with rushes and almost dry from the summer's heat. The tracks curved sharply to the left, skirting the marsh and vanishing in the wide plain that led to Boston and the sea.

Jack looked up at the church. The sun's glare hurt his eyes, but he sensed that something was wrong. He stopped walking and stared at the church. A strange cloud of smoke hovered over the ancient building—no, he suddenly realized, not over it but through it. The smoke must be drifting out of open windows. Then it struck him. Holy Christmas, there must be a fire! The windows sparkled like diamonds. But was that due to the sun or to flames?

As Jack stood looking up the hill, uncertain what he was seeing and undecided what to do about it, a figure emerged from the door of the church, running—stumbling, more like. Almost immediately, a second figure appeared, pursuing the first. The second figure caught the first, and there was a brief struggle. One of the figures fell—or was pushed—into the bushes that lined the church wall. Jack squinted to try to make sense of the distant images. The figure that was still on its feet turned away from the church, walked a few steps, and then stood motionless.

With a jolt, Jack realized that the figure was staring down the hill at him. Jack's mind filled with contradictory impulses, but he made no movement, and neither did the remote figure. Both waited for betrayal by motion. Jack was scared, and the fear sharpened his hearing. The air became filled with the sounds of fluttering insects. A hot breeze rumbled through the bulrushes and swept over him. He kept quite still and tried to breathe shallowly. Why didn't the figure on the hill do something? Who was it? Heat bubbled out of the thick vegetation and started to dissolve the distant outline.

A dull roar built up in his right ear, like the deafening sound of silence he could sometimes hear while trying to fall asleep at night. The sound grew more intense until with the crack of a whip, the lead RAF jet burst overhead on its return mission, followed rapidly by its two companions. Jack jumped on the spot, stifling a strangled cry, but that was nothing compared to what happened up on the hill. The remote figure lifted its head to watch the jets pass over then raised both arms to the sky and emitted a long, drawn-out howl like a lone, defiant wolf.

Jack was aghast. Was this man or beast? The howling ceased as quickly as it had begun, however, and without further hesitation, the figure began to sprint down the hill toward him. Jack turned on his heels and fled, not stopping till he reached the safety of the newspaper office. He went straight to the washroom and put his head under cold water. He surfaced with a gasp and dried off.

He looked at himself in the mirror, waiting for the heat and panic to subside. The chase must have been called off, he reasoned, and his confidence gradually returned. He pulled out a comb. "Well, well, well," he said to his reflection, "it looks like we finally caught up wi' them Kenning boys. The magic circle's in session this afternoon, I'll bet me boots on it." He combed his hair and smoothed it down with damp palms.

He turned and walked briskly out to his car. He exited the parking lot and took the narrow country lane back to Hoyland Church. As he approached a tight corner, a red sports car hurtled round the bend at tremendous speed, weaving from one side of the road to the other. Jack braked hard and pulled onto the grass verge. He watched stupefied as the car flashed past him, a lone figure hunched over the wheel. Jack stuck his head out the window and yelled, "Lunatic! Bloody loony!" at the trunk of the receding vehicle. He pulled back onto the road, thinking, *I've seen that car before. Parked by the church. It's that Prof. Kenning's car. I'm sure of it.*

Two minutes later, he was parked outside the lych-gate. He slammed the car door shut and marched confidently up the path. He didn't know if either of the Kenning brothers was still in the church. If they were, he wanted the matter settled quickly, but he was not at all sure how he would confront them. He had a scathing speech prepared, and at the very least, he would disrupt their latest performance. He also felt fairly certain that he would punch the elder brother. Beyond that, he was unsure. He decided to let the circumstances of the moment dictate his actions.

He passed Polly Coleby's grave. The polished marble headstone glittered in the sunlight like a beacon to his determination. "I'll put things right, ma," he muttered, spitting into his palm and making a fist. "Don't you worry." He entered the vestibule. The door into the church was wide open. Two hymnals were lying on the floor of the porch, and several more were scattered just inside the door. "Heathens," he said to himself, picking up one of the hymnals and smoothing the crumpled pages. *Look at this mess! What gives them the right to abuse our church like this?* He gathered up two more of the scattered books and placed them on a shelf.

As he walked to the center of the nave, he saw the smoke. The entire east end of the church was cloaked in an impenetrable bluish-gray haze. Neither the chancel nor the rood screen was visible. Only at the third or fourth row of pews in the nave did the smoke thin out. "Bloody hell," Jack cried out. "Will you look at that!"

Then with the thought that the brothers might still be in the chancel and might have heard him, he ducked down behind the font. Stealthily, he peered around it and stared at the smoke that hovered over the chancel and drifted up into the rafters. He heard sounds coming from beyond the curtain's edge—footfalls, scrapes, and grunts of pain. *They're still in there,* he thought. *Right!* The noises ceased, but the smoke didn't clear appreciably. He grew irritated. He hadn't come all this way to skulk like a frightened rabbit. He stood up and tiptoed down the aisle, body flexed to run in the opposite direction if necessary. He halted in front of the wall of smoke. He took a deep breath and pretended he was addressing the county council on a grave matter.

"Come on out, Kenning. The game's up!" he announced. His words were swallowed up by the smoke. "I know you're in there!" Jack screwed up his eyes but could distinguish no human shapes. He took off his jacket and began to fan the smoke, which swirled and dispersed a little. He tossed his jacket aside, rolled up his sleeves, and made two fists.

His shirt clung to his back with sweat, wide arcs of perspiration darkening the armpits. He peered into the haze and fanned the smoke some more. He could vaguely see a figure now, standing in the middle of the sanctuary. It was dressed from head to foot in some kind of dark clothing—medium height, stocky build, not moving a muscle. "Well, come on out then!" Jack struck a boxer's pose. "You've been asking for it."

The figure moved. It picked up a heavy large object. Brandishing it two-handed above its head, the figure strode confidently toward him out of the smoke. Jack turned tail instantly and sprinted out of the church. By the main door, he reached out and grabbed the doorpost to steady himself. He turned and listened for signs of pursuit. As he turned, he glimpsed something white sticking out from under a bush. With a shock, he realized it was a bare foot.

This was the man he had seen race out of the church and be pushed into the bushes! More than pushed, he now realized. He took a step to the side and drew back the branches of the bush. A bare leg came into view with a single streak of blood down the thigh. That was enough for Jack. He let the branches spring back into place and continued his flight down the church path as fast as his legs would carry him. He ran over to his car and tumbled into the driver's seat. The door slammed, the motor roared into life, and he was gone.

*****

He drove only half a mile then pulled off the road and into the parking lot of a pub. He sat quietly in his car for five minutes till his pulse returned to its normal rhythm and till he was satisfied that no one was chasing him. He should call the police right away, he knew that, and an ambulance, though that could surely wait, judging by the condition of the body in the bushes. And the fire department? The smoke wasn't the result of a normal fire. He was quite sure of that. Just what exactly ought he to do?

"My god," he said out loud. "What the hell happened?" It was all more, much more, than he had bargained for. His hands started to shake on the steering wheel. He wiped spittle off his lips, strode into the pub, and ordered a double brandy.

*****

The noise was deafening. So many voices were talking at once. They wanted to know his thoughts. Wouldn't he prefer to live freely and simply as they did? Therein lay the path to contentment. He tried to explain with tears in his eyes that he had always lived outside the world of such feelings. Like so many other men, he had been lost on a lonely road, not seeing, not hearing, and not knowing, searching in the dust at his feet, not raising his head to notice such things. They smiled sympathetically.

They leaned close to his face and told him of the life force in all things, how sometimes it appeared to be one thing and sometimes another, and how it was often hidden altogether but that however it appeared or did not appear, it was always present in every living thing. He wept, the tears streaming down his face and mingling with the sweat on his neck and the blood on his chin. It was as if he had suspected all along that he had gotten it wrong, and now finally, the dam was breached, and all his misconceptions were swept away in the flood. The catharsis sucked out his complacency and replaced it with humility. At last, he could lie peacefully under the sky and talk to them without shame, uncork everything that was bottled up. They nodded to encourage him, and he began to speak freely.

He told them about his life—from his childhood to the day of his entry into their realm. He told them of his family and friends, his adventures and misadventures. He returned over and over again to his guilt, stressing how misguided he had been and how he had wronged a great many of them. He resolved to change his life from that moment on. He patted their heads. He stroked their hair. They responded by kissing his hand.

He explained that the fault lay in his own selfishness. He had required all the effort to be given by others, not recognizing his own role in the mysterious drama of life. He knew now that you had to give of yourself to receive something of value in return. You had to break the shackles of human arrogance and be sifted and strained till the essence of your own life commingled with all life. The throng responded that, yes, they understood that; they wished every man felt as he did.

He grew sad again and apologized for those of them he had killed, those of them he had insulted and humiliated. They calmed him. They said it was a small matter. They explained to him that although the life of each one of them was precious, the essence of their life force resided in the group. Each one of them would die soon anyway, but the vitality of the group would endure and culminate in rebirth. They said they forgave him. They told him to be content to be broadcast with the wind. He smiled briefly and told them he understood. He was one of them now. The sun's rays began to lose their heat and light, and a breeze picked up. They asked if he was cold and closed around him. He was grateful. He asked their names. They laughed and said they had none.

*****

Jack Stephens walked out of the pub and got back into his car. He cast a quick glance up and down the road for further reassurance that he was in no danger, then he drove back in the direction of Hoyland. As he rounded a curve on the outskirts of town, he caught sight of a red car abandoned in the middle of a field. He pulled over, switched off the engine, and stepped out onto the road. Curious, he walked to the jagged gap in the hedge that the car had clearly cut. He stopped and looked over at the car. He recognized it as the one that had driven him off the road earlier.

"That's the bugger who almost killed me!" he exclaimed. "Looks like you came to a sticky end, squire. Not surprised, driving like that." Jack followed the tire tracks across the field with mounting concern. As he neared the vehicle, he saw that a wheel was missing, and the left front end was stove in. He saw, too, that the car was empty. He walked around to the other side. There, he found a man spread-eagled among the young shoots of barley, talking. "My god," Jack said. "It's you!" He stood over the man, looking down at him.

"Who are you talking to?" Jack asked. "The plants? Is that where all your fancy science leads you? Let me tell you something, chum. We simple country folks talk to nature as well. Did you know that? We understand it. It's like one of the family. But we don't expect it to talk back." He knelt down by the man's side and cradled his head in the crook of his arm.

"You see what happens?" he said to the unresponsive man. "You see what happens when you start to mess around with things that shouldn't concern you? Nothing but trouble." He wiped the blood and sweat from the man's face. "Don't worry, squire. I'll take care of you. I'll call an ambulance."

CHAPTER 35

London
July 2018

John was tapping away at his computer the next morning when there was a knock at his apartment door. He checked his watch. It was almost eleven o'clock. No callers were expected. He adjusted his disheveled clothing and opened the door cautiously. Two uniformed police officers filled the doorway, and his heart sank.

"Mr. John Kenning?"

"Yes?"

"I'm going to have to ask you to accompany us, sir."

"Where to? Why?"

"Up north, sir, to Lincolnshire."

"But I can't. I have to be in the lab this afternoon."

"You don't have no choice in the matter, son."

"But why? Can you tell me what's happened?"

"The county constabulary has requested that certain individuals be located and transported there immediately. We're expected soon after lunch, if you please, sir." The officer flipped his notebook open. "Ms., er, Sarah Harcourt is already in the car. And do you have any knowledge of the whereabouts of a Dr. Brian Kenning?"

"Your guess is as good as mine."

"Do you know of Dr. Brian Kenning's whereabouts?" the officer repeated sternly.

"No. No, I don't."

"He is your brother, is he not?"

"Yes, he is, but I don't know where to find him. I'm sorry."

"Very good, sir. Now if you'll just make ready to accompany us."

When he took his place beside Sarah in the back seat of the police car, John saw that she was white as a sheet. They exchanged formalities, and she confessed that she knew as little as he did about the reason for the summons. The car pulled away into traffic.

"Are we going to Hoyland?" John asked the policemen.

"Those are my instructions, yes," the officer replied from the front seat. His colleague, tight-lipped and black-gloved, kept his eyes on the road.

"Where precisely?"

"Detective Inspector Jamieson has asked that you be taken to the village church."

"St. Neot's?"

"Don't know the name of it, son, but I understand half the local force is there."

"Please tell us what's happened."

"Uniformed branch is just the taxi service here, mate," the driver said. "Hens loose in the vestry, I expect."

The two officers shared an abrasive chuckle. John and Sarah looked at each other. They were strangers to the world of law and order. They knew nothing about the police and its ways, and the police knew and cared less about them and theirs. John and Sarah realized they would learn nothing to allay their fears until they reached Hoyland.

*****

Two hours passed. The police car cruised through the flat Lincolnshire countryside along the same road they had taken the day before their first big experiment. The car kept fractionally above the speed limit. The law, it seemed, required respect rather than strict compliance. The interior grew stuffy, but no one lowered a window or turned on any fresh air. John's eyelids began to droop.

He looked down and noticed Sarah's hands clasped in her lap. As he watched, the wormlike fingers uncoiled and slid down to the hem of her skirt. They all pulled at once, tugging the hem down to her knees, straightening, smoothing. He looked at his watch. It was one o'clock. He stared at the grain on the simulated leather seat in front of him. His eyes lost focus and drifted into the interlocking patterns.

"Take this road on the left, Ted."

"Okay."

John wondered what could have happened in the church. Was it possible that Harry had gone crazy and attacked Brian? He had almost lost control during the previous experiments. Or what if Brian had taken some strange drug and turned on the others? What if Brian and Harry had been disturbed by the new vicar and assaulted him? John shook his head. Neither of them was capable of such a thing. And Frank Koslowski? He was an unknown quantity. But he was getting ahead of himself. He didn't know for sure that any of them had been in the church recently. Maybe it was a robbery or something. Maybe Brian, Harry, and the others weren't involved at all. Somehow, that one didn't ring true. Maybe, maybe, maybe—the possibilities swarmed in his head.

The car grew warmer, stuffier. John could feel himself beginning to doze off. Why couldn't he let go? That was what he really wanted to do. He was sick of the whole business. He needed to stretch out under some clean sheets and sleep for a week, to forget the dissertation, the ghosts, and Aunt Polly and just nestle into some cool white sheets, just let go. In a matter of moments, he dozed off. The car was headed for a church, a church under the… "This way." The church was beneath the waves. John could see the lead roof shining dull green beneath the waves, algae streaming from the parapet.

"John?"

The dead were everywhere. He could see the captain of the guard, sword in hand, swimming toward him, murder in his jade-green eyes. He couldn't breathe. The car was full of water. He was drowning. The killer raised his sword. John grabbed his arm as it began to descend. They grappled. He had no strength. The swordsman dived over the front seat of the car, and they fought. His foot cracked the windshield.

"What the hell's the matter with him?"

John held his breath till his head exploded. The swordsman gasped and spluttered. The sword spiraled over the front seat through the water.

"Help him!"

"Pull over, Ted."

John inhaled the ocean deep into his lungs.

"It's me—Sarah."

"Help me!" Wind blew into John's face. The sword faded from the floor of the car.

"What in God's name is the matter with him? Is he on something?"

Sarah patted John's hand. He shivered violently. The car had stopped, and the door was open. A breeze rustled through the tall grass in the dyke by the roadside. The wheat field beyond the dyke swayed gently. The car engine throbbed. He had escaped. The water had evaporated into the fenland afternoon. He had escaped death.

"Are you all right, son?" A blue uniform was bending over him. He saw brass buttons. "Okay?"

"I'm all right now." The wind blew in and ruffled the hair on the policeman's head. The other unfamiliar face stared at him over the back of the driver's seat. Sarah smiled encouragingly. "I'll be all right," John said. "I'm so sorry. Fell asleep."

"Are you sure?" the policeman asked. John nodded. "Let's push on then." A door slammed. The car pulled back onto the road and accelerated smoothly. John reached for Sarah's hand and held it tightly. She didn't resist.

*****

Soon, the car came to a halt outside Hoyland Church. With the two officers leading the way, they walked up the familiar cinder path and through into the back of the church. Sarah became increasingly agitated. Leaving the driver in the doorway, the other three walked over to the center aisle. All the lights were on. There were police officers in several parts of the church. Someone was dusting for fingerprints. At the intersection with the center aisle, they were met by the local detectives of their previous acquaintance, Jamieson and Carling.

"This is John Kenning and Sarah Harcourt," the London policeman said. "We're still searching for Brian Kenning."

"Yes. Ms. Harcourt," Jamieson said, "thank you for coming. And Mr. Kenning. You remember Detective Carling?" Sarah and John both nodded.

"Why have we been brought here?" John asked.

"What's happened?" Sarah added.

"Something very bizarre occurred in this church yesterday," Jamieson responded. "We're having a lot of trouble piecing it together. Try not to be alarmed." Sarah turned pale, and John supported her elbow with the palm of his hand. "We found a body in the bushes outside." Sarah's knees began to wobble.

"Whose?" John asked.

"We're not sure," Detective Carling replied. "The body was naked—no clothing or identification of any kind. Male. Severe blunt trauma."

"That'll do, Walter," Detective Jamieson interjected. "It was the body of a man in his late twenties or early thirties, I'd say. The corpse has been removed to the mortuary in Scardyke. I'd like you to take a look at these photographs if you would."

He handed John two Polaroids. They showed a face, or at least part of a face. The neck and left side had been discreetly covered with a white cloth. John took a quick look. "This is Frank Koslowski," he informed the detective. "He's an American scientist. He was over here with a team from Central Illinois University, near Chicago. They've been helping my brother with his studies." Sarah closed her eyes, overwhelmed with relief. "Who killed him?" John asked.

"We've not got anywhere near that far yet," Jamieson replied.

"Was he the only one here?"

"We found just the one body. We were called by Jack Stephens. You remember him, reporter from the local newspaper. He also said the church might be on fire. There was no fire, just a body in the bushes. Who else do you think might have been here?"

313

"I'm not sure."

"What do you mean by that?"

"Well, it's just that there were four of them on this ghost hunting team. There was the dead man, two other Americans, and my brother, Brian. But I don't know if any of the other three have been here."

"We found one body, nobody else. The church was empty when we got here."

"That doesn't make much sense."

"You're telling me. There's going to be a shitload of questions. Any idea where we might find your brother and the others?"

"I suppose you could try our uncle's cottage in Bittern Fen. A mile or so from here. We always stay there when we're in Lincolnshire."

"Walter," Detective Jamieson said, turning to his colleague, "check out that cottage. Then get McMillan to send a fax to the American embassy. Notify them of the death of this Koslowski fellow and see if they can be of any help."

"Okay," Carling replied. "Before I go, should I…?" He turned to his boss, and Jamieson nodded. Carling walked to the front pew while the others waited. "We found this beside the rood screen." He picked up a plastic bag, turned, and walked back to them. He held out the bag for John's inspection. In it was a severed human hand.

"Oh god," John spluttered, turning away.

"Any thoughts?"

It's the hand of Abbot Waltheof, John thought, *transported through time during a new experiment.* "I don't know quite how to say this," John began. "But is the hand—what's the word?—putrid? You know, decomposed?"

"No," Jamieson replied. "Why would it be? I'd say it's been cut quite recently."

John's mind was racing. *Perhaps a resonance was made with the time when Neot crept past his friend and stole the hand of the dead abbot. What was it that Sarah told us? Neot stole the hand to retrieve the holy ring of Waltheof.* "Is there a ring on one finger, an ancient sort of ring, old Anglo-Saxon style?"

"There is a ring. Take a look for yourself." Carling held the plastic bag closer.

John stared at the contents: a human hand with the bloody stump cleanly sliced and five thin white fingers. There was a ring on one finger. "It could be," John said.

Sarah took a step to John's side and looked over his shoulder. She shrieked and fell backward onto a pew. "That's my ring! That's the ring I gave to Brian! That's Brian's hand!"

"What?" Jamieson exclaimed. "You recognize it?"

"Oh god" was all that Sarah could say. "Oh no, no, no!"

Brian's hand? With creeping horror, another possible explanation came into John's mind. He ran to the chancel. There was blood on the floor. He turned and looked at the rood screen, feverishly examining the edge of the tracery. There it was, the cleft in the wood! But it was not the worn fissure that Brian had shown him before. This time, the wood was freshly cut. "Oh, Christ!" John exclaimed, leaning over and pressing his forehead against the screen.

While John was examining the screen, two plainclothes detectives entered the rear of the church. They sought out Jamieson and Carling, and the four of them huddled in a corner of the chancel. Then Jamieson broke from the group and returned to Sarah's side. He looked at John and said, "Mr. Kenning, would you join us a moment please?" John rubbed his finger once more across the splintered rail and then walked over to them with Sarah following. "Your brother owns a car, does he not?" Jamieson asked.

"That's right," John replied.

"A secondhand red MG TF?"

"Hmm. I'm not certain of the make. I think so. Why?"

"Apparently, Jack Stephens came across the car in a barley field just outside Hoyland yesterday afternoon. It had run off the road just north of the village, gone clean through a hedge. Front end pretty bashed up."

"Was anyone hurt? Who was driving?"

"Jack found a man lying on the ground beside the car. He had only superficial injuries. But the thing about him was, well, he was acting sort of crazy, spouting a load of gibberish to nobody. We only just now made the connection to this business here."

"Who was the man? Was it Brian?"

"An ambulance was called, and the man was taken to Stamford General Hospital. Apparently, the doctors can't get anything coherent out of him, not even his name. But it can't be Dr. Kenning. He speaks with an American accent."

"It must be Harry," Sarah said, turning to John.

"It would appear so, Ms. Harcourt, Harry Groh. The man was transferred this morning to Princess Alexandra Hospital on Ackerman Street. It's a sanatorium for patients recovering from mental illness. He's in some kind of amnesic shock, apparently."

"Can you find out from him where Brian is? And Karen Butler?" John asked him. "Look, Officer, it seems that Brian's hand was cut off. He can't have gone far in that condition. Won't Harry say anything?"

"Oh, quite the contrary, sir. According to these officers, they say he talks damn near all the time. They say he just goes on and on, spewing an endless stream of nonsense. No one can make heads or tails of it. Naturally, we need to confirm if this man is indeed Mr. Groh and find out what has led to his present condition."

"Naturally."

"Perhaps he was the one who killed the man in the bushes."

"Surely not."

"Well, somebody did. Anyway, Mr. Kenning, we're hoping you might be able to recognize some of the stuff he's saying. Maybe you can even get him to divulge something about what happened here."

"I can try," John said passively. He glanced at Sarah. Her eyes were wide, and she was staring at his face. It was a look of supplication, and he blinked under the force of her silent appeal. She was in desperate need of his help. Suddenly, the indecision that had dogged him for the last few months just melted away.

He realized for the first time that everyone else involved in the unfolding drama had suffered far worse than he had. Who was he to vacillate? Who was he to condemn and withdraw? He had come this far unscathed. Someone needed to pull together the threads of this grotesque show. There were wounds to be healed and minds to be put at rest, and there was no one left to do it but him. "I'll do my very best," John said.

"Come on then," Jamieson said. "Carling will take Ms. Harcourt to the Red Lion for the night and keep the pot boiling here. We're off to Stamford."

*****

By the time the tulip fields had given way to wet sidewalks, John thought himself sufficiently composed to be able to face Harry in his unbalanced state. They drove through the streets of the town in silence until the driver suddenly said, "This is Ackerman Street, sir."

The car nosed between a pair of wrought-iron gates and wound through a soothing garden of manicured lawns and regimented rose bushes. It came to a halt on a bed of multicolored stone chips, parallel to the long facade of Princess Alexandra Hospital. Fifty window-panes shone clean and bright in the late afternoon sunshine. Even the bricks looked to have been scrubbed.

John and Detective Jamieson got out of the car and climbed a flight of steps to the front door. Their inquiries brought forth a starched matron of agreeable disposition who led them down a long corridor, tiled underfoot in a soothing ivory and gray checkerboard and whitewashed pale green everywhere else. Neon lights buzzed in John's ears, and the smell of carbolic scoured his nose. The staff wore starched white uniforms and moved unhurriedly among the passive patients. The smoothness of the operation relieved John's mind as he prepared for the confrontation with Harry.

The matron reached the end of the hallway, smiled, and gave a little wave of her hand toward a door. It was closed and bore no markings other than the number 6. They entered. The room contained two hospital beds side by side, each flanked by small white pine tables. Over each bed hung cheap paintings of snow-covered mountains. In the two opposite corners stood simple pine chests, slightly scuffed. There was one window. Alongside the window was a chipped tiny porcelain sink with two plastic mugs on a shelf above it, a single toothbrush in each. The room contained nothing else. On each bed was a man stretched out full length. Both were dressed in plain gray trousers and white T-shirt. One of the men had two socks on; the other, only one, rudely violating the otherwise meticulous symmetry.

"Take Mr. Holmwood to the recreation area," the matron said to a nurse standing nearby. The nurse approached the man with one sock on and shook him. "Mr. Holmwood, come along now. Television time." The lethargic patient raised himself up on his elbows and watched with fascination as the nurse located the errant sock and began to pull it skillfully onto his bare foot. Toes were stuffed into a ball of wool, which was then stretched to encompass foot, heel, ankle, and calf. The man stared into the face of the nurse as if she was a magician. "Come along," she repeated. The man rose slowly from the bed, and the nurse led him out of the room.

The man on the other bed lay motionless, except that his lips moved almost imperceptibly, releasing a thin sound like air escaping from a puncture. John gazed into the man's eyes with great sadness; they had lost their sparkle and were hiding, fearful, in a thicket of facial hair. John turned to Jamieson. "It's Harry Groh, all right. Shall I talk to him?"

The matron nodded. When John hesitated, she smiled encouragingly. "Just say a few words, and he'll start up of his own accord."

John moved to the bedside and whispered, "Harry, it's me, John."

"Yesterday was such a gorgeous day," Harry began at once. "We went down to Dodger Stadium. The Dodgers were playing the Cubs. Sandy Koufax was pitching. Daddy says he has the most valuable arm in baseball. We sat in the bleachers—cheap seats—in the sun. Dodgers were ahead, one to nothing after six. Lou Johnson stole third in the fifth inning and came home on a wild throw. The sun was slipping down into the ocean. It was such a beautiful evening. The sun was like a big gold sphere, a sphere with all the planets circling it. Do you remember?"

"No, Harry," John said. "That was a long time ago. You're in England now. Tell me what happened to you and Brian in the church."

"See how he throws his slider? He holds it like this. He curls these two fingers like this, see? No one can spot it. Catcher gives him the sign, and he whips it by 'em. Do you like my mitt? Aunt Ellen bought it for me. It's big, and yet it's tight. If we get one hit out near me, I'll snag it for sure. It fits kinda snug. Feel the webbing."

"You don't have a baseball glove on, Harry. That's just your hand. You're in a hospital. Look around you."

"I know. Brian had the mitt, but he dropped it. I tried to save it for him. I knew he'd need it later on, but there was so much smoke that…that… I couldn't—"

"In the church?"

"The church? Daddy said to respect the Lord and his offices. We always go to church on Sunday. Daddy said they won't even hit one out of the infield today."

"What happened to Brian?"

"His hair stood up like a clown's."

The matron interjected. "You never know what he'll say next. He went on and on about the solar system this morning. Awful it was."

"Mercury, Venus, Mars, Jupiter, Saturn," Harry fired off rapidly without further prompting. "I know each one by heart. Emerald, diamond, ruby, sapphire, amethyst. The sun is a tiny gold sphere. I know where it is, but I'm not telling you. Mercury, Venus, Mars, Jupiter, and Saturn. And the sun is a…a giant golden ball sinking slowly into the Pacific, over left field."

Jamieson looked solemnly at Harry. "What made you run away, Mr. Groh?"

"I needed…time. The tree huggers were right, you see. Plants can talk, and they can hear too. Sophie can hear. Tex can hear. I've seen their voices on the graph paper. I used to rub gum on their leaves. Do you think they liked that? I've acted very ugly to Tex. I know that. I was so wrong. But they told me I was forgiven. They explained to me that God is in all of them."

"Who said that?"

"The bearded ones."

"Who?"

"They didn't want me to leave. They told me I was one of them. But I killed some of them. The road was wet, and I took the curve too fast. Oh, Christ!" He clamped both hands over his face and remained silent for a few seconds, then he looked up at John. "I'm sorry about your car, Brian."

"I'm John. Was Brian with you when you crashed the car?"

"No. He'd gone away."

"Where to?"

"Ascended into heaven, like Jesus."

"This is hopeless, Mr. Kenning," Jamieson said. "We're getting nowhere. We'll come back when he's more coherent."

"Give me a little more time. Harry, tell us why you ran away. What happened?"

"In the seventh inning, Ron Santo was called out on strikes, and Ernie Banks whiffed."

"Why do you keep talking about a baseball game? What was so special about it?"

Harry suddenly became very agitated. "Get away from me! You don't belong here. No, you can't have my clothes. Get away! Leave me alone!"

"Calm down, Harry. There's no danger here," John said, then as an aside to Inspector Jamieson, he said, "I think someone was chasing him."

"Ask him who it was," Jamieson said.

"Who was chasing you, Harry? Was it Frank?"

"I was hiding behind the chairs, watching where the sky fell. Mercury, Venus, Mars, Jupiter, Saturn. I memorized the spot. Emerald, diamond, ruby, sapphire, amethyst. But then he spotted me. Run, Frank, run!"

"What was the man's name? You do know his name, don't you, Harry?"

"It was Krug. Krug struck out in the top of the ninth. Daddy said it was history in the making. He was wearing his Bud T-shirt, a beer in one hand and a hot dog in the other. I wanted to catch a home run so bad. Have you seen my glove?" He looked down at the floor on both sides of his bed. "The Cubs brought in a pinch hitter.

What was his name? Daddy said, 'Uh-oh, this spells trouble.' T-R-O-U-B-L-E. I can't remember what his name was."

"It doesn't matter, Harry."

"Oh yes, it does. It has to be perfect. I have to remember everything, or it's not worth a—something or other. It's important to marshal the facts, organize them. Everything must fit exactly. The pinch hitter's name was—let me think."

"I told you, Harry, it doesn't matter."

"Nah! You're right. He struck out just the same. Harvey Kuenn was the last man up."

"Please get back to what happened in the church."

"They said he was a power hitter. What a joke! The crowd was going wild. One strike. Two strikes. Everyone was standing up. Hey, I can't see! I can't see!"

Harry struggled to sit up in bed. "Why is all this so important to you, Harry?"

"Strike three! He's outta here! We all went crazy. Daddy hugged me and laughed and laughed. He lifted me up on his shoulders so I could see it all. People running onto the field. It was bedlam. Daddy said it was history in the making."

"What's so special about this baseball game, Harry?"

"Don't you know?"

"No. Tell me."

"It was a perfect game."

"What?"

"Sandy Koufax pitched a perfect game—no hits, no runs, no errors, no men on base, twenty-seven up and twenty-seven down, perfect. Everything was perfect."

"What the hell?" Jamieson said.

"I think I'm beginning to understand," John said. "Harry's obsessed with perfect solutions. He has been from the very first. Harry told Brian that if there was the smallest loophole in our explanation, he wouldn't be able to accept the reality of ghosts. He'd have to gnaw away at it till he refuted it. His delusional mind must have picked up on this memory of witnessing a perfect game of baseball as something to cling to, to save his sanity."

"Who the hell cares about that?" Jamieson said. "Listen, Kenning, I need to know what happened in that church. I need to know where your brother is. I need to know who killed Mr. Koslowski. If this idiot's going to keep babbling on about baseball, then I'm going to try some other avenue."

"What happened to Brian?" John said pointedly to Harry, bending closer to his face.

"Bad shit," Harry repeated sourly. "No answer for it."

Jamieson sighed and turned away, saying, "This is completely hopeless."

"Did you try to help Brian?" John persisted.

"I've gotta save his mitt!" Harry replied, making a motion to get up, "before it gets burned. It's over by the screen there. I must get it for him!"

"That's not Brian's baseball glove," John said sadly.

"No, I know. It's his..." Harry became agitated once again. "Get away from me, you fucking bastard! Get the hell away from me! Run, Frank, run! You're not getting your hands on me! Run, run, run! I gotta get to the car. I gotta get it started." Harry thrashed his arms from side to side, knocking a jar of lubricant jelly off the bedside table. John grabbed his arm and held it against the head of the bed. Harry hit John with his free hand and cursed him roundly.

"Calm down, Harry," John said. "That's all over now."

"Hot-wire it! Faster, you son of a bitch! Quick! He's coming. He's coming!" Harry was fighting to get off the bed now, and Jamieson helped John to restrain him. It was all they could do to hold him down. The matron hurried from the room to get help. "Let me go! Let me go! The motor's started. I gotta get outta here!"

"You did escape, Harry. You got away. You're safe now."

"Look at that idiot in the brown car! Doesn't he know we're in danger? Get off the road! Get outta my way! It's that fucking newspaper man! Lunatic yourself! Asshole!"

"No, Harry, it's all right."

The matron returned with a nurse, who was pushing a low cart. The nurse quickly wheeled it to the side of the bed. She reached for a hypodermic and filled it with a colorless liquid. Harry scowled at her, nostrils flared. John and the detective pinioned his arms while the nurse injected him.

"Wait a minute," John said. "I've got an idea. Harry?" Harry turned to look at him. "Koufax pitched a perfect game, didn't he?" Harry nodded. "No imperfections. There can't be." Harry nodded again. "Not in the game itself or in the memory of it, right?"

"Right."

"So what was the pinch hitter's name?" Harry stared at him blankly. "It's not perfect until you remember every detail, Harry. It's not perfect for you until you remember the pinch hitter's name. It has no meaning without that, does it?"

"No."

"Think then! Remember!"

"It was Joe Alf—"

"Think!"

"His picture's on the wall of the barbershop in Joliet." A smile spread across Harry's face. "I remember now! It was… Joey… Joey Amalfitano." He began to relax, and they pushed him back down on the bed.

"Well done, Harry. And the ghost theory is almost perfect too, isn't it? Just one thing is missing. What was the name of the man who chased you? Who killed Frank?"

Harry smiled again. "It was Ironfist."

"Who? Who do you mean?"

"Ironfist." Harry closed his eyes and slept for eighteen hours straight.

CHAPTER 36

Hoyland Church
1583

Ezra Palethorpe, the sexton, leaned on his spade and gazed across the western fields. Sunset, a smear of mustard along the underbelly of distant clouds, was fast approaching. Already, the bushes at the edge of the churchyard and the wheel ruts winding up from the lych-gate had sunk into darkness. Soon, the day would be done.

He tapped his toe against the blade of his spade, fighting impatience and the first gnawings of fear. He very much wanted to be far away from this place at this time, but he was the sexton, and the grave had to be dug. He leaned sideways and shouted down into the pit, "Shagbag, thou hast no arms for the spade. At that snail's pace, this grave'll be dug come St. Geoffrey's Day. Put thy back into it. Death's head on a mop-stick!"

For the cursing of his young apprentice, the sexton employed a precise lexicon delivered with well-honed malice. He felt no compunction in treating the boy cruelly. To live one's life as a gravedigger was humiliating enough. To aspire to become one was contemptible. The sexton spat into the grave, not caring if his spittle hit the boy or not. "If this job not be finished in ten minutes more, I'll deliver thee to the cold cook, and thou wilt sleep the morrow night in the belly of thine own handiwork, 'pon my honor. Many's the worm'll thank me for its supper."

The boy didn't look up or alter the pace of his digging. His elbows wheeled at the same sad rate, and clods of earth showered onto the mound at the graveside with the same monotony. The sexton was always abusive to his apprentice, but at dusk, the threads of his abuse wove a more intricate pattern, embroidered with anxiety. For Ezra always made a point of leaving the churchyard well before nightfall, before the demons danced in the church.

Ezra was deeply superstitious. As he stood at the head of the grave, he recalled how the town crier had told the village that a wax image of the queen had recently been discovered on a dunghill in Spitalgate with a needle through the heart. The privy council had spread word that witchcraft was virulent in the body politic and must be cauterized. For the crime of the wax doll, four witches from Windsor had been burned at the stake. Ezra knew all about this. He also knew that one of the Windsor witches had kin in Boston. Covens were reported as close as Burstoft. The talk in the taverns was full of it.

Ezra knew what witches did after dark. He knew they fed toads with blood from their flanks. He had heard of the third nipple. And he knew they danced backward in church at night, the thought of which brought a particularly keen chill to his heart.

"Shagbag!" he shouted again into the grave. "Thou slackest a-purpose to keep me here after dark. No doubt thy wish is for Crossly and his sorcerers to catch me and wind me up in the cerecloth. Mayhap thou fancies to watch his devil's claw a-clutchin' my throat, thou lazy, good-for-nothing pissabed!"

Frustrated by the lack of progress, the sexton motioned the boy to step aside, jumped down into the grave with his own spade, and set to work with a will. The apprentice, covered from head to foot with dirt, climbed out the opposite end. But five minutes in the suffocating blackness of the grave was all that Ezra could endure; after that, though the hole was far from deep and precious narrow, he owned the work complete. He scrambled out and stood beside the boy, panting. They surveyed the grave's shortcomings. "Its intended won't complain nor nothin'," Ezra muttered.

With the departure of light, a raw clamminess settled over the graveyard. Mist crept out from behind the tombstones and oozed up from Friar's Swamp, spreading a white carpet on top of the grass. Sexton and apprentice stood shivering in the moribund silence, their eyes darting to the shadows, sorting and classifying the various shades of gray.

As they looked down the hill, over the old ruins of the monks' cells, they could see orange and blue lights twinkling at the edge of the marsh. "See the devils, shagbag?" Ezra said, pointing to the marsh and leaning so close that his breath warmed the boy's cheek. "See 'em yonder? See 'em sniffin' through the stones? In olden times, they'd creep up on a young monk asleep in his cot and drag 'im off into the bog."

"Nay, maister, it ain't true."

"Ain't it?"

"No, sir, I don't think it be."

"I think it be so. They say 'twas the worst thing in the world to be a 'prentice monk and have to take the cell nearest the bog. Many a novice didn't live through the first night, so they say. See 'em gatherin' there now? See the beads a-twinklin' on their horns? They can cart away thy sorry soul too if thy work don't improve."

"'Tis the marsh vapors, my father says."

"Oh, the marsh vapors, be it? Well, ain't heducation a wonderful thing, master gravedigger? Thy father is the schoolmaster, no doubt, and a student of the natural arts. Marsh vapors, eh? Well, maybe it is, and maybe it ain't. But I tell thee true. Many's the monk as has woke up under ten feet of mire. Mayhap they're a-risin' up this night at the beckonin' of the wizards."

"Nay, maister, say it ain't so, I prithee."

The sexton laughed nervously and tugged at the stubble on his weather-beaten chin. He was beginning to affright himself now, though, so he dropped the subject and helped his apprentice gather up the tools and carry them to a shed at the edge of the graveyard. With tools stowed and the bolt shot, they turned to face the church.

"There's them lights in the windows again, maister," the boy said, pointing ahead. "Where they come from?" The lad shuffled from one foot to the other. "The lights, maister?" The sexton did not reply. In an instant, the boy was down the path, over the gate, and halfway to the village. At first, the sexton was inclined to follow him, but then he was unexpectedly struck with pity for the lad, for his innocence and the hopelessness of his life and the dismay on his face as he begged for reassurance. No one had ever looked to him for protection before even though he was a strong man and unafraid to fight anyone in the village.

Ashamed and angry at the privileged wickedness that had made him behave so unchristianly, he began to sense the underpinnings of courage—or if not courage, at least curiosity about those who would manipulate him so. If he could discover who was responsible for the devil worship, perhaps he could consign them to the stake. Anonymous denunciations were commonplace in the county. Perhaps he could put an end to their frolic and make his and the boy's work tolerable in the future. *Thou shalt not suffer a witch to live,* he reminded himself.

He stared up at the church. Each window was now alive with flickering lights. Mediated by the small panes of colored glass, they danced like rainbows in a kaleidoscope. They seemed to mock him as they skipped up and down the side of the building. He could picture the devil dancing backward on the altar, cloven-hoofed. But did he have the strength to watch? If they spotted him, his days were numbered. A wax doll with his name on it would be found lying on a grave with a hawthorn prick in its chest. Or worse.

He decided he would stay well out of sight and steal just a quick look. He walked over to the immense wall of the church and considered how the spying was best accomplished. He crossed himself twice and climbed up a buttress. From there, he inched his way across the supporting span till he found a narrow ledge that ran the length of the wall of the nave. Shivering with cold and trepidation, he located a clear small pane of glass and peeked through.

A handful of men, perhaps six or seven, were assembled in the chancel. The man in the center of the group was most familiar to him: Richard Crossly. He was clearly the focus of attention and seemed to be directing the movements of the others. *Richard Crossly,* Ezra thought in wonderment, *the devil hath changed thee beyond all compass, though I cannot fathom how the magic was worked. Indeed, Satan did transmute the man that broke down the abbey doors when I were but a lad, for I saw thee then with mine own eyes as I stood by the side of Abbot Gervase with my father. I saw thee slap King Henry's warrant against the abbot's chest. Thou wert bewitched the day the abbey burned. Lord, deliver us all from such evil!*

Three other members of the group were also recognizable to him, most prominent among them being John Dee, the queen's astrologer. He was tall and thin and wore his white hair and beard extremely long. He was dressed from neck to toe in a loose-fitting black robe, densely woven with astrological symbols. Two others had visited the church several times before, and their names had been floated around the village: Edward Kelley and a foreigner named Laski. It was just as the sexton had suspected. The blasphemer and the necromancers had joined forces. Shivering frantically, Ezra clung to the wall like a beetle and watched.

Crossly and Dee stood to one side, communing privately, while the others were seated on the chancel benches. On a table at Crossly's side a single altar candle burned, its light refracted through an alchemist's glassware—retorts and sublimation flasks and a row of cobalt-blue bottles with Roman numerals stenciled on them. There were lengths of jagged glass tubing, corks of many sizes, and a dusty ledger. *The devil's potions,* Ezra reckoned. He saw that the flickering lights were caused by strange, luminous globes hovering within the airy void of the nave. *Familiar spirits!*

He watched the comings and goings of Crossly, Dee, and the other members of the coven for ten minutes or more. Some roamed about the church—changing places, changing positions—while others sat quietly under their spell. Several times, Crossly dipped the jagged tubes in potions and stabbed the arms of the sorcerers. The lights faded and brightened with regularity; but to the sexton's great relief, no hellish animals appeared, no horned demons cavorted backward, and only once did he think he saw wraiths from hell drifting within the candlelight.

At length, the lights faded entirely, and the enchanted sorcerers began to stir. Ezra knew then that the witching hour was over. Crossly conferred with Dee, his back to the window. Dee seemed to be confused, trying to explain something. Crossly remonstrated with him. Dee was apologetic. Then Crossly turned so that his face was visible, and the sexton was astonished to see tears rolling down his cheeks, his face contorted with grief. The sexton didn't know what to make of that, but then the other wizards rose, and all of them made their way to the back of the church and were lost to view.

No tears will glue Abbot Gervase's head back on his shoulders, Master Ironfist, Ezra concluded bitterly, *nor no devil will neither. Only God can work such a miracle. Thy crimes are well done these many years, and thou wilt pay the price in torment. And perchance I'll see thee burn afore that on a bonfire in the market square.*

CHAPTER 37

John Kenning wrote five letters on the chalkboard in a vertical line and spoke each one out loud: "L-A-S-E-R. This is an acronym for what?" He turned to face the sparse audience of students scattered around the university lecture hall. Several hands rose tentatively. He pointed to one of them.

"Light amplification by...something...energy of..." The voice trailed away.

"Light amplification by stimulated emission of radiation," John said. He spoke the words distinctly and wrote them after their initial letters on the board. "This is important stuff, people. It'll be part of the quantum physics course next term, so you need to get a good grasp of it." The advanced freshman class dutifully copied the words into their notebooks and laptops.

"The laser is one of the most powerful inventions of twentieth-century physics. It's used in a multitude of applications—surgery, welding, range finding." *Ghost hunting.* "It was postulated by Townes in the 1950s and then discovered by Maiman in 1960 using a rod of crystalline ruby." *A shaft of red light piercing the darkness of a church. Reflections twisting and squirming up massive stone pillars, melting into the void of the ceiling.* "The key word here is *amplification*." He drew a circle around the word. "The light produced by a laser is amplified tremendously, because each wave is in step with its neighbors. This is what we call coherent radiation."

John wrote the two words on the chalkboard underneath the acronym. He was finding it hard to concentrate. He had a single driving desire these days: to know what had happened in the church. It had been almost two weeks since the police had dismissed him and Sarah from their inquiries, and still, there was no trace of his brother—or of Karen Butler, for that matter. All local hospitals had been checked, train stations and ports were on alert, and air travel was being monitored. Nothing. Harry Groh had no more to say on the subject. He slept a lot and amused himself with baseball magazines provided by a hospital aide. Soon, he would be fit to return to the States. Frank's body had already been shipped back to Illinois.

Sarah had given John an icy farewell in a pub in Piccadilly that suggested they would not be seeing each other again. "It's over, John," she had said without tears. "The ghost hunting was one thing, but now that Brian's taken up with Karen Butler, there's nothing left for me to fight for. Wherever they've gone off to, I don't care. The south of France, Tahiti—I simply don't care. I've got to get on with my life. I'll be all right." John had been unable to come up with a rebuttal, so he just watched her finish her drink and walk out into the night. "It's been a wild ride," she said as she left.

And Hoyland Church was quiet at last.

So what was John to do? How did you begin to look for someone who had vanished from the face of the earth? His days had become long and painful. His dissertation had lain untouched on his desk since his return from Hoyland. He waited for the call from his brother that never came. He didn't know where to turn.

John resumed his lecture. "Let me explain to you how a laser works. Take notes on this, and it'll stand you in good stead come October. As I hope you already know, atoms and molecules normally exist in their lowest energy state, the ground state. If you excite them by application of heat or radiation, you can promote them to a state of higher energy. Usually, they relax back to the ground state at once. No big deal. In some substances, however, the atoms in these excited states transfer to an intermediate state that is relatively stable. The number of atoms in the intermediate state can start to build up. If you keep applying the incident energy, you, well, you pump it up, so to speak. It's a bit like pumping air into a football, I suppose." He took a question from a student and paused to collect his thoughts.

"If you keep applying this incident energy, you eventually get a much higher population of atoms in the intermediate state than in the ground state. Then if you stimulate the substance with light of the wavelength that corresponds to the energy difference between the two states, you get rapid cascading back to the ground state with an accompanying pulse of coherent radiation: the laser light. We call this process population inversion. The excited state empties all at once and spills over to the ground state. The frequency of the emitted radiation obeys the following equation."

He turned to the chalkboard and wrote: $f = \Delta E/h$ (h = Planck's Constant). Then he froze. *Population inversion.* "The frequency of the laser light is given by this equation. I'm sorry. I already said that. The parameter f is the frequency of the laser radiation, and E is the..." He heard one of the students cough and turned to find them all grinning at him. "Er, I'm sorry," John mumbled. "Where was I? The parameter E is the energy difference between the ground state and..." *Molecules cascading from one quantum state to another, spilling over.* "Look, people, I'm a bit under the weather this morning. Why don't we cut the class short today? We'll pick it up again next Tuesday."

A student whooped joyfully. Notebooks were slammed shut. Feet shuffled sideways. Voices faded away down the corridor. John was left staring at an auditorium of empty seats, his mind racing through the pages of their article on the ghost phenomenon and through Brian's lecture to him about how ghosts were formed. Energy diagrams and quantum mechanical equations flashed across his mind's eye. *Population inversion. Oh, shit!* He clung to the edges of the lectern, scared to death.

*****

It took John an hour to settle on a plan. Then he ran to his office, called British Airways, and tried to reserve a seat on the next flight to Chicago. It was standby only since it was the height of the season. He ran to his bank and withdrew all the cash from his checking account and retrieved his passport from the safety deposit box.

Fortunately, he had a visitor's visa for an upcoming quantum physics conference in Houston. He caught the subway to Heathrow Airport.

Twelve hours later, in the international terminal of Chicago's O'Hare airport, John fumbled through the local telephone directory. What was the name of the student who had participated in the sensory deprivation trials with Karen Butler? Brian and Harry had mentioned his name many times. Dan something. Passner? No, Patzer, something like that. Patzner, right. He prayed to God there were not a hundred Patzners in the city. There were seven.

His second call unearthed Dan Patzner's mother, who gave him Dan's address and phone number in Joliet. After a long and expensive cab ride, John stood in the porch of a drab apartment building, reading names off a directory on the wall. It was getting dark, and jet lag was creeping up on him. He found Patzner and Simpson and pushed the button. A voice answered, laced with suspicion. John said he was a friend of Karen Butler and had a message from her. He was buzzed up.

"You're a friend of Karen's?" Dan asked as they met in the doorway. "You a Brit?"

"That's right. My name's John Kenning."

"I'm Dan Patzner. Pleased to meet you. Wanna come in?" John entered and sat down in a lumpy armchair made of old tires. Dan brought him a soda. "So how's Karen doing? I haven't seen her in months. We had a falling out last Thanksgiving." Dan sat down opposite him on a couch made of old newspapers and took a slug from his own can. "You know, before that, we were big buddies on the ICPS sensory deprivation team. Cueball and Butthead we called each other"—he laughed—"because they made us shave our heads. They were just nicknames to needle Dr. Groh."

John returned his smile. "I know him too. I hear you got kicked off the team."

"Yeah, kicked off, quit, somewhere in between. Damn near got kicked out of school, to tell the truth."

"Harry told us you were scared of Karen. He said you thought she was a witch."

Dan colored. "Yeah, I did at that time. I'm kind of ashamed of it now. I was going through a bad time, and the experiments were getting real scary. I didn't know what the fuck was happening, man. Karen was pushing me to sustain this zeta thing longer and longer. I began to think she was the cause of it in some way. Dumb, really. I've had a couple of talks with Connie Cammaretta since then, and she's set me straight. Karen's all right. It was my fault. So how's she doing? Still working with Dr. Groh and that English professor guy?"

"You mean Brian Kenning. He's my brother."

"You don't say. What are you all up to?"

"Actually, the news is not good. Karen's disappeared. My brother has too. It's got something to do with a zeta experiment in England that went seriously wrong, but I don't quite know how. It's a mystery." Dan froze, and his amiability began to drain away. John continued. "The two of them have literally vanished. My brother's girlfriend— ex-girlfriend, I suppose I should say—thinks they've run off together to the south of France or somewhere, but I'm not so sure. And there's more. Harry Groh's had some sort of nervous breakdown, and Frank Koslowski's dead. You didn't know any of this?"

Dan shook his head. "I've been out of touch for months, even with Connie, keeping my head in the books and trying not to flunk out, you know. Koslowski's dead you say?"

"I thought you might've read about it in the campus newspaper or something."

"No. It doesn't publish during the summer." There was a moment of awkward silence. "But you didn't come all this way to deliver a news bulletin," Dan said. He rose from the couch and walked to the window.

"No, I didn't, Dan. I need your help."

Dan was on him in a flash. "Now hold your horses just a minute, chief. Hold 'em right there. Don't start asking me to do any more zeta stuff. I've had my fill of that mess. I'm sworn off it for life."

"You've gotta help me, Dan. I've nowhere else to turn. Two lives are at stake, and one of them is a good friend of yours. If you'll come back to England with me, we can save them both."

"To England? Are you nuts? Isn't there anyone else who can help you?"

"No. My aunt's dead, Brian's girlfriend's walked out on us, and I don't know how to locate the Scottish woman who helped us before. You're the only person I can think of."

Dan remained by the window, imploring the world with upraised palms. "Oh man, you can't ask me. You just can't. It damn near killed me last time. I swore, never again. Don't ask me please."

"Karen needs you, Dan. You can't let her down. You must come back with me."

"Anyway, I've got no time and no money."

"I've got cash. I'll buy your ticket."

"Oh man!"

"You ran out on Karen once, Dan. You can't do it again."

CHAPTER 38

Hoyland Church
August 2018

By the time their rental car came to a halt outside the church on a sultry Monday evening in late August, Dan and John were both uneasy—Dan because he didn't have a clue what was in store for him and John because he did. They got out of the car and stood for a moment under the canopy of the lych-gate. Darkness was almost complete, and rain was in the air.

"No one about," John said.

"Worst luck."

"No, that's good luck—good for us and good for them."

"Not for me, it's not."

John switched on the flashlight he had brought with him and led the way up the path. There were no lights on in the church, not a sign of a living soul within half a mile. Dan turned the handle, but the door wouldn't open.

"It's locked," Dan said.

"They don't lock churches."

"Well, they've locked this one."

"Let's try the vestry."

The eyeless stone heads on the cornices of the porch looked down on the futility of their efforts and ordered them out into the blackness again. They stumbled round to the vestry, where John tested the door. "This one's locked as well," he said. "Maybe the police locked it."

"Better leave it then."

"No. Come over here."

John approached the solitary window set into the vestry wall. He refrained from looking in for fear of seeing Applewhite's death mask smeared across the glass, this time a ghost for sure. He fumbled through the grass, looking for a stone.

"Hey, you can't do that," Dan said, even as the pane was shattering and John's hand was reaching through for the latch. "Jesus, we're in trouble now."

John turned to him angrily. "For Christ's sake, Dan, we're not here for choir practice! I've explained all this to you. It's a matter of life and death. Two people are missing. We're not going to stand back and tut-tut about the tragedy of it all. We're going to do something about it, so don't give me any crap about a broken window. Help me up onto this ledge." John climbed through the open window with Dan's help and then reciprocated by dragging Dan after him. They dusted themselves off and stood quietly in the darkness of the vestry.

"Can we switch the light on?" Dan asked.

"Better not."

"Okay, fine. So what do you want to do now we're here?"

"We're going to try a zeta experiment."

"Now? In the middle of the night? Can't we at least wait till it's light?"

"There'll be people here then, Dan. Think! There's an early morning service in the church every day. And the police will probably put a guard on it after tonight's break-in. We've got to do it now."

"What exactly do you have in mind?"

"I think that Brian and Karen must have established a strong resonance with the time of the destruction of the abbey, just like we all did back in April. They were taking special drugs to reinforce their innate ability. What precisely happened during their experiment I'm still not clear about, but we need to repeat it and find out, you and me. Brian believed that at least two people are necessary to get a strong resonance, like you and Karen did that time at the center."

"Yeah, I understand that, and I know how to reach zeta, but you don't."

"Oh, I'm beginning to think I do. Several incidents in the last few months have led me to believe that maybe I can do it. Anyway, we're all capable of it. Brian said so." Dan stared at him in disbelief. "Take my word for it, Dan. Brian and Harry have learned a lot since you quit the team."

"So do you want to do it here?"

"I want to look for a clue first."

"A clue to where Karen and your brother are?"

"Yes."

"Do you think they're still in the church?"

"They could be. I don't know."

"This is all beyond me. Where do you want to look?"

"In the crypt."

"Oh man, you're really insane," Dan said, turning in a complete circle. "I don't believe this. It's like a bad B movie without the pop-corn. Who in their right mind would want to go into a crypt in the middle of the night in an old church like this? Jeez!"

"Because that's where the clue is. I'm convinced of it."

"I'm outta here," Dan said without moving.

"You've got a debt to repay, so let's go." John walked over to the door into the church. "It's not going to be dangerous. Come on!" Dan shook his head but walked over to John's side nevertheless. John continued. "We can't risk turning on the lights. They'd be visible from the road. But I remember where the door to the crypt is. I saw it when my aunt and I walked through the church the first time I came here. It's on the south wall, in the middle of a line of religious paint-ings. We'll locate the door with the flashlight, and then we'll turn the light on in the crypt when we get inside. Okay?" Dan said nothing.

"Okay," John said for him. "Here goes." He took a deep breath and wished to God that it was his brother by his side instead of this unreliable stranger. He grasped the cold iron handle in his palm and turned it, and the door creaked open to reveal a cavernous black-ness. John waited in the doorway till his eyes grew accustomed to the dark. The only discernible feature was a row of gray rectangles that he took to be the windows in the opposite wall. He switched on the flashlight, and a feeble cone of light traced the crisscross of ancient flagstones. He swallowed hard.

"We cross the nave and hunt along that far wall," John said. He plunged into the darkness like a blind man with a cane of light and headed away from the vestry door. He tried to ignore the vast expanse of deserted church all around him, though it made him distinctly uneasy. The fall of his feet thudded starkly against the stone; the echoes that accompanied his own footfalls came from Dan's shoes he felt sure. The unseen and unseeing eyes of the huge crucifix burned into his cheek.

They passed a pillar, its transit marked solely by the eclipse of the lighter window shapes. John reached the south wall and turned to his right, bathing the wall with light as he went. He came to one of the paintings in the row that Polly had pointed out to him almost a year ago: *The Garden of Gethsemane.* He recalled it well but didn't dwell on it. Every object had taken on a disconcerting eeriness in the beam from the flashlight. He continued on. And there was the next painting: *The Raising of Lazarus. How appropriate,* he thought, *bringing the dead back to life.*

They skirted a section of chairs placed by the wall for use during services by the tardy and the timid. The sudden, irrational fear that the advancing beam of light would burst upon the bloodied corpse of Brian slumped in a chair took hold of John's mind and proved impossible to shake loose. He breathed regularly and deeply and tried to focus on the importance of the mission. He splashed light against the wall again. He saw *The Conversion of Saul.* Okay, he remembered that one. Behind him, Dan stumbled over a protruding flagstone and cursed under his breath. Raindrops began to patter on the stained glass windows above their heads.

As they inched their way down the wall, it seemed the darkness would never divulge the whereabouts of that little door. John began to worry. Had they passed it? Had his memory betrayed him? They were halfway down the nave, and there was still no sign of it. He kept walking, and the echoing footsteps followed. He knew that Frank Koslowski's body was no longer outside in the bushes. He knew the severed hand had been removed by the police. And Brian's corpse was not to be found in the next chair to swim into his pool of light.

They came to a gap in the rows of chairs, and John's flashlight hit upon a tiny door set into a Norman archway. This was it. He moved to the head of the steep and poorly cut stone steps that led down to the door. "Watch your footing," he whispered.

"Is this it?" Dan asked.

"My aunt told me this was the door to the crypt."

"If you're sure you know what you're doing..." John didn't know that he was sure. He had been sure. Just moments ago, he had been quite determined, but now it all seemed far-fetched. He could think of a hundred reasons to go no further, a thousand reasons to return to London at once.

Dan reached around him and turned the handle gingerly. "This one's not locked," he said. Dan stepped forward and leaned against the door, and it gave inward with a groan. John sprayed light into the doorway to prevent them from being unnerved by the blackness of the space beyond. But even as the door swung open and the torchlight struck the low ceiling, there came from within a sound that sent Dan jerking backward into John's midsection.

Something had moved in the depths of the crypt. Something had skittered across the ancient floor, knocking against something, grating against something else. Petrified, they listened to the ensuing silence. Dan's fingers gripped the arm of John's jacket. "What the fuck was that? Is there someone down there? Are you expecting someone to be down there, you fuck?"

"No, Dan, no. Who would be down there?"

"Your crazy fuck of a brother?"

"No. No, he couldn't be."

"Rats?"

"Mice maybe. Perhaps a bat."

"Bats? Oh man!"

"Mice, probably. That's all."

Musty air wafted up from the crypt and began to turn John's stomach. There was a taste of the dead in his mouth. His scalp was taut, ants crawling across it. He staggered as he stepped forward. *Easy does it,* he thought. *One step at a time.*

"Are you all right?"

"I feel a bit faint. The air's bad down here."

"Shit. That's just great. Here, give me the flashlight."

"Thanks, Dan. Sorry." John handed it over. Dan negotiated the threshold and ducked under the low arch. He looked down. The circular staircase dropped drunkenly away from his feet and into a well of darkness. "There's the light switch," John said, pointing to the wall.

Dan flipped it, and a faint illumination rose from the depths. "Are you coming then?" he asked. "This was your idea."

"You go ahead. I'll be right behind you." John steadied himself against the doorframe. The weak glow spreading up from the bowels of the vault highlighted the grimy, rough-hewn stones that lined the entranceway. Spiderwebs laced every corner. Dan had already disappeared around the first turn of the spiral staircase, and John had no choice but to follow him. Then with a horror that gripped his entrails and squeezed his courage into paralysis, John knew that Dan was about to speak, and he knew with absolute certainty what the words would be.

"This way."

Terrified, John began to descend the precipitous staircase. He ran both hands along the uneven walls, clutching at any projection to stabilize himself and calm the maelstrom in his head. The air was thicker now. It was like breathing sand. He continued his descent, turning dizzily, spiraling down into the bowels of the church.

"This way!"

He saw below him the pit of stone that was the crypt of St. Neot's. It was suffocating, claustrophobic. Narrow ranks of pillars stretched up from a checkerboard of flagstones to a vaulted ceiling. Every surface was crooked and cracked. Tombs lined the walls. Niches receded into blackness with their crusty dead. He tottered down the staircase, struggling to keep his balance, sucking fetid air into his heaving lungs, remembering his premonitions in the car, waiting for Dan's next words.

"Come down!"

He stumbled past the arched ceiling, down the pillars, down through the grainy air, down into the church beneath the sea. *I'm alive, but all down here are dead. See them arrayed along the walls! The fleshless, the dusty dead, rising to judge my complacency. Why did you kill Aunt Polly? I didn't. Why did you kill Nigel Applewhite? I didn't. Why did you kill Frank Koslowski? I didn't, I swear. Why did you kill Brian Kenning? I didn't, I didn't. He's not dead. Yes, he is!*

"John, man, are you all right?"

"I feel terrible."

"There's not enough oxygen down here. Let's rest a minute."

John sat down on the bottom step, cold and distressed. "My dreams have come true," he said.

"What dreams?"

"Oh, nothing. I'll be fine in a minute."

"It's like being buried alive down here."

Slowly, John began to recover. The light helped. Dan's sudden and unexpected courage helped. He swallowed hard and rubbed his cheeks. Fresher air drifted down out of the church.

Dan turned away and began to examine the dusty tombs. "So where do we find this clue to your brother's disappearance?"

"We have to find one particular sarcophagus."

"Which one?"

"The one that holds the remains of Richard Crossly and his wife. Many years ago, it was removed from the niche in the east wall of the church and stored down here."

"How will we find it among all these others?"

"It shouldn't be too difficult. It's wide enough for two people."

"I'll start on this side."

They searched the crypt, poring over stone carvings and Latin inscriptions. John began to feel a little better now that his brain was occupied, and soon, his fingers were white with stone dust. A mouse ran across the floor, and that further relieved his fears. He became aware of how quiet it was down in the crypt. The rain and wind outside were inaudible. "You could surely rest in peace down here. No problem."

"I think I've found it," Dan said after a while.

He was crouched beside a huge sarcophagus resting on the far side of the crypt at an angle. It looked like it had been discarded there carelessly. They examined it. On the top were two figures carved in relief: a man and a woman, side by side. Time had worn away the details of their features, but a curious, lifelike quality remained none-theless. John admired the artistry in the sculpted figures. It had cer-tainly once been a fine piece of work. "This looks like them," he said.

The man was dressed in light armor with a chain mail head-piece and a small breastplate. The right hand was covered by a wide gauntlet from which issued a sword that followed the line of the leg. The left hand was gripped by the right hand of the female figure. She was an elegant woman, clad in a full-length robe that stretched from the slender neck to the delicately pointed feet resting on a hassock. The couple seemed to be asleep, dozing in utter tranquility, while the world burgeoned above them.

"There's some writing here," Dan said. "I can't read it very well. It says *Sepul* something, and I think this says *Crossly* right here. Look. You read it." He traced the words with the tip of a finger and then stepped aside. John joined him and used the flashlight to illuminate the lettering, or at least improve the contrast. The inscription was a linear carving running around the perimeter of the upper part of the sarcophagus. The lettering was very ornate and bordered with finely carved dentals and double chevrons. Strands of ivy and honeysuckle trailed from the border, fading away in the plain marble block that comprised the bulk of the sarcophagus. John rubbed his index finger across the surface of the stone.

"This says Crossly, all right, just here. And the rest of the word-ing looks similar to what's beside the niche and on the plaque in the nave. Can you copy down the inscription while I read it to you? I brought my notebook and a pencil." He dropped to his knees. "It seems to start here. There's a big ornamental design in between these two words. That's probably the beginning." He paused. "My god, do you know what this design is?"

"What?"

"It's the solar system. Look! See the orbits of the planets? See the sun in the middle here? It's a representation of the Sphere of the Planets, the Crossly coat of arms. That's amazing. This is definitely the right tomb."

"Just read the words," Dan said.

John circled the tomb in a slow, crouching shuffle, reading out loud in halting Latin each word that he came across. "'Sepulchrum Richardi Crossly et Catherinae'—this seems to be identical to the wording on the plaque upstairs as far as I can remember. 'De Willugby Conjugum'—they were married at Willugby I suppose that means. Willoughby is a village not far from here. 'Ista obiit decimo nono Septembris MDLXXXVII'—that's 1587. 'Ille obiit nono Aprilis MDXCIII.' That's 1593. Those would be the years when they died. 'Tempus edax rerum.' I don't remember seeing this part before. I don't know what it means. 'Credite Ioanne non possum redire.' That's all there is. We're back to the Sphere of the Planets." John stood up and brushed dust from the knees of his pants. He came and stood by Dan, who was still scribbling in the notebook. "How's your Latin?" he asked.

"Nonexistent," Dan replied, staring down at the incomprehensible words. "How's yours?"

"Not bad. Three years of high school. Pretty pointless, as it turned out. Read me back that last bit, and I'll see if I can translate it."

"The part you didn't understand began: 'Tempus edax rerum.'"

"Let's see," John started, hesitantly. "That means 'time…something…things.'" He stopped speaking. A puzzled expression crossed his face.

"What is it?" Dan asked.

John picked up the flashlight and moved back to the sarcophagus. He stared again at the stone inscription. He traced each letter of the three words with his forefinger. "Edax…edax," he muttered. "I know that word. I know it. This is a famous quotation, something to do with eating. 'Tempus edax rerum.' Time, the eater of things. No. What's the word I'm looking for? *Devourer*, that's it. *Devourer*. It says, '*Time, the devourer of all things.*'"

"How did you know that?"

How did he know? Why was it familiar to him? "Oh, I remember now!" John exclaimed. "It's something Brian once said when we were walking on the beach last year. I think he said it was a quotation from Ovid. He was speaking about some old tree stumps submerged in the sea. It means that you can't prevent the ravages of time."

"Okay. So what about the next two words? *Credite?*"

"It's from the verb *credere*, meaning 'to believe.' It's the vocative form, I think. It means 'believe' or 'believe it,' like you're addressing someone."

"And *Ioanne?*"

"Another vocative form. I don't know this word. I know that the Roman letter *I* was used like our modern letter *J*."

They stared at the word in silence. Then Dan, hesitantly and without the slightest conviction, said, "It looks a bit like"—he looked up—"like... John." They stared at each other. Perhaps John had suspected all along what was now presented to his eyes in incontrovertible stone. He had believed that Brian would leave him a clue if it were humanly possible, but now that he saw the words with his own eyes, he desired desperately to be proved wrong.

"*Non possum redire?*"

John took out his cell phone and found a Latin translator app. He entered the three words. "I am not able to return." The message he had been given was at once vindication and repugnance. The words burned into his brain, burned through four hundred years he could never hope to span. He walked over and looked again at the figures carved in stone on top of the tomb. He stared at the face of the man but could recognize no features. Time had devoured them completely.

"Does it mean...you?" Dan asked incredulously.

"Yes. Don't you get it? This isn't Richard Crossly entombed here. It's Brian."

"It can't be. Don't be stupid!"

"It is."

"But—"

"It finally dawned on me last week when I was teaching a class about lasers. Population inversion—it means that all the molecules in one quantum state suddenly transfer to another. Somehow, Brian was projected into the sixteenth century during their last experiment. We knew there'd been some permanent transfer of material during the previous try, because Brian had found dust from the sixteenth century scattered around the church. When they did it this last time, the resonance must have been extremely powerful. Remember that Brian and Karen were taking drugs to intensify the zeta state."

"Wait, wait, wait! Hold up a minute. You're going too fast."

"Don't you understand what happened? The molecular concentration of Brian in the earlier time frame must have become extraordinarily high. Some sort of barrier was crossed with the result that all the molecules of his body cascaded over into the other temporal state rather than relaxing back to the present. They spilled over just like a laser pulse. Brian ended up in 1537."

"Oh, come on!"

"The history books record that Richard Crossly underwent a radical change following the overthrow of the monastery. They say he became a new man. I'll say he did! We'd assumed it meant that he changed his religious beliefs or his moral values, that he became remorseful for his wrongdoings, something like that. We didn't think it was literally true."

"Do you mean to say that your brother is…was—God, I don't know which—trapped in the sixteenth century?"

"I know it's unbelievable, but that's what appears to have happened. Brian found himself catapulted into the midst of the overthrow of the abbey, and somehow he managed to assume Richard Crossly's place. He made the locals believe it was magic or something like that. They'd have believed it back then. He lived out the rest of his life there and died there. Incredible! I knew he would want to leave a message for me, a message that would last for four hundred years. Paper would never survive. Metal would rust or be stolen. The surest way was to have it carved onto his tomb and hope I'd be smart enough to find it. I guess I was."

"I still can't believe it," Dan said. "Your translation might be—"

John stabbed his finger repeatedly toward the sarcophagus, on the verge of tears. "No! It's Brian who's buried in there. I know it is." All John could think about was what it must have been like for his brother to watch the ghostly contact becoming stronger and stronger until it finally became reality and to watch his friends and his whole life fade away into a ghostly, inaccessible future. John now knew for certain that the hand found in the church was Brian's. The molecules of Crossly's sword had been real as they sliced through Brian's wrist the second time. The severed hand had fallen on this side of the breached dam of time, and the rest of him had pitched onto the other side.

The hand! "Wait a minute!" John exclaimed. "I've just thought of something. Brian's hand was chopped off during their experiment. That means he had to live the remainder of his life with only one hand. If the skeletons inside this tomb are still intact, the male one should be missing a hand."

"Do you think we should take a look?"

"I don't know. What do you think?" They stared at the massive stone edifice. "The top looks like it might be a separate piece," John said. "Let's see if we can move it." They pushed up on the lid of the sarcophagus and, by applying all their strength, managed to lift it an inch or two. "Let's push it off to the side."

"It'll break."

"Then it'll have to break. Come on." They braced themselves at each end, and John counted down to the push. "Three, two, one, now!" The heavy slab jerked to one side and crashed to the floor, fracturing into three pieces. A cloud of dust billowed from the interior of the tomb. They waited at a distance till the dust settled then cautiously peered over the edge of the sarcophagus.

There were two skeletons inside, both greatly deteriorated. Each one was partially covered with strips of faded fabric. Around one neck was a gold chain strung with several bright jewels. That must be the female. John examined the spot where the hand of the man would have rested and could see no bones of any kind. But there was something else, something metallic, rusted through and thin as paper, a metal contraption with pincerlike appendages about the size and shape of a… John turned away.

"What is it?" Dan asked. "What?"

"Now we know the real reason why Richard Crossly was nicknamed Ironfist." John turned and walked to the wall of the crypt. He stood with his back to Dan, chewing on a knuckle, staring at the stones. He spluttered a mixture of tears and laughter. "It's really quite funny," he said, "in a way. Brian was always mechanically minded. That's just the sort of thing he would do. He made himself an artificial hand, a fist of iron."

"Oh man. I'm real sorry."

"And he made a life for himself in Tudor England, the stranger from the future."

Dan seemed genuinely moved by John's loss and the fate that had befallen his brother. He came over to him and put a hand on his shoulder. "Jeez, I'm so sorry, man."

John remained staring at the wall. But was there yet something he could do? Did the past have to be writ so tragically? An idea began to form in his mind, a million-to-one shot, a desperate plan to save Brian from his prison. He dearly wanted to prove the inscription wrong, to prove that time was not the devourer of all things and could be forced to regurgitate Brian into his rightful place and time.

"There's nothing we can do then," Dan concluded.

"Not necessarily," John replied, turning to face him. "There's something about these resonance experiments that doesn't make sense. It's bothered me before, and now that I know what happened to my brother, I'm even more puzzled. It's a paradox that just might give us a chance to turn this whole mess around."

"What do you mean?"

"During these temporal resonances, we link a present time with a past time. We did it once in this church and saw Abbot Gervase's miracle and subsequent execution. Then Brian and Karen did it again with disastrous consequences. To put it simply, which one of those two contacts really happened in so far as 1537 is concerned? That period of time only happened once. Which of the two contacts was witnessed by the monks and the soldiers? It can't have been both."

"I see the problem."

"Which one was real to them?"

"Evidently, the last one," Dan said, nodding in the direction of the sarcophagus.

"But why? Why should it have been that one and not the first one, when Brian was not transported back in time?"

"Maybe because it happened later and superseded the previous one?"

"Exactly. So why shouldn't there be a third contact? Why wouldn't that one stick, so to speak, and nullify the previous one? Perhaps one more benign contact would wipe out this horrible state of affairs and substitute a more acceptable one."

"But what about the inscription? Credite Ioanne—it's carved in stone. You can't alter that."

"How do you know? Maybe this carving, this whole travesty, would be wiped clean like a slate. Maybe we'll wake up to find that it's Richard Crossly buried here after all—no inscription, no message to me, no fist of iron. Dan, this is my brother we're talking about. If there's even a remote chance to bring him back, I've got to try."

"This is his message to you! He knew it was hopeless. He said so: 'Non possum redire.' I am not able to return."

"That just means that he wasn't able to bring himself back, though God knows he must have tried. I've been thinking back to what Sarah told us from the history books. She said that Crossly earned a bad name for himself by messing about in the church at night. The villagers thought he was trying to raise demons.

"But Crossly—Brian, that is—was just trying everything he could to bring about a strong zeta connection with the future, with our time, so that he could reverse the process and bring himself back. That's why he hung out with John Dee and the sorcerers of the day. They were helping him. But he didn't have anoxyseriphin, and there was no way to synthesize it back then. Without the drug, he was trapped. But just because he couldn't reverse it doesn't mean that we can't. He tried and failed. We can try and succeed."

"How, for Christ's sake?"

"By performing a third resonance with 1537. We'll reproduce the correct conditions and see if we can't replace Brian's disastrous contact with a harmless one."

"That's fucking insane! What if we end up in the past too?"

"That can't happen."

"Sure it could."

"No. You need the drug for that. Look, Dan, my brother's imprisoned in the sixteenth century. He's scared. He's alone. Imagine if it was you! We're going to take a sledgehammer and break down the door. Brian's going to wake up on the floor of the church, and the three of us are going to leave this stinking business to rot. Understand?"

"Jeez, man, you're fucking crazy!" Dan held his head in his hands and grimaced. "Okay, okay! Where do you want to do it?"

John looked up at the arched ceiling. "I figure we're no more than thirty meters from the chancel screen. Less. We'll try the experiment down here. If we're able to make contact, neither the soldiers nor the monks will see us. It will be as if we never interfered with the destruction of the abbey at all. The event will proceed normally, as was always intended."

"It's fucking impossible."

"This whole time distortion will be put right. Come on now. Let's give it a try."

"Fine, fine, but it won't work."

They sat down on the cold stone floor, facing each other. John could see the shattered lid of the sarcophagus out of the corner of his eye. He took a deep breath and let the seconds tick by. He recalled the feelings he had riding in the college van and in the police car, feelings of gliding smoothly across sand, of drifting out across the sea, floating on the ocean under a shimmering bowl of silver stars.

Dan seemed uncomfortable at first, uncommitted to the task ahead of them. But then he made a curious rocking motion of his head, and his eyes took on the familiar glaze that John had witnessed in the other sensitive subjects. John could feel his exhalations swirling around his cheeks in the thick, fetid air, curdling with the dust of time. He focused on the patterns on a nearby sarcophagus and let his mind ease itself around the intricate carving, tracing the labyrinth. He felt himself slipping away from reality, just like the other times.

Brian is not dead, he thought. *I can bring him back.* A sinew twitched in his neck. A paralyzing knot encircled his eyeballs, which quivered and began to roll upward into the tops of their sockets. The roof of the crypt seemed to drift away, and the stars seemed to replace it with a sudden, ringing clarity. John felt a tremor in the back of his head, like the activation of some electronic circuit. Then the axis of the universe tilted and threw him into a whole other reality. *I can do it. I have the power.*

There are ghosts in the niches, ghosts in the stone. We are all dead, thrown together in time's great mixing bowl, enfolded in the bowels of the church, wound together in communal shrouds. Our nostrils suffused with earth... What was that, over there behind the last pillar? A twinkling of silver. The rattle of steel against stone. No, no, that was just a dream. The air is not air, not air. The air is... water!

A strand of seaweed floated across his vision—transparent and gossamer but seaweed nonetheless. John watched it float in front of his face. It was almost real. They were almost beneath the sea. He tried to speak, but the words formed tiny bubbles and drifted up to the roof of the crypt. He couldn't move. He gasped for breath. A heavy weight pressed down on his chest. His lungs screamed.

A sword emerged from behind the last pillar, a hand, an arm, a man stepping out! The crypt wavered. The pillars quivered. A figure stood at the far end of the crypt, not transparent this time, not a ghost. He was a stocky man with tightly curled hair, wearing a jacket with a red cross on the chest and strange leather boots. He had Frank Koslowski's blue jeans on and the look of the cornered beast in his eye. Advancing through the air, the water, lumbering, swimming. The man was coming up behind Dan with his sword raised. John could see his lips move. He could faintly hear the words that he spoke: "Devils ye be! Wizards from hell!"

Richard Crossly, of course! He was transported forward into the future, crossing Brian in the deadly inversion. He was the one who chased Harry. He was the one who killed Frank. Just like Harry said, Ironfist! He's been hiding down here in the crypt since that last experiment, trapped in the future. That's why Brian was able to assume his identity after the assault on the abbey. Crossly had vanished into the future!

I'm choking. Drowning. Dan began to fall forward. Crossly's choking too. None of us can breathe. Crossly continued his approach, spluttering, sword swinging. The air slowly transforming into seawater.

"I am bewitched! For God and King Harry!" Crossly's sword descended onto the back of Dan's neck. John held his breath with a desperate determination. His premonitions had finally come true. He was in the church beneath the sea. The walls of the crypt had receded. There were no tombs anymore, no pillars. On all sides, the cold North Sea stretched far away.

But he was resolute. He would survive for the sake of all his dead friends. He could drown Crossly. He could win the game. Crossly's arms were tangled with Dan's legs. They were locked in a deathly embrace, spiraling slowly up to the surface, arms flailing in the icy water, slowly dying. They disappeared in the waters above his head. Only Crossly's sword remained, glittering faintly on the seabed. A transparent fish swam idly by.

There was nothing to save him now, nothing to save Brian. The flood had come to the fenlands at last. He slowly pitched forward and prepared for the end. He closed his eyes. His head exploded. *I will not die. I will not die.*

CHAPTER 39

The Lincolnshire Coast
Prehistory

Ten thousand years ago, the hill was nothing but an undulation in the floor of a shallow sea. Fish nuzzled its brow in search of tiny blue crabs, and the crabs tickled its scalp as they scuttled away through its weedy tresses. Sodden and ill-used, the hill muddled its way through the ages. With each day of each of the thousands of years that it withstood the pawing of the fierce undertow, however, its stature grew.

The climate cooled. Water was drawn away to be ice-fixed at the poles, and the rains that for centuries had swollen the sea off the eastern edge of Britain diminished. The hill inched its way toward the surface. The cliffs of Flamborough to the north now froze each winter, and their flanks were broken apart by the spring thaws, the crumbs fattening the sides of the hungry little hill. Then at low tide one fine August morning, the hill burst forth from the waves, shaking its mane into the unfamiliar wind.

As if to protect its offspring, the tide constructed a sandbar a little way out from the shoreline. Shells and driftwood accumulated between hill and sandbar till they were joined, at which point the tide withdrew. Another thousand years passed, and the hill scarcely saw even the highest tides of the spring equinox. Silt, washed seaward on the autumn rains, mingled with the ocean litter and held it fast. The hill was marooned.

When man first wandered into this remote part of Britain, the hill was a quarter-mile inland and a hundred feet tall. Only the marshes and perfidious quicksand preserved its solitude. Soon, the coarse saltwater grasses gave way to gentler varieties that bent under the force of the fen-sweeping gales. Seagulls dropped fertilizer on the hill, and water rats dug their burrows in it. The hill embraced them all, grinding their debris into rich humus.

The men who first ascended the hill were fiery hunters from across the North Sea. They brought with them a hardiness that respected the hill's splendid isolation. They knew it must have sprung out of the flatness for a reason. A cairn was built on the summit. Later, rocks were dragged from the Trent Valley to define a stone circle wherein the gods could feel safe to commune with them. The place was named Heighlendh, or simply the high land, and the sanctity of it grew with succeeding generations.

Hundreds of years later, a Mercian warrior named Guthlac sheathed his sword for the last time, paddled a coracle across the marsh, and built the first crude church on top of the hill. In the course of time, Heighlendh Abbey became the splendid culmination of the hill's ascendance from humble seabed to holy mount.

One particular morning, when the hill was still young and waves still lapped over its crown, a remarkable thing happened. A shoal of herring, nipping at the flanks of the hill, was astonished to see three large and unfamiliar creatures floundering at its base. The creatures were as big as dolphins but so awkward that they seemed not to belong in water at all. The herring backed off and watched the antics of these ungainly creatures as they beat the water with their long, thin fins.

In a matter of moments, two of the beasts died, and their bodies drifted up to the surface. The third beast pitched forward and floated motionless with its snout touching the sandy bottom. Slowly, all three faded from sight. The only thing left was a long, thin stick on the seabed, brightly colored in silver, red, and yellow. The herring feared it was a sea snake of a species they had never before seen, so they kept their distance. But it was stiff and straight, and it did not move. Then it, too, vanished. The herring hesitated only a moment then resumed their quest for food.

CHAPTER 40

Hoyland Church
August 2018

John regained consciousness to find that the waters had receded to their rightful place in time, and the crypt was dry once more. He realized that he and Dan had not succeeded in making contact with the time of the destruction of the abbey but rather with some much more ancient time when the whole area had been underwater. He groaned aloud when he saw the bodies of Dan Patzner and Richard Crossly entwined in the corner, drowned and at peace.

He cried for a long time over Dan's death, for which he felt directly responsible. But he felt less anguish over the passing of Crossly—not because he judged him an evil man but because he felt sympathy for his predicament. Crossly was freed from the terrible circumstance of being thrust alone and unprepared into the distant future. No wonder he had fought and killed and hidden deep underground, away from the growling automobiles and the huge metallic birds that flashed across the sky. It was a mercy he was gone.

John lay for a long time among the dead. He tried to visualize that fateful moment when Crossly and Brian had faced off as equals in front of the chancel screen, each half flesh and half ghost, speeding past each other in time, the fearless despoiler confronting the fearful Christ-image. He tried to imagine how each of them must have felt to be thrown up on an alien shore.

Brian had survived there for fifty years by virtue of his superior knowledge and an ability to manipulate the superstitions of the local people. Crossly had lasted just a few weeks. John pictured his brother's fruitless attempts to reconstruct the zeta experiment with the help of the spiritualists of the day. It was hopeless. Brian Kenning, Poing de Fer, was long dead.

John stood up, dusted himself off, and ascended the spiral staircase into the silent church. He drove through the night to Calais and caught the early morning ferry to France. By the evening of the next day, he was in Provence. He never returned to England to claim his doctoral degree. He took a temporary job at a country inn and eventually became a teacher of English at a primary school. He married a French girl, started a family, and put the past behind him.

*****

Six months after arriving in France, John was reading the arts section of the *Sunday Times* in a quiet corner of the inn when an article caught his eye. A wonderful new treasure had recently been discovered in England; it had been identified as the Sphere of the Planets, one of the finest examples of French metalwork of the fifteenth century. The piece had been dug up under the floor of a church according to the instructions of an American scientist who had expressed a conviction that the piece had been abandoned there during the time of the dissolution of the monasteries. John dropped the newspaper onto the table. Harry Groh! He had seen where the treasure had fallen and been buried under the tons of roof material! The old bastard had finally completed the puzzle. Maybe now he, too, could find some semblance of peace.

John never heard anything more about Karen Butler, but on the occasional evenings when he had no homework to grade and the family was quiet, his thoughts drifted back to the events in Hoyland Church, and he wondered what had happened to her. He supposed that she might have been unlucky enough to be close to Brian during their last experiment and transported back in time with him. Maybe her molecules had been scattered to a continuum, and she had simply ceased to exist. Or perhaps the solution was much simpler. She had been so distraught by what had happened to Brian that she had simply fled and started a new life just like he had.

But for John, none of these options seemed to be a suitable fate for such a remarkable woman. He preferred to imagine that she had achieved resonance with some other past time and linked up with one of the great mystics with whom she believed she shared the power of zeta. He saw her sitting beside Nostradamus in a French castle, staring into a mirror of the future. He saw her in the temple of Apollo on a sunny Greek mountainside, intoning the oracles for the priests. Sometimes, he saw her lying with Coleridge in his opium-scented Xanadu. It was just idle speculation.

CHAPTER 41

Ketteringham Lodge
1587

Ketteringham Lodge passed into the hands of the Crossly family in the same year as the jeweled Sphere of the Planets, 1492, and for the same reason—as reward for Sir Adam Crossly's diplomatic skill in establishing the Treaty of Étaples, which ended a perfunctory English invasion of France. While the latter prize was awarded honorably by the foreign protagonist King Charles VIII, the former was seized from a wealthy Catholic family by King Henry VII and slid sub rosa to the Crosslys.

It was across the sward of Ketteringham Lodge and in and out of the ornamental maze with its great privet hedges that Richard Crossly learned his war craft with wooden sword and paper helmet. It was in the oak-paneled library there that he learned politics and in the dining room that he learned statesmanship from his mother and father respectively. And it was cloaked at night in the darkness of one of the high-ceilinged bedrooms that he dreamed of chivalry in foreign lands.

When Sir Adam Crossly died, the estate was bequeathed to his elder son, Richard. This happened only two years after the dissolution of Hoyland Abbey and Richard's magical transformation, which undoubtedly contributed to Sir Adam's demise. Richard and Catherine took up residence and lived there contentedly, though somewhat isolated, for fifty years.

Upon the death of her husband from choleric fever in September of 1587, Catherine withdrew to a small apartment at the rear of the house and shut up the other rooms. She spent much of her time that autumn at the west window, gazing across the fenlands toward Lincoln, the River Trent, and beyond. Her sole companions were a young maid and a pair of beagles.

It was now December of the year 1587. Christmas was struggling to disperse the somber air. The apartment was decorated tastefully with paper chains and Chinese lanterns, and red coals smoldered in the hearth. A small fir tree in the corner of the room sported lit tiny candles. Catherine was at her writing desk, but not writing. There was a knock at the door.

"If thou wilt, ma'am?" The maid appeared in the doorway.

"What is it, Alice?"

"Please, ma'am, Edward Kelley hath arrived."

"Show him in."

"Very good, ma'am," the maid replied with a curtsey. "This way, sir."

A stooped man, somewhat heavy about the waist, entered the room. His thin gray hair and general physical disrepair suggested a man of about sixty years. The outmoded cut of his dress betrayed him as not one of the professional or landed classes. And with a stretch of the imagination, the clashing colors and threadbare patches might have suggested that he was not wed either. He approached Catherine and bowed deeply. She rose from her desk and walked over to him, smiling. "Edward, I am delighted to see thee again. It hath been three months since we were at Richard's funeral. How goeth thy world?"

"As gladsome as an old man might perceive it, Lady Crossly— Catherine, if I may."

"By all means."

"Though I must confess that my investigations into the astrological and alchemical sciences have been unrewarding of late, and I begin to fear that I will accomplish little of lasting value ere I depart this world. The dread of it weighs heavily on my shoulders. Still, I try to be diligent. I rise early each morning, put on a stolid face, and work in the laboratory till my energies fail me. I spend much of my time in Bohemia these days, and King Rudolph hath promised to knight me in a year or two."

"Truly?"

"I shall become Sir Edward Kelley of Imany and New Lüben!"

"Wherever they may be!" And they both smiled.

"But enough of me. I trust thou art in good health?"

"Tolerably, Edward, but my husband's death hath left me dreadful low. I have the edge on thee in years, I believe."

"By the calendar only, Catherine. In no other wise. But hearken, I may dally only a short while in the county. I am expected at York late in the day. John Dee hath contrived a conversation with an alchemist there who claims to have found vulgar gold in a vial of molten lead and mercury. I doubt it to be true, but I will join them anyway. I have contrived this diversion to talk briefly with thee. For I needs must relate that there is news of John White."

"He hath been heard from?"

"Indeed, ma'am, he hath returned! He made landfall in the west of Ireland on the sixteenth day of October. He made his way to London by way of Cornwall and granted me an audience not a week ago. Is it not wonderful news?"

"It is. It is."

"Though his voyage was uncomfortable in the extreme. A small party set sail in the flyboat at the end of August, but they encountered such storms and unfavorable winds that they were much delayed and like to have all perished from want of drink. Many were dead or dying when they sailed into Dingle Bay."

"Most distressing, Edward. Only God's grace delivered them. But tell me, did they bring news of Sir Richard Grenville's party?"

"Alas, ma'am, Governor White could find no trace of them—neither at the Roanoke village nor at Ralph Lane's stockade. Only the bones of one long slain by the savages. Mayhap the rest were butchered too."

"Through their own duplicity, I'll warrant. Thou wilt recall the arrogance of Lane and Grenville at the subscribers' meeting."

"Aye, they rated the natives very low."

"Indeed, they did, and it sorely troubled me."

"And thou the main subscriber to their undertaking! Mayhap all thy investments are lost."

"I think not in the eventual outcome. It is a cause close to my heart."

"Though the first of Roanoke might be lost, the news is good in other wise. Governor White replenished the colony tenfold. More than one hundred settlers disembarked from the *Lyon* and began to rebuild the cottages and stock them—resourceful men, hardy wives, and hale children. Good souls all."

"Ah, yes, the fateful hundred."

"And this, too. A child was born to the colonists on the eighteenth day of August, the first English and Christian child born in the Americas."

"Yes, Virginia Dare."

"Ma'am? How so?"

"What?"

"How canst thou know this? Hath some bearer delivered this news to thee afore me?"

"What? Ah, no! As I recall, the news was vouchsafed to me that the governor's daughter was with child afore sailing, at the subscribers' meeting in Gould Street. Perhaps Ananias Dare told me. I forget."

"Yes. Somehow, thou art correct. A babe named for our virgin queen."

"E'en so. But, Edward, it must have been a great sorrow for John White to leave his daughter and granddaughter in a savage land."

"He did not complain to me, but I feel his grief is only hid. He explained that the greatest benefaction he could do for his kinfolk was to return to England to ensure that the colony was quickly refitted with all requisites and strengthened in numbers. That would best aid their security. He hath already convened with Sir Walter Raleigh, and they together instructed Grenville to ready vessels and stores for a voyage in the spring. For this reason alone did the governor abandon his heirs. So rest assured, he will see them again afore long."

"No." Catherine turned away and looked again out her west window, this time far beyond Lincoln and the Trent, beyond the ocean even, to America.

"Ma'am?"

"I do not think that John White will set foot in Virginia again for quite some years."

"How canst say such a thing? He is most determined."

"Yet I feel it is so. King Philip already masses his Spanish galleons to sail on our island. Every stout ship and able seaman will be needed for its defense. It will happen next year mayhap."

"A few flyboats and a pinnace can be spared."

"No. I fear that John White will not see his granddaughter again. I do truly grieve for him."

"Ma'am, sometimes, thy words astonish me. Though I am experienced at the astrological arts and know the ways by which the stars can foretell coming events, yet sometimes do I feel that thou hast powers unknown to the rest of us, that thou knowest what the future will bring."

"Fiddle-faddle."

"And in this particular matter, I am sure thou art wrong. An English colony will prevail in the Americas."

"Yes. In time, it will." Catherine's eyes were moist now, and she could no longer clearly see the fields outside her window.

"There is one other matter," Edward Kelley said, then he also turned away. He addressed the fireplace. "Catherine, I wish to tender again the offer I made thee in the summer, when Richard was on his deathbed with the choleric humors. In hopes that the mild summer and crisp autumn hath caused thy heart to soften, I wouldst say, again, that I promise to care for thee in thy widowhood. My thoughts have not swerved. In truth, I would that we should wed, mayhap next autumn, when the mourning period is well ended. When thou judges the time to be right."

"Edward, I—"

"We are neither one of us in our nonage, if I might press my case, and neither of us hath bred children to ease our passage to paradise. I see our union as a vessel for companionship and solace. As for romance, ah, well, I think it matters less with the years. Solitude will tax thee sorely anon, as it doth me."

Catherine turned to face her suitor, wiping her eyes with the back of her hand. "Edward, I—Edward, thou knowest I respect thee dearly. Thou wert one of my husband's dearest friends. I know that thou and John Dee and Laski and the others did aid him most earnestly with his experiments in the church of St. Neot, fruitless though those long nights were. I am aware also that thou wert most solicitous at his death and showed great kindness to me thereafter. For all these things I am greatly indebted, but—"

"But?" They turned to each other and their eyes met.

"But marriage between us cannot be," Catherine explained. "I can have only one love in this life. That is the way it is with me. My heart will not permit entry of another even though my husband hath gone on ahead. The intrusion would seem treacherous to it and would draw from it only coldness. I speak not of my mind, you understand, or indeed my body. It is my heart that saith nay, and as I have discovered during the course of my life, over that organ the rest of my being holds no sway. As for solitude, well, it hath become a friend these last months."

"I must tell thee, Catherine, that this news redoubles the pain within me. Yet do I still pray for a reversion in due course."

"Do not. It will not happen in this lifetime. Recall that Richard's sarcophagus was built for two people. I will lie beside him in death."

"Ah. E'en so, I will remain thy friend and will continue to visit thee and bring thee news of the Americas, in which I know thou holdest a deep interest."

"Thou art most obliging. And if Sir Walter or Sir Richard wants for more subscriptions, my purse is ever open. Please tell them this. And Edward, Edward, I do—" She touched his sleeve.

"Yes. I see," he said, averting his eyes and pulling away. "Your husband was—I do see." He turned and made to leave. "Now cometh the lonely ride to York. Adieu."

"Adieu, Edward."

"The Lord be with thee."

"And with thee." Edward Kelley left the room and Catherine Crossly returned to her writing desk.

So, she thought, *the lost colony of Roanoke is established—Virginia Dare's fate to be forever unknown. Soon, Jamestown. Soon, Plymouth Rock. The misfits of England will be surging across the Atlantic and spreading westward like the locust. But the waves of Iowa prairie grass will not be parted by white hands for another two hundred years. Two hundred years till the scythe is taken up and that wonderful rolling land is cut and blocked into farms. The black sky and the silver stars yet untainted by the lights of man.*

She stared into the mirror above the desk. Sixty-eight years had been kind to her. But this was no longer the face that the boys had lusted after. And yet what had Brian once said? Her smile held the promise of dimples, which was so much more appealing than dimples themselves. The promise of dimples remained, but so much else had been wiped away. She was reminded of some words of Brian's favorite poet, Ovid: "Poor Helen weeps at the looking-glass, asking how she could ever have been carried off as prize—not once, but twice."

The loss of her good looks she could accept, but time had robbed her of so many other things. In fact, it had stolen all the touchstones of her youth—friends, family, home, culture, and even her very name, which she had been forced to change to Catherine, the root of the name Karen, which was unknown in these times. Yes, time had devoured almost everything.

She turned to the framed likeness of Brian that had been painted by Hans Holbein the Younger at the request of Sir Richard Rich. "I have no regrets, Brian," she said to him. "You know that. We were both young and brave and willing to take risks. And even though my present situation is most appalling and never before experienced by any living soul, I can bear it. You were as kind to me as you knew how to be and loved me as much as you could love any woman, and though both might have been less than a wife dreams of, I always knew there were no guarantees. Under the circumstances, I had no right to expect more.

"Your obsession with returning us to our own time was admirable. I often think you worked so hard at it more for my sake than your own, even when we both knew it was futile. But we should have accepted the fact that we were trapped here. We should not have continued to see ourselves as mere visitors to this alien world, soon to depart. We should have embraced the society we found ourselves in, not shunned it. We should have salvaged our lives. We should have had children."

She pinched the bridge of her nose and closed her eyes tightly. "Ours was a rare love, wasn't it, Brian, one that didn't press for favors or bear malice for slights? A love that asked for only one thing: time in the other's company. Presence brought contentment. Absence was borne with a heavy heart. Could anyone want for more? With the other boys, I used to ask myself, 'Is this love? Now is this love?' With you, I forgot to ask the question.

"It was best, you know, that I had so little time to choose at that moment in the church. There were no agonies of decision-making, no weighing of future lives unlived. All answers were shades of the same color. When I was roused from the zeta state and saw your spreading arms, I knew that they were extended to me, not to Abbot Gervase.

"Hearing that single word—'Karen!'—slip faintly from your fading lips, your body disappearing into the wood of the pews behind you, that blue halo embracing you and Richard Crossly, well, it was my test, wasn't it, the bed of hot coals I had asked for?"

She ran her fingers over the glass of Brian's portrait, tracing the lines of his eyes and mouth. "What did the others think, I wonder, John and Sarah, Harry and Frank. That I was sucked into the whirlpool, a poor sacrifice to science? Can they have known that I was not pulled, that I jumped into your arms, into the desperate future, because I could not live without you?

"To your credit, Brian, you understood this and never again asked me if I loved you, so no, I have no regrets. We drank the milk of paradise together."

"Alice!" she cried.

"Yes, ma'am?"

"A glass of claret, if you will. I feel a little faint."

ABOUT THE AUTHOR

 David Streets was born in England but has lived in suburban Chicago for most of his life. He is an environmental scientist with advanced degrees in physics. He specializes in the study of air pollution and how to control it so that we can all breathe easier. He has helped to improve the air in many parts of the world, particularly Asia. He is a world-renowned researcher with more than three hundred publications in the scientific literature. He was a named contributor to the work of the Intergovernmental Panel on Climate Change, which was awarded the Nobel Peace Prize in 2007. In his childhood, he spent many hours in gloomy churches, wondering if they were haunted, which has led to this first foray into the world of fiction.

CPSIA information can be obtained
at www.ICGtesting.com
Printed in the USA
LVHW110756250123
737628LV00002B/12/J